A Home *in* Drayton Valley

Books by Kim Vogel Sawyer

FROM BETHANY HOUSE PUBLISHERS

Waiting for Summer's Return
Where the Heart Leads
My Heart Remembers
In Every Heartbeat
Where Willows Grow
A Promise for Spring
Fields of Grace
A Hopeful Heart
Courting Miss Amsel
A Whisper of Peace
Song of My Heart
When Hope Blossoms
A Home in Drayton Valley
Sweet Sanctuary

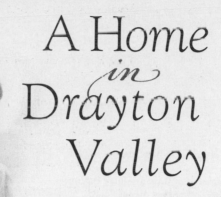

A Home *in* Drayton Valley

Kim Vogel Sawyer

A Novel by

BETHANY HOUSE PUBLISHERS
a division of Baker Publishing Group
Minneapolis, Minnesota

© 2012 by Kim Vogel Sawyer

Published by Bethany House Publishers
11400 Hampshire Avenue South
Bloomington, Minnesota 55438
www.bethanyhouse.com

Bethany House Publishers is a division of
Baker Publishing Group, Grand Rapids, Michigan

Printed in the United States of America

Library of Congress Cataloging-in-Publication Data
Sawyer, Kim Vogel.
    A home in Drayton Valley / Kim Vogel Sawyer.
        p.   cm.
    ISBN 978-0-7642-1054-9 (hardcover : alk. paper) —
    ISBN 978-0-7642-0788-4 (pbk.)
    1. Pioneers—Kansas—Fiction. 2. Wagon trains—Kansas—Fiction. 3. Life change events—Fiction. 4. Man-woman relationships—Fiction. 5. Domestic fiction. I. Title.
PS3619.A97H66 2012
813'.6—dc23   2012013131

Scripture quotations are from the King James Version of the Bible.

The poem Tarsie sings in Chapter 8 is from "The Last Rose of Summer" by Thomas Moore.

Cover design by Lookout Design, Inc.

12   13   14   15   16   17   18   7   6   5   4   3   2   1

For *Deena*,
who knows without doubt
". . . it was then that You carried me."

"Fear not: for I have redeemed thee,
I have called thee by thy name;
thou art mine.
When thou passest through the waters, I will be with thee;
and through the rivers, they shall not overflow thee:
when thou walkest through the fire,
thou shalt not be burned;
neither shall the flame kindle upon thee.
For I am the LORD thy God, the Holy
One of Israel, thy Saviour . . .
Fear not: for I am with thee."

Isaiah 43:1–3, 5

❋ 1 ❋

Tarsie Raines clutched the collar of her cloak beneath her chin and prayed the gusts of wind tugging at the patched bombazine wouldn't carry her away like a kite before she reached her destination. Dark clouds hovered above the rooftops, promising a shower and giving the filthy city streets a gray cast that masked the midmorning hour.

The heels of her shoes *tick-tocked* against the cobblestone, steady as a clock's pendulum, despite having to wend between vendors' carts, groups of begging urchins, and the endless throngs of milling humanity. Odors—fish, rotting vegetables, bodies too long unbathed—assaulted her nose, stirred by the damp breeze whisking from the bay. Her cloak slipped from her shoulder and its tail slapped the leg of a man leaning negligently on a rickety stair railing. She jerked the fabric back into place but not before the man sent a leering grin that traveled from her unraveling braid to the scuffed toes of her well-worn boots. Tarsie hugged the leather pouch containing her herbal cures to her bodice and shivered, but not from cold.

How she wanted out of this city! Mary did, too. *Oh, Lord, please . . .*

7

The prayer, a helpless plea, winged from her heart as more than a dozen others had since she'd found the tattered copy of James Redpath's *Handbook of Kansas* in an alley a week ago. Although her deepest yearnings found no utterance, she trusted that the Lord she loved and served could read the wordless groanings of her heart and would answer in a way perfect for Mary. But so much rested on Mary's husband, Joss, and what he would say. And Joss had no use for the Lord.

The first cool raindrops plopped onto the dirt-crusted cobblestone as Tarsie reached the brick tenement that housed Mary's family. She darted inside, grateful to have escaped a dousing. Her wool-and-cotton cloak was far too heavy for balmy springtime. But Tarsie owned no other covering, so she wore the cloak year-round. It helped hide the sad dress beneath it.

Tarsie made her way up the narrow concrete stairway littered with food scraps, crumpled paper, and animal droppings. Somewhere in the building, a baby's weak cry tore at Tarsie's heart. Such suffering. Wasn't there a better life waiting elsewhere? Her fingers curled around the booklet in her pocket. Yes, a better life awaited . . . in Kansas. Somehow she must convince Joss of that truth.

The door to the Brubachers' apartment stood open, inviting Tarsie's entrance as it always did on Wednesdays. The children, Emmy and Nathaniel, dashed to greet her the moment she stepped over the threshold. Tarsie gave the towheaded pair a hug, then glanced around the sparsely furnished but clean room. "Where's your mama?" Tarsie hoped her friend hadn't ventured out for shopping. The rain would surely bring on another cold, and Mary's weakened lungs couldn't abide one more illness. Tarsie marveled that the woman had survived the winter.

"Sweepin'," Nathaniel said, tucking a finger into his mouth.

Five-year-old Emmy wrinkled her nose at her little brother. "*Still*-eeping." She squared her skinny shoulders and beamed at Tarsie. "I fixed biscuits an' jam for Nattie an' me. Mama said I'm her best helper."

Tarsie gave the little girl's tangled hair a pat and managed a smile, but inwardly she quaked. If Mary still lay in bed, something was amiss. With trembling hands, she draped her cloak over the single chair in the room. "You two stay out here and play quietly. I'll be seein' to your mama." She pinched the precious pouch between her elbow and ribs and scurried into the sleeping room beyond the living quarters, certain the children would obey. They were bonny youngsters—in all the months Tarsie had visited, she'd rarely found a need to scold them.

As the children had indicated, Mary lay on the lumpy bed that filled the corner of the small room, eyes closed and lips slightly parted. The pale pallor of her skin concerned Tarsie, as did the sheen of perspiration on her brow. Another fever? Tarsie sat on the edge of the bed, causing the springs to creak. Mary's eyes fluttered open as Tarsie placed the back of her hand gently against the woman's moist forehead.

The heat from Mary's skin seared Tarsie's flesh. Her heart tripped in worry, but she clicked her tongue on her teeth and shook her head, assuming a teasing tone. "Look at you now, sound asleep in the middle of the mornin'. Such a lazy one you are."

The corners of Mary's mouth twitched upward in a feeble smile. "So you don't agree I've earned a rest after doing laundry yesterday for my own family plus four others?" A sigh heaved, carried on a wheezing breath. "I have two more loads to do today, though, so I should rise."

"And why are you still takin' in laundry?" Tarsie scowled, all pretense at teasing forgotten. "Didn't I tell you the lye fumes an' plungin' your hands again an' again into water isn't good for you? If you're wantin' to get better for good, you cannot—"

Mary struggled to prop herself up with her elbows. "I have to work, Tarsie. I've told you so." Her arms gave way, and she collapsed against the soiled pillows.

"Well, you won't be doin' any laundry today." Tarsie flopped her age-worn pouch open. Her most valuable possession, she always kept her great-aunt's medicinal pouch with her. She never knew when the cures inside might offer comfort and healing to some poor soul. The cures had been used for Mary more than anyone else. If only something in the leather pouch would heal Mary for good.

Tarsie's fingers sought the small packet of holy basil. The herb had effectively reduced Mary's fever in the past. "I'm thinkin' this new illness ought to tell you leanin' over a washtub does you no good."

"It wasn't doing the wash that caused my sickness," Mary said.

Tarsie whisked a glance around the room and noted the window opened at least six inches. She pointed. "Did Joss leave the windows open all night again? I've told you, the night air . . ." Tarsie shook her head, too frustrated to continue. She stomped to the window and gave it a push that settled the frame against the sill with a thump. Sometimes she wondered if Joss had no interest in keeping his wife healthy. He stubbornly refused to follow any of her directions. Hands on hips, she faced Mary. "I'll be havin' a chat with him, an'—"

"No." Mary's voice, although weak, sounded firm. "He works so hard during the day. He needs his rest, and he sleeps better with a little cool air in his face."

Tears pricked Tarsie's eyes. Mary was the most giving, unselfish person she'd ever known. Why couldn't Joss pander to Mary the way she pandered to him? She moved to the bed and seated herself again. "But what of you? Is your sleep not important?"

"I'll be all right." Mary's chapped lips curved into a weary smile. "You'll make me well again, as you always do."

Oh, how Tarsie prayed Mary's words proved true. She loved this dear woman—had ever since their very first meeting across the apple vendor's cart on the street not quite a year ago. God had orchestrated the crossing of their paths days after she'd laid her great-aunt to rest, just at the time Tarsie desperately needed a friend. Her eyes slipped closed. *Help me get Mary out of this city, Lord—away from its damp breezes that bother her lungs an' from the vermin that crawl through her bed at night. Help me send her to a better place . . . even if it means I never see her again.*

She rose, holding the little drawstring bag of crushed holy basil in her fist. "Then I better be brewin' you some tea that'll rid you of the fever, hmm?"

Mary's hand snaked out and curled around Tarsie's wrist. "And something for my strength? So I can work this afternoon?"

Tarsie frowned. "You can't be up workin'—not when you're sick. The people can wait for their wash."

"But they won't wait." Desperation colored Mary's voice. "They'll find someone else to do their washing, and I'll lose the money."

"Joss earns a decent wage at the docks. You shouldn't need to be worryin' about money."

Mary pursed her lips and turned her face away, falling silent. Rain splatted against the closed window, and the children's muffled voices carried from the other room. Tarsie hated hurting her friend, but she knew Joss squandered a fair amount of his wage in the drinking and gambling saloons that lined the docks. If he used his money for his family instead, they could live in a better apartment and Mary would have no need to bring in extra funds.

11

The booklet in her pocket pressed against her thigh, reminding her of Kansas and fresh opportunities. Away from New York and the immoral businesses that tempted coins from a man's purse, would Joss finally become the kind of husband and father Mary and the children needed? She ought to brew the tea, but she sank back down on the mattress and took Mary's hand. The hot, dry skin with its calluses and broken, brittle nails pained Tarsie. A gentle soul like Mary deserved so much better than she presently received.

"Mary, I know you're wantin' to leave this city—you've told me often how you pray more than dirty streets an' a lifetime of living near the docks for your wee ones."

Mary shifted her face to meet Tarsie's gaze. Longing glimmered in her blue eyes, the wordless beseeching creating an ache in the center of Tarsie's chest.

Tarsie pulled the yellowed *Handbook of Kansas* from her pocket and opened it. "Listen . . ." She began to read. "'Drayton Valley, it is admitted by everyone, has the best rock-bound landing, and is the best town site on the Missouri River. We say to the emigrant, come to Drayton Valley; believe as we do, that it is destined to be the great emporium of the upper Missouri.'"

Mary plucked the booklet from Tarsie's hands and squinted at the cover. Her brows crunched low. "Kansas?"

"To be sure." Tarsie's heart pounded, hope swelling. She jabbed her finger at a paragraph farther down the page. "See there? It speaks of the busy steamboat trade. Joss knows dock work, so he'd surely find a job. A town of two thousand, Mary, instead of this crowded, dirty city. Wouldn't it be a fine place for you an' for Emmy an' wee Nathaniel? And maybe . . . maybe . . ." She swallowed. How she hated to remind Mary of Joss's shortcomings, but her Bible taught her to always speak truth. "Far from here, maybe Joss'll lose his taste for frequenting the saloons."

12

Mary sucked in her lower lip. A single tear trickled down her wan cheek.

Tarsie squeezed her friend's hand. "It'd be a healin' place for you. For all of you. I feel it in the very center of my soul."

Mary pulled her hand free and rolled to her side, taking the booklet with her. "Brew my tea, please, Tarsie."

With a sigh, Tarsie scuffed to the main room, where the children played in the middle of the floor with a simple doll made of rags and a tumble of discarded chunks of wood. She paused long enough to praise them for being so good, then tossed a scoop of coal into the stove's belly and poured the remaining water from a bucket beside the stove into a pan. While the water heated, she hurried to the rain barrels behind the building to refill the bucket.

To her relief, all four barrels were half full. With the morning's steady rainfall, they'd easily overflow by midafternoon, guaranteeing more than enough water for her to fill a tub and do the laundry Mary had promised to customers. Trudging up the three flights of stairs with the full bucket gripped in both hands, she wondered how Mary in her weakened state had managed to make this trek so many times. Why didn't Joss insist she rest?

Back in the apartment, Tarsie steeped the tea and carried a mugful of the strong-smelling brew to Mary. Expecting to find her sleeping, she gave a jolt when she spotted Mary propped against the pillows, the *Handbook of Kansas* open beneath her palms.

Mary looked up at Tarsie and released a sigh. "I've been reading. And praying." Tears flooded her eyes. "Tarsie, this place . . . the town called Drayton Valley . . . it seems to be everything I want for my family. So far from here . . ." Her gaze drifted to the window, where raindrops chased each other down the cracked pane.

Tarsie scooted to the edge of the bed and pressed the mug

into Mary's hands. "Drink." She waited until Mary took a hesitant sip of the steaming liquid, hiding a smile at her friend's grimace. The tea tasted dreadful, but it worked, and that was what mattered. Retrieving the booklet from the rumpled bed cover, Tarsie held it tight between her fingers. "After I found this book lying in an alley last week, the pages wavin' in the wind as if beckonin' to me, I did some checking at the railroad station. A man there told me groups leave New York on the iron horse every week to join up with wagon trains headin' for Kansas towns. I wrote his name in the back of the book, see?" She indicated the back cover, where her pencil smudgings spelled the name *Charles Driscoll*. "He can tell Joss everything that needs knowin' about joinin' one of the wagon trains that'd take you to Drayton Valley."

"It'll cost so dear," Mary whispered.

Tarsie swallowed. She'd done little else but think of how to help Mary since she'd found the book. She prayed her friend would be able to set aside her fierce pride and accept Tarsie's help. Slipping to her knees beside the bed, she cradled the booklet beneath her chin and offered her most imploring look. "I've been savin' up the money from my sewing. I want you to take it, to use it to help pay for—"

Mary's eyes flew wide. "No!"

Tarsie ignored the fierce objection. "—whatever your family needs to get established in a better place. I'm all alone. I have no need for more'n what I already have."

Images of the filthy street, the leering men, the hopelessness that permeated the tenements flooded Tarsie's mind, but she pushed them resolutely aside. Mary had offered friendship when no one else extended so much as a kind glance in her direction. As much as Tarsie longed for escape, Mary *needed* escape. The city would kill Mary one day.

Tarsie gulped down her own desire to flee this vile place

and gazed fervently into her friend's tear-filled eyes. "Don't rob me of the blessin' of helping one who's so dear to me." Behind her, the patter of little feet signaled that Emmy and Nathaniel had tired of being left alone. They charged into the room and flung themselves onto the foot of the bed, giggling and wrestling like a pair of puppies. Tarsie flicked a smile in their direction before looking at Mary again. "Let me help send you an' these precious wee ones to a place where happiness dwells."

Mary's warm gaze embraced her children. The stubborn lines around her mouth softened, and she released a deep sigh. "Oh, Tarsie, how would I have managed this past year without you?" She stretched out one hand and cupped Tarsie's jaw. "My angel . . . that's what you've been." Her hand fell away. "I feel a tug toward Drayton Valley, I won't deny it. But I can't take your hard-earned money."

"But—"

Mary shook her head, her forehead pinching. "There's no use hoping, Tarsie. Joss . . ." She sighed. "He'll never leave New York City."

Tarsie pushed to her feet and strode stiffly from the room, leaving Mary and the children alone. She crossed to the window and stood before the rain-speckled glass, peering into the narrow alleyway between the buildings. A sad view. An empty view. So different from the green fields and wide, sunshiny sky of her native Ireland. So many years had passed, she barely remembered the place of her birth or the ones who had birthed her. She'd planned to save enough money to get her and Great-Aunt Vangie back to Ireland one day, but for what purpose?

Ma and Da had passed when Tarsie was but a small child. Aunt Vangie now lay in a pauper's grave. No whitewashed cottage with thatched roof awaited her return no matter how many times Tarsie tried to imagine it. Her life was here now.

15

She was young and strong and could make the most of it. But Mary needed more.

Giggles carried from the sleeping room, followed by Mary's soft reprimand. She sounded tired. Would she last through another damp New York spring? Tarsie's heart caught.

The apartment door banged open, and Mary's husband stepped into the room. Tall and raw-boned, Joss Brubacher filled the doorway. Whipping off his hat, he sent water droplets across the clean floor. In two wide strides, he reached the stove and peered into the pot. Then he sent a scowl in Tarsie's direction. "No lunch ready? Where's Mary?" He started toward the sleeping room, but Tarsie darted across the floor and blocked his progress.

Although he frowned at her, silently demanding she move aside, she held her ground. Looking into his sunburnt, irritated face, she said, "Sit down, Joss. I have need of talkin' to you."

❊ 2 ❊

Joss balled his hands into fists and planted them on his hips. Just what did this little Irish snip think she was doing, delivering orders? He followed demands at the dock—he had to if he wanted to keep his job—but this was his home. Here, he was in command.

"Lemme by."

Mary's friend lifted her chin. "I'll not be budgin'."

"You can move or I'll move you." An idle threat. In his thirty years of life, Joss had never raised his hand to a woman, and he wouldn't now. But she didn't know that.

"Not 'til you've listened to me."

Men quaked beneath Joss's scowl. The girl's refusal to kowtow earned a grudging admiration, but he didn't have time to argue with her. Thirty minutes—that's all he got for a midday break. If Mary didn't fetch his dinner soon, he'd have to return to the docks hungry. And Joss had vowed a long time ago he'd never face hunger again.

He tried to step around her, but quick as a cat she blocked his passage. He tried the other way. With a nimble leap, she waylaid him again. He released a grunt. Had he ever met a more stubborn female? "Girl, I—"

"My name is Tarsie, as you well know, Joss Brubacher. I'll be thanking you to make use of it. Now . . . if I fix you

17

some sandwiches, will you hush your bluster and hear what I have to say?"

His stomach rumbled. If it meant getting fed, he could listen. He stomped to the trestle table in the corner and plopped onto a bench. "Hurry, then. I don't have time to yammer."

Tarsie gathered items from the little cupboard in the corner and set her hands to work slathering butter on halved biscuits. She layered the biscuits with cheese and slices of meat leftover from last night's beef tongue, then carried a tin plate stacked with the biscuit sandwiches to the table. Plunking the plate before him, she sat on the opposite bench and folded her hands.

Joss reached for a biscuit, but Tarsie began to pray, freezing his hand mid-reach.

"Our lovin' Father in heaven, we thank Thee for giving us our daily bread. Bless this food that it might bring nourishment. Please grant listening ears and a sensible spirit"—she peeked at him through one squinted eye. He snapped his eyes closed—"so we might do what's most pleasin' to You. Amen."

He opened his eyes and quirked a brow at her. Was she finished?

She pointed to the plate. "Eat now."

He needed no further prompting.

"Your Mary is sick again."

The dry biscuit tried to stick in Joss's gullet. His Mary was always sick. Hadn't he worried having children would bring ruination? Day after day, his own father had told him kids were the scourge of a man's life, but Mary had insisted on birthing five of them. Three hadn't lived past the suckling age, and the two who'd managed to survive drained her of energy. His chest constricted. If only she'd listened to him . . .

He jammed another biscuit in his mouth and spoke around the lump. "So doctor her."

"I've given her my herbal medicine, just as I've been doing these past months. But she's in need of more."

Defensiveness raised the fine hairs on the back of Joss's neck. He did his best by Mary. "You think I can afford a real sawbones on my measly wage? It's all I can do to pay for our apartment, food, and shoes for those kids." He yanked up another biscuit and took a mighty chomp.

Tarsie's fine eyebrows pulled into a frown. "Didn't I ask you to listen? Hush now."

With his mouth full, Joss couldn't snarl. But he could scowl. So he did. Fiercely.

But Tarsie didn't cringe. To his consternation, she didn't even blink. "I wasn't speakin' of calling in a doctor. When I say she's needing more, I'm meaning she needs clean air, a bed free of vermin, a home away from the crowded city. You've already buried three wee ones, Joss Brubacher, an' if you don't get your Mary to a better place, you'll be burying her, as well. Is that what you want?"

The biscuit turned to sawdust in Joss's mouth. Although two more sandwiches remained on the plate, he pushed it aside. In a lifetime of disappointment and misfortune, Joss had found only one good: Mary. The thought of putting her in the ground sickened him. How dare this girl—this self-possessed stranger—try to frighten him? He jolted to his feet, the bench legs screeching against the planked floor, and pointed his finger at her face. "I'm done listening."

She leaped up as well. "But—"

"No more!" He thundered the words, and finally the girl ceased her blather. With firm stomps against the floorboards, he charged into the sleeping room. He swept his arm, silently commanding the youngsters to leave the room. They skittered out the door. Dropping to one knee beside the bed, he took his wife's hand. As always, the difference between his wide, thick palm and her fragile, slender fingers gave him pause. Such a delicate, lovely woman, his Mary. He didn't deserve her.

He looked into her pale face, and Tarsie's statement swirled through his mind. *"You'll be burying her, as well."* Anger rose in his chest, pushing the fear away. "Sick again?" Worry tangled his tonsils into a knot, and the words came out harsh. An imitation of his father's voice.

She nodded, her little hand quivering within his grasp. "I'm sorry, Joss."

"That Irish friend of yours demands I take you out of the city." Releasing a derisive grunt, he shook his head. "Where does she think we'd go?"

Mary's free hand slipped from beneath the rumpled bed-covers. She held out a small book, its cover stained and torn. She pushed the book open with her thumb, revealing one dog-eared page. "To a place called Drayton Valley. In Kansas." Her expression turned dreamy.

Joss stared at the page where tiny lines and squiggles marched in straight rows. His inability to make sense of the marks reminded him of his insignificance. Another wave of anger rolled through his gut. He snatched the book from Mary's hand. "Why does she plant ideas in your head?"

He started to fling the book across the room, but Mary's fingers curled around his wrist. "Joss, please—" A coughing spell cut her words short. Joss gritted his teeth, watching helplessly as she struggled to bring the cough to an end. Finally she flopped back on the pillow, spent. Tears swam in her eyes as she begged, "Please think about it. The town has active docks where you could work. But we'd be away from the . . ." Her voice dropped to a rasping whisper. "Saloons." Her fingers tightened on his wrist, her strength surprising him. "You aren't your pa, Joss. You don't need the drink. Or the gambling. But as long as we stay here, it will always pull at you."

Of course it would. What else did he know? He had no other securities. Except Mary.

She went on, her voice dropping so low he had to strain to hear her. "Promise me you'll think about it. Please?"

Pa's voice echoed from the past. *"Never make a promise, boy. Who keeps 'em? Nobody. Promises disappoint."* Joss made promises, but only to people who didn't matter to him. He pulled his arm free of her grip and set his jaw.

The hopeful light in her eyes dimmed, and Joss looked away to avoid witnessing a flood of tears. His gaze landed on the elaborately carved clock on the dresser. He hissed through his teeth. Late! Ignoring Mary's soft sniffles, his children's wistful farewells, and the Irish girl's disapproving frown, he charged out of the apartment, down the stairs, and into the street. Not until he neared the dock did he realize he still held the Kansas book in his fist.

With a muffled oath, he gave the book a toss. No sense keeping something that would only encourage Mary to dream about what could never be.

The six o'clock whistle signaled the end of the working day. Joss plopped the fifty-pound burlap bag of seed corn from his shoulder onto the stack and brushed his palms together, dispelling dust. He fell in line with the other jostling men, listening but not adding to their ribald comments. He hoped Tarsie's cures had worked well enough to get Mary out of that bed. Worried him to see her laid so low. And he needed a good meal.

"Brubacher!" His boss's voice blasted over the other noises. "Wait up."

Joss shifted out of the flow and turned to face the man, holding back an annoyed grunt.

"You still owe fifteen minutes."

Joss frowned.

Marsden raised one eyebrow. "Thought I didn't see you creep in late after the dinner break, huh? Well, if you wanna draw a full day's wage, you hafta give a full day's work. So head back up there and finish unloading that corn."

Joss bristled, but he couldn't argue. Not with the boss man. But he let his bootheels show his aggravation, thumping them good and hard as he returned to the end of the pier and yanked up a bag by its tied corners. Thirteen years on this job—thirteen years of showing up day after day, no matter the weather, even headachy and sick from too much drink the night before—and they couldn't allow him one time of showing up late?

Marsden stood watching, boots widespread, a timepiece pinched between his fingers. Joss gritted his teeth and held his grumbles inside as he hauled the remaining bags of corn from their spot on the pier's end to the waiting wagon. Finally Marsden barked, "Good enough. You can go."

Joss let the final bag slide from his fingers and drop beside the wagon. Without even a glance in his boss's direction, he aimed his feet for home. But Marsden's hand bolted out and captured Joss's shirtsleeve.

"Got a message for you from Lanker."

Joss's mouth went dry, but he held his shoulders erect and set his face in a disinterested sneer. "That so?"

"Uh-huh. Said he'll be here on payday, an' he expects every penny. No more delays."

With a little shake of his arm, Joss freed himself from Marsden's grip. If only he could rid himself of the gambler's hold as easily. He forced a wry chuckle. "If you're servin' as one of Lanker's errand boys, you must owe him, too."

Marsden blanched. "You know as well as I do nobody crosses Lanker—not if they wanna see tomorrow." He glanced around as if seeking listening ears. "How much you in for?"

Joss clamped his teeth together. Too much. More than he could possibly repay. What had compelled him to join that game last month? Stupid, stupid, stupid. "Enough."

Marsden clicked his tongue on his teeth. "I don't envy you, Brubacher. Come next Friday, you best be ready to hand over your wages." His gaze whisked from Joss's scuffed boot toes to his little wool cap. "Even a fella as big as you won't be standing when his gang is finished with you. Lanker gets his due one way or another."

Joss didn't need the reminder. "Can I go now?"

Marsden waved his hand in dismissal. "See you tomorrow. On time."

Spinning on his worn heel, Joss took his leave. Damp air scented with fish and salt chilled him, and he jammed his hands into his jacket pockets. His fingertips encountered a few coins. As if of their own accord, his feet slowed. An idea filled the back of his mind. One lucky roll. That's all he needed to turn those cents into dollars. If he had to hand Lanker his entire pay envelope on Friday, he'd need something to carry his family through the next weeks. Even though his stomach rumbled, he changed direction and entered the closest saloon. One he rarely frequented. Safer to go where he wasn't known, just in case some of Lanker's men loitered about. They'd rid him of his meager coins if they caught sight of him.

An hour later, raucous laughter chased Joss from the saloon. One of the revelers staggered to the doorway after him, his foul breath wafting to Joss's nostrils. "You need to find a differ'nt game if you can't toss dice any better'n that."

Joss whirled, his fists clenched. "Leave me be."

The man's eyes widened in mock innocence. "Just givin' you some advice, friend." He offered a taunting grin. "You sure could use it."

Joss raised his fists. "I'm not your friend, and I don't want your advice."

The drunken man took a stumbling step in reverse, holding up both palms. "Awright, awright." He raised his bony shoulders in a shrug. "Don't gotta get sore, fella. Shee, some people can't take help when it's bein' offered." He turned a clumsy half circle and reentered the saloon, muttering.

Shoulders hunched and fists tucked in his empty pockets, Joss scuffed his way along the docks. He was in no hurry to get home. Mary would take one look at him and know where he'd been. The hurt in her eyes always stung more than his pa's belt ever had. His stomach churned. Partly from hunger, partly from worry. So far he'd managed to hold Lanker at bay by handing over a portion of his pay and promising more the next week. But next Friday, his time was up. He owed Lanker. He owed the tenement owner. And Mary would need money to buy food. Could he sell something? The only thing left of value was the mantel clock Mary's grandfather had brought over from England. Mary wouldn't part with it—and even if she did, no pawnshop owner would give him what he needed to pay his debt to Lanker.

Mary'd done her best over the years to convince Joss that God would meet their needs. But no God—not even if He was as loving and giving as his wife proclaimed—would help a man who'd done as many wrongs as Joss Brubacher.

With a strangled moan, Joss kicked at a clump of papers lying along the filthy boardwalk. He expected them to separate and scatter in the wind, but instead the entire clump rolled over twice and then settled with a stained, worn, brown cover facing up. Joss sucked in a breath—Mary's book about Kansas.

He bent over and yanked it up. His cold fingers trembled as he clung to the book. Maybe there was an answer to his problem.

❋ 3 ❋

The pain that never left Mary's side stabbed as she bent over the children's sleeping mats and tucked a soft quilt beneath their chins. *Strength, Father*, her heart begged as she forced a smile to her lips. "Sleep well now."

Emmy and Nathaniel murmured a sleepy response, and their eyes slipped closed, thick lashes casting shadows on their rounded cheeks. Mary's heart swelled as a lump filled her throat. Such beautiful children. Such blessings.

Mary struggled upright. The pain intensified with the movement. She ground her teeth together to hold back a moan. Each day the burden of pain, which had begun in her right breast more than a year ago and trailed beneath her arm and into her ribs over the ensuing months, became harder to bear. Having watched her own mother travel this pathway—although the pain had found Mary years earlier than it had gripped Mama—she knew what awaited.

Strength, Father.

Clutching her threadbare robe around her shoulders, she scuffed to the main room of the apartment and sank down at the trestle table. She rested her elbows on the scrubbed, scarred surface and let her face drop into her hands. How much time did she have? Weeks? Months, maybe? She hadn't yet told Tarsie about the pain that held her captive. Her friend would try her best to cure her, but Mary knew far too well there was no cure for this illness. It would take her soon enough. No need to leave Tarsie feeling guilty for something over which she had no control.

Tarsie had called Kansas the place where happiness dwelled. Mary's gaze drifted to the doorway of the sleeping room. She envisioned Emmy and Nathaniel, snuggled together on their mat, blond, curly heads tipped close. The children deserved a place of joy. Somehow, she had to get them out of this tenement before her time to leave the earth came. Her head low, she began to pray, asking God to protect her children, to move in her husband's heart, to make it possible for the ones she loved more than life itself to find joy together when she could no longer be with them.

Lost in her prayer, she gave a start when someone viciously wrenched the doorknob. Then a voice called, "Mary? Unlock the door." *Joss.* Releasing an involuntary groan, she pushed herself off the bench and shuffled to open the door. She searched Joss's face as he entered the apartment, seeking signs that he'd been imbibing liquor. Seeing none, she nearly sagged in relief.

"You missed your supper. Sit down. I'll get you a plate."

Joss's heels dragged on the floor as he crossed to the table and eased himself onto the waiting bench. She sensed his eyes following her as she scooped beans seasoned with pork fat onto a speckled plate. One biscuit from yesterday's baking remained in the tin, so she tucked it next to the beans. Such a sad offering for a man who'd spent his day laboring.

She planted a kiss on his temple, inhaling his unique aroma of sweat, sea, and musky skin as she placed the plate in front of him. He picked up the fork, but then sat with it in his fist, staring at the beans.

"Aren't you hungry?" She ran her fingers through his thick hair. She'd always loved Joss's hair—thick and dark and laden with natural waves that rolled away from his forehead like the ocean rolled toward shore. But also soft. Surprisingly so, considering how gruff he could be. But she understood his crustiness was a mask—a barrier he used to protect himself. Although at times she longed for tenderness, she loved him anyway, because she knew he loved her the best way he knew how. What would he do when she was gone? Her fingers coiled around the silken strands and clung.

He dropped the fork and reached up to grasp one of her exploring hands. With a tug, he drew her onto the bench beside him. "Mary, tell me . . . about Kansas." He slapped the little book onto the table.

Although his tone sounded more weary than eager, her heart leaped with hope. She sought the section Tarsie had pointed out about Drayton Valley and read slowly, emphasizing the points she thought Joss would find the most interesting. While she read, she couldn't help imagining her children running along a grassy riverbank or ambling toward a little schoolhouse, slates tucked in the bends of their arms. She pictured Joss coming home at the end of the day, tired but smiling, satisfied with the toil of his hands, his eyes clear and his face tanned from the sun. But she didn't put herself in the fanciful imaginings.

She finished reading every detail, then told Joss about the man at the railroad who could help them purchase tickets. Placing her hand over his, she sighed. "Doesn't it sound like a fine place, Joss? A place for a family to prosper." Slipping her eyes closed, she allowed one more picture to form in her mind—of Joss leading the children up the steps of a clapboard chapel. Tears stung behind her closed lids. *It could happen, Lord, couldn't it?*

"It's far away from here, this Kansas?" Joss's low, serious tone drew Mary's focus.

"Yes, Joss. Far away."

His jaw jutted. "This, then, is what you want?"

Mary held her breath, afraid she might still be caught in her wistful dreaming. Her vocal cords seemed tangled in knots, unable to deliver words, so she gave a nod.

Joss's head sagged. "But money for tickets . . . I don't have it."

As much as Mary wished she could refuse Tarsie's offer to give over her saved earnings, she wouldn't be taking it for herself. This was for her children. For Joss. For a better, richer, more joyful life. She could swallow her pride for the sake of her loved ones. She only prayed Joss's pride, which was much larger than hers, could be overcome.

In a mere whisper, she said, "I do."

His head shot up, one wavy strand of dark hair flopping across his forehead. "You have money?"

The glimmer in his eyes frightened her. Desperation tinged with fury. But she couldn't retreat now. "Y-yes."

"How much?"

Tarsie hadn't mentioned an amount, but she had indicated she'd spoken to the railroad man and knew her funds were adequate for the journey. Mary chose a simple reply. "Enough."

"Fetch it for me."

"I . . . can't. It isn't here."

"Where is it?"

Mary swallowed. "Tarsie has it." Should she tell him it was Tarsie's money, not hers? But Tarsie was willing to give it to her, which made it hers, didn't it? Her pain-muddled brain tried to reason, but rational thought wouldn't form.

Joss chewed his lower lip, his gaze aimed somewhere behind Mary's shoulder. She'd learned over their years together that it was best to let Joss ruminate. If she pushed him, his defenses would rise. While he thought, she prayed, and after several silent minutes he blew out a mighty breath.

Face still averted, he said, "Pack, then. We'll go."

With a joyous cry, Mary threw herself into Joss's arms. The sudden movement brought a new, excruciating crush of pain. She muffled her gasp with his shoulder. He'd change his mind if he knew how sick she was. And she couldn't let him turn back now. Struggling against waves of nausea, she forced herself to speak. "I can be ready by Monday if need be."

"Monday, then."

Joss's arms held her tight, the pressure painful but still welcome. He so rarely cradled her, seemingly afraid of gentleness being misconstrued as weakness. She relished the feel of his firm, sturdy arms encircling her frame, and although the pain continued to stab with a ferocity that brought tears to her eyes, she refused to wriggle loose of his snug embrace. Mary sighed in contentment as Joss ran his big, warm hands up and down her spine.

With a final pat on her back, he disengaged himself from her hold. He picked up his fork, scooped a bite, and swallowed. "I'll go to Tarsie's after I finish work tomorrow and get the money so I can purchase tickets."

"That's a fine idea." Mary drew in a slow breath, gathering courage. Her next request would surely be met with resistance, but somehow she had to convince him. "And . . . would you tell her to pack, too?"

The fork clattered to the tabletop as Joss spun to face her. "Why?"

Tarsie had no family, nothing to hold her here. And Tarsie loved Mary. Tarsie would do anything to honor her friend— Mary knew this from the depth of her soul. Did Joss love Mary enough to honor her desire? She tested his love with a simple statement. "Tarsie must come with us. I won't go without her. I . . . I need her, Joss."

And you and the children will need her soon, too.

⁕

Tarsie snipped the thread with her teeth and let the heavy velvet skirt flop across her lap. She'd finished with hours to spare before the Saturday-morning deadline. She sent up a silent prayer of gratitude then balled her hands into fists and stretched, releasing the tense muscles in her shoulders.

In a chair across the table, one of her roommates, Agnes, lifted her gaze from the camisole in her hands and sent Tarsie a narrow-eyed scowl. "All done? I wish I could sew as quickly as you. Mr. Garvey always berates me for being behind quota."

Their boss was a stern taskmaster, and often Tarsie's heart lurched in sympathy for workers forced to endure the sharp side of his tongue. But sometimes, Tarsie had to admit, Agnes deserved it. Of the six young women who shared the little apartment and worked as seamstresses for August Garvey, Agnes was the only one to fall below expectations. Mostly because she piddled rather than used her time wisely, claiming the work "boring." But Tarsie's Bible admonished her to work as unto the Lord rather than men. Her conscience wouldn't allow her to shirk, no matter how uninteresting the task.

Tarsie rose and shook out the skirt, admiring the glint of deep purple in the lantern light. "Speed comes with practice, Agnes. You'll be catchin' on soon enough, I'm sure."

Agnes sniffed and leaned back over the camisole.

Tarsie folded the skirt and laid it carefully on her chair. Massaging her lower back, she moved to the stove. A peek in the tall enamel pot revealed at least a cupful of brackish liquid. She poured it into a tin mug and raised it to her lips, grimacing as the bitter brew hit her tongue. The coffee had sat on the back of the stove all day, gaining strength, and the taste turned her stomach, but she drank it anyway. Her empty stomach needed filling. After draining the mug, she carried it and the pot to the dry sink where more dirty mugs, plates, and silverware waited in a basin.

When Mr. Garvey had assigned the girls to this apartment in his building, he'd instructed them to take turns with housekeeping, each pulling an equal share. But she'd discovered the other girls could ignore piles of dirty dishes, crumb-scattered floors, and dust-covered furniture. So frequently, Tarsie—the eldest of the girls at twenty-four—performed the others' tasks rather than live in a messy apartment. She couldn't prevent rodents and vermin from creeping in under the door or from holes in the walls, but she could at least make it harder for them to hide by keeping things tidy.

She picked up the water bucket and headed for the door, intending to venture to the pump in the alley. When she opened the door she discovered a large man, fist upraised, on the opposite side of the threshold. She let out a squawk of surprise and nearly threw the bucket at him. But then lantern light from the apartment reached his face, and she blew out a breath of relief.

"Joss Brubacher, you came close to scaring the life out of me. Why've you come?" A second bout of fear—this one much more intense—gripped her. She grabbed his shirtfront and dragged him through the doorway, her heart pounding.

The other girls paused in their stitching, curious gazes aimed at Tarsie and their unexpected visitor. Joss swept from his head the little plaid hat he always wore and flicked a glance at the circle of seamstresses. Apparently intimidated by his unsmiling countenance, they bent back over their work. But their usual chatter ceased, and Tarsie sensed their ears tuned to her conversation with Joss.

"Is it Mary? Should I fetch my medicinal herbs?" Thank goodness she'd finished that skirt early. She'd be free to go with Joss if need be. She turned toward the sleeping room, ready to retrieve the leather pouch of cures.

Joss held out his hand, sealing her in place. "Mary's fine. Least, as fine as she ever is." His brow crunched—in worry or consternation? Mary claimed Joss cared beneath his bluster, but Tarsie wasn't so sure. He was a difficult man to read. "But we're leaving come Monday. For Kansas."

Tarsie clasped her hands beneath her chin and gasped. "Oh, praise be!"

"So we're needing the money . . . for tickets and such."

Joy exploded through Tarsie's middle. A miracle! She was witnessing a miracle! She waved both hands at Joss, encouraging him to wait. "I'll be gettin' it for you. Stay right here."

She dashed to the sleeping room, aware of six pairs of eyes staring after her. Dropping to her knees beside her cot, she lifted the lumpy mattress and pulled out a woolen stocking containing the carefully hoarded bounty of nearly eight years' labor. Bouncing to her feet, she darted to Joss and jammed the sock at him. "There you are. Thank you for agreein'." She'd never have imagined Joss Brubacher accepting her help. His willingness to do so—to set aside his fierce pride—softened her toward him. He did care for Mary. He *did*.

He gave her a puzzled look, but he took the stocking and shoved the wad into his jacket pocket. She expected him to take his leave, but instead he twiddled the hat in his hand and stared off to the side. From the circle of girls, a nervous titter sounded. It seemed to bring Joss to life. He jerked his face around to scowl down at Tarsie.

"As I said, we're leaving come Monday. I'm hoping to get us tickets on the eight o'clock train to Chicago. So be packed and at the station early. Only take what you can't do without. One trunk—that's it. Won't be space for frippery." He snorted. "Won't hardly be space for the *people* I need to take, but Mary says she won't go without you. So . . ." He slapped the hat onto his head. "Be there." He turned and stomped off, disappearing into the shadows of the hallway.

❊ 4 ❊

Joss lifted Emmy onto the step leading to the passenger
car, then reached for Nathaniel. He gazed up and down
the Grand Central Depot's boarding platform, searching
the crowd for any of Lanker's henchmen. If the gambler got
wind that Joss had collected his pay a week early, he'd be on
the prowl. What with Mary giving away all but their most
important belongings to anyone in need, word was out that
they were leaving. It was only a matter of time before Lanker
came to demand his money.

Granted, the pay envelope held precious little compared
to what Mary had squirreled away. How had she managed
to accumulate such a sum? The things he could've done with
that money if he'd known about it! But now, if Lanker's men
caught him, they'd take every penny, whether he owed it to
Lanker or not. Nobody bested that former riverboat rat.

Someone in the jostling crowd bumped him, and Joss jerked
around, his heart in his throat. But to his relief, it was only a
hunchbacked old man, who waved a gnarled hand in silent
apology. Joss's shoulders sagged. He was far too jumpy. They
needed to get out of here—and quick.

Mary touched his arm. "Have you spotted Tarsie?"

"Not yet." To be honest, he hadn't been looking for Mary's
friend. "Don't worry. She'll be here." He'd seen where she

lived. He'd always thought the tenement he and Mary occupied was sad, but it seemed a palace compared to the one
Tarsie shared with so many others. Kansas probably sounded
like the promised land to the girl. "Come on—let's get you
on board."

He lifted Mary the same way he had the children, surprised by how little effort it took. She'd never been a robust
woman, but when had she grown so slight? She grimaced as
his hands cupped her rib cage, her pale cheeks turning an
ashen gray. He set her down gently, concerned. Readying the
family for the journey must have worn her out even more
than he'd realized. But their four days on a train—one to
Chicago, then three more to reach Des Moines, Iowa—would
give her time to rest.

Joss waited until she took hold of the children's hands.
Then he pressed their tickets into her skirt pocket. "Find us
seats. I'll keep a watch out for your friend."

She gave a weary nod and guided the children inside the
car. Joss paced, his head low, his eyes flicking this way and
that. He'd always been proud of his stature. By the time he
was sixteen, he'd stood an inch taller than Pa. The man had
never laid a hand on him once he had to look up at him—a
huge improvement over the previous years of his life. Standing tall made others think twice about challenging him in a
fight. But now, with his head a good two inches higher than
any other man on the busy walkway, he'd be easily spotted
by Lanker or his cronies. Would that Irish girl hurry already?

A blue-suited conductor walked from the caboose toward
the engine, swinging a brass bell. Its clang competed with the
blast of steam from the engine. As he neared Joss, his steps
slowed. "Got a ticket, mister?"

Joss nodded.

"Best get aboard, then. Pulling out in less'n five minutes."
He headed on, the bell clanging out its warning.

Mary's worried face appeared in the window above Joss's head. He shrugged at her. If Tarsie didn't hurry, they'd have to go without her. They could all catch a train tomorrow—trains left for Chicago every day now, thanks to Cornelius Vanderbilt's ingenuity—but he couldn't give Lanker a chance to catch up with him. He had to go *now*.

Another cloud of hissing steam, accompanied by a shrill whistle blast, chased Joss to the passenger car's step. Mary'd be crushed, and Joss wasn't thrilled he'd squandered money on a ticket that wouldn't be used, but they couldn't wait for Tarsie. He'd told her eight o'clock. Wasn't his fault she couldn't follow directions. With a resigned huff, he heaved himself into the car.

❋

Tarsie collided with a wall of steam. Temporarily blinded, she ceased her headlong dash. Agnes's tattered carpetbag, which she'd traded for Tarsie's good pair of shoes and the quilt off her bed—an uneven trade, to be sure—bounced against Tarsie's knees, throwing her off balance. She staggered two steps to the side, coughed, then squinted and plowed on through the steam. Just ahead, a conductor waved a tarnished brass bell by its wooden handle. She dashed to his side.

"Excuse me, sir, I'm not in possession of a ticket, but—"

The man gave her an imperious look. "If you don't have a ticket, you can't board."

Panic seized Tarsie's breast. "But I must be boarding, sir! My friends and me, we're going to Kansas!"

"Not without a ticket you ain't." He took hold of her arm and steered her toward the depot.

A *tap-tap-tap* captured their attention. The conductor halted and looked upward, as did Tarsie. To Tarsie's great relief, Mary peered at them through a passenger-car window. She gestured with both hands, her meaning clear: *Stay put!*

The conductor growled under his breath, but he hesitated long enough for Joss to burst from the car's doorway.

Joss held a square of paper in his hand. "I've got her ticket. Let her come aboard."

The conductor looked Joss up and down. Seemingly deciding he'd rather not tangle with the big man, he abruptly released Tarsie's arm. Without a word of apology, he gave his bell a swing and plodded on.

"What kept you?" Joss grabbed Tarsie's bag and herded her toward the step. "You worried Mary half sick."

Tarsie lifted her skirts out of the way and struggled to mount the high step. She'd donned two dresses beneath her black cloak, and she felt thick and bulky. Joss let out a huff and caught her elbow, giving a push that launched her onto the little platform. She gasped in surprise and skittered out of his way as he leaped up behind her, his motions as lithe as a cat's.

Still panting from her wild dash to the station, Tarsie leaned against the doorframe. But Joss didn't give her time to rest. Once again grasping her elbow, he propelled her through the narrow aisle to a tall wooden booth where Mary, Emmy, and Nathaniel crowded together on a green-velvet-cushioned seat. The children smiled greetings, and Mary reached both hands toward Tarsie. "Oh, Tarsie, thank the good Lord you made it."

The conductor bustled up the aisle with a wide-legged gait, the bell sticking out of his pocket. "Sit, sit! We're leaving the station."

Joss tossed Tarsie's bag onto the floor, then plopped onto the bench opposite his family. He filled the half near the window. Tarsie looked uncertainly at the open space beside him. Was she to share a seat with Joss?

Mary released a soft laugh. "Here. You sit with the children." As stiff as an elderly woman, she eased out of her bench and slipped in beside her husband.

A high-pitched whine sounded, followed by a *chug-chug*, and the train lurched. Tarsie, turning toward the bench, was thrown smartly onto her bottom in the spot Mary had abandoned. Emmy and Nathaniel hunched their shoulders and tittered. Tarsie flashed a grin at the pair. The train picked up speed, and both children clambered onto their knees to peer out the window and wave at people standing on the platform. Joss sunk low in the seat and tugged his hat over his brows, his furtive gaze aimed at the passing crowd. Tarsie had no one to bid farewell, so she looked across the narrow gap to Mary.

Mary smiled, her lips white in an equally colorless face. "Did you find it difficult to leave your employ?" Sympathy tinged Mary's voice.

Tarsie considered Mr. Garvey's fury—ear-singeing expletives followed by a wheedling series of threats—when she'd told him she'd be leaving. When those tactics failed to sway her, he'd set her roommates to condemning her for leaving them holding her share of the rent. Then he'd insisted she honor her responsibility to clients who'd commissioned articles of clothing. By putting off sleep, she'd managed to complete the lace-bedecked shirtwaist and sweeping multi-layered skirt for one of Mr. Garvey's most particular patrons. The past days had been her most trying since her arrival in New York with her great-aunt a dozen years ago. But she gave Mary a warm smile. "Not at all."

"Good." Mary yawned, wriggling into the corner of the bench. Even before the view outside the window indicated they'd left the city behind, she was sound asleep.

Tarsie watched Mary, noting her white, firmly set lips. She'd crossed her arms over her middle and her thin hands gripped folds of her loose dress. Her brow remained puckered, as if unpleasant dreams held her captive. Even in sleep, Mary didn't relax.

Tarsie's stomach twisted in worry. She faced an arduous

task, nursing Mary back to health, but her herb packets were tucked safely in the carpetbag at her feet. Now she'd be with Mary every day, not just once a week, giving her better opportunity to minister to her friend. During their journey, she'd ply Mary with slippery elm or perhaps cardamom to increase her appetite, ginger and garlic to improve her constitution, and goldenseal to prevent further illnesses from taking hold.

The train rocked, an occasional whistle blast drifting through the crack in the window. Tarsie settled more comfortably in the seat, her plans lifting the burden of worry. By the time they reached Kansas, Mary would be hale and hearty. She'd see to it.

Mary leaned over the spittoon provided by the conductor and retched until what little she'd eaten for supper found its way up again. Even if Joss begged, she would refuse food until they'd left the train. Hunger would be far easier to bear than the nausea the train's rocking created in her belly. Completely spent, she collapsed into the seat.

Tarsie pressed a handkerchief into Emmy's hands. "Go dip this in the water bucket, darlin', and bring it back for your mama." Emmy scampered up the aisle, and Tarsie leaned in close to Mary, touching her forehead with the backs of her fingers.

Even through her watery gaze, Mary read the deep concern on her friend's face. She forced herself to smile. "You needn't look so guilty. My sickness isn't due to your cooking."

Tarsie didn't laugh. "The sandwiches we've purchased from the conductor haven't been the freshest, but they've not made the rest of us sick." She shook her head, her brow furrowing. "My ginger tea should be settling your stomach, but you've not kept down a bite since we left New York. Three days of heaving!" She leaned closer, her gaze briefly flicking toward

Joss, who leaned toward the opposite corner of the bench as if afraid of contracting whatever illness plagued his wife. "Could you be with child?"

Joss sat bolt upright, his horrified gaze landing on Mary's face. Mary started to reply, but Emmy bounded over and shoved the dripping handkerchief into Tarsie's hands.

"Thank you, darlin'. You're a big help, you are." Tarsie began dabbing at Mary's cheeks and mouth with the moist cloth.

Emmy climbed back into the seat next to Nathaniel and engaged her brother in a finger game. While Tarsie ministered to her, Mary watched the children, an anguished lump in her throat. As much as she'd longed for a large, boisterous family, God hadn't seen fit to grant her desire. And He'd made the right choice. He'd known her time on earth would be short and that Joss wouldn't be able to handle the burden of more than two children on his own. Yes, God always knew best.

Tarsie finished wiping Mary's face and sat back, placing the limp handkerchief over the armrest to dry. Then she opened the bag that rested between her feet and began pawing through the contents.

Joss nudged Mary lightly. "You're not expectin' another one . . . are you?"

Despite the pain that throbbed through her midsection, she winged upward a short prayer of gratitude. When she left this earth, at least she wouldn't be taking a second life with her. "No, Joss. I'm not expecting."

He heaved out a mighty breath, and his obvious relief pierced her heart. As much as she knew he loved her, he'd never seen the children as the blessing she believed them to be. Oh, how she prayed he'd find comfort when her time came, knowing a piece of her still lived in the forms of Emmy and Nathaniel.

Tarsie held up a small bag and bounced from the bench.

"I'll be begging some hot water from the conductor and brew you up a cup of chamomile tea. Maybe it'll settle your stomach better than the ginger."

Mary wanted to tell Tarsie not to bother, but the young woman shot up the aisle before Mary could form a word of protest. She leaned sideways, her shoulder connecting with Joss's arm. He lifted his arm, and she tucked herself against his side, the warmth of his body familiar and comforting. His elbow curved around her, his big hand cupping her waist. She pressed her face to his chest and closed her eyes against the pain that throbbed fiercely from her breast all the way to her hip. If only the pain would abate. She didn't want to wake the others another night by crying in her sleep.

Strength, Father. The simple plea left her heart without conscious thought. Nestled in Joss's arms, she focused her pain-fuzzy brain and offered another request. A selfish one, perhaps, but she needed to cling to an element of hope. *I know this sickness will have its victory, Lord, and I accept Your will. But could You let me live long enough to reach Kansas—to see with my eyes the place where my children will grow to adulthood? Give me a glimpse of their home, Lord, before You take me to Your home.*

❀ 5 ❀

Des Moines, though not as big and bustling as Chicago or New York, still offered a city view. And city smells. Tarsie wrinkled her nose as she scanned the clusters of tall buildings, some of which bore smokestacks belching gray puffs into the pale blue sky. She hoped the Kansas landscape near Drayton Valley proved more pleasing to the eye and fresher to the nose.

She pulled a restless Nathaniel against her skirts lest he become lost amongst the travelers rushing to and fro on the planked boardwalk. Her days of sharing the single bench seat with both Emmy and Nathaniel had bonded her to the children in ways a year of weekly visits had not. The little boy tipped back his head and grinned up at her, his endearing dimples flashing in his apple cheeks.

"Do you suppose Joss will find a train of wagons leaving yet today?"

Idly smoothing Nathaniel's tousled hair away from his face, Tarsie turned to Mary, who slouched beside Emmy on a slatted bench pressed against the depot wall. The tiredness in Mary's voice matched her drawn face. Tarsie prayed wagon travel would prove easier on her friend than the train's rocking motion—poor Mary appeared to have aged ten years in the past few days.

"Mr. Driscoll told me wagons travel every week toward the western states, so I'd be thinking there's a good chance we'll soon be on our way to Drayton Valley." As eager as she was to reach Kansas, Tarsie secretly hoped they might have a day or two of rest before climbing into a wagon and heading out. Mary would benefit from a comfortable bed in a warm hotel, if Joss were willing to spend the money.

Mary draped her arm over their pile of belongings—two trunks and three carpetbags—and then rested her cheek on her bent elbow. She looked as worn out and sad as Tarsie's crumpled bag, stirring Tarsie's sympathy. Might the depot-master be willing to share a tin cup and hot water so Tarsie could mix a potion to improve Mary's constitution? Now that they sat on steady ground rather than in a rocking train car, surely her stomach would hold it down.

Tarsie pressed Nathaniel into Emmy's arms. "You children stay here with your mama. I'm going to—"

"Mary!" Joss's booming voice carried over the discordant melody of hissing steam, whistle blasts, and conversation. Tarsie searched the crowd and spotted his hat-covered head. He emerged from the flow of people and stood before them, his hands on his hips. "Sorry it took so long. Had to walk near a mile to reach a livery, but I found us a wagon. It's a sorry-looking thing, but the livery owner insists it'll get us to Kansas without breaking down." He swept off his hat and ran his hand through his thick, unruly waves. "I'm not as certain about the pair of nags he convinced me to buy to pull it, but I couldn't afford any of the other horses in the corral." He jabbed his thumb over his shoulder. "It's waiting on the other side of the block. Couldn't get it closer with all the fancy carriages cluttering up the street."

Mary wearily pushed to her feet, reaching her hand toward the children. "Well, then, let's each take a bag and—"

Tarsie pressed forward. "You sit back down with Emmy

and Nathaniel. Joss'n me will cart our belongings to the wagon and then come fetch you." She sent Joss a stern look, daring him to argue with her. Her gaze on Joss's unsmiling face, she added, "After these past days of turning your belly inside out, you're in no shape to be lifting anything heavier than a bird's feather."

Silent communication passed between Tarsie and Joss, and although he hesitated for several seconds, he offered a brusque nod. "I'll take the trunks. Tarsie can take the bags. You stay here with the young'uns until we're loaded." Bending forward, he pushed the bags from the trunks' tops and lifted the biggest one. He sent a quick glance at Tarsie. "Follow me."

By filling their arms to overflowing, Tarsie and Joss transported all of their possessions from the depot to the wagon in three trips. Tarsie agreed with Joss about the wagon being sorry looking. With unpainted, weathered wood held together by rusty hardware and bent nails, the wagon appeared ready to rattle apart. But the boards supported the trunks and bags, and Tarsie had to trust that the human cargo wouldn't fall through the bed, either.

Tarsie remained with the wagon while Joss fetched Mary and the children. Her heart gave a funny flip when she saw them approach. Joss held Mary in his arms, the children scuttling along beside him, each holding to his jacket tails. What a picture they presented—a groom carrying his bride, attended by cherubs in homespun. Tears pricked her eyes, and she knew the image would be forever burned in her memory.

Joss placed Mary gently into the bed of the wagon, then swung the children over the warped sides. He turned to Tarsie and offered his hands. She'd always viewed his broad hands—callused from years of toil—as hard and stern. But having seen them hold Mary with such tenderness, they seemed vessels of kindness. Of caring. Of love. Suddenly shy in his

presence—but uncertain why—she allowed him to assist her
into the wagon.

The wagon creaked and complained as Joss coaxed the
team into the cobblestone street. He called over his shoulder,
"The livery owner told me where to buy provisions for the
trail. He said wagonmasters gather at the store. We should
meet up with others heading toward Kansas."

Mary's head bobbed as if her neck were too weak to hold
her head steady. "Then we'll leave today?"

Joss's broad shoulders lifted in a shrug, stretching his jacket
taut across his back. "Don't know. If we can't leave today, we'll
just bed down at the livery—the liveryman said he wouldn't
mind. Not fancy, but a pile of straw makes a good enough
bed for a day or two."

Tarsie wanted to suggest getting Mary and the children
a hotel room. Hotels dotted the streets, varying from fancy
to plain. But her tongue refused to cooperate. She held to
the side of the wagon and sat in silence until Joss pulled up
in front of a large, false-fronted store with a painted sign
boasting *Franklin's Emporium*. On the outskirts of town,
with wood siding nearly as worn as that on the wagon, it
hardly resembled an emporium. But Joss set the brake and
hopped down.

He strode to the back and reached for Mary. "Come help me
buy supplies. Tarsie can stay in the wagon with the young'uns.
No sense in having them underfoot while we shop."

Being spoken about as if she weren't there chased away
the fanciful feelings that had held Tarsie captive for the past
minutes. She gave Joss a meaningful look. "The children and
I are tired of having to sit. With another long ride ahead of
us, we'll be getting down and running about in that cleared
area beside the store."

Ignoring his low-browed scowl, she scooted to the end of
the wagon and climbed over the edge without assistance.

"Come along, children. There's a nice shady spot over here just perfect for a game of tag."

※※※

Joss slipped his arm around Mary's waist and guided her onto the planked floorboards of the emporium's porch. He sent a glowering look over his shoulder to Tarsie, but she was already engaging the children in a chasing game and missed his silent reprimand. With a huff, he gave the glower to his wife instead. "That Irish friend of yours has a sassy tongue in her head."

Mary glanced in Tarsie's direction. Affection rather than indignation glowed in her eyes. "She's a good friend. The best I've ever had." She shifted to look up at him. "Don't begrudge her presence, Joss. Be thankful for her. She's . . . a gift."

Something in her gaze made Joss's mouth go dry. He'd never backed away in fear from anything, but he discovered he was afraid to pursue the meaning behind her words. So he gave a little nudge with his hand, urging her forward. "We need supplies enough for a month, but no extravagance. It'll take a fair amount of money to rent a place and set up a household when we reach Drayton Valley."

They stepped from the midmorning sunshine into the shadowy depths of the store. A husky voice called out a welcome. Joss blinked several times, letting his eyes adjust to the dim interior, and he finally spotted an apron-clad man behind a tall, warped counter.

The man waved a beefy hand. "Howdy. Welcome to Franklin's. You homesteaders?"

"That's right. Need to buy provisions." Joss nudged Mary forward. Dust coated the floor, stirring as they walked. Joss glanced around, noting the livery owner told the truth about the place being well stocked. The wood shelves bowed beneath the weight of their bounty. They should be able to find everything they needed for the journey.

Mary's steps dragged, her movements so jerky it seemed her joints were rusty. Joss frowned as worry gripped him. She'd never survive several trips up and down the aisles. He spotted a barrel near the counter, and he ushered Mary to it. "Sit here. Tell me what we'll need, and I'll fetch it."

She sank onto the barrel with a sigh. Her weary smile thanked him.

The jovial man behind the counter held up a tattered sheet of paper. "This here might help you. It's a list o' what most folks buy before settin' out with one o' the trains. Wanna make use of it?"

Joss shrugged. "Why not? Give it to my wife." Mary would have to read it—Joss didn't possess the ability. But the emporium owner didn't need to know that.

The man ambled around the counter. His shape reminded Joss of the Humpty-Dumpty character in Emmy's storybook. He was bald as an egg, too. "Tell you what. Stay here with your missus an' I'll do the fetchin'."

"You charge extra for doing the gathering?"

The man laughed, apparently unaffected by Joss's blunt question. "Nah. I know where everything's at anyways, so why not save you the trouble o' huntin'? By the way, folks call me Fat Frank." He patted his ample belly and laughed again.

"We're Joss and Mary Brubacher," Mary said. "It's nice to meet you, Mr. Frank."

The man's jowls flushed pink. "Oh, now, Miz Brubacher, no need for mister. Just Frank'll do. So . . . want me to fill that list for ya?"

Joss flipped his hand outward, giving Frank permission, then leaned against the counter. He fidgeted in place, discovering it difficult to stand idle while someone else did the work.

While Frank shuffled between aisles, carting back bushel baskets or plump bags, he kept up a steady flow of talk. "Where you folks plannin' to settle?"

Mary answered, "A place called Drayton Valley. Have you heard of it?"

"Yup. Drayton Valley's in Doniphan County, right on the Missouri River. Good cropland in those parts." Frank plopped a bag marked FLOUR onto the counter. White dust rose, and he snuffled. "You plan on farmin'?"

Joss snorted. "Not me. I was a dockworker in New York. Hope to find the same work in Drayton Valley."

"Ahh." Frank shuffled off again, his throaty voice drifting over the shelves. "Heard tell the busiest docks in the whole state are right there in Doniphan County—an' they might be gettin' the railroad, too. Promisin' community, to my way o' thinkin'."

Mary smiled up at him, and Joss nodded at her.

Frank dragged a bushel basket containing dried apples across the floor, raising a small cloud of dust. "Quite a few folks headin' for Kansas these days—whole groups of 'em." He turned a clumsy circle and set off again. "But most o' them aim to snatch up some o' that free farmland in the middle o' the state."

He added another bushel basket—this one half full of navy beans—to their growing pile of goods. "'Course, that won't matter none to the wagonmasters. They'll still guide you where you want to go. Reckon they'll just leave you off an' mosey farther on west." Hands on hips, he surveyed the gathered items. "Let's see now, you got a hunnerd fifty pounds o' flour, twenny-five pounds bacon, ten pounds rice, fifteen pounds coffee, half bushel o' apples an' half bushel o' beans, ten pounds salt, fifty pounds cornmeal, two pounds saleratus . . . Still need a jug o' vinegar, twenny-five pounds o' sugar, an' a big tin o' pepper. Smart to take a few loaves of hard bread, too, for the days cookin' just ain't an option. This bein' spring, there'll be some rainy ones, most likely."

Joss fingered the wad of bills in his pouch, envisioning how it would shrink after paying this tab. "Throw in the bread," he said, "but we can do without the pepper."

Mary sat up, angling her head to peer at Frank. "What about canned milk? The children will need milk."

Frank gave a hearty laugh. "You don't need to worry about that none. Ever' one o' these trains, somebody's got a cow. You'll be able to barter milk without no trouble at all. How many young'uns you got?"

Pain crumpled Mary's chin. Joss knew she'd say five. She always counted the three they'd buried. Then they'd have to explain why only two were in the wagon. He blurted, "Two."

"Well, then . . ." Frank popped open a round glass jar and withdrew a pair of fat, sugarcoated gumdrops. He plunked the candy into Mary's hand. "A treat for your little ones."

Tears winked in Mary's eyes. "Thank you, sir. You're very kind."

"Oh, now, it ain't much." Frank grinned and backed away, wiping his hands on his stained apron front. He waddled behind the counter and retrieved a small tin box. Its hinges creaked when he lifted the lid. "Let's get you all tallied up here. Then we can load your wagon."

Joss paid the bill—to his relief, a lesser amount than he'd expected. Then, with Frank puffing along beside him, he carted everything to the waiting wagon. Mary stood beside the wagon while Tarsie climbed inside and organized the sacks, boxes, and bushel baskets, leaving space in the center of the bed for the children and her to sit.

Frank frowned at the wagon. "Don't you got a cover for this thing? Bound to hit rain on the trail. You'll need a cover." He slapped Joss on the back. "Tell you what, I got a canvas big enough, and there's a broken-down wagon out back. Been tearin' it up and usin' the wood in my cookstove, but the ribs're just lyin' there. No use for 'em. You can have 'em if you buy the canvas."

Tarsie's face lit. "What a generous offer! We'll be thanking you kindly."

Joss harrumphed. Friend of Mary's or not, this girl would have to learn her place. *He* was in charge, not her. "Go check on the kids," he told her. She frowned, but she climbed out of the wagon and bustled away. Turning to the store owner, Joss squared his shoulders. "'Preciate the offer. But I wouldn't know how to fit the wagon with ribs."

"Why, that's no problem at all, mister!" Frank beamed. "Any o' the wagonmasters'll be able to attach the ribs an' stretch a canvas over to keep the sun an' rain off your family. Most of 'em are right good wainwrights—have to be to take care o' those they're leadin'. 'Sides, you get rain on them sacks, that cornmeal, sugar, an' flour'll be ruined. *Gotta* have a cover."

Swallowing an irritated grunt, Joss surrendered. If the wagon had a cover, they could use it as a temporary shelter tonight instead of paying to sleep in the liveryman's barn. "All right, then. Where'll I find one of the wagonmasters so we can get a cover on this thing?"

Frank's deep chortle shook his belly. "You're in luck, mister. Right there's Tate Murphy, one o' the most reliable wagonmasters I've ever known." Lifting his thick arm, he waved. "Tate! Over here! Got some folks—Joss an' Mary Brubacher an' their young'uns—wantin' to join up with your train!"

Joss squinted up the road and spotted a man on horseback. His dusty plaid shirt and brown trousers spoke of days in the saddle. Leather gloves covered his hands, a bandana circled his neck, and a battered hat tugged low hid everything but his thick black beard. Except for the bandana and cowboy-styled hat, he might have been one of the dockworkers from New York.

The man reined in the horse next to the emporium's hitching rail and swung down. With a deft flick of his wrist, he wrapped the reins around the rail, then aimed the toes of his scuffed boots in Frank's direction. His head low, he batted at his britches while he walked, and not until he reached Frank's side did he lift his head. He smiled, his teeth a slash of white against his walnut-husk-colored skin.

Tate Murphy stuck out his gloved right hand to Joss. "Pleased to have you join my train, Mr. Brubacher."

Joss kept his arms stiffly at his side. He glowered at Frank. "Just what do you take me for? I won't travel with"—he raked a derisive glare from the brim of Murphy's well-worn hat to his boot-covered feet—"the likes of *him*."

✳ 6 ✳

J oss!" Mary sent an apologetic look to Frank and Mr. Murphy. Both men aimed their gazes downward, hiding their expressions, but Frank's slumped back and wringing hands denoted worry. In contrast, Mr. Murphy communicated controlled fury with his clenched fists and tense shoulders.

Joss whirled on her, waving his hand toward Frank. "He's wanting us to trust our passage to a—"

Mary pressed her shaking fingertips to her husband's mouth.

He jerked away from her touch but kept his lips clenched together. With a growl, he marched from the wagon to the shaded area beside the store where the children continued to run and play, their bright laughter an ignominious pairing for the tension emanating from the men.

Mary clasped her hands to her ribs. Now the deep hurt throbbing through her middle was more than a physical pain. "Mr. Murphy, please forgive my husband's outburst. He . . . he isn't an evil man. But his father . . . he . . ." She couldn't bring herself to complete the statement. Such ugliness should never be spoken aloud.

Slowly, Mr. Murphy raised his head. Although he held his jaw at a stern angle, understanding glowed in his soft brown eyes. "It's all right, ma'am. Children don't come into the world hatin'. It's taught." He looked toward Emmy and Nathaniel, who scampered uninhibitedly in a splash of sunshine, their sweaty faces alive with joy and innocence. A smile quivered on his lips, making his thick beard twitch. "I'll be prayin' the lessons for those little'uns are more in keepin' with the Good Book than what your man was fed."

Mary's heart leaped. "Are you a believer, Mr. Murphy?"

He swept his hat from his head, revealing a bald pate. "Yes'm. Learned about Jesus an' His sacrifice for men—*all* men—from my granny when I was still a young'un. The Lord's seen me through some mighty troubled times. Wouldn't wanna walk this world without Him."

"Nor would I." Mary nibbled her lower lip. Given Joss's behavior, Mr. Murphy could refuse to allow her family to join his train. Yet she believed God had brought this man into her pathway for a purpose. She wanted him to be the one to lead them to Kansas. Breathing a prayer for God's will to be done, she skittered forward a few inches and looked directly into Mr. Murphy's dark face. "My family needs to reach Drayton Valley, Kansas. Will . . . will you guide us to our new home?"

Mr. Murphy's expression didn't change. For several seconds he stood so still and unmoving, he gave the appearance of a statue. She waited, her breath caught in her lungs, her hands twined together in hope. *Please, please, God. Let him say yes.*

At last the man drew his shoulders back, his chest filling his shirt and straining against his striped suspenders. He seemed to examine Joss's stiff figure across the yard as he spoke. "I got a group camped east o' town—eight families in all. We're leavin' first thing tomorrow for Kansas. Easy thing for you to join up. But, ma'am . . ." He faced Mary. His gaze bore into hers. "They's all colored families. Not a white face among us. Is your man gonna be willin' to be part o' a train full o' . . . ?"

The unspoken word stung her heart. Mary winced. Joss would certainly fuss. His father'd had no use for men of color, whether black, yellow, or red. Mary never understood her father-in-law's vile opinions, and she'd prayed when he died that his offensive ideas would be buried with him. But they lived on, through Joss. How often had she begged God for the means to rid Joss of his unfounded prejudice? Now it seemed the answer to her prayer stood before her dressed in a patched plaid shirt and dusty brown trousers.

Her legs trembled from standing so long under the sun. A decision had to be made. She didn't know this man, but he loved the Lord. That made him her brother in Christ. She drew in a sharp breath as a fresh stab of pain, seeming to sear her insides, stirred nausea. They had to reach Drayton Valley. Soon.

She fixed Mr. Murphy with a determined look. "If you'll have us, my husband and I will join your wagon train. And"— she shifted to peer at Joss, who leaned against the corner of the store with his hands thrust deep in his pockets, his head low—"I promise Joss will give you no trouble."

Mr. Murphy whipped off his glove and extended his hand. Without a moment's hesitation, Mary placed her hand in his leathery palm. He gave a firm shake, his grip warm and solid. "Welcome aboard, Miz Brubacher."

Mary lifted her chin, swallowing the moan of pain that strained for release. "Please, call me Mary."

"Thank you, Miz Mary. An' you call me Tate."

"Very well, Tate."

A smile creased his face, relaxing the worry lines that created furrows in his forehead.

Frank gave Tate's shoulder a clap, his jovial nature restored. "Well, now, since that's all settled, can you help these folks afix some ribs to their wagon so we can put a cover on it? Then they oughta be set to go."

Tate slapped his hat into place and tugged his gloves over his fingers. "Let's get to it."

※

Joss held the reins and watched the puff of dust rising from the scrub brush on either side of the road a quarter mile ahead. For three days he'd followed the wagon train's silent signal, keeping his family on course. For three days, he'd sat silent on this warped, creaky seat, teeth aching from being ground together. Another ten days of travel awaited. He'd surely explode before they reached Kansas.

Not once in all their years together had Mary defied him. Until now. Everything inside him wanted to rail at his wife. But something held his tongue.

In his mind's eye, her fervent expression rose again. She hadn't begged. Just outright stated, "We have to get to Drayton Valley. Mr. Tate is willing and able to guide us. We're going, Joss." Yet something akin to desperation had tinged her tone and glimmered in her blue eyes. And that very desperation had made him swallow his pride and agree to follow Murphy's train. But he wouldn't be a part of it. Not even Mary's begging could make him camp with that bunch.

He glanced skyward, noting the descent of the sun. They'd be stopping soon. Each of the previous nights, Murphy'd led them to a clearing with a nearby water source—creek, lake, or hand-dug well—where they could circle their wagons. Joss couldn't deny the man seemed to know what he was doing. But he also couldn't deny relief that none of his dock buddies could see him now, mindlessly following a former slave like a lamb follows its shepherd.

He'd taken to parking his wagon on the opposite side of the water source, in sight of the train's glowing campfires and within hearing of their voices, but separate. Mary and Tarsie seemed to enjoy listening to the nightly singing that came from the camp. The whole lot of them from youngest to oldest gathered together before bedtime and delivered song after song in low-toned, husky voices. It was haunting. Joss shivered despite the early evening warmth.

From behind him in the wagon bed, beneath the stained canvas covering, one of the children began singing, "Go down, Moses, way down in Egypt-land . . ." Joss jerked upright and barked out his first words since they'd left Des Moines. "You hush that up right now!" The song ceased, followed by a childish whimper and Tarsie's soothing voice. Joss didn't turn around to determine which child he'd wounded with his harsh command. Didn't matter, as long as he was obeyed. He'd never laid a hand on Emmy or Nathaniel—he wasn't like his pa when it came to using a strap—but if either one of his young'uns picked up any habits from those people in the wagon train, he'd cut a switch and chase it right out of them again.

The dust cloud ahead settled. Murphy must've brought them all to a halt. Joss squinted at the sun, then frowned. Stopping early tonight. He preferred pressing onward till dusk. Sooner they reached Kansas, sooner he could be shed of their company.

As Joss had come to expect, Murphy'd led the wagons off the road a piece. The wagons formed a rough circle with children darting here and there between the wheels, braids bobbing and squeals ringing. Women with kerchiefed heads gathered twigs and buffalo chips for fires. The men unhitched mules or oxen from wagons and led them to a trickling stream. Murphy separated himself from the group and jogged to meet Joss's wagon. Although he didn't smile, neither did he avoid Joss's eyes. Joss's fiercest glares hadn't managed to intimidate the wagonmaster. Another reason Joss resented the man.

"Hold up a minute," Murphy called, jamming his palm in the air.

With a grunt, Joss drew his wagon to a halt. Tarsie leaned over the back of the seat, her shoulder brushing against Joss. "What is it, Mr. Murphy?"

Murphy removed his hat when addressing Tarsie. "Wanted to let you folks know, might be delayed in startin' out tomorruh mornin'. One of the women—Minnie Jenkins—is near her time. Wanna give her at least a few hours' rest before jostlin' her around in a wagon aftuh her babe is born."

Joss let out a mighty huff. The woman better drop her whelp soon. He didn't have the patience to sit around waiting.

Tarsie clicked her teeth with her tongue, a sympathetic sound. "Are you needin' a midwife? My great-aunt did midwifery and taught me what she knew. I'd be pleased to see to the mother."

Murphy shook his bald head. "Appreciate the offer, Miss Tarsie, but Minnie's mama is travelin' with her, and she'll see to the birthin'."

"All right, then. If something changes and she has need of some extra hands, please tell her—"

"Yah!" Joss brought down the reins on the horses' rumps, and the beasts lurched forward, sending Tarsie into the wagon bed. She let out a disgruntled squawk, but Joss ignored her and guided the team upstream of the circled wagons. He brought the horses to a stop and set the brake, then turned and scowled into the back of the wagon. "You won't be going to that camp."

Tarsie folded her arms over her chest and matched his glower with one of her own. "Joss Brubacher, the good Lord gave me an ability and He expects me to use it. I brought my medicinal cures, and if someone in the Murphy wagon train has need of tending, I'll be tending 'em and that's that!" With her nose in the air, she flounced to the back of the wagon and climbed out. "Come along, Emmy and Nathaniel. You can help me gather fuel for our cooking fire." The children scrambled after her.

Joss clutched the hair at his temples, stifling a snarl. That woman! He couldn't wait to be rid of her and her sassy, argumentative tongue. He glared at Mary, who lay on a pile of quilts draped across the trunks. Three days' worth of frustration rose up, ready to spew from his mouth. But one look at his wife's white, drawn face, and his fury flickered and died.

Crawling into the back, he touched her cheek. "That Tarsie and her talk of medicinal cures . . ." His words growled out. "That's all it is, is talk. She's done you no good."

Mary's face puckered as if discomfort gripped her, but a weak laugh left her throat. "She's done me much good, Joss, just being here." She clutched his hand, pressing his palm more firmly to her face. "Don't torment her. It grieves me to hear you two fussing at one another. Can't you be friends?"

Joss had no desire to grieve Mary, but he couldn't admit to any hankering to befriend the Irish girl, either. "I need to unhitch the team. Do you want to stay here and rest, or would you like to get out?"

"I'd like to get out and enjoy the evening breeze." She tried to push herself upright. Her face contorted, and she dropped back onto the rumpled quilts with a strangled moan.

Joss reached for her. So much effort just to sit up. No matter what Mary said, Tarsie's cures were useless. He scooped her into his arms and eased her over the edge of the wagon. He followed with the quilts and laid them out in the shade of the wagon. When she'd settled herself, he crouched before her. "You all right there?"

She offered a gentle smile. "I'm fine, Joss. Go about your business."

His legs stiff from hours on the wagon seat, he scuffed to the horses and released them from their rigging. He tethered the pair within reach of the creek and left them contentedly munching tender shoots of green along the bank. By the time he returned to the wagon, Tarsie had already started a fire. A coffeepot sat on one side of the crackling flames, a covered kettle on the other. She held a bowl between her skirt-draped knees and stirred cornmeal into a mushy mess with a wooden spoon.

Joss stifled a snort. Beans and johnnycakes for supper. Again. The aroma of roasted meat drifting from the campfires of the wagon train made Joss salivate. He paused, lifting his face to inhale the scent and let it flavor his tongue. Then, without warning, something else drifted from the camp. A scream.

Tarsie leaped up. The bowl tumbled from her lap and its contents splattered across the ground. A second scream rent the air, this one even more piercing than the first. Nathaniel and Emmy raced from their playing spot nearby. Tarsie held out her arms, and the children clung to her.

Mary struggled to her feet and staggered to Joss's side. She clutched his arm, her fingers digging into his flesh. "W-what do you suppose is happening?"

Joss shook his head. "Nothing good, that's for sure."

Tarsie separated herself from the children and scuttled to Mary. "It must be the woman straining to deliver her babe. I should fetch my pouch and go over. Maybe—"

"You stay here," Joss ordered.

A third scream, long and anguished, carried to their ears. The hair on Joss's neck prickled. He curled his arm around Mary's waist and turned her toward the quilts. "Sit and rest. No matter what's going on over there, there's nothing you can do."

Tarsie let out a little huff. "There's somethin' *I* can be doing!" She grabbed up her skirts, darted to the wagon, and clambered into the bed. Moments later she emerged with her pouch tucked under her arm. "I'm going over to see if I can help."

"I told you—"

Mary grabbed Joss's arm. "Let her go, Joss."

Joss ground his teeth as Tarsie dashed toward the circle of wagons.

❄ 7 ❄

Tarsie stood with the other solemn travelers, watching as Mr. Murphy emptied shovelful after shovelful of dirt onto the blanket-wrapped forms of Minnie Jenkins and her newborn son. A mighty lump filled her throat. *It shouldn't be, Lord. Birthings should be times of celebration, not times of mourning.* But sounds of sorrow filled her ears—low moans, soft sobs, whispered prayers seeking comfort, and the *skritch-skritch* of a shovel's blade digging into dirt, followed by soft plops of earth falling.

The rosy pink of a new dawn highlighted the scene, and birds chirped a cheerful song from nearby brush. The sweet promise of the blossoming day seemed a bitter insult to the too-soon ending of two lives. Tarsie hugged herself, blinking hard against tears.

Mr. Murphy used the back of the shovel to smooth the dark mound of dirt, then stepped aside. Minnie's husband, his steps slow and plodding, separated himself from the throng. He gripped a crude cross fashioned from two thick twigs bound together by a rawhide strip. Using a rock as a hammer, he dropped to one knee and pounded the cross into the newly turned dirt. Each strike of the rock on the wood sent a shaft of pain through Tarsie's heart. Oh, why couldn't she have saved them?

The cross secure, the man rose and stood silently, staring down at the cross with his wide shoulders slumped and tears swimming in his brown eyes. A woman—Minnie's mother—broke from the crowd and staggered forward. She held out her arms to her son-in-law. The rock fell from his hand as they clung to each other. In unison, cries wrenched from their mouths. From their souls. And then the others joined in, giving vent to their sorrow in a grief-laden melody that rose from the earth all the way to the heavens, where, Tarsie prayed, God would hear and rain down blessed comfort.

Tarsie wanted to cry, too. But she realized her tears were as much out of guilt as sadness. She'd failed Minnie Jenkins and her baby. She had no place in this circle of mourners. Yet she couldn't bring herself to leave. She stayed until the song of sorrow died to sniffles and muted moans. The people shuffled away one by one until only Minnie's husband and mother, still locked in a tight embrace, and Tarsie remained on opposite sides of the fresh mound.

Mr. Murphy propped the shovel on his shoulder and inched to Tarsie's side. He spoke in a near whisper. "Gonna let Harp an' Judith take a little more time here, then we'll pull out."

Tarsie nodded, her throat so tight no words could escape.

Mr. Murphy's thick hand descended onto Tarsie's shoulder. "Don't be blamin' yourself now. Minnie's mama tol' me that babe was fixed to come out wrong-side first. Nothin' you coulda done. Your bein' here, your carin', was a blessin'. You think on that, you hear, Miss Tarsie?"

Tarsie offered another miserable nod, then scuffed her way back to Mary and the waiting wagon, cradling her bag of herbs in her arms. Mary greeted her with a warm hug, then pulled back, her hands clamped over Tarsie's shoulders as her empathetic gaze searched Tarsie's face.

"We heard the wailing. Did she lose the baby?"

"The babe died. And his mother did, too." Tarsie separated

herself from Mary's tender grasp. "I need to put my medicine pouch in the wagon."

Mary grabbed Tarsie's arm, holding her in place. "It wasn't your fault, Tarsie."

Tarsie looked away, unwilling to accept the tenderness in her friend's eyes. She didn't deserve kindness. Not when she'd failed so miserably.

"Death . . . happens. Babies die. Mothers die. And we simply have to trust both life and death to our loving heavenly Father's hands." Mary's tone changed from compassionate to contemplative, sending an uneasy chill across Tarsie's scalp.

Tarsie gently removed her arm from Mary's light grasp. "Let me put away my pouch, and then I'll be seein' to breakfast."

She scurried off, eager to put her hands to work. If she were busy, she wouldn't have to think. When she'd finished frying cornmeal cakes in bacon grease, she tossed a quilt on the ground to serve as their table and called everyone to breakfast.

Joss, who'd kept himself occupied with the horses while Tarsie prepared their morning meal, ambled over after Mary had prayed and served the children. He crouched at the edge of the quilt, selecting one of the remaining crisp cornmeal cakes in the skillet. He sent Tarsie a low-browed look while he chewed. "You were out all night."

Tarsie poked at the browned cake on her tin plate. She couldn't bring herself to swallow. "Yes. It was a hard birthing." She flicked a glance at the children, hoping Joss would read the warning in her expression. Why subject the little ones to unpleasantness? "And it ended in the worst possible way."

He nodded, popping the final piece of cake into his mouth. "Figured as much from all the caterwauling." He glanced toward the other camp, a flicker of something unreadable squinting his eyes. Then he squared his shoulders and rubbed his palms on the thighs of his britches, leaving streaks of grease on the heavy duck fabric. "Since the new mama won't need time to rest up, guess we'll be pulling out early. Glad I hitched the team." He pushed himself upright.

Tarsie bit down on the end of her tongue to prevent herself from unleashing a torrent of fury at the man. How could he be so unfeeling? He himself had lost three babies. His wife sat now, pale and with barely enough strength to lift a fork. Didn't he possess even an ounce of charity?

She spoke through clenched teeth. "Mr. Murphy intends to give Minnie Jenkins's husband and mother a proper time of mourning before we set out again."

Joss looked again toward the gathered wagons, as if seeking evidence that contradicted Tarsie's statement. Finally he nodded and hunkered down again. "Well, then, reckon I'll have another cup of coffee." He held out his tin cup.

Tarsie rose with a rustle of skirts. "Pour it yourself." She stomped away, her hands clenched into fists and her teeth clamped so tightly her jaw ached. Mary called after her, but she ignored her friend and continued to the creek, where she plopped down on the bank. She tore loose a few sprouts of green and gave them a vicious toss into the sunshine-speckled water, watching as the slow-moving stream carried the scraps out of sight. If only her own feelings of inadequacy could be so easily discarded.

"I'd also like to be sending *Joss* downstream, the insensitive oaf!" She muttered the words to the passing breeze. It replied by tossing loose strands of hair across her cheek. With a grunt, she anchored the strands behind her ear and folded her arms over her chest. She sat stiffly until Joss hollered they were pulling out.

After thanking Mary and Emmy for seeing to the breakfast cleanup—something she should have done instead of skulking off in a cloud of anger—she huddled in the corner of the wagon bed and fell silent. She wanted to sleep, as she'd gotten no rest the night before, but the jouncing progress over stones and ruts in the road jarred her from sleep every time exhaustion coaxed her eyes closed.

Mary, seemingly oblivious to the jolts and bumps, napped off and on. The children entertained themselves with some rocks they'd picked up along the way that left whitish marks on surfaces. By the end of the day, they'd decorated every exposed inch of the wagon's planked sides, earning a scolding from their father. Tarsie bristled at his harsh words. The wagon was old and battered. The simple drawings and attempts at the ABCs did no harm. But she held her tongue and spoke not a word to Joss, fearful she'd say things that would distress Mary and displease her Lord. That man ruffled her feathers worse than anyone else she'd ever known.

At suppertime, a rustle in the brush near their wagon stilled everyone's forks above bean-filled plates. Tarsie instinctively reached for the children, but Mary had already tugged them snug to her sides, so she hugged herself instead.

Joss snatched out the pistol he wore in the waistband of his britches and aimed it at the shadowy patch. "Who's there? Make yourself known before I lose my patience and pull the trigger!"

A hatless form in dark trousers with ragged holes where the knees used to be stepped from the shadows into the flickering firelight. "No need to shoot, mistuh. It's just me, Harp Jenkins—from the Murphy train." He inched closer, bringing his face into view, but stopped well away from the quilt that served as their table. "I ain't armed. Just brung somethin' for Miss Tarsie. A payment for her service to . . . to my wife. Can I give it to her?" He held out a bandana-wrapped packet with both hands.

Joss shoved the gun back into its hiding spot. He bobbed his head at Tarsie. "Go ahead." Bending over his plate, he resumed eating but kept his wary gaze pinned on the other man.

Tarsie skittered across the short distance to Harp, her heart twisting in her chest. "You shouldn't be giving me anything, Harp. I'm not deserving of payment."

He shook his head, his expression serious. "Yes'm, you are. You done us a favor, spendin' the night easin' Minnie's pain an' bein' a comfort to her mama. This ain't much . . ." He pressed the packet into Tarsie's hands. "But I hope it'll serve as a thank-you. You's a nice lady, an' we's honored to know you." He swallowed, his voice dropping to a throaty whisper. "It weren't your fault, Miss Tarsie, that Minnie an' our baby boy died. So don't be blamin' yourself now." With a respectful bow of his head, he turned and slipped away into the shadows.

Tarsie stood, clutching the lumpy packet—she didn't have the courage to open it yet—and stared at the spot where Harp had disappeared. He'd told her not to blame herself. Both Mr. Murphy and Mary had told her the same thing. She sighed, lifting her gaze to the sky where a few bright stars winked white against the pale gray expanse. *Lord, how many times will I need to be told it wasn't my fault before I finally believe it?*

The morning of their eighth day of wagon travel, Mary awakened in such intense pain she couldn't hold back a cry of anguish.

Tarsie, lying in the narrow gap between crates, bolted to her knees and gripped Mary's shoulders. "What is it?"

The flap of canvas serving as a curtain at the back opening whisked aside and Joss peered in. His dark hair drooped across his thick brows. "Mary?"

Mary wanted to reassure both of them, but when she

opened her mouth only a groan spilled out. Nausea—the worst ever—rolled through her belly. Panic-stricken, she gasped, "I . . . I'm going to be sick."

Joss unhooked the back hatch and let it drop open with such force it rocked the wagon. Tarsie's arm slid behind Mary's back and urged her upright. The moment Mary raised her head, the earth spun, throwing her back again.

"Joss, be helping me!"

At Tarsie's shrill cry, both children, who'd been put to bed in the space under the wagon last night, began to cry. The sounds of their distress carried through the floorboards and stung Mary's heart. How she wanted to comfort her babies, but she could only hold her stomach and hope the bile filling her mouth wouldn't spew across their belongings. She closed her eyes and prayed for strength.

The wagon rocked again, forcing another groan from her mouth. Then Joss's terse voice barked, "Get out of my way, girl!"

Scuffles let Mary know that Tarsie was scrambling to obey. Firm arms slipped beneath Mary's shoulders and knees, lifting her from the makeshift bed, and moments later a cool morning breeze heavily scented with dew caressed her hot face. She gulped the moist air, letting it wash away the foul taste that flooded her tongue.

Joss paced with her, the movements causing further queasiness but also distracting her from the intense pain that radiated from her chest all the way to her hip. She lacked the strength to cling to him, but she trusted him to hold her securely. Her head lolled against his shoulder, her arms lying limp across her middle and her legs dangling over his bent elbow. Such pain. Such weakness. Would she die right here in Joss's arms? Part of her wished she could so she'd be released from the pain, but the greater part of her longed for life.

The children's wails calmed to hiccupping sobs, and Mary

realized a murmur followed her and Joss—Tarsie addressing God in prayer. *Yes, pray, Tarsie. Remind God I've not yet reached Kansas. I want to see it before I cross to glory.* Just as she trusted Joss to hold her body, she trusted Tarsie to lift her soul. Slowly, although the pain continued to pound like stormy waves against a shore, the nausea eased.

Eventually Joss's frantic march around the campsite slowed, too, and she opened her eyes to meet his worried gaze. She wanted to smile, but the pain turned her smile into a grimace. Even so, she forced her thick tongue to say what he needed to hear. "You can put me down. It's . . . it's passed."

Joss sank onto a barrel and settled her in his lap. He cupped her face between his palms and looked deeply into her eyes. "You scared me, hollering out like you did."

"I'm sorry."

The children scrambled to their father's side, holding hands and staring at her as if afraid to come too close. She reached out and smoothed Emmy's tousled curls, then tweaked the end of Nathaniel's nose. The three-year-old giggled, hunching his shoulders. The sound was music to Mary's mother-heart. She prayed her children would always have reasons to laugh.

Tarsie crossed behind the pair, curling her hands over their shoulders. "Come, you two. Let's wash the sleep from your faces and give your hair a brushing. Then we'll fix our breakfast, hmm? You can stir the cornmeal mush." She led them away, her troubled face angled to peer at Mary over her shoulder.

Mary drooped against Joss's frame, tucking her head beneath his chin. His arms circled her. She pressed one palm to his firm chest, listening to the steady *thump-thump* of his heart in her ear. Would his heart shatter when she left him? "Joss?"

His fingers twined through her tangled hair, cupping the back of her head. "Hmm?"

"How much longer . . . 'til we reach Kansas?"

"Murphy said last night, three more days." His hand crept around to lift her chin. The concern in his eyes spoke love to Mary. "Can you last three more days bumping around in the back of the wagon?"

Oh, how she prayed so! With effort, she bobbed her head in a nod.

He kissed her forehead and drew her close again. "I'll try to find the smoothest spots in the road. Make it as easy on you as I can."

"Thank you," Mary whispered. *And when my time comes to slip away, I pray I find a way to make it as easy on you as I can.*

❋ 8 ❋

Joss couldn't eat breakfast—his stomach held a boulder of dread. For the first time in his adult life, he ignored food. Instead of eating, he strode determinedly to Murphy's camp, passing the wagons where families sat in small circles, enjoying their morning meal. Black faces lifted, watching him. Some nodded a silent greeting. Others only watched with wary eyes. He ignored them all, even the man who'd brought that chunk of salted ham to Tarsie after she'd spent the night seeing to his wife. He had nothing to say to any of the travelers. He needed the leader.

He finally found Murphy saddling his horse on the far side of the circled wagons. He trotted the final distance, calling, "You. Murphy."

Murphy kept a grip on the horse's reins with one hand, stroking the animal's glossy nose with the other. "G'mornin'."

Joss didn't have time for pleasantries. "My wife, she's not feeling good. The bumps in the road hurt her stomach." Recalling the tormented wail that had jolted him awake less than an hour ago, he grimaced. Mary hadn't hollered during childbirth, which was supposed to cause women great pain. Whatever troubled her now, it was bad. "Wondered what we had ahead—whether it's gonna be as rough as what we crossed the last couple days."

Murphy rubbed his forehead, pushing his hat askew. "Hard to say. Wasn't so bad the last time I came through, but if they've had a lot of rain, or if heavier wagons've passed since then, it might've changed the trail." He quirked his lips to the side. "We can take it slower if we need to—don't reckon the folks'd mind accommodatin' you an' your missus."

Something ugly welled in Joss's chest. Even though Murphy's tone was congenial—even though he was willing to offer assistance—it grated that Joss had to ask a favor of a colored man. He balled his hands into fists and pressed them to his thighs. "Nah. Don't bother. Quicker we get to Drayton Valley, the better."

"You sure?"

"I'm sure."

Murphy settled his hat back into place above his brows. "All right, then." He scanned the sky, the blue hidden behind a shield of thick gray clouds. "Might end up movin' slower'n usual anyway if the wind don't blow them clouds away. Looks like a rainstorm's brewin' up there." He swung into the saddle and gave a nod. "Be pullin' out in 'bout half an hour."

"We'll be ready."

The rainstorm Murphy predicted hit midmorning. Big drops, cold and carried on a gusting northern wind, pelted the ground and soaked through Joss's jacket and wool hat. He wished he'd spent money on a leather broad-brimmed hat like the one Murphy wore—least his head would stay dry. Raindrops ran down his face in rivulets. Miserable, he shivered on the seat and encouraged his team to continue plodding over the muddy pathway.

The horses' hooves sank into the muck, slowing their passage. Without the guiding cloud of dust ahead, Joss couldn't be sure he was still trailing Murphy's train. He searched for fresh ruts in the road, signs of recent passage by other wagons, but the heavy rainfall distorted his vision. He faced forward and brought down the reins with a mighty crack. The horses strained against their rigging, then broke into a clumsy trot.

The wagon rocked from side to side, and once Joss thought he heard Mary groan. His heart twisted in his chest—he didn't want to cause her undue pain—but what good would it do her if he got them all lost? Disregarding the horses' slipping hooves, he flailed the pair of tawny hides with the reins and hollered "Yah!" again and again. He needed to reach Drayton Valley soon, needed to find his wife a doctor. Mary needed more help than the Irish girl could offer.

⁂

Mary lay on her pile of quilts atop the trunks with her face to the wagon's side. She pressed her fist to her mouth to hold back agonized moans. On the floor behind her, Tarsie sang hymns and ballads to the children. The sweet Irish lilt combined with the *rat-a-tat-tat* of plump raindrops against the canvas cover offered a comforting harmony. If only the stabbing pain would allow her to enjoy the gentle lullaby.

Joss had said he'd drive carefully, but he seemed to be setting a reckless pace. The wagon rocked, the old wood creaking. Mary feared she'd be tossed from her perch. Tucking her knees toward her chest, she curled one hand over the edge of the trunk and held tight. Eyes closed, she focused on listening to Tarsie's song.

"'Tis the last rose of summer left blooming alone; all her lovely companions are faded and gone . . .'"

Tears stung behind Mary's closed lids. Tears of pain, yes—she could scarcely bear the tormenting shards of agony piercing her middle—but mostly tears of sorrow. Why did the sickness that stole her mother have to rob her of life, as well? She didn't want to leave her children alone, motherless, to bloom into adulthood without her watchful gaze and petitions to God on their behalf.

Tarsie's voice lifted, rising above the patter of rain. "'When true hearts lie withered and fond ones are flown, oh! who would inhabit this bleak world alone?'"

The melody faded, and Tarsie began singing a silly nonsense song. But the final words of the tender ballad reverberated through Mary's mind. A strange peace flooded her frame. The pain still pounded, but beneath the pain a recognition dawned. Her children wouldn't be left to inhabit the bleak world alone. They'd have their father, and Tarsie, and they'd always have God. Didn't God promise He would never leave nor forsake His children? Perhaps in moments of weakness the illness made her feel forsaken, but being taken to Him—to bask in the promise of residing forever with Him where no pain would ever again touch her body—was glory.

Thank You, my dear heavenly Father, that this pain is only for now. Thank You that soon . . . very soon . . . You'll take it away. Just please let me see Kansas first.

For two days, the sky "leaked," as little Emmy described it. Dousing rain delivered sideways on a stout wind, drizzling rain that hung like a mist, gentle rain falling straight down to patter softly on the canvas cover. Rain both day and night slowed the wagons' progress and made everyone miserable with the constant dampness. The gray gloom dampened their spirits, as well, bringing out crankiness in the children and an increased surliness from Joss. But on the third morning, when Tarsie stretched awake, her eyes were assaulted by brightness. Sun!

She bolted to the back of the wagon and threw aside the flap. Blue skies, dotted with a few wispy clouds, hung overhead. Tarsie released a cry of exultation and spun to shake the children awake. "Emmy! Nathaniel! Come look—the rain's stopped!"

The children sat up, rubbing their eyes with their fists, then crawled to the opening and peered out. Delight lit both faces. Tarsie laughed, watching them. They acted as though they'd never seen sunshine before. But after their long days of being trapped inside the wagon, she understood their elation.

Joss stepped to the opening. His clothes were caked with mud from sleeping beneath the wagon, but his usually dour face wore a relieved grin. "Glad all that rain didn't put out the sun." He held his hands to Emmy. "C'mon out."

With a huge smile, the little girl catapulted into Joss's arms—an action Tarsie had never witnessed before. She marveled not only at the glistening sunshine sending fingers of light across the brightening sky, but at the change in the man. Perhaps he did harbor some kindness beneath his gruff exterior.

Joss swung Nathaniel out, then looked at Tarsie. "Can't get a cookfire going—too wet out here—but maybe scout around for a spot we can throw out a quilt and eat the last of the hard bread and some dried apples. I'll take the bucket and get milk for the young'uns."

Each day, he'd shoved the bucket into her hands and sent her after the milk, unwilling to spend time with their fellow travelers. Tarsie gawked at him in amazement. "You—*you're* fetching the milk today?"

He rubbed his whiskered cheek. "Yeah. Gotta talk to Murphy anyway." He turned and clomped off.

Tarsie started to climb out, eager to stand in the morning sun, but she checked on Mary first. Her face, even in sleep, bore a furrowed brow and firmly pressed lips. She'd eaten nothing during the rainy days, claiming it would be a waste of food, since it would only come up again, and her pale skin stretched over her cheekbones, making her seem even more fragile. Reluctant to disturb her friend, Tarsie gathered the last portion of hard bread and a few handfuls of dried apples. With the food items bundled in a checked napkin, she inched toward the opening, moving slowly to avoid rocking the wagon.

But as her weight left the bed, the wagon shifted, and Mary stirred. She peered around in confusion, blinking. "J-Joss?"

Tarsie leaned in and touched Mary's foot. "He's gone to fetch milk. Were you needin' something?"

"Are we there? Is this Kansas?"

The weak quaver set Tarsie's pulse pounding. "Not yet. But we're close. Very close, Mary."

Mary licked her dry lips, her eyelashes fluttering as if her lids were too heavy to hold open. "Am I imagining . . . sunlight?"

Tarsie let her gaze drift from east to west, admiring the emerald green of leaves on scraggly brush, the radiant pink of wildflowers dotting the countryside, and the robin's-egg blue directly overhead. Such beauty. "The sun's shining as bright as a new penny."

A soft sigh escaped Mary's throat. "A blessing."

"Would you like to come out and be seeing it for yourself?" Hope coursed through Tarsie's chest. The sun had brought a smile to Joss's face. Might it bring a touch of healing to Mary?

"I want to rest."

Tarsie's hope plummeted.

"But the moment we reach Kansas, wake me. I want to see Kansas." Mary once again coiled into a ball.

A weight pressed so hard on Tarsie's chest it hindered her breathing. She turned away from the wagon into a splash of sunlight so bold she had to squint. But Tarsie's pleasure in the sun had dimmed.

❋ 9 ❋

D ay after tomorrow?" Joss blasted the words, impatience and aggravation puffing his chest until his shirt strained against its buttons. Each added day on the trail meant more discomfort for Mary and a delay in reaching a doctor. Besides that, he needed to get Mary and his kids out of that wagon. It wasn't a fit home.

"That's the soonest, I reckon."

Joss blew out a mighty breath. "It's too long."

Murphy shrugged. "Can't change the land, Mr. Brubacher. Them days of rain got things all sloppy. Scouted ahead last night an' seen how the trail's plumb under water on my usual route. Gotta do a little windin' off course or our wagon wheels'll get caught in the goo an' none of us'll get where we're goin'."

Joss yanked off his hat and whacked himself on the leg. He glowered at Murphy. "But my wife needs a doctor!"

"'Scuse me," a hesitant voice intruded.

Joss whirled around. The young black man who'd entered his camp and given Tarsie the ham stood a few feet away. Harp, he'd called himself. Joss growled, "Whatever you need, boy, it can wait. I'm talkin' to Murphy right now."

Harp lowered his head but kept his dark eyes pinned on Joss's face. "I wa'n't needin' to talk to Mr. Murphy, suh. I was wantin' to talk to you."

Joss squinted at the man, suspicion rising in his chest. "What do you want with me?"

"Heard what you was sayin' . . . 'bout your wife needin' a doctor." He inched closer and gestured toward the circle of ragtag wagons. "Thought mebbe Mr. Murphy could drive my wagon, an' I'd take his horse an' ride on ahead to one o' the towns 'round here. Fetch you a doc an' bring 'im back to meet up with our train."

Murphy made a face. "Dunno, Harp. Folks in these parts are used to me comin' an' goin'—they don't give me trouble. But you're a stranger. A *colored* stranger. Might could meet with some unpleasantness."

Harp gulped, but he squared his shoulders. "If Mr. Brubacher's missus is ailin' bad enough to need a doc, somebody oughta fetch one." His gaze bounced sideways, as if he knew he'd overstepped boundaries, but he added, "I'd be willin' to risk it to help his missus . . . an' him."

Joss barked, "Why're you so interested in helping me, boy? What do you want from me?"

The man's head hunkered low again, and he pressed the toe of his scarred boot into the mud. "Don't want nothin', mistuh. Just . . . I know how it feels to see the woman you love hurtin'. Good Book says 'do unto others,' so I thought to spare another man puttin' his wife in the ground."

An ugly picture formed in Joss's head. His gut clenched. Balling his hands into fists, he angled his body toward the smaller man. "My Mary ain't gonna die." She wouldn't. She wouldn't! He stormed away as fast as the rain-soaked ground beneath his feet would allow.

※

Nineteen days after setting out by wagon from Des Moines, Joss got the promised view of the Missouri River—the final barrier between his family and Kansas. One by one, Murphy's wagons drew to a stop along the bank. An excited chatter carried on the crisp breeze of the late-spring afternoon. As he pulled back on the reins, halting their wagon at the tail end of the train, Emmy and Nathaniel grabbed the back of the seat and leaned out, their faces eager.

"Is this it, Papa?" Emmy tugged Joss's sleeve. "Are we here?"

"We here?" Nathaniel echoed. The boy reminded Joss of a parrot he'd seen in a saloon one time, always repeating what he heard.

The youngsters had asked the same question at each stop the past two days. Their impatience wore on Joss, but he held back a sharp retort. They were as tired of being in the blasted wagon as he was. "Not yet. Gotta cross the river." Murphy had indicated he'd make arrangements with the ferry owner to transport the wagons and people to the other side.

"Then we'll be there?" Emmy asked.

Nathaniel rested his temple against his sister's shoulder. "We'll be there?"

"Still got a little ways to go. But we'll be in Kansas. Kansas is on the other side of the river."

The children squealed in excitement, and Joss's lips twitched into a smile at their reaction. Up ahead, folks spilled out of wagons. The children dashed toward the edge of the water and their mothers ordered them to come back. Emmy pointed at the hustle and bustle. "Papa, can we get out, too?"

"Reckon so."

"Hurrah!"

Joss grabbed Emmy's arm, keeping the little girl from leaping over the wagon's seat. "But you keep hold of your brother and stay away from the water." The river moved fast, sloshing high on the bank. Last thing he needed was one of them to drown. Mary couldn't take losing another one.

"Yes, Papa! C'mon, Nattie."

The two clambered over the seat and used the wagon wheel

as a ladder to reach the ground. They scampered off hand in hand, their yellow hair shining in the sun. Joss watched them for a moment, noting how little his kids resembled him. They had Mary's hair, Mary's eyes, Mary's slight build. But he had no doubt they were his. Unlike his ma, who'd dropped a red-headed drummer's whelp and then died, Mary was faithful.

Twisting to look into the back, he called, "Mary, come on up here. You can see it now—Kansas—on the other side of the river."

From her makeshift bed, Mary lifted her head. Her pain-dulled eyes flickered with interest. "Kansas?"

Tarsie, kneeling on the floor beside Mary, offered her arm. "Come. I'll be helpin' you so you can get a look."

Joss bit down on his lower lip, watching Mary rise up and slide her feet to the floor. She reminded him of an old, crippled woman the way she moved so slow and bent over. Tarsie guided her to the opening, and then Joss caught hold of her under the arms and lifted her onto the wagon's seat. It took no effort at all—she'd near wasted away to nothing over the past few weeks.

Swallowing his worry, he pointed to the wide river. "See there? The Missouri. Murphy's hiring the ferry to take us over, and then we'll be in Kansas, just like you wanted."

Mary sagged against Joss's chest, but her drooping eyes darted everywhere, seeking, seeming to drink in the view of rushing water, the rolling grasslands that held the wagons, and the sharp rise of brush-covered land on the other side. "It's beautiful, Joss, just like I knew it would be."

Joss tightened his grip on her thin shoulders, wincing at how her bones poked against the cloth of her dress. "Wait 'til we cross over. I'll get you out and let you stick your feet in the grass. Reckon it'll tickle?"

Mary laughed softly, but the tinkling sound ended with a sob. "It will. I know it will."

Tarsie reached for Mary. "Here. You be lyin' down again. Rest up for the ferry ride."

Joss scooped Mary into his arms and lifted her over the seat and back into the wagon's bed. He chewed his dry lower lip and watched Tarsie tuck Mary beneath the quilt. Mary's eyes—they'd almost looked yellowish out here in the sun—slipped closed. Her lashes threw a shadow on her waxy cheeks.

Tarsie skittered to the opening and fixed Joss with a worried look. "Just moving from there to here wore her out." She spoke in a frantic whisper. "She's doing poorly, Joss. More poorly than even she's willing to admit, I'd wager."

Joss looked past Tarsie to Mary. The worry he'd pushed aside returned, gnawing at his insides. "We'll be across the river soon."

Tarsie wrung her hands. "Look at all these wagons. It'll take three trips for sure to get us all across. Can you be asking Tate Murphy to let us cross first? I . . . I don't have anything more to offer her. My herbs aren't enough." True remorse pinched Tarsie's face. "She's needing a *real* doctor, Joss."

Joss shot one more look into the back. His wife's shoulders rose and fell in shuddering heaves, causing her tumbling hair to stir. He'd always loved Mary's bright hair, but now it was thin and without luster, the color and texture of old straw. If he didn't know better, he might think a much older woman lay there instead of his not-yet-thirty-five-year-old wife. Tarsie was right—Mary needed help *now*.

He wrapped the reins around the brake handle. "I'll talk to Murphy about getting us across. Stay with her." He leaped out of the wagon and took off at a run.

Tarsie observed Joss's dash through the middle of their fellow travelers. Usually he skirted the colored folks. He might scowl and talk gruff, but his love for Mary was stronger than his prejudice. The thought gave Tarsie's heart a lift.

"T-Tarsie?"

She scooted to Mary's side, touching her friend's dry, sunken cheek. "Are you wantin' a drink? I can fetch it."

"No. No, I . . ." Mary's eyes fluttered half open. "Where's Joss?"

"He's gone to talk to Mr. Murphy and get us to the other side of the river so you can be seeing a doctor."

"There's no need." She angled her head to peer into Tarsie's face. A weak smile tipped up the corners of her chapped lips. "Tarsie, it's my time. 'The Lord giveth, and the Lord taketh away. Blessed be . . .'" Her words faded with a grimace of pain.

Tears flooded Tarsie's eyes, distorting her vision. "No, Mary! You have to hold on. Joss, he's going to—"

"There's nothing Joss or a doctor can do. I *know*, Tarsie."

Tarsie swiped her hand across her lashes, groaning. "But there must be somethin' someone can do. Somethin' *I* can do . . ." Flopping open her leather pouch, she scrambled through the bag of cures.

Mary's arm extended slowly, her hand hovering in the air like a butterfly caught on a slight updraft. The sight of those thin, white, reaching fingers stilled Tarsie's frantic search. She slipped her hand beneath Mary's and clung.

Mary wheezed, "There is something . . . you can do."

Tarsie leaned forward, peering into Mary's pale, pain-riddled face. "What? Anything, Mary."

"Take care of my loved ones." Mary's clammy fingers tightened, surprisingly strong for a woman whose very life was ebbing away minute by minute. "See to my children . . . and to my Joss. Minister to them, Tarsie, just as you've ministered to me. They'll need your love."

Tarsie swallowed. Loving Emmy and little Nathaniel would come easy. But Joss? How could she love Joss?

"Yes, Joss."

Tarsie blinked in surprise. Had she spoken aloud? But no, Mary knew her so well. She'd never had a closer friend. Oh, how she would miss this woman.

Mary's lips trembled into a tender half smile. "I know you think he's hard and unfeeling, but you're wrong. He feels deeply. He's just afraid to let it show—afraid it isn't manly to let it show. His pa . . . the man tried to whip the tender out of Joss. But underneath his bluster, Joss is a good man."

"Is he?" Tarsie heard the sarcasm in her tone, and she flinched. She shouldn't be hurtful. Not while Mary lay dying.

But Mary—either unwilling or unable to read Tarsie's cynicism—released a gentle sigh. "He is." Her eyelids drooped, her blinks so slow Tarsie could count to three during one up-and-down sweep of her brittle lashes. "Tarsie, when our heavenly Father looks at us, He loves us enough to see . . . what we were meant to be. I've prayed for the Father to let me view Joss through His eyes instead of my own, to let me love my husband unconditionally, the same way God loves us, hoping my love would one day awaken Joss's heart to the love of God. But now . . ."

She took a hollow, shuddering breath that reminded Tarsie of stones rattling in the bottom of a can. "Now I'll be gone." The fingers held in Tarsie's grip trembled, their grasp weakening. "You're my dearest friend, Tarsie, and I . . . I know I'm placing a tremendous burden on your shoulders, but who else can I ask? My children need a godly father. Someone must show Joss the way. Will . . . will you be God's love on earth . . . to my precious children . . . and to Joss?"

Tarsie bit back sobs. Although it would tax her to the height of her abilities, she would honor her dear friend's request. "Yes, Mary. I will."

"You promise?"

"I promise."

Mary's hand fell away from Tarsie's wrist. Her face relaxed as her eyes slipped close. "Thank you." Air escaped Mary's lips, a whisper-soft sigh of satisfaction. And then silence fell.

Tarsie stared into Mary's sweet face, holding her own breath as she waited for her friend to pull another life-giving breath into her lungs. But Mary lay still. Tarsie's chest burned with the effort of withholding her own breath—*Breathe, Mary! Breathe!*—but eventually the air whooshed from Tarsie's lungs on a tormented moan of sorrow. Sobbing, she threw herself across Mary's lifeless body, willing the warmth and life she possessed to somehow transfer to her friend. Emmy, Nathaniel, Joss—they needed Mary so badly. How could God take her?

Over her heartbroken sobs, the echo of Mary's voice reverberated through her memory. *"Will you be God's love on earth to my precious children and to Joss?"* With stiff, painful movements, Tarsie forced herself upright. She'd made a promise, and with God's help, she would honor it. Her first task would be finding a way to tell Emmy, Nathaniel, and Joss that Mary's spirit had slipped away.

Swallowing her tears, she gently covered Mary's face with her apron. Then she turned toward the wagon's opening and borrowed a prayer she'd heard Mary whisper many times. *Strength, Father.*

❋ 10 ❋

His Mary would never know if Kansas grass tickled her feet, but at least she'd been put to rest in Kansas soil. Joss swallowed the massive lump that filled his throat and hoped his wife would be satisfied with the simple grave on the far fringes of White Cloud, Kansas.

Strangers surrounded the mound of dirt that covered Mary's body—all of the black travelers from Murphy's train, Murphy himself with his hat in his hands, the doctor Joss had summoned but who'd arrived too late, and a solemn-looking preacher the doctor had dragged out to perform a simple ceremony. Joss reckoned he should appreciate their presence, but resentment churned through his gut. These people didn't know Mary. They didn't belong here. But a weariness heavier than anything he'd ever known held him captive, and he couldn't dredge up enough energy to send them away.

The preacher's voice rose with conviction as he read from the Bible. "'Surely goodness and mercy shall follow me all the days of my life: and I will dwell in the house of the Lord for ever.'" The Bible's pages fluttered in the wind, and the man smoothed them back into place. His head low, he closed his eyes and offered a prayer.

Joss shut his ears to the petitions, the same way God

must've shut His ears to Tarsie's prayers and the prayers Murphy said his people sent up to the heavens for Mary. A God who'd take a woman like Mary before her time wasn't worth beans in Joss's estimation.

The preacher concluded his prayer with a deeply intoned "amen," and the folks gathered behind Joss echoed it before they ambled away. Tarsie stretched out her hand to the minister and thanked him for coming, but Joss kept his hands clamped over Emmy's and Nathaniel's small shoulders. He wouldn't offer a thank-you he didn't mean.

The moment Tarsie stepped back from the preacher, Joss pushed the youngsters in her direction. "Take 'em to the wagon and stay put. I got me some business in town. I'll meet up with you later."

Tarsie's eyebrows crunched. "What kind of business might you be having in town?" She tugged the children snug to her sides, her eyes widening. "You aren't fixin' to"—her voice dropped to a raspy whisper—"drown your sorrows?"

Joss snorted. "A man's got a right to pickle his insides after layin' his wife to rest."

Tarsie tipped her head. A strand of red-brown hair, loosened from her braid, danced in the breeze. "And would that be what Mary would have you do on her buryin' day?"

Pain stabbed Joss's stomach, as fierce as the ache that must have tormented Mary these past weeks. The doctor who'd come had said she'd probably died of a cancer—the kind of sickness no doctor could cure. He'd told Joss, "It would've taken a miracle to restore your wife's health, Mr. Brubacher." Well, the Miracle-Maker hadn't seen fit to heal his Mary, so why shouldn't Joss dull his pain in the only way he knew how?

"I don't reckon Mary'll know one way or the other," Joss growled. "Just do as you're told." He smacked his hat onto his head and stomped away.

In his dash through White Cloud yesterday afternoon in

scarch of a doctor, he'd spotted a billiard hall. A place for men. If he didn't miss his guess, there'd be spirits served there. He patted his pocket, noting the clink of coins. He'd drink till his pocket was empty or his brain was numb, whichever happened first.

The hinges on the screen door creaked when Joss threw it open. Four men, each with a long pole in his hands, surrounded a green-flocked table. They turned from the table as Joss stepped over the threshold. The one closest to the door said, "Howdy, mister. You come for a game?"

Joss shook his head. "Came for a drink. Whatcha got?"

The man looked Joss up and down, smirking. "From the looks of you, you need a bath more'n a drink. You been rolling in a pigsty?" His cohorts guffawed.

Joss glanced down his length. He hadn't paid much attention to the dark stains that blotched his pants and shirt. The nights of sleeping under the wagon on soggy ground, even with a protective strip of canvas around him, had left him disheveled and filthy. Then digging Mary's grave had added more dirt to his hands and clothes. But what difference should that make? His money was clean.

Ignoring the sniggering bunch, Joss clomped to the long counter that ran along the south wall and slapped his hand on the sleek wood top. "I'll drink anything. Beer. Whiskey. Rum." He glowered toward the men who remained like guards on duty around the table. "Make it quick."

One of the men—the one with brown hair so coarse and curly it resembled coiled springs shooting from his head— separated himself from the others and scooted behind the counter. He grabbed a white cobbler apron from a hook and tied it over his shirt and trousers. "Whiskey's two bits a shot."

Joss tossed a few coins onto the counter. They rolled across the polished wood, circled, then settled. "Pour."

The curly-haired man removed a bottle from a shelf and

slid a short glass toward Joss. He glugged the first shot into Joss's glass, then extracted two dimes and a nickel from the coins scattered on the counter.

Joss lifted the glass, licking his lips in anticipation of the first taste of liquor. He'd need at least four shots before he'd start feeling good, but the first one always tasted the best, before his tongue lost track of flavor. Just as he touched the glass's rim to his lower lip, a voice whispered through his memory.

"You aren't your pa, Joss. You don't need the drink."

Sweet. Beseeching. Mary's voice.

His hand trembled. Liquid dribbled over the rim onto his thumb and finger. For long moments he stared at the little glass and its contents, a war waging inside of him. Desire to lose himself in numbness battled against desire to please his wife. Which was more important to him—the drink or Mary?

He plunked down the glass, sending up a spray of gold-colored liquid that doused his hand and puddled on the wooden counter. Wiping his wet hand on his shirtfront as he went, he aimed himself for the door.

"Hey, mister—your money!"

Joss ignored the call and careened into the street. So he'd left a good six bits behind. It was a small price to pay for— just once—putting Mary first.

Tarsie tucked the children beneath the quilt Mary had used every day during their journey. Perhaps the scent of their mother caught in the fabric would help them sleep. Little Nathaniel was too young to understand what had happened, but he'd cried all afternoon because Emmy cried. The little girl's inconsolable sorrow and Nathaniel's repeated demand to go back to the cemetery and "dig Mama up" nearly broke Tarsie's heart.

She leaned forward and kissed their foreheads, then whispered, "Get a good rest now. God's angels'll be holding you tight all through the night."

"Like they're holdin' Mama tight?" Emmy's voice quavered.

"Holdin' Mama?" Nathaniel mimicked.

Tarsie forced her lips into a smile and brushed Emmy's curls away from her tear-moistened cheeks. "Your mama doesn't need angels to hold her anymore because she's with Jesus."

Emmy blinked, her blue eyes so like Mary's. "And she's not sick no more?"

"She'll never be sick again," Tarsie said. As much as she missed Mary, she couldn't help but send up a silent prayer of gratitude that her dear friend's pain was forever gone.

Emmy snuggled closer to Nathaniel, who appeared to have already drifted off to sleep. "I wish I could go to Jesus, too." She sniffed. "I wanna be with Mama."

"I know, darlin'." Tarsie adjusted the quilt beneath Emmy's chin. "And you will be someday. But you have to wait 'til God calls you. He has a perfect time for you to go be with Him, and you mustn't want to go ahead of His plan. All right?"

Emmy yawned, her eyes crunching closed. "All right, Tarsie. G'night."

Tarsie remained on her knees beside the children's pallet, alternately singing and praying, until Emmy's deep, even breathing matched her brother's. Then she carefully climbed out of the wagon into a starlit night. The fire she'd started earlier to cook their supper no longer snapped, but coals glowed. She added a few twigs, stirring the fire to life again. When Joss finally stumbled back into their camp, he might need the coffee she'd left in the pot.

A few yards downriver, the canvas covers of the Murphy wagons hunkered like a circle of ghosts in the muted light. Campfires glimmered, and mumbled voices drifted to Tarsie's ears, a comforting reminder of someone's presence. But here, in her silent camp, she felt alone. Tate Murphy had come over after supper to tell her that he and the others would head on come morning. She'd thanked him for staying long enough to see Mary buried. Even if Joss didn't appreciate their attendance at the graveside, Tarsie did. And Mary would have, too.

She glanced toward the town, searching the shadows for Joss's return. She shivered despite the warmth from the fire. What if he didn't come back? What if he decided to abandon his children now that Mary was gone? What would she do if—

She refused to continue pondering what-ifs. He'd come back. Everything he owned was in the wagon. He had to come back. But the fire had died to smoldering coals a second time and the other camps had fallen silent before the sound of footsteps alerted Tarsie to someone's approach.

Straightening from her hunkered position beside the soft orange glow, she aimed her face toward the deep shadows. "Joss?"

"It's me."

He stepped fully into the camp. As he passed her, a telltale odor tickled her nose, and she resisted pinching her nostrils shut. She watched Joss cross to the opposite side of the rock circle she'd built to contain their fire. He crouched, resting his elbows on his bent knees, and stared at the glimmering coals. His face, lit from beneath by the feeble glow, appeared harsh, his thick mustache a slash of black above his firmly set lips.

Tarsie shivered again. Hugging herself, she jolted to her feet. "Now that you're back and can keep a watch over your children, I'll be taking myself to sleep." Accusation colored her tone.

He lifted his head sharply, pinning her with a stern frown. "Nobody told you to wait up for me. I'm no boy in need of tending."

Tarsie angled her chin high and peered down her nose at him. "For sure you aren't a boy, but in need of tending? I'd be arguing that with you. The way you smell, you could stumble and roll yourself into the water and be drowned before anybody knew you were gone. And then what would wee Emmy and Nathaniel do?"

He rose in one smooth, menacing motion and towered over her. "Not that I have to answer to you, but I ain't been drinking. Got some spilled on me—that I won't deny. But not one drop made it past my lips to my throat. So you can just climb down off your high horse."

He'd been gone for hours and the smell following him spoke of time tipping a bottle. Yet his movements were sure rather than clumsy, his eyes clear rather than red-rimmed. Could he be telling the truth?

Tarsie tipped closer, examining his face. As she leaned in, he leaned back. "Step back, woman. What ails you?"

The odor was stronger up close to him, but it wasn't coming from his breath. Satisfied, Tarsie retreated a step. "Then where've you been all this time if you haven't been drinking?"

Joss jammed his hands into his pockets and turned away, staring toward the river. "Walkin'. Thinkin'. Figurin' what to do next."

Tarsie tugged her cloak higher on her shoulders and inched to his side. "What do you mean, figuring what to do next? You're going to Drayton Valley, that's what you're doing next."

"Why should I?" A derisive snort followed the words. "What's there for me now, Tarsie Raines?"

Tarsie grabbed his sleeve. "The fresh start your wife wanted for you and her children. Making a home in Drayton Valley was Mary's dyin' wish. You'd dishonor her memory by changing your plans now." Heat rose in her cheeks as she considered Mary's other dying wish. What would Joss say if she blurted out that Mary had begged Tarsie to love Joss?

Joss jerked free of her grasp. "How can I?" He waved his hand toward the wagon. "I got two young'uns in there too small to fend for themselves. If I'm working the docks all day, who's gonna watch 'em?" His voice broke. He drew in a shuddering breath, stalked several feet away, and turned his back on her. "Got to talking to some folks in town. They told me there's an orphans' home in Kansas City. I can put the kids on a steamboat and send 'em."

Tarsie gaped at his stiff back, unable to believe she'd heard correctly. "Y-you'd give your children away? Your only tie to Mary . . . you'd be sending them away?"

He spun around and glared at her. "I got no choice. Don't you see that? I can't work *and* nursemaid two kids! They'll end up runnin' the streets, gettin' into trouble, probably being hungry and dirty and . . ." Something akin to agony creased his face, but he gritted his teeth and replaced the pained expression with a fierce scowl. "And I got no use for kids anyway. Never did." His tone turned hard, but Tarsie sensed regret hiding beneath the bitter utterance. "Mary's the one who wanted 'em. Well, she's gone now, and I got no way to take care of 'em. So they're gonna have to go."

He headed for the wagon, but Tarsie stepped into his pathway and pressed both palms to his shirtfront. She felt his pounding heartbeat beneath his solid bulk. "I don't believe you, Joss Brubacher. I've watched you on the trail, answering their endless questions and even smiling at their antics. You let Mary see to their needs, but you care about those wee ones. I know you do."

His jaw jutted and his face angled away from her, but he remained frozen in place, as if the light touch of her palms held him prisoner. He swallowed, the sound louder than the crickets chirping from beneath a nearby shrub.

"Do you really want to give them away, Joss?" Tarsie

whispered the question, fearful of his honest reply, yet compelled to make him face his own deepest feelings.

He swallowed again. His lips pressed into a thin, firm line. His body quivered like the lid of a boiling pot. After several seconds of strained silence, he spoke past clenched teeth. "I got no other choice."

Mary's voice echoed through Tarsie's memory—*"Take care of my loved ones."* Resolutely, she stepped back, linking her fingers together in supplication. "There is another choice, Joss."

He sent her a withering look, but she gathered her courage and met his gaze. "You could let me take care o' your wee ones—and you. Marry up with me."

✳ 11 ✳

Joss stared at Tarsie. Her skin was so pale it appeared colorless in the moonlight, but she faced him squarely. Her big eyes bored into his, and her unsmiling lips formed a determined line. She wasn't joshing. She really meant he should marry her. Apparently, Mary's death had robbed her of her senses.

He edged around her, heading for the wagon. "You're out of your ever-lovin' mind."

She dashed after him and caught his sleeve. "Emmy and Nathaniel know me. I know them. I . . . I love them." She spoke softly but with an intensity that sealed him in place. "I'd be caring for them as if they were my own wee ones. You could keep 'em—keep your tie to Mary. You're not really wanting to cast 'em aside, Joss. I know you're not. You're just scared and uncertain and feeling alone. Let me help you."

"Fine." He jiggled his elbow, eager to be shed of her, to lose himself to sleep and forget the happenings of this day. "Instead of sending them to the orphans' home, you can keep 'em."

She gripped so hard the fabric cut into the opposite side of his arm. "I can't keep 'em on my own. I have no way of supporting them. Besides that, they need a father. They need *you*."

With a mighty wrench of his arm, he freed himself from

her grip. He jabbed his index finger at her. "I made my decision." The hardest—and most selfless—decision he'd ever made. He wouldn't turn back now. "If you want 'em, fine, you can have 'em, but I—"

"What I'm suggesting is what Mary wanted. Would you be denying Mary's wishes?"

Her calm utterance took the bluster clean out of him. He stared at her again, his heart pounding hard against his rib cage, his skin tingling. "She—she wanted me to marry up with you?"

For the first time since he'd returned, she lowered her gaze. She toyed with the skirt of her apron, her braid slipping over her shoulder to fall across her bodice. The pose made her seem shy and very, very young. "Before she stepped into glory, Mary asked me to see to her family. *All* of her family." Slowly, Tarsie lifted her face. Tears glimmered in her eyes. "I promised her, Joss. I can't go back on my word. P-please don't make me break my promise to Mary." One tear broke free to slide down her cheek in a silvery trail.

Joss clenched his fists and growled low in his throat, frustration rising from the depths of his soul. He spun to face away from her, but the image of her begging expression played before his eyes, flashing in and out with an image of Mary's joy-filled face when he'd agreed to take her and the youngsters to Kansas. Saying no to Tarsie was like saying no to Mary. He groaned again.

A hand touched his arm. He glanced at Tarsie, who stood timorously beside him. "What?" he growled.

She didn't cringe at his harsh tone. "Be thinking on it, Joss, and tell me in the morning. The minister who buried Mary could speak the words, and then we could continue on to Drayton Valley. We could do it . . . to honor Mary." Clutching her shawl at her throat, she turned and scurried to the wagon.

❋

"Tarsie? Tarsie, wake up."

The voice filtered through Tarsie's dream, chasing away the hazy images. She rubbed her eyes and blinked into the murky morning light sneaking through a crack in the canvas flap at the back of the wagon. She glanced at Emmy and Nathaniel, who continued to sleep soundly, their heads tipped together. Tears stung her eyes as she gazed at the motherless children. Would they soon be fatherless, too?

She wrapped her cloak over her dress, scooted to the back of the wagon, and peeled the flap aside. Joss stood just outside, attired in a fresh pair of trousers and a green plaid shirt. His hair glistened with water and lay slicked away from his face in thick waves. Apparently he'd shaved, because his cheeks were red and smooth, making his mustache seem even darker. She gave him an up-and-down look and gulped. "D-does this mean you . . . we're . . . ?"

He gave a brusque nod. "Reckon so." No joy lit his face. Or his voice. Instead, he spoke in a flat tone. Emotionless. Dead. "If Mary wanted it, then . . ."

Realization of what she was giving up to marry Joss hit hard, carried on a wave of intense disappointment. She'd never be wooed, never indulge in tender glances or stolen kisses, never hear a shyly uttered request for her hand. Marrying Joss would give the children a caretaker and continue Mary's determination to see Joss accept God's love in his life—good things—but it meant a sacrifice Tarsie hadn't understood would cost so dear until that moment.

She swallowed the knot that formed in her throat. "Will you bring the minister here for our nuptials, or—"

"Don't want that preacher who spoke over Mary's grave."

From behind her, Nathaniel mumbled in his sleep. Tarsie quickly climbed out of the wagon and led Joss several feet away to prevent disturbing the children. "But he'd do a fine job, I'm thinking."

Joss shook his head. "Huh-uh. Won't have the man who did the service for Mary's burying be the one who binds me to another wife."

Tarsie's heart turned over. She wouldn't have thought of Joss as sentimental, but his reluctance to have their wedding attached to Mary's burial touched her. "I understand."

He stared off to the side, giving her a view of his chiseled profile. His Adam's apple bobbed in his throat. "White Cloud's big enough to have more'n one man who can take care of things for us. I'll walk to town, make the arrangements. While I'm gone, you get cleaned up and ready the young'uns. Soon as we're . . . done . . . we'll set out again." He heaved a huge sigh. "No need to stick around here any longer." Without a glance in her direction, he strode off, arms pumping with determination.

Tarsie watched his broad back disappear over the gentle rise in the road leading to town. A fierce ache rose from the center of her chest. Longing—to love and to feel loved—nearly strangled her. Her groom-to-be, although spit-shined and handsome, had barely looked at her. She'd witnessed intense reluctance—even resignation—in his eyes. He'd agreed to her proposal, but only out of obligation to Mary.

She gave herself a little shake. Hadn't she only suggested marriage out of obligation to Mary? Of course she had. So why should she expect more? She looked to the east where fingers of sunlight poked through a bank of purple clouds and pointed to the peach-colored sky. "Father, when I speak the words 'I do,' I'll be making a commitment. To Mary. To Joss. To Mary's children. But most of all, to You. Give me the strength to honor it." Hot tears burned in her eyes, and she blinked them away. "Let this union be pleasing to You."

The prayer complete, she scurried to the wagon to wake the children. Within an hour, she'd fed Emmy and Nathaniel a simple breakfast of johnnycakes, dressed the pair in clean clothes from the trunk, and washed and packed the dishes and pan. While Tarsie went about her morning chores, the Murphy wagons departed. The children waved good-bye, and loneliness rolled over Tarsie as the last wagon disappeared around the bend. They were truly on their own now.

With everything packed, Tarsie instructed the children to sit on a quilt outside the wagon and look at a picture book together. Then she climbed inside and gave herself a cursory wash with water drawn from the river. She opened her bag to remove a clean dress, and her fingers found her Bible.

She lifted out the book and opened it to the section marked "Family Record." Using her finger to underline the words, she read aloud, filling in the blanks with the information that would be recorded in black ink by the end of the day. "This certifies that Treasa Raines and Joss Brubacher were united in holy matrimony on the 21st day of April in the year of our Lord 1880 in White Cloud, Kansas."

The ache in her chest increased. Her hands began to tremble. She closed the Bible and hugged it close. She was doing the right thing, wasn't she? Giggles erupted from outside. She peeked out the flap to see Emmy tickling Nathaniel. The little boy's gleeful chortle, coupled with Emmy's teasing grin, brought an answering smile to Tarsie's lips. Yes, this was right. She'd do it for the love of Mary and her children.

Without further rumination, she donned her nicest dress—the green-sprigged calico—then brushed out her hair and tied it in a tail at the nape of her neck with a satin emerald ribbon. Even though both frock and ribbon were rumpled, they were the best she could offer. And they'd go nicely with Joss's green-checked shirt. Even if their hearts weren't in this union, at least they could offer a pretense of unity.

When Tarsie emerged, Emmy looked up and smiled. "You look pretty, Tarsie."

"Pretty," Nathaniel repeated, his blue eyes wide and bright.

Their sweet words served as a balm. She gave them each a hug, then knelt before them. "Children, today your papa and I will be saying some special words in front of a preacher. And when we're done, I'll be your new ma."

Emmy drew back, scowling. "I don't want a new ma."

Nathaniel, apparently sensing the panic in Emmy's tone, puckered up.

Tarsie pulled Nathaniel into her lap and took Emmy's hand. "I know you're wanting your mama. She was the dearest woman in the world, and she loved you so much." Both children stared at her, and Emmy sniffled. Tarsie forced her lips into a wobbly smile. "Right before her spirit slipped away to heaven, she asked me to take very good care of you, and I promised her I would. You wouldn't be wantin' me to break a promise to your mama, would you?"

Nathaniel leaned against Tarsie's shoulder. His hair tickled the underside of her chin. She smoothed the tousled blond wisps into place and looked at Emmy, waiting for the little girl's reply.

Emmy sucked on her lower lip, her brow furrowed. "Do we hafta call you Mama?"

Tarsie shook her head. "You can call me Tarsie just like you always have."

Emmy's thin shoulders lifted and lowered in a resigned shrug. "I s'pose it's all right, then. But it feels funny."

Tarsie couldn't argue with Emmy's conclusion. Becoming wife to Mary's husband and mother to Mary's children felt funny to her, too, but she believed she would grow into the roles over time. Maybe, someday, would she have a wee one of her own who wouldn't balk at calling her Mama?

Nathaniel raised up in Tarsie's lap, pointing. Emmy turned and looked, and she pulled in a deep breath. "There's Papa. An' some man."

"Must be the preacher," Tarsie said. She set Nathaniel

aside and stood on quivering legs. She smoothed her hands down her skirt—if only the wrinkles would magically disappear. Then she stood with the children on either side of her, waiting for Joss and the preacher to reach them.

Joss stopped a few feet from Tarsie and jerked his thumb toward the other man. "This here is Stanley King. He's gonna speak our words."

Tarsie stepped forward and shook the man's hand. Dressed like a workingman, with a thick thatch of brown, curly hair, Stanley King didn't look like any minister she'd seen before. But she supposed a man of the cloth might dress humbly on a day he didn't need to step behind a pulpit. Even so, she found it strange that he hadn't combed his hair or donned a nicer-looking suit to officiate a wedding. Regardless of her inner ponderings, she gave the man a respectful nod and thanked him for coming.

"Weren't no, er, wasn't any trouble, miss." He toyed with one of the buttons on his brown shirt and shot a quick look at Joss. "Well, let's go ahead an' get the words spoke, huh?"

Joss lifted his chin and squared his shoulders. "That's what we're here for." In one stride, he moved beside Tarsie. But he didn't take her hand. Or even her elbow. Apparently a pretense wasn't important to Joss. Tarsie blinked back tears as her groom folded his arms over his chest and aimed his unsmiling gaze at Stanley King. "Let's get this over with."

✳ 12 ✳

Joss gripped the reins so tight his fingers ached. Had they fooled her? The billiard hall bartender had done a decent job of remembering the right words for a wedding. Joss had stated his "I do," knowing it didn't matter, since Stanley King had no authority to bind a man and woman together. Even so, Joss had caught himself hesitating, a prick of guilt at his deception causing his tongue to stumble.

But Tarsie hadn't hesitated. She'd promised right there under the sunshine and without so much as a stammer to love, honor, and obey him for the rest of her earthly days. Joss stifled an amused snort, imagining Tarsie being obedient. She had a lot more sass in her than he preferred—but that was the only reason he could carry through with the mock ceremony. When the truth came out—and it would as soon as he got her and the young'uns settled in Drayton Valley—she'd have the gumption to see to herself, Emmy, and Nathaniel without him sticking around. A woman with sass had backbone. She'd be fine.

But would he? Ever since they'd put Mary in the ground four days ago, he'd felt empty. Like something that'd made him whole had been plucked out. Would he be forever hollow and aching? He wasn't one to cry. Pa had chased away his desire to let loose with tears when he wasn't much bigger than Nathaniel. But keeping the hurt bottled up inside was harder than he'd figured something could be. He missed Mary. Missed her something fierce.

Tarsie and the young'uns rode in the wagon bed, their soft voices keeping company with the clop of the horses' hooves and the wind's whistle. It was cooler today, and the air smelled like rain. He wanted to reach Drayton Valley before those clouds billowing in the east opened up. Sooner he could get there and get Tarsie settled, sooner he could hightail it out of here. He couldn't go back to New York—not with Lanker waiting—but Chicago seemed like a good place. Lots of jobs available, and lots of saloons where he could keep himself so pickled he'd forget he once had a family.

He cleared his throat and called out hoarsely, "Tarsie? Come up here."

Within seconds, she poked her head from the gap in the canvas. "Yes?"

Would she be so johnny-on-the-spot if she knew those vows'd been recited to a bartender instead of a minister? He cleared his throat again. "Climb on the seat. Need to talk to you."

She wriggled her way over the seat's back, keeping a grip on her skirts. Even so, he got a quick glimpse of her unruffled petticoats. He jerked his gaze forward and focused on the horses' rumps until she settled herself.

"Yes? Is there something wrong?"

There were lots of things wrong. Mary was dead, he was heading to a town where he didn't know a soul, he had a woman for whom he didn't give two beans in a pot relying on him . . . He resisted a snort. "Just wanna tell you we'll be reaching Drayton Valley by tomorrow evening, for sure. Fella in White Cloud told me there's houses built for dockworkers' families an' we oughta be able to rent one of 'em without too much trouble. Thing is . . ." He angled a look at her attentive face. She appeared to be memorizing his every word. Did she have to look so . . . wifely?

He harrumphed and continued. "Them houses'll be small. Sitting room and sleeping room all in one—that's it."

She turned abruptly forward. Sunshine splashed her cheeks, which blazed red. Her fingers wove together in her lap. "Oh."

Joss waited a few seconds to see if she'd say anything else. But she sucked in her lips and sat silently, staring ahead without blinking. He gave the reins a flick. "You gonna be all right sharing a little house like that with me? Or should I see about renting two of 'em? That'd mean less money coming in, of course, but if you'd rather—"

The coils of hair that always worked loose from her braid bounced against her pink-stained cheeks as she shook her head. "No. No, that'd be foolish, wouldn't it, to spend money on two houses when . . . when we're . . . a family?" Slowly, she turned her face and met his gaze. "We'll make do."

Joss's chest pinched. "All right, then. We'll stop in an hour or so for some lunch and to stretch our legs." He bobbed his chin toward the wagon bed. "Go on back with the young'uns now."

Without a word, she followed his direction. Alone on the seat again, he considered her halting response to his question. Apparently when she said she'd be his wife, she meant in every way. Pa would probably smack Joss on the back and crow about how lucky he was, having a woman as easy on the eyes as Tarsie willing to offer herself to him. But something sour rose from Joss's belly and settled on the back of his tongue. He might've faked that wedding ceremony, but he wouldn't take advantage. As Mary'd said, he wasn't his pa.

✳

Just as dusk was falling on the twenty-fifth day of April 1880, they reached Drayton Valley, Kansas. Tarsie held the canvas flaps wide as Joss drove the wagon down the middle of the town's main street. She didn't want to miss a single inch of the place she'd dreamt about for so long.

Built in an area with close-fitting, rolling hills, the town reminded Tarsie of a tiered cake. The lowest, flattest portion stretched the widest and contained the businesses, with each subsequent level scattered with houses in uneven rows. Woodshake roofs glowed gold, gilded by the descending sun. Glass windows glimmered like diamonds. Water from the recent rain stood in the ruts carved by wagon wheels and reflected light, becoming streaks of silver.

Tears pressed for release, but she blinked them away and focused on the sights. She examined the town for herself, but also for Mary, who would never see it.

By the time they reached the edge of Drayton Valley that butted against the banks of the Missouri River, Tarsie was convinced the *Handbook of Kansas* had aptly described the town. Such a nice place. A clean place. A cheerful place with proud trees standing guard on every corner and clustered in thick stands around the town. Surely she, the children, and Joss would find happiness here.

She pressed her fist to her mouth. "Oh, Mary, I wish you were with us."

The wagon rattled to a stop, and Emmy and Nathaniel scrambled to the back hatch. Emmy turned a hopeful gaze upward. "Can we get out, Tarsie? Huh? Huh? Can we?"

Nathaniel adding his begging. "Out? Can we?"

Joss hollered over the fray before Tarsie had a chance to respond. "Not sure where we'll end up tonight. Stay in the wagon 'til I get back." His gaze bounced to Tarsie. "All of you."

The children moaned, and Tarsie bit back a word of protest. They'd spent so much time cooped up in this small space—what would it hurt to let the children run around a bit? But remembering her promise to Mary to show God's love to Joss, she offered a nod rather than an argument. Joss strode toward the only house on this block with a railed porch, and Tarsie shifted her attention to the children. "While we wait for your papa to come back, how about a game? I'll pretend to be an animal, and you can be guessing what it is."

Neither child expressed great enthusiasm, but Tarsie played the game with them until footsteps signaled Joss's return. He poked his head through the gap in the canvas. Although Emmy and Nathaniel bounced to the end of the wagon like a pair of eager puppies, Joss looked past them to Tarsie. "Talked to the dock manager—he said there's a house we can rent, but it's been empty for a while and is plenty dirty. Has a couple broken windows, too, so it might be wet inside. Guess they got the same rain we did on the trail."

A house—no matter how dirty or damp—would be better than remaining in the back of the cramped wagon one minute longer. Tarsie said, "I can be sweeping dirt and blotting up water. As long as it has a good roof, we can make do." She hoped her positive attitude might relieve the slump in his shoulders and ease the deep crease in his forehead, but he merely offered a weary nod.

"I'll tell him we'll take it, then." He patted the lump beneath his shirt where the money pouch rested. "Gotta pay him for the first month's rent. Eight dollars."

Tarsie gasped. "Oh, such an amount!"

Joss grimaced. "I know. But once I start working, it'll come out of my pay, so . . ." His brow furrowed as if something pained him. But then he drew in a breath that erased the odd expression. "Lemme get him squared away. Then we'll head to the house."

Tarsie let the children climb onto the wagon seat so they could see their surroundings. When Joss returned, he squeezed in between them and drove the wagon to a tiny clapboard house identical to more than three dozen others, with dirt pathways separating them and small yards climbing upward behind them. Joss set the brake and looked at the children. "Out of the way, now. We got a wagon to empty." They scooted to obey.

The sun had slunk behind the trees while Joss made arrangements for their new home, and Tarsie squinted through the long shadows as she carried her carpetbag across the mushy ground to the little wooden stoop that served as a porch. Joss followed with one of the trunks. When he set it down on the wide-planked floor, dust rose.

Tarsie covered her nose. "Could you be bringing in the lanterns right away? I'm thinking some light might help us get settled in." But when she lit a lantern and got a look at the house in full glow, her spirits sank. She'd thought her apartment in New York a dreary place, but the walls of this little house had never even been plastered. She held the lamp aloft and turned a slow circle, examining her new domicile.

Bare wood—some planks with exposed openings where knotholes had been knocked free—surrounded the room, which was no more than six wide paces across front to back and side to side. Muddy-looking water puddled below the broken-out west window, and wet stains ran down the wall below the south window thanks to a jagged crack in the pane. The east and north windows were intact, although the frames didn't fit snug to the openings, warning Tarsie that wind and insects could easily enter. The planked floor held a good quarter inch of dust, as did the shelves built into the wall near the rusty cookstove that filled one corner of the room. In her imaginings, Tarsie had never pictured such a dismal little house as the one in which she now stood.

Emmy tugged on Tarsie's skirt. "Is this where we're gonna live now?" Uncertainty pinched the child's face.

Tarsie set the lantern aside and embraced the little girl,

seeking comfort as much as trying to bestow it. She adopted her cheeriest tone. "Yes, darlin', and a fine place it'll be just as soon as I give it a thorough scrubbing and put all of our things away. You and Nathaniel will help me, and we'll make it the nicest house ever, won't we?"

"Yes." Emmy yawned. Nathaniel leaned his head on his sister's shoulder and tucked a finger in his mouth, his eyelids drooping.

Tarsie pursed her lips. She hated to toss the children's pallet onto the filthy floor, but what choice did she have? The cleaning would have to wait until tomorrow.

Emmy and Nathaniel sat on a trunk, silently observing while Tarsie and Joss emptied the wagon. They stacked their belongings in the northeast corner, where the floor was driest, but then Tarsie had to shift several things to lay out the children's pallet. Both of them tumbled onto the simple bed without a fuss, not even bothering to remove their shoes. Tarsie knelt at the end of the feather-stuffed, blue-and-white-striped pallet and gently tugged their shoes free.

Joss stood beside her, his hands on his hips and his unsmiling gaze pinned to her hands as if ascertaining she performed the task correctly. When Tarsie straightened with the two little pairs of shoes in hand, he gestured to the open doorway. "Gotta find a place to tether the horses, and then I'll just sleep in the wagon." He glanced around. "Won't be room to set up beds until everything gets put away. Where're you gonna sleep?"

She blinked rapidly, her pulse skipping into double-beats of worry. Although they'd entered their third day as husband and wife and spent two nights on the trail, he'd continued to sleep under the wagon while she stayed beneath the canvas cover with the children. Now that they'd reached their destination, would he expect her to lie with him?

Clutching the shoes to her trembling tummy, she lifted her

shoulders in a nervous shrug. "I, um, thought to throw out a few quilts on the floor and—"

"Fine." Joss turned and clomped toward the doorway, his bootheels stirring dust. "Soon as the sun's up, I'll come knocking at the door for breakfast. Need to meet the dock manager first thing to get started working." He paused in the doorway, sending a dubious look around the cluttered, dirty, water-splotched room. "You'll have plenty to do, too."

Tarsie released a nervous titter. "Oh, yes. The children and I will be busy tomorrow, putting our house in order." Her face flooded with heat at the word *our*. She drew in a ragged breath and held it.

Joss grabbed a quilt from the tumbling stack near the door—the very one Mary had favored when she lay so ill—and wadded it in his hands. "Tomorrow, then." He stepped out.

Tarsie eased the door closed behind him. She leaned against the solid wood, allowing the air to whoosh from her lungs. When she had the items organized and everything neat, would Joss sleep in the house with her and the children?

❈ 13 ❈

After Tarsie served a simple breakfast from the last of the dried apples and a lump of cornmeal mush directly from the pan, Joss pressed a few crumpled bills into her hand and said, "There's a mercantile 'bout a quarter mile down the street—only buy what you can't do without but"—he glanced around the filthy, cluttered space—"get some cleaning supplies." He grabbed the packet containing the final portion of jerked beef, informed her not to expect him for lunch, and headed out.

Tarsie woke the children, washed the sleep from their eyes, and fed them. Then they set off through a dew-kissed morning for the mercantile. Tall trees lined the winding pathway, holding back all but slivers of sunlight and making the air seem chilly, but the children's high spirits warmed her. Nathaniel hopped like a little toad from one dappled splash of sunshine to another. Emmy sang an Irish ballad, her childish tremolo hauntingly sweet.

They reached the back edge of Drayton Valley's business district, and just as Joss had indicated, a mercantile with a cheerfully painted porch sat on the first corner. Tarsie ushered the children inside, and a thin man with several missing teeth scurried over.

"Good mornin', good mornin'. Out bright an' early, aren't

ya? Haven't seen ya before, but it'th good to have y'all here. I'm alwayth fair in my prithin'. Uh-huh, alwayth fair."

Although both Emmy and Nathaniel stared at the man in openmouthed amazement, to Tarsie's relief neither snickered. She listened attentively as the man continued speaking.

"Lemme tell ya 'bout thith week'th thpecial itemth."

Tarsie had no interest in a whistling teakettle or French perfume, no matter how "thweet" its "thmell," but she eagerly claimed two of the sturdy straw brooms—"Only thirteen thenth today!"—so she could have one for inside and one for outside use. The house only had a small stoop rather than a porch, but she would keep it swept clean. She also purchased a bucket, soap, and a few groceries, including two loaves of bread that seemed fresh and a good-sized round of cheese so she could send sandwiches with Joss the rest of the week. She stacked all of their items except the brooms inside the bucket, gave one broom to each child, and waved good-bye to the owner, who followed them onto the porch and hollered out, "Y'all come back thoon!"

Emmy and Nathaniel carried the brooms like fishing poles over their shoulders, whacking Tarsie with the prickly straw bristles more than once on the way back to their little house. She didn't complain, but she did hurry them, noting gray clouds building once more over the river. By running the last few yards, they reached the house before raindrops began pelting the ground.

After covering the broken window with their most tattered wool blanket—an inept barrier but better than nothing—Tarsie set the children to work scrubbing the shelves, and she put one of the bargain-priced brooms to use. She couldn't dispose of the ridiculously large accumulation of dirt until the rain stopped— if she opened the door to sweep out the pile, the spattering raindrops would turn the dust into a mud puddle—so she built a mountain beside the door and then turned to other tasks.

By noon, with the children's assistance, Tarsie had put away their belongings either on the shelves or inside the trunks, lined the trunks and crates neatly against one wall, and made their bed pallets in opposite corners on one side of the room. Satisfied with the morning's accomplishments, she turned her attention to lunch. She'd used the few twigs left by the previous occupants in the stove at breakfast, so she couldn't prepare a hot meal, but the children seemed satisfied with cheese sandwiches. They complained, however, about drinking cold leftover coffee. Tarsie couldn't blame them. Growing children needed milk. She'd need it, too, for baking. Now that she had a stove, she didn't intend to continue to purchase bread.

With their tummies full, the children stretched out on their pallet and looked at the few picture books they'd brought from New York. They especially enjoyed *The House That Jack Built*—Tarsie thought it clever that Emmy could already recite most of it from memory. While the children entertained themselves, Tarsie located a scrap of paper and a pencil stub to make a list of the things she needed so she'd remember to share them with Joss. She wrote in her careful penmanship: *Arrange milk delivery or buy cow; purchase icebox; arrange ice delivery . . .*

Within half an hour, she'd filled both sides of the slip of paper. She stared at the list, aghast at its length. But when she tried to eliminate items, she discovered each was important to establishing a comfortable household. Nibbling the end of the pencil, she examined the list again. Perhaps if she were to prioritize the items and suggest they be gathered two or three at a time rather than in one fell swoop, he would be more agreeable.

Bending forward, she flattened the paper against her knee and began organizing the listed items in order of importance.

Joss trudged through the rain, his boots sticking in the muck and slowing his pace. Had there ever been a longer day than this one? The rain that started before nine o'clock continued to fall in a solid curtain, even though the supper hour had passed. Two ships had arrived at the Drayton Valley dock despite the rain, and he'd kept up stride for stride with the other workers, transferring the cut lumber from the first one and the boxed fine furniture from the second to a holding warehouse near the dock. How many times had the dock manager hollered, "Keep those deliveries dry"? Joss had lost count. But he'd thought it a foolish demand. How could a body keep anything dry in weather like this?

After working all day, wet and weary, he'd gone to the livery where he'd boarded the horses to ask the liveryman to purchase the team, since he had no further use for the beasts. Over the roll of thunder and steady thrum of raindrops hitting rooftops, Joss could still hear the man's uproarious laughter.

"Mister, you are a caution, that's for sure. What would I do with tired old nags like these?"

Joss had shrugged. "Sell 'em to somebody else. They can pull a plow or something."

The liveryman snorted. "They should've been put out to pasture years ago, an' that's a fact." Then, apparently seeing Joss was ready to blow, he'd slapped Joss on the back. "Tell you what, I'll keep 'em here an' post a notice that they're available for sale. Might be somebody'll want a horse to pull a youngster's cart or something. Check back next week."

So Joss had no extra money in his pocket as he'd hoped. He'd wanted to give the money to Tarsie. If he could get back what he'd paid for the team, the amount would be enough to see to her and the young'uns' needs for a couple of months at least. He needed what remained in his money pouch to get himself to Chicago.

Groaning under his breath, he hunched into his jacket and tried to speed his feet. Drenched to the bone, all he wanted to do was get someplace dry, sit back with his boots off, and warm his feet in front of a roaring fire. But all he had waiting for him was a wagon with a leaky canvas top. At least Tarsie'd have supper ready for him. His stomach growled in anticipation. Maybe he could dry out by the stove before bedding down in the wagon for the night.

He reached the boxy little house, identical to all the others huddling on the sloping landscape—except for its broken window—and hopped onto the stoop. Rain poured from the wood-shaked roof, dousing him anew, but he paused long enough to stomp his feet a bit to knock off at least some of the accumulated mud. Then he reached for the string that would lift the crossbar on the other side. Before he could touch it, though, the door swung open.

Tarsie stood in the doorway. Her green eyes flew wide. "Oh, be looking at you, wet as a drowned rat!" She caught his coat sleeve and tugged him over the threshold. Giving the door a slam, she flapped her hands at Emmy and Nathaniel, who stood staring up at Joss. "Quick, fetch your papa a quilt so he can bundle himself."

Emmy dashed to the corner and returned with the quilt from her bed. She thrust it at Joss. "Here, Papa."

Joss shook his head. "I'll just soil it. Lemme sit by the stove awhile. I'll dry."

Tarsie grimaced. "A cold stove'll do you no good."

Joss frowned at her.

She shrugged. "I have no fuel for a fire. You better take the quilt."

Stifling a growl, Joss complied. While he wrapped the colorful patchwork quilt around his shoulders, he glanced toward the center of the room. A blanket lay on the clean-swept floor, dotted with plates holding what appeared to be

111

slices of bread and cheese and the contents of a tin of peaches. His frown deepened. "Is that supper?"

"And how can I be cooking if I cannot start a fire?"

Joss caught a hint of defensiveness in Tarsie's tone. It raised an answering irritability in his own voice. "And how can I chop wood or fetch coal when I have to work? You've been here all day. Why didn't you ask one of the neighbors where to get fuel?"

She squinted, and he waited for a verbal assault. But then, to his surprise, she drew in a breath, held it for a few seconds, and released it slowly. She tipped her head in a sign of meekness. "I should've thought to seek out a neighbor's advice. I'll be seeing to that first thing tomorrow." She lifted her face to meet his gaze. "But for now, I can't be offering you a hot cup of tea or even a hot supper." A halfhearted smile quivered on her lips. "But I suppose a cold supper'll fill your stomach just as well as a hot one. Come. Sit."

She gestured to the blanket, and Joss scuffed forward and plopped down. The children scurried after him, perching at the opposite side of the blanket and smiling at him. Emmy said, "We had a picnic for supper."

"Picnic," Nathaniel echoed. He reached for a slice of cheese.

Tarsie leaned in and caught his hand. "You've already had plenty. You let your father eat. When he's finished, if anything remains, then you may have the leftovers."

Nathaniel pouted, but he sat back on his heels and placed his hands in his lap. The little boy's eyes followed Joss's every move as he dumped the peaches onto a plate and then stacked bread and cheese over the mound of yellow fruit. Joss lifted a folded slice of bread to his mouth.

Emmy pointed her finger at him. "Papa! You need to pray first."

Once again, Tarsie intervened with a gentle hand on Emmy's head. "We blessed the food already, Emmy. Hush now."

Embarrassed, but uncertain why, Joss took his first bite. The food, although simple, tasted good after his long day of work. He ate ravenously, his empty stomach eager for filling. The children continued to watch him and, uncomfortable beneath their scrutiny, he angled his attention away from their matching pairs of blue eyes that reminded him too much of their mother.

His gaze encountered Tarsie, who sat on a crate with one of Emmy's dresses in her lap. A silver needle flashed in and out of the blue-checked cloth, repairing a small tear in the skirt. Tarsie's busy hands—sturdy and sure, accustomed to working—reminded him of Mary's hands before the illness took hold and weight dropped from her bones. Thinking of Mary brought a stab of pain, so he quickly turned his attention elsewhere.

While he continued to chew, he examined the shelves, where new kitchen supplies now rested in an orderly row. Just to the right of the shelves, the stove gleamed beneath a fresh scrubbing and a coat of oil. A soggy blanket hid the broken window from view and held back most of the moisture. The other windows each sported squares of yellow calico suspended by string—the simplest of curtains, but offering privacy and a bit of color to the bland backdrop of unpainted wood.

Tarsie might not have gathered fuel, but she got plenty accomplished. Perhaps she'd worked as hard as he had. He finished the food on his plate and picked up the last two pieces of cheese. A small movement caught his eye—Nathaniel, licking his lips. The simple gesture transported Joss backward in time so quickly he dropped the yellow wedges. In that moment he was four years old, hunkered on his louse-ridden bed, holding his empty, aching belly and crying without a sound so Pa wouldn't hear him and come give him a different reason to cry.

With a jerk of his arm, Joss yanked up the cheese and thrust both chunks at Nathaniel. "Here, then. Eat it."

Nathaniel's face lit with joy. He snatched the pieces and started to shove them into his mouth. But then he paused. With his lower lip caught between his teeth, he offered one hardening wedge to Joss. "Share?"

Emotion roared through Joss's middle. Anger, humiliation, or overwhelming love—he couldn't determine what propelled the wave, but it hit with such force he feared his chest would turn inside out. He bolted to his feet. "Just eat it, boy." He tossed aside the quilt he'd used to warm himself and charged toward the door.

Tarsie dropped the little dress onto the crate and scampered after him. "Where're you goin'?"

He held to the crossbar, every muscle quivering. "To the wagon. I'll sleep out there."

Her cheeks flooded with pink and something akin to relief broke across her face. Then she scuttled forward and thrust a paper at him. "B-before you go, I'd be asking to speak with you. There are some additional things we need, and—"

He glanced at the sheet, all covered with words. Although he couldn't read the page, he understood. She'd made a list of items to purchase. A long list. A list that would require a tidy sum. He clenched his fists, forcing down a frustrated groan.

Why did so many things come down to money? He'd had to leave New York because of his poor use of money. If he hadn't wasted his wages in the gambling hall, he could've taken Mary to a doctor months ago, before the illness got so bad it couldn't be cured. Now he was stuck here in Drayton Valley—maybe for months—with a pair of towheaded kids who made him yearn for his sweet wife and a woman who wanted to act like a wife . . . all because of money.

He wrenched the door handle. "Not now."

Tarsie held out the list. "Will you take it and look at it tomorrow? I've marked the most important things with a little star. Surely you'd be agreeing the children need milk each day.

And I'm needing food stores as well as fuel so I can use the stove for cooking." She bobbed the paper, encouraging him to take it from her. "It'd be nice, eventually, to have a table and chairs where we can sit together and eat our meals. I can make do without furniture and such for now, but food . . . We have to have food and a way to prepare it."

Her reasonable tone—not begging but simply stating a truth as she saw it—should have calmed Joss. But it didn't. It added to his guilt. If she'd get feisty, if she'd rail and screech at him, then he'd have a reason to charge out the door and ignore her. But her calm sensibility only made his aggravation appear more irrational. From the blanket on the floor, Emmy and Nathaniel began to whimper, apparently frightened. He should comfort them, assure them, but he couldn't. His frustration with himself—and with Tarsie—was too high for sensible behavior.

He spun from the door and jammed his finger in Tarsie's direction. "I said I don't wanna talk about this right now. You'll do well to keep your tongue in your head and not goad me."

Finally, an answering spark ignited her eyes. She angled her chin and shot him a flinty glare. "Fine." She folded the paper and stuffed it into her apron pocket. "Maybe after tomorrow's breakfast, which will be dry bread and more cheese, you'll be ready to open your purse." She reached past him and yanked open the door. Fat drops fell steadily from the dark sky. "Sleep well, Joss Brubacher."

Tugging his wet cap over his nearly dry hair, Joss gritted his teeth and stepped into the cold rain shower.

❋ 14 ❋

Long after the children had fallen asleep, Tarsie lay awake listening to the rain's patter on the roof and repeating her conversation with Joss in her mind. She'd failed. She'd failed Mary, and—even worse—she'd failed her heavenly Father. Why had she lost her temper with Joss?

She shifted to her knees, tugging the quilt with her to stave off the nighttime chill. With her fists holding the quilt tight beneath her chin, she raised her face to the shadowed ceiling overhead and addressed God in a soft whisper.

"He's the most confusing man, God. Did You see him at suppertime, giving the last bites of cheese to wee Nathaniel? A kind gesture, but then he used a blustery voice and spoiled the tenderness. He works hard—I could see the weariness in him when he came in tonight—but he doesn't seem to appreciate anyone else's hard work. I want to find the good in him, as I promised Mary I would, but I'm going to be needing Your help. My eyes only find the bad. Give me *Your* eyes, Lord."

Closing her eyes tight, she searched for images of what Mary must have seen in Joss. Mary was the dearest, kindest soul Tarsie had ever met. And she'd loved Joss with her whole heart, which meant there must be good in him. Slowly, memories crept to the surface—Joss cradling Mary in his arms on the train; carrying her around their camp the morning her pain drove her to wails of agony; his big hands gently smoothing the tangled hair from Mary's wan cheeks; those same hands lifting Emmy high in the air, making the child squeal in delight; and finally the tortured anguish in his eyes the day he ran for a doctor.

Tears stung behind Tarsie's closed lids. *Lord, thank You for these reminders. A good man does indeed lurk beneath the prickly exterior he chooses to show to the world.* Popping her eyes open, she gasped as realization dawned in her spirit. "He needs examples, Father, doesn't he? I recall Mary telling me he was raised without a mother's tender care, by a father who was gruff and even cruel. He means to do right, but how can he when he hasn't been shown the way? This is why Mary begged me to be You to Joss—so he'll learn how to show Nathaniel the kind of man You mean him to grow to be. So little Emmy will learn what to seek as a husband someday."

Considering her own failings, Tarsie knew she was inadequate to the task Mary had given her. Although she'd pledged her troth to Joss, she didn't love him. Sometimes she didn't even like him. But she also knew God gave strength when human strength was gone. Drawing in a deep breath, she made one more request. "Help me, my dear Lord and Savior, to be a holy example before Joss. But don't leave the full responsibility to me. I fall short far too often. Joss needs other examples—men who serve You—to show him how to be a man of God. Bring godly examples into his pathway, Lord. Show Joss the way."

She continued to pray until her eyelids grew too heavy to hold open. Curling back onto her pallet, she finally succumbed to blissful slumber.

***

Show Joss the way.
Tarsie kept up this constant prayer in the back of her heart.

She begged it of God, and she admonished herself with the statement. She uttered it as relentlessly as the rain that continued to fall daily. The prayer winged upward while she gathered wet branches to dry in the house and then break into kindling for the stove, while drawing water from the well, while caring for Joss's children, washing his clothes, and cleaning the little house he only entered to consume the meals she prepared.

The final Friday in May, Joss entered the house shortly after dawn, as had become his custom, for breakfast. Emmy and Nathaniel still slept peacefully on their pallet, and Joss sent a brief glance in their direction before plopping onto a crate. Tarsie placed thick slices of fried mush swimming in sorghum on a plate and handed the plate to him along with a cheery smile. He balanced it on his knee with a mumbled, "Thanks."

As Tarsie had come to expect, he didn't bow his head to pray—he never asked God's blessing for his food. He forked up a dripping bite and ate in silence. She went about her morning duties—wrapping two sandwiches in paper for him to take along for lunch, heating water in which to wash the dishes, straightening her bed, adding wood to the stove to keep the fire hot. She longed for conversation—for companionship from her husband—but she'd learned over their weeks together that Joss didn't speak until he'd filled his belly and downed a cup or two of coffee. So she hummed, puttering about as quietly as possibly to avoid disturbing the children, and waited until he'd finished.

He used one finger to blot up the last few drops of sorghum and licked it clean, then rose. Placing the plate on the corner of the stove, he turned to her. "Not raining today." He made a face. "Yet." He kept his voice low, barely above a whisper, but cynicism colored his tone. "Be nice if it'd stay clear for a few days."

Tarsie released a wistful sigh. She'd grown weary of the

constant damp, as well. "I wouldn't be opposed to seeing the sun peek through the clouds."

Joss went on as if she hadn't spoken. "Need to put a garden in. There's a plot of ground out back pretty much cleared—looks like the people who lived here before planted there. Do you know how to grow vegetables?"

When she was a girl, still in Ireland, she'd helped her great-aunt keep a garden. After they'd come to New York, she'd purchased her vegetables from street vendors, since they had no spot of ground to cultivate. But she didn't think she would have trouble putting seeds in the soil and coaxing them to grow. This was Kansas, after all—hadn't she assured Mary this was a growing place? "I can grow vegetables."

"I'll buy seeds, then." He stood next to the door, one hand on the warped crossbar and the other tucked in the pocket of his trousers. His little plaid hat sat snugly on his head and his thick hair curled up around his ears. Were it not for his hardened features and rakish slash of dark hair above his lips, the untamed hair and casual pose would give him a boyish air that Tarsie felt certain most women found appealing.

Realizing where her thoughts had taken her, Tarsie experienced a rush of heat in her face. She waved her apron skirt, stirring the air. "That's fine. As soon as the ground's dry enough, I'll see to the planting." She ducked her chin, suddenly shy. "I-I'm partial to tomatoes and parsnips, if you'd be so kind."

"Parsnips." He snorted softly. "I'd sooner eat bark."

Her face shot up, a sharp retort forming on her tongue. But she thought she glimpsed a teasing glint in his eye. Uncertain, she decided to test it. "And if you keep up your complaining, I can fill your supper dish with boiled bark instead of good, fresh vegetables from my garden."

His mustache twitched. No smile creased his chiseled cheeks, but the barely discernible twitch meant his lips had curved just a bit—a small sign of humor that made Tarsie's heart leap in her chest. She held her breath, wondering what he would say next.

He cleared his throat and lifted the crossbar. "Better get to work. Today's payday, so get out that list of things you need. We'll shop tomorrow."

"All right."

He started out the door.

"Oh! Wait!" At Tarsie's insistent whisper, he paused. She tiptoed to the stove and retrieved the cheese sandwiches she'd wrapped for him. Another rush of heat filled her cheeks as she placed the package in his outstretched hand. "There you are. H-have a good day now, Joss."

He bobbed his head in reply and stepped out the door. Tarsie closed it, then leaned against the cool wood, eyes closed, heart pounding. They'd had a conversation. A real conversation. With a bit of teasing. And no sharp words. She'd prayed for a glimmer of hope, and God had provided.

With a little giggle, she pushed away from the door and spun a happy circle. Her feet came to a stop when she realized both Emmy and Nathaniel had awakened. They sat up on their pallet, curious faces turned in her direction.

She plunked her hands on her hips, feigning indignation. "And at what are you two gawking? Have you never seen a morning jig before?"

In unison, they shook their blond heads.

Tarsie held out her hands. "Well, then, come. The clouds have passed, the sun is showing its face, and it's time you learned to greet the day in the happiest of ways."

The pair dashed across the brief expanse of floor and caught Tarsie's hands. She led them in a merry dance that sent their nightshirts flying around their knees. Then they tumbled to the floor in a tangle of arms and legs and melodious giggles. Tarsie hugged the two tight, tears stinging her eyes, and planted a kiss on each tousled head. Good things were coming. She just knew. *Good* was coming.

※※

The jumbled confusion of voices reached Joss's ears long before he turned the final corner to reach the dock. Fear struck—an almost feral reaction—and without conscious thought he broke into a run. Mud spattered his pants and coated his boots, but he ignored the slop beneath his feet and pounded the final distance.

On the shore, men milled in a mob, those at the back of the crowd straining to see over the shoulders of those in front. Had a steamship sunk? Had someone drowned? Joss puffed to a halt at the rear of the group and jabbed the closest man on the shoulder. "What's going on?"

The man turned a dumbfounded face in Joss's direction. "Dock's gone. It plumb tore loose and floated downriver last night. Steamship's out on the water, wantin' to leave its load, but there's no way for us to reach it. Boss says it's gonna have to go on to White Cloud an' unload there."

Joss jolted. If the steamships couldn't dock, they wouldn't have work to do. And no work meant no pay. He shouldered his way through the muttering crowd to the front, searching for the dock manager, John Stevens. He located the man at the edge of the shore where the jagged ground showed where the dock had once stood. Joss rushed toward him.

"You can't send the ships on to White Cloud." Joss waved his hand toward the group of men who lingered uncertainly several yards upshore. "What're we all s'posed to do about drawing a wage if the ships pass by Drayton Valley?"

Stevens balled his hands on his hips and glowered at Joss. "You think I'm addlepated? I know what it means to send that ship on, but how'm I supposed to get to the goods with no dock? You got the means of walking on water?" He huffed derisively. "Get back with the others, Brubacher."

Joss bristled, but he returned to the gathered men, listening to their complaints and worried remarks but keeping his lips tightly sealed. A few minutes later, steam coughed from the ship's stack and the paddlewheel heaved into motion. The men groaned as the ship continued upriver.

Stevens slowly crossed the ground and faced the workers. He held up both hands, waiting until everyone quieted. "We're gonna hafta get a crew in here to rebuild the dock before we can bring in any more steamers. 'Til it's built, there won't be any work for you fellows, so—"

Someone yelled out, "What're we s'posed to do about feedin' our families?" An angry murmur rose from the crowd. Joss leaned forward, eager to hear the boss's response.

The man sent a sympathetic scowl in the direction of the question asker. "I don't like it any better than you do, Caudel. I won't be earnin' any wage until the dock's up again, either."

His statement calmed the men a bit, but Joss gritted his teeth. He had to make money. He called out, "What about rebuilding the dock? Can't we help?"

"Not unless you've got construction experience. Takes special skill."

One of the men pushed to the front. "I've done lots of buildin'. Helped build two hotels in St. Joseph."

Stevens nodded at the man. "We'll talk."

Joss kicked at the muddy ground. He'd never built so much as a chicken crate. They wouldn't put him on the construction crew.

"Head up to the warehouse office, men," Stevens instructed, "and I'll divvy out your wages for the days you worked. Sorry I can't do more for you."

Joss followed the others to the warehouse, holding back his irritation, even though those around him voiced their concerns and aggravation. Anger smoldered inside his chest, but what would fussing do? Wouldn't put that dock back, so why bother?

He accepted his six dollars from Stevens and jammed it into his pocket without a word of thanks. With nothing to do, he angled his feet toward the rental house. He'd told Tarsie to get out her list for the mercantile. She'd have to do a lot of trimming, though. They'd need to make this six dollars stretch, since he didn't know when he'd work again. His head low, he dragged his heels, reluctant to return to the house.

Someone plodded up alongside him. "Hey, Brubacher. Tough break, huh?"

Joss glanced at the short, stocky, redheaded man. "You Wells?"

The man grinned. "That's right. Dick Wells. Came here a year ago from White Cloud." He made a face. "Thinkin' now I should've stayed. I'd still be workin' if I had."

Joss didn't answer.

"Got a brand-new baby at home. Colicky. Been buyin' that Soothing Baby Syrup every week. My wife's not gonna be too happy when I tell her we can't afford it 'til I start earnin' again." He shook his head, whistling through his teeth. "Don't reckon either of us'll be gettin' much sleep without that bottle."

Joss wished he could buy a bottle, too—but not of Soothing Baby Syrup.

They reached the corner and paused, Wells looking left and right. No wagons in sight, so they stepped into the muddy street. Wells continued. "Wonder if work's to be had at the vineyard. Scrabblin' in the dirt ain't my idea of the way to spend a day, but it'd be better'n nothin'."

Interested, Joss shot the man a look. "Vineyard?"

Wells nodded, his hair flopping on his forehead. "South o' town. Big operation. Grapes for wine, as well as some fruit trees. Ship all over the country." He shrugged. "This time o' year might not be much to do out there, but I plan to ride out and ask around anyway." He snickered. "Beats sittin' at home listenin' to my baby howl an' my wife complain."

Joss forced a short laugh. "Reckon you're right."

The man inched sideways, heading east. "Good luck to you, Brubacher." He lifted his hand in a wave and trotted off.

Joss watched him go, his mind ticking. A vineyard . . . where they made wine. A familiar hunger rolled through his belly. Maybe that dock breaking free wasn't such a bad thing after all. There'd be certain benefits to working at a vineyard. Anxiety pricked. If the other dockworkers knew about the vineyard, they'd certainly hightail it out there and snatch up any jobs before Joss had a chance. He shouldn't waste time.

Turning on his heel, he reversed his steps and trotted toward the livery stable. His horses hadn't sold yet. He'd take one and ride out to the vineyard. Anticipation sped his pulse. If anybody was going to grab an available job out there, it would be him.

✳ 15 ✳

You's in luck, mistuh." The worker at the edge of the vineyard leaned on the handle of the pitchfork he'd been using to arrange dry straw beneath some twisted-looking short trunks. His dark face showed a sheen of sweat despite the morning hour and cool nip in the damp air. "The boss man was plannin' to go into town this aftuhnoon an' put up a notice at the post office for another hand since ol' Zeke passed on. We buried him yesterday under the trees yonder, just like he wanted." The man pointed, releasing a heavy sigh. "Ol' Zeke, he was a good man."

Almost against his will, Joss's eyes drifted to the cleared spot where a crude cross marked a grave. For a moment, he questioned the wisdom of working at a vineyard and winery. Mary wouldn't approve. And from the looks of things, many of the workers here were colored. Gave him a twitchy feeling to think of working side by side with them.

He rubbed his jaw. Maybe he should move Tarsie and the young'uns to White Cloud, where he could work the dock there and be close to Mary's resting spot. But then he shook his head. He didn't intend to stay in Kansas, and he needed money before he could leave. He'd better grab the quickest means of adding to his coffer.

The horse shifted beneath Joss, and he gave the animal a

few pats as he faced the worker again. "So where do I find the boss?"

The man pointed to a big house at the end of the lane. Tall trees blocked most of it from view, but even from the distance and with the shielding trees, Joss could see it stood two stories high and sported a railed balcony above the porch. He blew out a little breath. The owners must be doing well to afford a house like that.

Without thanking the man for the information, Joss tapped the horse's sides with his heels and urged the animal up the lane. At the porch, he swung down and tied the reins to the ring imbedded in a limestone post near the porch. He gave the tired horse another quick pat before stepping onto the porch.

He glanced down his length, cringing at his stained trouser legs and mud-caked boots. Would the owner take one look at his slovenly appearance and send him packing? But he wasn't asking to be a house servant—only a worker in the field. He'd get plenty filthy out there, and his clothes would let the owner know he wasn't afraid of dirtying himself up when he worked. Raising his fist, he drew in a breath and then gave the door several good thumps.

Moments later it swung open, and a fine-dressed man with white hair and a lined black face peered out at Joss. "Mornin', suh. Can I help you?"

Joss looked past the man at a sizable foyer where wood floors gleamed, a spindled stairway curved upward, and a brass lamp with more than a dozen glowing candles lit the room. The candlelight bounced off little crystals hanging from the brass arms. Wouldn't Mary love to see something like that lamp? She'd always loved shiny things. Not that he'd been able to buy many for her. But she'd admired them in store windows. Joss swallowed a lump of longing.

"Suh?"

The man's simple query brought Joss back to the present.

He peered down his nose at the well-dressed servant. "I need to talk to the owner."

"Can I tell Mistuh Tollison what it is you're wantin'?"

"A job."

The white head bobbed in acknowledgment. He gestured Joss inside and closed the door. "Wait here, suh. I'll fetch Mr. Tollison for you." The man disappeared through a wide doorway draped with heavy curtains.

The faint aroma of onions reached Joss's nose, and his nostrils twitched in response. He fidgeted in place until he realized every shift of his boots left dirty marks on the polished floor. He forced himself to stand perfectly still, determined not to sneeze, while he waited for the owner—Tollison—to join him.

The sound of footsteps reached Joss's ears, and then a tall man in black trousers and a white shirt with the sleeves rolled up breezed around the corner. He came at Joss with his hand outstretched. The scent of onions clung to him. "Hello. I'm Edgar Tollison. And you are . . . ?"

Joss whipped off his cap and gave the man a firm handshake. "Joss Brubacher."

"Brubacher . . . Brubacher . . ." Tollison frowned, as if searching his memory. "I haven't heard the name before."

"Just moved here from New York. Came to work the dock in Drayton Valley." Joss briefly explained the morning's calamity, then said, "No guarantee when they'll be able to receive steamers, and I need a way to take care of my family. So I came out here to see if you might need another hand."

Tollison hooked his thumbs in his pockets and looked Joss up and down. "As it stands, I lost a worker yesterday, Zeke Foster. Good man—experienced. So I could use another worker. But I don't want to hire someone for just a week or two. I want someone permanent. You planning to return to dock work in Drayton Valley when they've got things rebuilt?"

Joss rubbed his dry lips together. He hoped to return to dock work, but not in Drayton Valley. "Not if I don't have to, sir." Guilt pricked. He hadn't spoken the full truth and he knew it, but if he told this man he'd be skedaddling to Chicago as soon as he had enough money set aside, he wouldn't get the job. So he held further explanation inside and waited for Tollison to decide whether or not to put him to work.

"Well, then, Mr. Brubacher, I'm willing to give you a try. Can't start you out with the wage I'd been paying Zeke, since you don't have experience, but does two dollars a day sound fair?"

Fifty cents more a day than he'd drawn in town! He'd have the money he needed in no time. Joss turned his cap into a wad, reining in his elation. "Yes, sir. That sounds just fine."

Tollison smiled, showing even white teeth. "Good." He turned to the servant, who stood in the doorway behind the men. "Wilson, take Mr. Brubacher out to the field and introduce him to Simon." He looked at Joss. "Simon is my vineyard manager. You'll follow his directions. He'll be the one to pay you, too. Simon reports to me, and if there's any trouble, he'll let me know."

What kind of trouble could there be? Joss nodded. "Yes, sir."

"All right, then." Tollison extended his hand again. "Welcome to Tollison Vineyard."

※

Tarsie stepped out onto the tiny stoop and looked up the street. Still no Joss. Where was he? During the morning, the other dockworkers had returned to their houses, and she'd overheard the frustrated murmurings about the dock breaking free and the men being sent home. But even though she'd asked, none of them seemed to know what had happened to Joss.

Here it was, noon already, and no sign of him. Tarsie nibbled her lower lip. In the past, Joss had tried to drown his disappointments. Had he found a place in town that served liquor? She wanted to ask one of her neighbors about such an establishment but was fearful they'd surmise she was seeking refreshment for herself.

Behind her, Emmy and Nathaniel chased around the small space, their loud voices echoing from the wood walls. She whirled and snapped her fingers at them. "You're behaving worse'n a pair of hooligans. Stop that running at once."

At her sharp tone, they came to a startled halt and stared at her. Tears welled in both sets of blue yes. Nathaniel's chin quivered.

Emmy wrapped her arms around her brother. "It's all right, Nattie," she whispered, her gaze pinned on Tarsie's face. "I won't let Tarsie yell at you no more."

Remorse smote Tarsie. For weeks, the children had been cooped up. First in a wagon and then in this small house. Until the ground dried, they wouldn't be able to run outdoors. She needed to be more patient.

Crouching down, she held out her arms. "Come here, wee ones." They scuffed their feet, clearly reluctant, but they came. She drew them close, kissing first Emmy's cheek and then Nathaniel's sweaty head. "'Tis sorry I am that I hollered. I took out my worry on you, and it was wrong of me. Will you be forgiving me?"

Nathaniel wove his skinny arms around Tarsie's neck and planted a moist kiss on her cheek. Emmy hesitated but then offered a small nod.

Tarsie sighed. Mothering was much harder than she'd imagined. "Thank you, wee ones." She pushed to her feet.

Emmy caught her apron and gave a tug. "Why are you worried?"

Tarsie didn't care to discuss her fears with the little girl. To distract the children, she made a suggestion. "There's enough flour and sugar in the bags to stir up a batch of cookies. If you two will break some twigs for me and choose the driest ones, we'll feed the stove 'til it's good and hot and then do some baking. Does that sound good?"

Both children let out squeals and darted to the corner where Tarsie had piled their wood supply. Relieved, she turned to the shelf and began removing the needed items for sugar cookies. The recipe would take most of what remained of their flour and sugar, but Joss had indicated they'd go to the mercantile tomorrow to purchase supplies. Her hands stilled mid-task, worry returning. If Joss had crept away to lose himself in a bottle, would there be money remaining for food?

"Tarsie? The wood's ready!"

Tarsie forced a smile in response to Emmy's excited voice. "You're such fine helpers. We'll make the best cookies ever tasted in Drayton Valley." The pair beamed at her, all former hurt forgotten. Tarsie began layering wood in the stove, humming to cover the fear that rolled in her belly.

Dear Father, please put Your protective hands on Joss and hold him back from doing something foolish.

Joss wrapped the pale green vine—which Simon had called a cordon—carefully around the wire strung along the row of plants. In early spring, with only a few buds forming, the empty trunks of the grapevines reminded Joss of a forest fire's remains. Simon had said these were Cynthiana vines, which would bear purple grapes to make red wine. Joss tried to envision a full, leafy plant with clusters of purple grapes hanging beneath thick greenery, but the picture wouldn't set in his head.

"That's good, that's good. Treat them li'l vines just like you'd cradle a newborn babe 'cause they's fragile as a newborn." Simon's slow drawl drifted on the breeze to Joss's ears. "Now use the cutters I gib you to trim back them two shoots unduhneath. They's dead—no sense in leavin' 'em where they do no good."

While Joss followed the man's instructions, Simon chuckled, a low, throaty sound. "You know, Joss, my pappy tol' me prunin' grapevines is a lot like how the Lawd works in the lives of His chillun. He looks down at us, sees how we's supposed to be bloomin' an' what's standin' in the way, an' He takes His mighty cutters an' snips off the parts that would keep us from doin' good."

Joss tossed aside the brown, brittle bits he'd removed and remained on one knee on the scattered straw that lay like a mat around the base of each vine.

Simon went on, his voice as patient as a preacher in a pulpit. "Yessuh, that trimmin', it can pain us when it happens, but later we come to know it was for our own good. An' when we start blossomin', bearin' fruit for the Lawd, then we find out what it means to be joyful." A warm hand curled over Joss's shoulder, and Joss stiffened. The fingers tightened, and the chuckle rumbled anew. "You done good today, Joss. Real good. You'll make a fine workuh here. Thank the good Lawd He seen fit to send you our way just when we was needin' somebody."

Joss jerked upright, shaking loose the hand. He held out the cutters, his gaze aimed off to the side so he wouldn't have to meet the man's watery brown eyes. "What time should I be here Monday?"

Simon hitched his way down the straw-covered path between the wires and Joss trailed him. "Seben 'clock sharp, that's when the others're here." He sent a one-eye-squinted-shut look over his shoulder. "That gonna suit you?"

The ride from town took ten minutes on horseback. He'd have to leave earlier than he had for the dock job, but he'd manage. "Yep." When he returned to Drayton Valley, he'd have to let the livery stable owner know not to sell both horses. At least, not yet.

"Good, good. S'pose I oughta tell you, though, spring an' summer we work six days a week, so we need you here tomorruh. But we don't never work on Sunday. That be the Lawd's day, an' we honor it by visitin' a house o' worship an' then restin'. Good Book says to keep the Sabbath day holy." Simon's left leg—a good two inches shorter than the right—dragged a bit by the time they reached the end of the row. A gray-muzzled mule and two-wheeled cart waited, and with a little grunt, Simon heaved himself into the seat. He patted the spot beside him. "Climb on in. Ransom here'll tote you back to the big house."

Joss planted his boots in the muddy roadway. "Don't mind walking." A hard edge sneaked into his tone, although he'd managed all day to keep his resentment to himself. If he'd known he'd be following directions from a crippled black man, he might not have been so eager to take this job.

Simon stared at Joss, his dark eyes seeming to examine him from the inside out, as if he knew why Joss wouldn't sit on the seat beside him. Joss squirmed beneath the other man's gaze. He forced a weak laugh. "Been stooped over most of the day. Feels good to stand straight and stretch my legs."

A smile broke across Simon's round face, but his eyes continued to bore into Joss. He took up the reins and gave a slow nod. He lifted the reins, but then he paused. His left eye squinted shut again. "You bein' new in these parts, you found yo'self a church home, Joss?"

Joss snorted. "I haven't darkened a church doorway in years." Mary'd gone to Sunday services when she felt well enough to walk down the block, and she'd taken Emmy and Nathaniel, leaving Joss alone. Stifling another snort, he added, "But I do lots of resting on the *Lawd's* day." He deliberately drawled the word the way Simon did.

He expected the vineyard manager to frown or berate Joss for his disrespectful tone. But to his surprise, Simon's watery eyes softened, and he slowly shook his head. His rounded shoulders drooped, and Joss read sadness in the gesture. "Joss, Joss, Joss . . . 'Pears to me the good Lawd's got some trimmin' to do in your life. Well . . ." Looking skyward, he spoke to the wisps of clouds overhead. "Trustin' You to do Your work, Lawd, in this man's heart." Then he gave Joss that one-eyed look again, like he was taking aim on Joss's soul. "I'll be a-seein' you tomorruh mornin'. Have a good evenin', Joss." He flicked the reins, and the cart squeaked away.

Joss stared after him, fury writhing through his middle like a spitting snake. Just who did Simon think he was, telling Joss he needed improvement? He stomped up the lane, ignoring the happy chatter of the other workers who also filed out of the fields.

He jerked his horse's reins free of the iron loop and swung himself astride the horse's back. Simon'd told him the workers would be paid tomorrow, and he'd get to collect for the time he'd worked. So he'd come tomorrow, put in his hours, and collect his four silver dollars. But then he was done. The pay wasn't enough to take orders from a gimpy colored man who acted like a preacher.

❊ 16 ❊

Simon leaned over the wash bucket on the bench outside the door of his simple clapboard house set well behind Tollison's mansion and splashed water on his face. All the rain lately'd kept the temperature pleasing, but he still managed to work up a sweat. Ruth'd say it was a good day if he'd brought forth honest sweat—he'd wager she was the most uncomplaining woman in all of the United States of America. And she'd chosen him. He sent up an oft-repeated prayer of gratitude for his beautiful wife, then dried his hands on his shirtfront while gazing at the little house a few yards to the right of his.

His chest tightened. How he missed Pappy. Smelling the smoke from his old corncob pipe drift across the breeze each evening, hearing him greet the day with songs of praise, seeing his face light with pleasure when little Naomi skipped across the yard to give him a howdy . . . Slipping his eyes closed, Simon clasped his hands beneath his chin and spoke to the only Father he had left.

"Dear Lawd, I thank You an' praise You for the years I had with Pappy, even if thirty-two just don't seem long enough sometimes. But I know me an' him an' Mama'll have eternity togethuh with You, so I ain't gonna complain none 'bout spendin' the rest o' my earthly years without 'im next door. Still, Lawd, my heart's just achin' at missin' him, an' my chilluns're gonna miss 'im, too, so gib us comfort an' strength to face these days without 'im. Amen."

"Amen."

Simon popped his eyes open and found Ruth beside him, her dark eyes looking at him so tenderly it made his throat ache. He held open his arms, and she settled herself against him. Where he was slight, she was robust, but they still fit together like two halves of one whole. The red bandana tied over her wiry hair brushed against his cheek, holding the smells of her cookstove. Corn bread, pork, and onion. Good smells.

He sighed. "Ah, woman, nothin' beats comin' home to you, you know that?"

She chuckled sweetly as her hands roved across his shoulder blades, calluses catching on the flannel of his shirt. "Nothin' beats seein' you come home to me, an' that's a fact, Simon Foster."

Simon marveled anew that Ruth could find such pleasure in him—scarred and crippled and imperfect him. God-planted love surely made a person see things differently from what they really were. Slipping his arm around her waist, he guided her over the threshold. A glance around the little room proved they were alone, so he stole a quick kiss before sending her back to the cookstove with a teasing pat on her behind.

He shuffled to the bed in the corner and sat to yank off his shoes. His misshapen foot always ached horribly at the end of his working day. "Where're the young'uns hidin'?"

She stirred a pot, her apron strings swaying with the movement and steam swirling around her chin. "Sent 'em to the garden plot to carve out furrows for plantin'."

Simon propped his foot on the opposite knee and massaged, wincing. "Awful muddy out there. You know how them boys are. Gonna create a lotta washin' for you."

She shrugged, flashing an impish grin over her shoulder. "Keeps 'em outta mischief. An' since when've I evuh minded washin'? Gibs me pleasure, it does, to see stains come outta shirts an' britches. Reminds me o' the good Lawd takin' away the stains o' our sins."

Simon rose and limped to the stove. Wrapping his arms around her middle from behind, he rested his chin on her shoulder and nuzzled her ear. She tipped her head slightly, returning his affection in the only way she could with her hands busy flipping pieces of salt pork in a skillet of sizzling grease.

After a few minutes, she gave a little shrug that urged him away. "Time to eat. Go fetch the chillun an' have 'em wash good. Tell them boys to use the lye soap, too."

Simon's stomach rolled over in eagerness. "Yes, ma'am."

He headed outside and shuffled around the house on bare feet, enjoying the feel of cool, moist earth beneath his soles after hours in the hot, confining boots. Just as Ruth had said, all three youngsters worked busily, hoes in hand. Crooked furrows marched from one end to the other in the large patch of mud behind the house. E.Z. and Malachi had done a right fine job, readying that ground for planting. Simon chuckled, noting little Naomi's tongue poking out in concentration while she hacked ineffectively at the edges of the plot, using a rusty hoe with a handle three times her height to chop away bits of weeds.

He stood for a moment or two, enjoying the sight of his children—dark hair glistening in the fingers of sunlight that peeked between clouds, their hands set to constructive tasks. Then his stomach growled, reminding him Ruth was waiting. He called, "Young'uns! Time to eat!"

All three faces turned to him, three pairs of dark eyes lighting at the sound of their pappy's voice. Hoes fell in the mud with soft plops and they all came running on healthy legs, hands extended, smiles beaming. Simon braced himself for their hugs, laughing as their sturdy bodies plowed against his.

Ah, Lawd, such blessin's, such blessin's—more'n I deserve. Thank You, dear Lawd.

✳

Joss entered the house without knocking. Before he could close the door behind him, Emmy and Nathaniel dashed across the floor and wrapped their arms around his legs, crying in shrill unison, "Papa! Papa!" The force of their greetings nearly toppled him. Grunting in aggravation, he caught hold of their shoulders and peeled them loose. He steeled himself against their hurt expressions and looked across the room at Tarsie, who stood with a skillet in one hand and a wooden spoon in the other. Her face pursed in disapproval.

He grunted again. "You just now putting supper out?" He glanced at Mary's clock, which stood proudly on a warped shelf alongside a few sparse grocery items. "It's near seven o'clock."

Her faded skirts swirling around her ankles, Tarsie charged to a trunk she must've pulled to the center of the room during the day and plopped the skillet onto the wooden top. Hands on hips, the wooden spoon still wrapped in one fist, she glowered at him. "'Tis near seven o'clock, an' ever since noon I've been worryin' an' wonderin' where you've been keepin' y'rself."

Her Irish brogue thickened with ire. She was in full temper right now. Despite himself, a grin tickled Joss's lips. He drew his hand over his mustache to hide any sign of humor, thumped his way to the wash bucket beside the stove, and dunked his hands in the tepid water. He angled a glance over his shoulder and noted she'd followed, wielding the spoon like a weapon.

"All the other dockworkers came wanderin' back midmornin', fussin' about how the dock washed away an' no work was to be had. I watched an' watched for you . . ."

Straightening, he plucked a length of toweling from a nail and dried his hands, his eyebrows high. "Don't s'pose it occurred to you I'd be looking for another job, seein' as how my first one went floating downriver?" The moment the words left his mouth, he regretted them. Now, come Monday morning, he'd have to explain why he didn't keep the new job.

Tarsie squinted. "You went job seekin'? You weren't . . . ?"

Her disbelieving tone stirred Joss's irritation to life. What gave her the right to throw accusations at him? She wasn't anything more than his children's nanny and his maid. He smacked the towel onto the nail and marched to the trunk, where four tin plates formed a circle around the skillet. "We gonna eat or not?"

Tarsie drew in a breath, as if preparing to release a torrent of words, but then she waved her hands at the children. "Come. It's late, and I know you're all hungry." Her eyes spit fire at Joss, telling him she wasn't finished with their conversation.

They had no chairs, so they knelt beside the trunk, except for Nathaniel, who remained on his feet. Tarsie scooped servings of beans and chunks of ham swimming in a thick gravy onto their plates. She sent him a warning glance when he reached for his spoon, and with a disgruntled snort he waited until she offered a brief prayer before yanking up his spoon and digging into the mound on his plate.

His mouth full of the flavorful beans, he mumbled, "No biscuits?"

Tarsie swallowed. "No flour."

Emmy sent a shy look at him. "We used up the flour makin' cookies. Tarsie says we'll have 'em for dessert."

Nathaniel waved his spoon. "Cookies!"

Tarsie caught the boy's hand and drew the spoon toward his plate. "But not 'til you've eaten all your beans."

With a grin, Nathaniel jammed the spoon into the mound of beans.

Joss frowned. "You wasted the flour on cookies?"

Tarsie raised one brow. "I didn't consider it wastin' when your children were in need of a distraction while wonderin' where their papa was. Besides . . ." Her expression softened. "Every wee one needs a treat now and then." She shrugged and took another bite. "We'll buy more flour at the mercantile, an' I'll be sure to fix a batch of biscuits for tomorrow's supper."

Joss bent over his plate, thinking. His knees hurt after his day of stooping next to grapevines. He didn't care to eat every meal kneeling at this crate. They needed chairs. And a decent table. He had the six dollars from his dock work, and after tomorrow he'd have another four dollars for his time at the vineyard. Ten dollars in all—not an insignificant amount, but not enough to buy furnishings. It'd be enough, if they were careful, to keep them in groceries till the dock was rebuilt and he could take up there again. However, he'd fill a purse faster, furnish this little house quicker—and be able to beat it to Chicago sooner—if he continued working at the vineyard.

An image of Simon's dark, smiling face filled Joss's memory. Hadn't he decided he couldn't work with that man? He clanked his spoon into his empty plate and lurched to his feet.

"Gonna head to the wagon and change my clothes." He gestured to his mud-stained trousers. "I'll bring these dirty ones back in for washing."

Emmy blinked up at him. "Don'tcha want a cookie, Papa?"

"Every wee one needs a treat now and then." Nobody'd ever treated him when he was a youngster. A band wrapped around his chest, restricting his breathing. "No." He headed for the door.

"If you're done eatin', I'll be speakin' with you, Joss Brubacher!"

The command in Tarsie's voice stopped Joss midstep. He

aimed a glower in her direction, which she didn't acknowledge. She rose and offered quick instructions to the children to finish eating and then they could each have two cookies from the tin. She scurried to his side. "Let's be steppin' outside, you an' me."

Joss yanked open the door and swept his hand in a grand gesture of invitation for her to precede him. Skirts pinched between her fingers, she flounced past him with her chin set at a determined angle. Stifling a grunt, Joss followed.

On the porch, she whirled on him. The feistiness that had sparked in her eyes earlier had fled, replaced by a glimmer of concern. "Joss, when the other men came back, all a-flutter about the dock being gone and no work to be had, I feared for you. I've spent the whole day pacin' and prayin' . . . remembering how you'd take to drink when things went wrong."

Heat filled Joss's face. Partly shame, partly fury, and partly desire to lift a glass and feel the burn of whiskey draining down his throat followed by blissful numbness.

Tarsie touched his arm, her fingers resting gently on his sleeve. "I'm proud to see you didn't go searching for a bottle. Mary'd be proud, too."

The mention of Mary sent a shaft of pain through Joss's middle. He stepped away from Tarsie's light touch. "Yeah, well, I found a job, but—"

"Where?"

He shook his head. Couldn't the yappy woman let him finish his sentence? "At the vineyard south of town. As a field worker. But—"

"A vineyard?" Tarsie's voice turned shrill. "You didn't take a job at a vineyard, did you?"

Defensiveness straightened Joss's spine. "I did."

"Oh, but, Joss . . ."

The disapproval in her tone raised Joss's stubborn pride a notch. "And just why shouldn't I work at a vineyard?"

She fluttered her hands, her lips pursed. "You know why. They'll be brewing wine at a vineyard. Why be placing yourself in the midst of temptation?"

"We're makin' wine out there, not drinkin' it." Joss growled the words, determined to put her in her place.

"But it'll be easily available to you."

Joss clenched his fists. He leaned close, lowering his voice to a grating growl. "You got no say in this, Tarsie."

She turned sharply away and sucked in several little breaths, her chest heaving with each intake. Her eyes snapped closed for several terse seconds, and when she opened them again, she met his fierce gaze with a calm resolve. "As your wife and the caretaker of your children, I should be havin' a say, Joss. I'm concerned for you, putting yourself in such a place. We came here to Kansas to help you lose your taste for the drink. But if you—"

Joss held up his hand, stilling her words. "I gotta earn a wage. Dock's gone, so I'm gonna work at the vineyard an' that's the way it is. No more talk."

He ignored her sharp gasp of frustration and stepped off the porch. As he strode around the house to the wagon to fetch another pair of trousers, it occurred to him he'd just trapped himself. He slapped his forehead, inwardly berating himself for letting his pride run ahead of his mouth. With a growl, Joss heaved himself into the wagon and flopped onto his back on the quilt.

He was stuck with that job now, or Tarsie'd think she'd been the one to change his mind. Which would be harder to tolerate—following Simon's directions, or having Tarsie believe he cared about her opinion? He'd either be kowtowing to a black man or appearing to kowtow to a woman. Both ideas soured his stomach.

"Well, Brubacher," he muttered to the flapping canvas cover above his head, "you got yourself in a fine pickle now."

❀ 17 ❀

That man's gonna be gettin' himself pickled every day, workin' at a place that makes wine," Tarsie murmured to herself as she followed Emmy and Nathaniel down the mucky roadway toward the mercantile. Joss had given her three dollars and instructed her in his typical dictatorial tone to be careful with it because she wouldn't be getting more for another week at least.

Gray skies loomed overhead, promising another bout of rain. Tarsie heaved a sigh, already weary, even though the day had just begun. She'd lain awake last night, praying, asking God to give Joss the good sense to quit that job where he'd be tempted to succumb to foolish desires. But Joss had headed off to the vineyard anyway.

Tarsie ushered the children through the mercantile door and offered a quick warning. "Don't be touching anything. Be good children, an' when we get home we'll have a cookie with some milk." Fortunately, one of her neighbors had agreed to barter a quart of milk a day in exchange for laundry services, so she needn't purchase canned milk, which was, in her opinion, overpriced.

The patter of footsteps and giggles erupted outside the store. Emmy dashed to the window to peer outside. She spun to Tarsie, her expression beseeching. "There's some kids on the porch. Can we go out an' play with 'em?"

Tarsie hesitated. She didn't know any of the town children. As she considered the request, a woman with a bright red bandana tied over her hair and a round, cheerful face stepped inside the store. She glanced at Emmy, who stood with her fingers and nose pressed to the glass, and released a low chuckle.

"You watchin' my chillun out there bein' plumb silly?"

Emmy nodded. "I wanna play, too. But Tarsie didn't say yes." Emmy's lower lip pooched out in a pout.

The woman swung a basket on her arm, her dark eyes twinkling. "An' they'd be right pleased to have a new playmate or two." She held out her work-callused hand to Tarsie. "I be Ruth Foster—me 'n' my fam'ly live out south o' Drayton Valley. Don't b'lieve I evuh seen you befo'."

Tarsie took the woman's hand and offered a shy smile. Friendliness radiated from this colored woman, drawing Tarsie in. "We're new in town. My . . . my husband"—fire seared her cheeks, speaking of Joss in such a personal manner—"had been working at the docks 'til the rain washed the dock away. But now he works at a vineyard."

Ruth's thick eyebrows shot upward. "Tollison Vineyard?"

Tarsie searched her memory. Joss hadn't given a name, but he'd told her the location. "The vineyard south of town."

The woman's face lit like a Fourth of July firecracker. "Ooh, now you got me all curious. Yo' husband he be named Joss?"

It was Tarsie's turn to raise her brows in surprise. "How did you know?"

A deep, rich chuckle rumbled from the woman's throat, bringing an answering smile to Tarsie's lips. "I knows it, girl, 'cause he be workin' fo' my husband."

Tarsie's mouth dropped open. "W-what?"

143

Pride lifted Ruth's chin. "That's right. Simon Foster—he be manager o' Tollison Vineyard, an' aftuh supper last night he tells me he gots a new man on the job. Says his name is Joss, an' that he's big as a mountain an' smart as a whip an'—" She fell abruptly silent, lowering her head to fiddle with the eggs in the basket.

Emmy darted to Tarsie's side and tugged on her elbow. "Can't me an' Nattie go out an' play with those kids? Pleeeeease?"

Apprehensive, Tarsie glanced at Ruth. The woman still looked down, clearly flustered. To give the other woman time to collect herself, Tarsie took both children by the hand and led them to the porch. Two boys—slightly older than Emmy—and a little girl close to Nathaniel's age ran back and forth from one spindled porch post to the other, their giggles running the scales. The oldest one caught the post with his palm and whirled around. He spotted Tarsie, Emmy, and Nathaniel and halted, holding out his arm to stop the younger two.

The three dark-faced children stared at Emmy and Nathaniel, who stared back, Nathaniel with one finger in his mouth. Before Tarsie could offer an introduction, Emmy took a step forward.

"I'm Emmy, an' that's Nattie." She jammed her thumb at her little brother.

The oldest boy pulled his brother and sister forward. "This here is Naomi an' Malachi. I be Ezekiel, but folks call me E.Z."

Emmy twisted her hands together and rocked from side to side. "Can me an' Nattie play, too?"

E.Z. broke into a broad grin. "We's just chasin', seein' who can get from one pole to the othuh the fastest." He shrugged. "If'n yo' mama don't care, you can play."

Joss might object, but Tarsie knew Mary wouldn't mind

Emmy and Nathaniel playing with these little Negro children. She gave the towheaded pair a gentle nudge forward. "Go ahead. I'll be right inside."

With a joyful hoot, Emmy grabbed Nathaniel's hand, and they joined in the fun.

Tarsie watched for a few minutes, smiling at their antics. Satisfied they'd be fine, she reentered the store. Ruth browsed the aisles, her basket now empty of its eggs. Tarsie approached the woman. "Thank you for letting your young'uns play with Emmy and Nathaniel. Poor wee ones, they haven't met any friends here yet. It'll do 'em good to play with someone besides each other for a change."

Ruth's smile returned, whatever had caused the shyness to surface forgotten. "Oh, those chillun, they do love to run an' shout. I's hopin' they'll get wore out good so they'll gib me some peace this aftuhnoon." She laughed, the sound reminding Tarsie of molasses dripping slowly across a biscuit. "So I know yo' husband's name, but I didn't catch yours."

Tarsie bobbed her head in greeting. "I'm Tarsie."

Ruth's eyebrows rose. "Tarsie? That be a mighty unusual name. Cain't say I evuh heard of it before."

"My real name is Treasa, but my da nicknamed me Tarsie when I was just a wee girl." Tarsie's chest constricted, loneliness for her parents still strong even after so many years. She shrugged. "I like it."

Ruth's eyes crinkled with her smile. "Why, Miz Tarsie, I b'lieve I do too."

The two fell into step together, Ruth filling her basket and Tarsie filling her apron, which she held outward by the corners to create a pouch. Ruth examined Tarsie's apron, her full lips quirking into a grin. "You gon' carry ever'thing home thataway? I reckon it works, but it sho' look ungainly."

Tarsie couldn't resist a chuckle. The teasing twinkle in Ruth's dark eyes invited gaiety. "I hope the proprietor will have a crate I can use. I might be tearing my apron strings clean off if I load it too much."

"Need a basket like I got—somethin' with a handle made for totin'."

Tarsie admired Ruth's basket. Large, tightly woven of creamy bands, and with a thickly wound handle, it seemed capable of carrying nearly everything she'd need. "Yours is very nice, but I couldn't be affording such a luxury right now. It's more important to buy food than a vessel for carrying it."

"Ooh, I didn't buy this basket. I made it." Ruth plucked two jars of pickled pig's feet from the shelf and settled them in her basket.

Tarsie came to a stop in the aisle and stared at Ruth. "You did?"

Ruth sent a twinkly grin in Tarsie's direction. "Sho' did. Y'see, durin' the spring an' summuh, I collect reeds from down by the rivuh. Then, come wintertime when I cain't be out workin' the garden, I takes those reeds an' I make baskets. All shapes an' sizes. Gots plenty of 'em sittin' aroun' my house. If you like, I can gib you one for shoppin'."

"Oh, no." Tarsie shook her head hard, once again admiring the workmanship of Ruth's basket. "I couldn't take something that cost you so much time and effort. And I have no money to pay for one." She bobbed the corners of her apron. "I'll make do."

Ruth shrugged. "Suit yo'self."

They finished their shopping. The lisping proprietor recorded Ruth's purchases against a credit in an account book, offering a thank-you for her bringing in fresh "eggth." Then Tarsie laid out the items she'd chosen, praying she'd have enough money to cover it all. To her relief, the money Joss had given her proved more than adequate, but the proprietor didn't have a crate for her to carry the purchases home. With a sigh, she removed her apron, tied everything into a lumpy bundle, then gathered the bundle in her arms.

Ruth raised one brow at Tarsie's makeshift package, but she didn't comment. The women trailed outside where the children sat in a row on the edge of the porch, bouncing their feet on the muddy street below. None of Ruth's youngsters wore shoes. For some reason, the sight of those dirty, bare feet with broken, dirt-rimmed toenails made Tarsie's heart hurt.

"Come, Emmy and Nathaniel." Tarsie nodded her head at the Foster children. "Tell your new friends good-bye. We must be goin' now." The bundle weighed heavily in her arms, making her impatient to get home.

A chorus of childish good-byes rang, each voice tinged with regret. Just as the children pushed to their feet, the bell on the schoolhouse up the hill began to clang. Tarsie smiled as the doors burst open and children spilled out, lunch buckets in hand. She heard a sigh and shifted to look at the oldest of the Foster youngsters. The boy gazed up the hill, longing in his eyes. He turned to his mother.

"Cain't I be goin', Mama? Huh? Huh?"

Ruth cupped the boy's dirt-smudged cheek. "Now, E.Z., we done talked 'bout this befo'. You know that school's only fo' the white chillun. You's gon' hafta wait 'til somebody comes along willin' to make a school for the black chillun, too."

E.Z. scuffed his toe on the porch floor. "Ain't nevuh gon' happen."

Ruth swatted his bottom, and E.Z. yelped in surprise, holding his rear. Ruth pointed her finger at him. "Now you quit that kind o' talk. Yo' pappy an' me, we's prayin' ever' day 'bout school, an' God's gon' answer by an' by. Don't you be disbelievin', boy."

E.Z. nodded solemnly. "I's sorry, Mama."

Ruth's smile returned. She bounced it from E.Z. to Tarsie. "It was right nice meetin' you all. I hopes to cross paths with you'uns again soon." Waving her arm, she turned to her children. "Well, come along now, no dallyin'. We gots work to do at home." The four traipsed off, the little girl skipping ahead, the youngest boy holding on to his mother's skirt, and E.Z. scuffing behind with his head low.

Tarsie watched them for a moment before she turned toward the house and headed up the road. Emmy and Nathaniel followed, chanting a nonsense song as they walked, but Tarsie paid little attention to their voices. Her thoughts were inward, churning. She'd heard mutters from her neighbors. Although many colored people resided in Drayton Valley, often working side by side with white men at the docks or in the warehouses, their homes were far separated. They attended different churches, buried their dead in different cemeteries, and apparently had a rule against colored children sitting under the same school roof as the white children. The white business owners had no trouble taking the blacks' money, however. It didn't seem fair.

By the time they reached their little house, Tarsie's arms ached from carrying the heavy load, and her heart ached from the seeming inequities between whites and blacks. Joss would certainly have much to say in defense of the current system. In fact, Joss would—

She gave a start, the bundle dropping from her arms to spill its contents across the clean-swept floor. She clutched her hands to her heart, her soul rejoicing. Ruth had indicated Joss worked under a black manager. Joss Brubacher—working for a black man. She shook her head, marveling. Hadn't she prayed for Joss to change? And apparently he had in some wonderful way or he'd never have taken that job at the vineyard. Although it still worried her to have him working in a place where wine was produced, she chose to push the worry aside. Perhaps this was God's way of softening Joss's heart.

※

Tarsie honored her conviction to hold her tongue concerning Joss's place of employment, trusting God had a reason for placing Joss at the vineyard. She waited for him to admit— or even bemoan—working for a colored man, but he never spoke of work. She supposed she shouldn't expect him to. Joss wasn't much of a talker, and even though she was his wife, he held his distance in every way. But she kept her ears tuned for any comment that might lead to conversation concerning Ruth's husband and how Joss was getting along with him.

On Sunday, she and the children attended a red-brick chapel set on a little rise overlooking the cemetery. Joss stayed at the house to cover the broken window with some scrap lumber he'd dragged home from the vineyard. Although Tarsie came close to informing him, rather tartly, that he'd make better use of his day attending church, she held the words inside. Mary had let her kind actions and attitudes speak to Joss, and Tarsie would follow the same example.

Rain fell both Monday and Tuesday, turning the garden plot into such a mucky mess Tarsie feared she'd never be able to put the turnip, carrot, cabbage, tomato, and bean seeds in the ground. Having the youngsters constantly underfoot in the small space made work difficult, and she searched for ways to occupy them. Remembering how they'd drawn all over the sides of the wagon with bits of white rock, she gave them each lumps of coal and permission to use one wall of the house as a blackboard. They cheerfully entertained themselves most of the day Wednesday, allowing Tarsie to bake bread and do laundry without interruption.

On Thursday morning, after Joss left and while the youngsters still slept, she sat on the little front stoop with her Bible in hand. The minister had admonished the congregation from the pulpit about the importance of spending time each day with God. Tarsie prayed daily—many times each day, as needs arose—but she'd neglected the Bible reading her aunt had encouraged. Determined to do better, she flopped open the worn book and hunched forward, drinking in the beautiful words of promise found in the forty-third chapter of Isaiah.

Birds sang from treetops, oblivious to the gloomy sky painted the same color as an old iron washtub. Tarsie read aloud, her whisper joining with the birdsong to create a sweet melody of praise. "'Fear not: for I have redeemed thee, I have called thee by thy name; thou art mine. When thou passest through the waters, I will be with thee; and through the rivers, they shall not overflow thee . . .'" She took comfort in the words, knowing how the rains filled the rivers and brought the banks to the edge of town.

She read on, and when she reached verses eighteen and nineteen, a tremor of delight wiggled its way up her spine. Her heart skipping cheerfully within her chest, she read the words in a strong, sure voice. "'Remember ye not the former things, neither consider the things of old. Behold, I will do a new thing; now it shall spring forth; shall ye not know it?'"

Closing the Bible, Tarsie hugged it to her chest and looked out across the burgeoning day. So many "new things" were springing up—a new place to live, a new family to claim as her own, Joss taking on a new job, all of them meeting new people . . . Immediately, in her mind's eye, an image of Ruth and her three barefooted, bedraggled children appeared. Something niggled in the back of Tarsie's heart. She pursed her lips, squinting skyward. "Are You tellin' me something important, dear God? Somethin' new I'm to know . . . or do?" The idea quivered beyond her reach.

"Tarsie? Tarsie, where are you?"

Emmy's panicked voice carried from inside the house, chasing Tarsie's thoughts away. She rose, calling, "I'm out here, Emmy." She entered the house, ready to face the day, but as she stepped to the cookstove to boil water for the children's mush, she sent one more prayer up to the heavens. *God, if You've got something else in mind for me to be doin', make it clear to me so I can be about Your business.*

❋ 18 ❋

The vineyard's lunch bell clanged and, with a sigh of relief, Joss set aside his hoe. Simon limped ahead of Joss and climbed into his little mule-pulled cart. He lifted his hand in a wave before flicking the reins and rolling past the lines of workers filing out of the fields and making their way up the lane toward the Tollison mansion. Joss joined the ranks, eager to get out of the muggy air that buzzed with mosquitoes and sit for a while.

To the west of the big house, Tollison had constructed a barnlike structure sporting rows of square windows on all four sides where the men gathered for meals or to get out of the rain. Behind the building, Joss's horse grazed with a half dozen other horses owned by white workers and a goodly number of mules belonging to colored workers. Joss glanced into the corral, noting how the horses clumped together on one side, the mules on the other. Separate, just like their owners. Funny how even dumb animals knew things weren't equal, no matter what Lincoln said or how Tollison tried to run this place. Joss didn't know of any other operation that put colored men in authority over white men.

Pushing the thought aside, Joss entered the building. Tollison's house servants always set out jugs of water and baskets of fruit or pans of cobbler for the workers, and men

151

swarmed the table containing the items. As much as Joss's parched mouth longed for a cup of water, he wouldn't battle the crowd, putting him elbow to elbow with the black men. Pa'd always said to be careful—the black could rub off on him. He'd fetch a cup of water and maybe an apple or two when everyone cleared out.

He made his way to one of the roughhewn tables, his paper-wrapped cheese sandwiches in hand, and plopped onto a bench. Others joined him, tired-looking men with lines etched into their sunburnt foreheads. None of them spoke—they were too interested in guzzling water from tin cups or digging through whatever their wives had sent in their lunch pails. That suited Joss. He'd listened to Simon's blather every day since he'd started out here, from morning to late afternoon. The man seemed to have nothing better to do than follow Joss and oversee his every move. When would Simon finally trust Joss to do the job on his own?

He finished his first sandwich in four big bites, nearly swallowing the chomps whole. The dry bread tried to stick in his throat, but he swallowed resolutely and reached for the second sandwich. Just as he lifted it, a hand shot over his shoulder. A black hand, curled around a shiny tin cup filled to the brim with clear water.

"Here you go, Joss. You ain't stopped for a drink all mo'nin'—need to have yo'self some watuh."

Joss nearly groaned. He grabbed the cup and plunked it onto the table, chagrined as droplets spilled over the rim. "Thanks."

"Sho' thing." Simon stood at the end of the bench, beaming down at Joss. "Mistuh Tollison's cook done outdid herself today with peach 'n' berry cobbler. It be 'most gone a'ready." He bobbed a small plate under Joss's nose. "If'n you want, I'll gib you this portion an' fetch another plate fo' myself."

Joss squeezed his sandwich in both hands, his mouth

watering at the sight of rich juices oozing from a thick, flaky crust. Tarsie was a good cook, but she'd never made anything more than some crispy cookies for treats. He wanted that cobbler so bad his insides nearly quivered right out of him. But he couldn't bring himself to take that plate from Simon.

"No, thanks."

Simon's wiry eyebrows shot up. "You don't like peach 'n' berry cobbler?"

Joss waved his sandwich, keeping his eyes averted from the tempting plate. "Got this to eat."

"A'right then." Simon shrugged, his brown face still wreathed in a smile. "Just hope they's still some waitin' when you git that sandwich all et. Enjoy yo' break, Joss. We'll take up again when lunch is over." Finally, he ambled off to a lone table near the colored workers, the shorter leg giving him a painful-looking hitch.

The man on Joss's right snorted. "That Simon . . . thinks he's somethin' 'cause the boss made him foreman. Don't got nothin' to do with him bein' able. Got everything to do with his pappy pullin' Tollison's brother from a ragin' creek when they were young'uns. Tollison thinks he owes the family."

Joss sat straighter. "That so?" He hadn't realized how long the vineyard had been in operation. "Their families go way back, huh?"

"Way I understand it," the man continued, his derisive tone reminding Joss of his pa, "Tollison's pa came from Virginia in the 1850s an' brought a whole passel of workers with him—slaves he bought off o' plantations. He gave all them slaves their freedom papers an' put 'em to work here, plantin' vines an' peach trees alongside the berry brambles. Simon's pa was one of the workers he freed, so Simon was born a free man." The man narrowed his eyes, peering across the room at Simon. "Makes him uppity, to my way o' thinkin'."

"Aw, Stillman, Simon ain't so bad." A man across the table

pushed his spoon through the crust of his fist-sized serving of cobbler. "He don't lord his position over anybody. An' he knows grape-growin'—spent his whole life in the vineyard—so why shouldn't he manage things? He's got more sense'n you an' me when it comes to what's needed around here."

Stillman rose half out of his seat and clenched his fists. "You sayin' a colored's smarter'n me? That what you're sayin', Rouse?"

Joss leaned away, tense and ready to join a fracas if it erupted. But on which side would he fight—Stillman's or Rouse's? Part of him agreed with Stillman, but as much as it irked him, he also saw sense in Rouse's viewpoint. Uncertain, he held his breath, waiting to see what would transpire.

Rouse dropped his spoon and held up his hands in surrender. "Ain't gonna fight. You know Tollison's rule—fightin' gets instant dismissal." He lowered his voice. "I need this job. Same as you do, Stillman."

As quickly as he'd flared, Stillman settled down. He plopped onto the creaky bench and snatched up an apple. Joss relaxed, turning his attention to his uneaten sandwich. It'd all happened so quickly, no one besides those at their table seemed to know a fight had nearly erupted.

Stillman bit into his apple, chewed, and swallowed, his narrowed gaze pinned on Rouse, who went on eating with a hand that now trembled. After a few tense seconds, Stillman spoke again. "Ain't Simon's color bothers me so much as him drivin' all over the place in that blamed cart. Rest of us hafta walk—Tollison don't want us tramplin' his 'tender vines' with wooden wheels or horse hooves. But Simon . . . he gets special privileges."

Rouse shook his head. "You holdin' a grudge 'cause Simon uses that cart? Don'tcha think he'd ruther have two good legs to tote him from place to place?" The man shoved the last bite of cobbler into his mouth, then stood, his face sad. "There're some things folks don't got no choice over, Stillman, but we all choose how we treat people. Might do you some good to find a little Christian charity in your heart 'stead o' bein' so plumb hard-nosed." He walked off and joined another table.

Stillman muttered a foul oath and bolted off the bench. He tossed his cup onto the table near the double doors and stormed out. Joss watched Stillman go, relieved he hadn't gone after Rouse. Stillman seemed to have a temper, so he'd best mind himself around the man—try not to rile him. Especially since he now knew Tollison would dismiss any man who started or participated in a fight.

He faced forward, and his gaze landed on Simon, sitting at a table by himself. Behind him, black workers huddled together on benches. In front of him, white workers did the same. But there Simon sat, a part of neither group. Joss finished his sandwich, but more out of habit than hunger. His hunger had slipped away. Sympathy—a feeling he would never have expected—replaced the desire to eat.

Rouse had asked whether Simon would choose to have a gimpy leg over two whole, hale legs. Even Joss, an uneducated dockworker from the poor side of New York, recognized no man would make such a choice. Joss paused, stopping to contemplate for the first time in his life that Simon had no choice over something else. His skin color.

✳

On Saturday morning, as dawn painted the sky all pink and soft, Ruth pressed Simon's lunch bucket into his hand while planting a lingering kiss on his lips. He raised his empty hand to cup her cheek, using his thumb to caress the little hairs that curled tightly at her temple. So hard to leave her every day, especially so early, but he wouldn't begrudge the job that required he be the first man to arrive and the last to go home. Pappy'd always said Edgar Tollison was an angel walking the earth, and Simon had to agree. What other white man would give a colored cripple such an important job? He wouldn't let Mr. Tollison down.

"Packed you the last o' the sliced ham an' three big chunks o' corn bread." Ruth pulled away to point at the little bucket, her eyes sparkling with mischief. "Put a li'l surprise in there, too. Somethin' to make you think o' me when you oughta be thinkin' o' work."

Simon chuckled, giving her full cheek a soft pinch. "You tryin' to get me fired, thinkin' on you 'stead o' my job?" He bounced the bucket, pretending to try to peek beneath the frayed square of cloth hiding the contents. "Nothin' in there gon' jump out at me, is there?"

She slapped at his chest, her deep chortle making him smile. "Only thing gon' be jumpin' is your heart, wantin' to hustle on back here to me."

Simon tipped forward for a second kiss. "Woman, when the good Lawd handed out wives, He done saved the best o' all for me. I love you, Ruth."

Her arms slipped around him, her face burrowing into the bend of his neck. "An' I love you, too, Simon." She stepped away, a grin giving her an impish look. "Now off to work with you."

Simon coiled his arm around her waist and drew her with him as he made his way to his waiting cart. "What're you gon' do with your day? Bakin'?" He smacked his lips, thinking about the rich molasses cakes and egg custard pies that often greeted him from the windowsill at the end of a Saturday, a treat for their Sunday dinner.

"Goin' to town. Gon' try to look up Joss's wife an' chillun."

Simon's steps halted. "What fo'?"

"Just a visit." Ruth's expression turned wily. "Her bein' new in town, she might could use a little woman-talk. 'Sides, our young'uns got along right good. She didn't blink an eye at lettin' hers run an' skip on that porch with E.Z., Malachi, an' Naomi right there in front o' the whole town. Gon' take her a present, too. Feel like I owe her a li'l somethin' for favorin' our'n."

Simon chewed his lower lip, concern rolling through his middle. "Jus' be careful, will you? That Joss, he ain't come right out an' said he don't want nothin' to do with coloreds, but his standoffishness sho' speaks it for him. Don't wantcha gettin' yo'self hurt, bein' pushed aside by some snooty white gal."

Ruth toyed with the mismatched buttons on Simon's shirt, her lips pooched in disapproval. "Don't you be worryin' none about me an' my feelin's. I's tough as ol' boot leather, an' you knows it." A teasing glint came into her eyes. "Hafta be to put up with you an' your sass."

Simon laughed aloud. The only sassy one in his house was Ruth, and they both knew it. And he wouldn't have it any other way. "All right, then, woman." He plopped the little bucket on the cart seat and heaved himself over the edge. Reins in hand, he asked, "Whatcha givin' her?" They had little of value to share.

Ruth stepped back from the cart, flapping her apron skirt at him. "Nevuh you mind that. Just git on now befo' you's late. I be tellin' you how she liked her present when you come home tonight."

***

Tarsie wrung the excess water from Emmy's dress and then flipped the little frock over a bush in the side yard. She sneaked a quick look at the sky—huge white puffs hung high on a pale-blue backdrop, allowing the sun to poke through. If she were lucky, the sun would chase away those clouds. Or at least keep them from leaking, as Emmy put it, until the laundry was dry. She could hang everything inside on cords strung from one side of the room to the other if she had to, but it made it difficult to move around in there.

Turning back to the washtub, she plunged one of Joss's shirts into the water and began to scrub. Filmy soap clung to her arms, and water dampened the edges of her rolled sleeves. The strong smell of lye soap filled her nostrils while the children's giggling voices carried from the little patch of grass at the front corner of the house, where they hopped in a circle in a made-up game. Perspiration trickled down her forehead, but she sped her pace. She still had the neighbor's laundry to wash, and she wanted it all finished before noon.

As she lifted the final item—Nathaniel's small britches—from the now murky water, the children's joyful squeals abruptly dropped to hissed whispers. Puzzled, Tarsie tucked a stray wisp of hair behind her ear and looked toward the yard. She gave a start. Three little black children hunkered in a circle with Emmy and Nathaniel, their heads close together. Although the two biggest ones had their backs to her, partially hiding the others from view, she thought they were the same children she'd met outside the mercantile last week. She tossed the water-logged trousers over the closest bush and trotted in their direction only to have her pathway blocked by the children's mother.

Ruth Foster broke into a huge smile and thrust out a finely woven basket, its opening so large Tarsie would have difficulty stretching both arms around it. "I brung you this. Fo' when you go shoppin' next so's you won't have to wear out your apron strings."

Something tapped together in the bottom of the basket, and Tarsie inched forward to peek inside. Six eggs—two brown, four white—rolled against one another. Tarsie wove her fingers tightly together to keep from reaching for that beautiful basket and its bounty. "B-but I told you, I be having no way of paying you for a basket. An' certainly not for eggs, too!"

Ruth's brown eyes squinted as she gazed toward the little house. "You gots coffee brewin'?"

Tarsie gulped. At least half a pot sat cooling on the back of the stove, leftover from breakfast. She drank it off and on all day. "It needs heating, but I have some, yes."

"Cup o' coffee'd be a fine exchange for them eggs."

Tarsie tipped her head. It hardly seemed a fair exchange.

"An' mebbe . . ." Shy hesitance dimmed the woman's bright eyes. "We could just set an' talk a spell? The way friends sometimes do?"

Looking into Ruth's round, hopeful face, Tarsie suddenly realized the colored woman was offering much more than a shopping basket and a few eggs. She was offering a piece of herself—risking rejection to do so. How could Tarsie refuse?

Tarsie gestured to the children, who remained in a little circle poking twigs into the ground to form a miniature fence. "What about the youngsters?"

Ruth shrugged, swinging the basket slightly. "Ground's soggy, but the sun's shinin' down. Do 'em some good to feel it on their heads, don'tcha think?"

With a grin, Tarsie nodded. "Come inside, then." She led her new friend over the threshold.

❈ 19 ❈

Tarsie unrolled her dampened sleeves back down to her wrists as she crossed to the pile of twigs in the corner. Squatting, she gathered an armful and glanced over her shoulder to Ruth, who stood in the middle of the room, seeming to examine every corner of the little house. Embarrassment heated Tarsie's cheeks as she considered the trunk that served as a table, the piles of blankets thrown on the floor for beds, unplastered walls and boarded window. The house was clean thanks to Tarsie's diligence, but the lack of furnishings gave it a rustic appearance. What was Ruth thinking as her dark-eyed gaze roved from corner to corner?

Laying the twigs on top of the remaining coals, Tarsie blew gently until a fire flared. She closed the stove door and turned to face her guest, wadding her apron in her hands and releasing a nervous chuckle. "It'll take a bit for the coffee to heat. I'd like to say sit and make yourself comfortable, but as you can see, I . . ." She held out her hands in a gesture of futility.

Ruth grinned and plopped onto the trunk, placing the basket on the floor beside her feet. "This'll serve me jus' fine as a sittin' place."

Relieved at Ruth's easy acceptance of their stark surroundings, Tarsie drew up a crate for her own chair. The moment she settled herself, Ruth pointed to the faded marks on the

160

wall left by Emmy and Nathaniel's enthusiastic application of the pieces of coal.

"What be all this?" Her face held curiosity but no condemnation.

Tarsie grinned. "That's the wee ones' attempts at writing letters and numbers."

Ruth shot a startled glance at Tarsie. "You teachin' 'em? To write an' all?"

Shrugging, Tarsie laughed lightly. "I was just trying to keep them out from underfoot one rainy day."

Ruth didn't chuckle in reply. She leaned toward Tarsie, her eyes wide and fervent. "But you knows how? To write? An' read? An' do numbers?" She seemed to hold her breath.

Understanding bloomed through Tarsie's mind, followed by a wave of guilt. It wasn't fair that Ruth's children were denied an education just because their skin was brown instead of white. She'd always been proud of her education, limited as it was due to needing to help provide for Aunt Vangie. But being able to read, write, add, and subtract meant no one could cheat her. At least not easily. But Ruth, her family, and her neighbors had no such advantage. How helpless they must feel.

Tarsie swallowed, battling both shame and sympathy. "Yes. I know how."

Ruth gave a long sigh, her shoulders wilting. "Lawsy, girl, such a fine thing to know." Her gaze drifted to the little crate that stood between the two piles of blankets where she and the children slept. She rose and crossed to the crate. Tarsie's Bible lay on the slatted top. "You can open that book anytime you please, cain't you, an' read the words fo' yo'self?"

Ruth picked up the Bible and held it against her middle, turning to face Tarsie. "I gots a Bible. Ol' Mistuh Tollison give it to Simon's pappy a long time ago as a gift. Didn't make much sense to my way o' thinkin', givin' a former slave-man somethin' he gots no way o' usin', but Pappy, he treasure that Bible, an' he carries it to service ever' Sunday just proud as can be, even though he just holds it 'stead o' readin'. When Zeke died, Simon brought the Bible home an' tol' me to keep it as a sign o' God's promises, so I gots one. Just cain't do nothin' more'n look at it. Cain't read one word on the pages."

She raised Tarsie's Bible to her cheek. Her eyes slid closed, and she drew in a deep breath as if trying to absorb its contents. "That's what I hunger for, to read God's words fo' myself." A tear trickled down Ruth's plump cheek. "An' I wants it fo' my chillun even more'n I want it fo' me."

A deep ache filled Tarsie's breast as she listened to Ruth's impassioned yet low-toned desire. The woman could long for a fine home, fancy clothes, even to be white instead of black. But what she wanted was to read so she could study God's word on her own.

Almost without conscious thought, a suggestion poured from Tarsie's lips. "I could be teaching you. And then you could teach your children."

Ruth's eyes flew open. She placed the Bible, just so, in its spot on the crate and then stumbled across the floor toward Tarsie with her hands outstretched. She grasped Tarsie's hands and pulled her to her feet, her expression so hopeful it pierced Tarsie to the center of her soul. "You'd be doin' that fo' me?"

Tarsie squeezed Ruth's hands. "You brought me a basket and eggs. You offered me friendship. Your husband's making sure my h-husband has a means of carin' for his family. I'd be sayin' it's the least I can do for someone who's given so much to me."

Ruth flung her hands upward, laughter pouring from her throat while tears rained down her cheeks. "Oh, praise the Lawd, He done answered our prayers!" She threw her arms around Tarsie and hugged her hard, rocking from side to side. "Girl, you's an angel. An angel, fo' sure."

Then Ruth pulled back, her joy fading to worry. "But don'tcha need to be askin' yo' husband first? Teachin' me, it'll take a heap o' time, I reckon. He . . . he might not like the idea o' you spendin' so much time with a colored woman."

Tarsie ducked her head. What would Joss say? He worked uncomplainingly under a black man's leadership, and she continued to pray daily for Joss's heart to soften toward his children. But hadn't she also prayed for God to answer Ruth's prayer? Surely the idea to teach Ruth so she could teach her children had been God-planted. And if God had planted the idea, He'd find the means to make it blossom.

She raised her chin and fixed Ruth with a determined look. "Don't you be worrying about what my husband says. God wants me to do this, and if I'm honoring God, He'll honor me." The coffeepot's lid began to rattle. Tarsie grinned. "Now, how about that cup of coffee?"

Joss, with a gunnysack dangling from his hand, trudged up the hill toward the house, where a hot meal waited. Tarsie'd told him that morning she'd traded some stitching for a nice pork roast, which she intended to fix for their supper, so Joss should hurry home after work. He still couldn't think of the place as *home*, although Tarsie and the youngsters called it such. The only place that had ever been home to him was the apartment in New York, dismal as it might've been. Mary was there, and that made it home.

He drew in a sharp breath, grief capturing him anew. He'd held thoughts of Mary at bay by staying busy, but now pain— fierce and all-consuming—seared him from the inside out. How he missed her. He missed her tender touches, her sweet smiles, her soft laugh. He missed watching her go about her tasks, always humming, never complaining. He missed the weight of her body rolled next to his, her breath teasing his cheek at night. He missed how she made him feel like the most important person in the world—valued, cherished, loved. Despite his faults and grumbles and lack of appreciation, she'd still loved him. Mary made life worth living.

His steps faltered, a thought tripping him. Whether in Kansas, Chicago, or any other place on earth, he'd never feel at home again. He was fooling himself, thinking going to Chicago would make him happy. But what else could he do? Nothing held him here except responsibility, and he'd see to that before packing up and taking off.

Despite imagining his carefully made plans come to pass thanks to the money he'd be able to squirrel away from his wages at the vineyard, he couldn't dredge up a smidgen of joy at the prospect of leaving. What was wrong with him?

The sack tugged at his shoulder, reminding him he'd been standing idle too long. He set his feet in motion, holding the bag away from his body to keep from bruising the contents. At the end of the day, Simon'd handed every worker his week's pay plus a bag of last year's apples, which had spent the winter in Tollison's wine cellar. They were shriveled up some but still plenty good for baking in pies, stewing, or drying. He had no doubt Tarsie would make good use of them. She was a fine cook, same as Mary'd been. She was a lot spunkier than Mary, but she had Mary's patience with the young'uns, which was good, since Joss had none. And his eyes didn't mind looking at her, given her physical appeal, even if she didn't have Mary's golden hair or blue eyes.

And what was he thinking now? He muttered a mild oath and sped his pace, determined to leave the wild notions about Tarsie behind. The door to the house stood open in silent greeting, the aroma of roasting meat drifting on the breeze. Saliva pooled under his tongue, and he trotted the last few feet. As he stepped into the house, Emmy looked up from placing silverware beside plates on the trunk and grinned.

"Howdy, Papa. Whatcha got?"

Nathaniel galloped over and tried to take the sack. "What got?"

"Apples." Joss wrestled the sack free of Nathaniel's little hands and placed it on the floor near the door, then hung his hat on a nail pounded into the wall. He turned toward the center of the room and spotted Tarsie at the stove with her back to him. She wore one of Mary's aprons—the rose-sprigged one Mary'd always liked best because it reminded her of a garden. The early evening light slanting through the open window fell on her braided twist, bringing out the gold highlights in her reddish hair. For a moment, Joss could almost believe it was Mary at that stove stirring a pot, and it was all he could do to resist moving up behind her and slipping his arms around her waist, pressing his cheek to hers, and greeting her the way a man greeted his woman at the close of a day.

Pot in hand, Tarsie moved toward the trunk. Her gaze lit on him, and a smile lifted her lips—a smile of welcome. Joss's breath caught, old memories tumbling over the present picture and getting all muddled in his mind.

Tarsie paused midway between the stove and trunk, her brows coming together. "Joss, is somethin' the matter?"

He shook his head hard, dispelling the images of Mary. "'Course not." He inched in the direction of the wash bucket. "Just hungry's all. Been a long day. I'll get washed an' . . ." Leaning over the bucket, he soaped up good, drawing in several breaths to get himself under control. What was he doing, looking at Tarsie that way? She wasn't Mary. Couldn't ever be Mary. Even if a very small part of him might wish she could be *like* Mary to him. Maybe. Someday.

Towel in hand, he froze, realizing where his thoughts had

just carried him. He spun around, gawking at Tarsie in horror—would she guess the errant ideas tripping through his mind? She met his gaze, her lower lip caught between her teeth and a look he could only define as consternation marring her face. His muscles began to quiver, and it took two tries to hook the towel back on its nail.

Ignoring her discomfiture, he plodded to the trunk and knelt, nodding to the two youngsters. "Well, c'mon, you two. Tarsie's got a fine dinner prepared. Git over here before it grows cold."

The towheaded pair dashed to the trunk. His command seemed to bring Tarsie back to life, too. She hustled to the trunk and set the pan containing boiled potatoes before him. Then she fetched the roast, knelt, and offered a familiar blessing for the food. She carved the roast and dished up potatoes as if nothing were wrong, but she didn't speak. Her uncustomary silence held the children's tongues, as well, and Joss grew more uncomfortable by the minute. With no cheerful blather to distract him, he found himself doing too much thinking. And all that thinking led to nothing good.

He swallowed a flavorful bite of roast, swished his hand over his mouth, and looked across the trunk to Emmy. "So . . . what'd you young'uns do today?"

Emmy wriggled in place. "We had a fine time, Papa! E.Z. an' Malachi an' Naomi came to play, an' we built a fort an' made cowboys an' Indians outta little sticks! Tarsie gave us scraps to put clothes on 'em, an' we—"

Joss held up a hand, confused. He'd learned the names of their nearest neighbors, but he didn't recognize those Emmy had mentioned. "Who're you talking about?"

"Miss Ruth's chillun." Emmy's childish voice took on a distinct twang.

Joss put down his fork and frowned at the little girl. "An' who's Miss Ruth?"

Emmy hesitated, and Tarsie cleared her throat. She gestured to Emmy's plate. "Finish up your supper, Emmy. You, too, Nathaniel." She waited for a moment, watching the children until they moved to obey. Then she shifted to look Joss full in the face. "Miss Ruth is Simon Foster's wife. E.Z., Malachi, and Naomi are their children. We met in the mercantile on Monday, and today they came by the house to pay us a visit."

"An' guess what, Papa?" Emmy bounced on her knees. "Tarsie's gonna teach Miss Ruth how to read an' write!"

❋ 20 ❋

You's gon' do *what*?" Simon stared at Ruth. He must've heard wrong—Ruth had more sense than to take up lessons with a white woman. Especially Joss Brubacher's woman.

Ruth set her lips in that way of hers that let Simon know she didn't intend to say another word. At least not until they were alone. Deciding it best not to argue in front of the boys and little Naomi, he held the rest of his protests inside. They went on eating their supper in silence, the youngsters finishing first and dashing outside to play away the remaining hours before sundown. Clouds building in the east warned of another storm coming—might as well let the children enjoy the sun for as long as it lasted.

Simon stayed at the table, sipping a final cup of sassafras-root tea, while Ruth cleared the pans, plates, battered silverware, and cups. But before she filled the tub for washing, he said, "All right, woman. Set yo'self down ovuh here an' 'splain this thing to me."

Ruth came at him in a rush, settling her bulk in his lap rather than taking her own chair. She toyed with his earlobe—something she always did when she was trying to wheedle him into her way of thinking—and spilled out the whole plan for Joss Brubacher's woman to teach Ruth how to read, write, and cipher.

"When I gots the lessons down real good myself, then I can be teachin' our chillun. Maybe even all the colored chillun from Drayton Valley. Don'tcha see, Simon? Our prayers've done been answered."

"How you gon' be able to do all that?"

Ruth gave him a sour look. "You sayin' I ain't smart enough to learn what needs learnin'?"

"That ain't what I'm sayin' at all, an' you knows it." Simon shifted, his foot aching from supporting her weight. But he didn't push her from his lap. He'd never minded sharing a chair with Ruth. "I's just saying learnin' takes time—a heap o' time. What's gon' happen when that husband o' hers says he don't want her spendin' so much time with the likes o' you?"

Ruth pinched his earlobe. Hard. "You sayin' the good Lawd'd take away His gift right aftuh He done give it to me? Where's your faith, Simon Foster? Your pappy'd have your hide to hear you talkin' thataway."

Simon couldn't hold back a chuckle. He rubbed his ear. "Reckon you're right. But Pappy nevuh got the chance to meet Joss Brubacher. Matter o' fact, Joss wouldn't even be hired on if Pappy hadn't died." He sighed ruefully. "That Joss, he be a good workuh, I'll give him that. But he sho' ain't got Pappy's easy way o' livin' a life." Simon pictured Brubacher, tall and sturdy, with lips that never smiled. "That man, he carries a grudge. A mighty big grudge. And it seems to be aimed at peoples like you an' me."

Simon burrowed his face against Ruth's cheek, seeking to soften the impact his words could have on her hopeful heart. "Don't wantcha gettin' all worked up, thinkin' you's gon' get somethin' that don't nevuh come." Lord knew she'd had enough disappointments in life between losing her mama and pap when she was but a girl, burying two babies before her twenty-first year, and marrying up with a man with a crippled foot. She'd already borne more than a body should.

Simon would have a hard time staying pleasant with Joss if the man did anything to hurt his Ruth.

Ruth smacked a kiss on Simon's lips and pushed up from his lap, her smile wide. "Don't you be worryin', Simon Foster. I gots faith in Tarsie. She be a good woman with a good heart—I can see it in her. The Lawd done tol' her to teach me, an' she's a gal who does what the Lawd say, so she's gon' teach me. You just wait. Uh-huh, you just wait an' see."

Joss paced beside the wagon, listening to the distant rumble of thunder and waiting for the windows to go dark. As soon as Tarsie put out the lamp, he'd know the young'uns were sleeping. And then he and Tarsie would have themselves a talk.

He couldn't let her make a commitment to that Negro woman. Soon—another month, maybe a little more—he'd have enough set aside to hightail it out of here. With him gone, she'd need to find herself a job. And if she took up with a colored woman, nobody in town would hire her. Prejudices ran deep. He'd have to make Tarsie understand how she was hurting herself to make friends with a Negro family.

The sky's grumble increased in volume, flashes of sheet lightning turning the clouds into Chinese lanterns. Wind gusted, rocking the wagon. Josh shoved his hands into his pockets, stifling the desire to let loose a string of curses. It was mid-June already. When would these storms leave for good? They'd gotten so much rain the ground was too soft to support a new dock, leaving the dockworkers without a means of caring for their families.

Talk around the vineyard had it a railroad was thinking of bringing a line through Drayton Valley, which would take the place of the dock. Men hoped it would happen—there'd be jobs laying the lines, and the railroad always brought more businesses and people to a town. But unless the rain stopped, removing the threat of flooding, nobody'd take a chance on running rails through town.

More flashes illuminated the sky, the bursts of light bouncing from east to south and back again. The thunder rolled with such intensity Joss's chest tightened. He needed to get inside the wagon before the storm let loose. Would Tarsie ever turn out that light so he'd know it was safe to talk to her?

After another twenty minutes of pacing, during which time the wind rose to a howl that raised the hairs on the back of Joss's neck, the glow behind the windows finally died. Blowing out a breath of relief, Joss trotted to the front door and tapped. "Tarsie? Open the door. It's me, Joss."

Moments later she cracked the door a scant six inches. A burst of lightning illuminated her figure, her disheveled braid tumbling across the bodice of a belted robe.

Joss gulped. "Didn't know you'd already dressed for bed." He aimed his gaze at the murky sky where clouds hid the stars from view. "Need to talk to you."

"Can it not be waitin' until tomorrow? The children'n me will be risin' early to prepare for service in the mornin'."

Her thick Irish brogue let him know it unsettled her to be caught in her nightclothes. If he possessed an Irish brogue, he'd be using it himself, considering how flustered he felt seeing her with her hair all billowy around her face and her bare toes peeping from beneath the hem of her robe.

He took a backward step. "M-maybe that'd be best."

She creaked the door open a bit more—wide enough to poke her head out. "Would you be goin' with us? Emmy an' wee Nathaniel, they'd find such pleasure in goin' to Sunday service with their papa."

"No," Joss barked over a roll of thunder. "I'll talk to you tomorrow when you get back." He charged around the house to his waiting wagon without giving her a chance to speak again. He climbed into the wagon, tying the canvas cover

171

closed at both ends just before the clouds opened and rain pelted the earth. Carried on a gusting wind, raindrops found their way between cracks, spattering Joss. He hunkered as low as he could and pulled the blanket clean over his head. He found it stifling underneath the heavy wool, but it blocked the water and also muffled the howl of wind, crashes of thunder, and *rat-a-tat-tat* of raindrops on the canvas.

The wagon rocked in the wind, and soon Joss fell into a fitful sleep, wrapped in his blanket like a caterpillar in a cocoon. He dreamed he sat high on a wagon seat, driving through a gray, gloomy countryside. The road was rough, the wheels bouncing over rocks, nearly jarring him from the seat. But in the distance he caught sight of a slight figure. Shining blond hair blew in the wind, and deep blue eyes beseeched him to come nearer, nearer. His heart pounding in eagerness, Joss encouraged the horses to hurry, which increased the jolts and bumps of the wagon. But no matter how much distance the wagon covered, the woman remained far away. Heart thudding, breath coming in heaves, Joss leaned forward and forced the horses faster. The wheels hit a boulder, and the wagon tipped, tumbling end over end.

Joss jolted awake, gasping as he realized the tip of the wagon was reality, not a dream after all. He reached for some kind of handhold but found none. Curling into a ball to protect himself as best he could, he rolled with the pitch of the wooden box, jarring his knees and elbows and banging his head as he went. The wagon came to a rest on its side, the canvas cover torn and flapping in the wind that continued to blow. Rain pelted him, dripping into his eyes and drenching his clothes.

He lay for a moment, trying to gather his senses. His forehead throbbed, and he gently fingered the area. Already a lump was forming. He'd have a goose egg for sure. His pants were torn at the knee, and it hurt to bend his right arm. Rain lashed him, the drops stinging his flesh. He needed shelter. But the only place to go was the house. Would Tarsie let him in?

Using flashes of lightning to guide him, he limped his way around the house to the front, his feet slipping in the mud. His first knock went unacknowledged, but the second—harder and more insistent—brought a rasping query. "Who's out there?"

"Lemme in, Tarsie." Joss hugged himself, shivering from the rain and the shock of the past minutes.

"Joss?" She sounded dumbfounded. He heard the scrabble of the cross-latch, and then the door swung wide. She held a lantern high in one hand and clutched her robe at her throat with the other, gawking at him. "What happened to you?"

He stumbled over the threshold and sank onto the closest surface—the trunk where they ate their meals. Keeping his voice at a whisper to avoid waking the children, he said, "Wind blew the wagon clean over. The cover's all torn. I'm gonna have to stay in here."

She stared at him, her lips pressed tightly together, as if struggling against a mighty argument. Then she let out a whoosh of breath. "Well, then, I guess there's no choice in the matter, is there?" She set her shoulders square, peering down her nose at him. "No one can be looking askance at us, considering we were joined by a clergyman. It's not unseemly, is it, for a man and his wife to reside together under the same roof." She spoke as though convincing herself.

Joss, listening, wished he could crawl inside his own soggy shirt and disappear. If she knew the truth, she wouldn't be so stalwart.

"I'll just climb in with the wee ones," she went on in that same no-nonsense tone. "You . . ." Under the glow of the lantern, her face bloomed bold pink. "Be changin' into dry clothes and take m-my sleeping spot. Good night, Joss." She leaned forward and deposited the lantern next to his hip, taking care that her fingers avoided contact with his wet trousers. Then she scurried to the corner, slipping beneath the quilt with Emmy and Nathaniel.

Joss started to unbutton his shirt, then he flicked a glance at the corner. Tarsie's eyes were shut, but her eyelids quivered. He drew in a deep breath, then used the air to extinguish the lantern. Fumbling through the dark, he located the trunk that held his clean clothes. He changed, flicking furtive glances toward the corner, then left his wet clothing in a pile on the floor.

Dry again, he snuggled into the pile of blankets, still warm from Tarsie's body. An uneasy chill worked its way up his spine. Come tomorrow, there were lots of things he and Tarsie would need to discuss. And she wasn't going to like any of them.

❋ 21 ❋

Sunday morning dawned rosy and calm, the fury of last night's storm chased away by cheerful fingers of light spreading across the horizon like a fine lady's jeweled fan. Tarsie tiptoed, barefooted, over soggy ground strewn with scraps of green leaves to the well and lowered the bucket into the cool depths.

She wore her robe over her nightclothes, just as she had all night. Where would she find the privacy to change into her church dress? If she asked, would Joss step outside and allow her to disrobe without audience? As her husband, he had every right to remain inside. To even observe her, if he desired. The thought of Joss's eyes on her sent tremors through her belly.

She pulled the full bucket upward on its squeaky rope as heat built in her face. "He's never once demanded his rights as husband," she murmured, trying to reassure herself. "Surely a tipped wagon won't be changin' how we've done things in the past. He'll just set it back to right again an'—"

"Tarsie?"

Tarsie let out a yelp of surprise and released the rope. The bucket plummeted downward and landed with an echoing splash. She whirled around, her mouth open, to find Joss a few feet behind her. His tan trousers and blue untucked shirt

175

were rumpled. A dark shadow filled his lower face, and his thick hair stood in untidy tufts, signifying a rough night's sleep. For one brief second, Tarsie found herself wanting to smooth his hair into place. Her hand lifted, but she caught herself in time and linked her fingers together, pressing her joined hands to her ribs, where she felt the pound of her heartbeat.

Joss strode toward her, the ties of his boots flopping against the moist grass. He tugged the bucket upward, then sloshed water into her waiting pail. Tossing the empty bucket back into the well, he studied her solemnly. "Did you take a look at the wagon?"

"N-no."

He pursed his lips, his mustache forming a grim line. "It's ruined. Cover's shredded, front axle broken, box all busted up. It's nothin' more'n scrap lumber now."

Although he didn't come right out and say so, she knew he'd be residing in the house from now on. She lifted the pail and started for the house, Joss on her heels. His hand curled around her elbow, halting her progress. She looked up at him, her mouth dry. Although they'd exchanged vows nearly two months ago, they'd never stood so close. She could see her own reflection in his pupils.

"Before you go inside and wake the young'uns, let's talk."

Tarsie swallowed. Her attire and his sleep-tumbled appearance lent too much intimacy to the moment. She didn't think she'd be able to form a coherent sentence. "C-can't it wait . . . 'til later?" After breakfast. After worship service. After she was dressed and had gathered her wits about her.

He scowled. "Puttin' it off won't change anything. Just listen. I don't think you oughta teach that colored woman to read."

Tarsie drew in a breath, an argument forming on her tongue, but before she could speak he went on.

"Folks won't look kindly on you, taking up with her. An' if you're gonna make your home in this town, you don't want to be branded a Negro sympathizer. It'll cause all kinds of trouble for you."

She huffed. "I can't be livin' my life worryin' about what pleases or displeases narrow-minded people. In the end, the only opinion that matters is the one held by my Lord, an' He's the One who gave me the idea of teachin' Ruth."

His lips curled in derision. "Lord oughta have sense enough to know something like that would put you in disgrace with your neighbors."

She wrenched her arm loose and pointed one finger at him. "Don't you be spewin' insults toward the good Lord Almighty, Joss Brubacher!"

"Just speaking the truth." Joss balled his hands and plunked them on his hips. With widespread feet and arms held akimbo, he created a formidable figure. "You think your neighbors are gonna trade milk or pork roasts with you once you've tainted yourself? You're walking a dangerous road, woman. And what's worse, you're dragging my young'uns down with you. Your actions'll affect them."

As much as Tarsie wanted to deny Joss's claims, she feared he could be right. People's prejudices were never rational. Might Emmy and Nathaniel suffer as a result of her reaching out to Ruth Foster? But how could she possibly refuse after making a promise? After seeing Ruth's face light with pleasure—after experiencing the rush of peace that only came when one followed the Lord's prompting—she couldn't retreat from her commitment.

Tarsie drew in a breath and then let it rush out, her shoulders wilting. "You know how much I love those wee ones. I'd never want to bring hurt on their little hearts."

Joss folded his arms over his chest and peered down at her. "So it's settled, then."

"Yes, Joss. It's settled."

"Good." He took one step toward the house.

"I'll be prayin' for God to wrap His arms of strength and protection around Emmy an' Nathaniel so if anyone flings an arrow of criticism, the wee ones won't be pierced by ugly words."

He whirled to face her, his gaze narrowing. "What?"

"I've got to do what God asked me to do no matter what it might cost."

Fury sparked in his eyes. "You mean to say you're gonna teach her even after I said not to?"

Tarsie lifted her chin. "That's what I mean."

Joss growled low in his throat. He clenched his fists again and leaned toward Tarsie, his pose menacing. But then he spun, presenting his stiff back. "No colored woman oughta be able to do somethin' more'n what I—" His voice stopped so abruptly, it seemed as though someone had ripped his tongue from his mouth.

Tarsie's heart skipped a beat. "More than you . . . ?"

But Joss charged toward the corner of the house, calling over his taut shoulder, "Get inside, get dressed, an' you an' the young'uns skedaddle outta there. I got work to do this morning, and I don't want any of you underfoot." He stormed from view.

Tarsie stood in the morning sunshine, staring after him, her lip caught between her teeth. She repeated his unfinished sentence in her mind, considering possible completions, and when realization hit, her knees nearly buckled. She stared at the corner of the house where he'd disappeared, remembering his tense shoulders and tightly clenched fists. Anger—and pride—had pulsed from him.

"Joss can't read." She whispered the words, her stomach churning with both sympathy and embarrassment for him. Little wonder he'd gotten so frustrated with the children for leaving all those marks on the wall. Little wonder he pressed bills into her hand and sent her to do the shopping. Little wonder he'd never picked up a storybook to read to the children.

She pictured the page in her Bible where she'd filled out the marriage certificate. Heat rose from her middle and seared her all the way to her scalp as she recalled him turning away when she'd asked if he wanted to sign his name on the page. "Just do it," he'd said, stinging her with his disinterest. But it wasn't disinterest that kept him from writing his name—it was inability.

A proud, independent man like Joss . . . unable to read. Her heart ached for him. Just as God had placed Ruth's plight on her conscience, Joss's need weighed heavily on Tarsie. But Ruth had begged for teaching. Joss would certainly refuse any offer. His fierce pride would hold him back.

Heaving a sigh, Tarsie scuffed toward the house, water pail in hand. She'd do as he said for now—ready the children for service and leave. And when the minister had them all kneel to pray, she'd ask God to reveal a way for Joss to learn to read and write so he needn't hang his head in shame. She'd have a time of it, convincing Joss to bend his pride enough to admit he needed help. But God answered prayers.

Strength, Father . . .

❋

When she and the children returned from church, Tarsie paused in the yard, puzzled by a strange banging coming from inside the house.

Emmy glanced at her, obviously worried. "Is somethin' getting broked? Like Papa's wagon got broked?"

Joss had been so angry with her that morning. Surely he wouldn't destroy their little house out of spite, would he? The peaceful feelings from hearing God's words spoken followed by a time of prayer and reflection fled. She grabbed Nathaniel's hand and urged Emmy, "Come along, now. Let's go make sure your papa's all right in there." She stepped over the threshold, the children crowded so close she nearly tripped over them, and she let out a little gasp of surprise.

Joss rose from his haunches beside the most ungainly-looking table Tarsie had ever seen. He bounced a hammer against his thigh and sent her an unsmiling look. "Borrowed a hammer and nails from Bliss next door. Figured I better get as many favors as I can before you turn all the neighbors into enemies with your harebrained scheme."

The tenderness she'd felt for him when considering his illiterate state washed away on a wave of defensiveness. "I won't be discussin' that with you in front of the wee ones." She took a step forward, examining his project. Weathered strips of wood, some of which bore pale scuffs left over from a white rock wielded by a child's hand, formed a square with posts stretching upward from each corner. Her gaze bounced to Joss, surprise replacing irritation. "You made a table from the wagon boards."

Joss plopped the hammer on the floor and turned the table right side up. He pressed both palms to the top. It wobbled some, the legs uneven, but it supported his weight. "Nothing fancy, that's for sure." His voice held disdain, but his eyes traveled over his handiwork, satisfaction glimmering in the dark depths. "But it beats that trunk. I'll build a couple benches, too, so we can sit instead of kneeling to eat."

"You did a fine job, Joss. I've been longing for a table. Thank you."

He barely flicked a glance at her. Scooping up the hammer, he headed for the open door. "I'll work on the benches outside so you can put dinner together. Make it quick. I'm half starved."

They sat on crates to eat their Sunday dinner—chunks of

leftover pork roast on thick slices of bread with rich gravy poured on top. Joss gulped his food, using a spoon to scoop up every drop of gravy. The moment he finished, he stood and aimed himself for the door again, his arms swinging and chin jutted forward as if marching to war. Tarsie, watching him, couldn't help but think he found pleasure in building. In creating something useful. She filed the thought away to reflect on later, when she needed reminding of his good traits.

The children stretched out on their makeshift bed after filling their tummies, and soon they napped, oblivious to their father banging boards together and hammering nails outside the window. Tarsie washed and dried the dishes, then returned them to their spot on the shelves, humming the morning's hymns and reflecting on the sermon. Reverend Mann had preached from Psalm 138, and snippets from the Scripture played through Tarsie's mind. She liked the reminder that God gave strength when it was requested. When the minister had read "Though I walk in the midst of trouble, thou wilt revive me," she'd shivered with delight. Joss predicted trouble would come from her reaching out to Ruth, but the Scripture assured her God would prevent it from overwhelming her.

Her cleanup tasks complete, she scurried to her Bible and opened it to the psalm, wanting to recall the entire passage. She read straight through, appreciating more than ever her ability to make sense of the words on the page. Reading in a whisper, she finished, ". . . forsake not the works of thine own hands."

Closing her eyes, she asked God once again for the strength to complete the work He'd given her in teaching Ruth. She asked comfort for the family, understanding from her neighbors, and acceptance from Joss.

With the mention of Joss, a picture formed in her mind of his hands pressed to the table's top. She sat upright, her eyes popping open.

A giggle burbled from her throat. Of course! Why hadn't she thought of it before? Lifting her gaze upward, she praised, "Thank You for givin' me the idea. It comes from You, I've no doubt."

Setting the Bible aside, she hurried out the door and around the house, to where Joss used the clawed end of the hammer to pry apart the remains of the wagon. "Joss, I'm wonderin', since you've borrowed that hammer, if you might be doin' me a favor."

❋ 22 ❋

Simon tugged the reins, and his mule obediently halted outside the dinner barn. He let the reins drop, knowing Ransom wouldn't wander, and heaved himself onto the ground. His lunch bucket waited under the seat, as always, and he reached for it, eager to see what Ruth had packed for him today. He chuckled in anticipation, recalling past lunches with little surprises like bites missing from his sandwich—"So's you know I sampled it an' found it pleasin'," she'd later teased, or sugar cookies carved into the shape of a heart—"'Cause the heart means love, an' I love you, Simon Foster." That Ruth, she knew how to make a man feel special.

He hitched his way toward the barn, lunch bucket in hand, but before he stepped inside, he heard someone call his name. Edgar Tollison trotted toward him, waving his hand. Generally Simon met with Mr. Tollison on Saturday mornings, since Saturday was payday and he needed the pay envelopes. They always talked over the week's accomplishments and what needed to be done in the coming week on Saturday after the rest of the workers had left. He couldn't remember the last time his boss had sought him out on a Monday.

Worry tried to wiggle its way through his mind, but Simon pushed the unwelcome emotion aside and limped toward his boss as quick as he could. He met Mr. Tollison halfway across the yard beneath a towering elm that spread heavy shade over them both.

Simon squared his shoulders and stood as tall as his uneven legs would allow. "Mistuh Tollison, what can I do fo' you?"

"I need a favor."

Anything Mr. Tollison needed, Simon would do it. "Sho' thing. What you needin', suh?"

Mr. Tollison slipped his thumbs into the little pockets on his vest and drew in a ragged breath. "I suppose you've heard about the vote coming up to establish prohibition in our fair state."

Simon crunched his brow. "Pro'bition?" He scratched his chin, chuckling. "Cain't rightly say I know what that is."

"It means taking away people's right to purchase alcoholic beverages. Like wine."

Simon dropped his jaw. Although the Tollison Vineyard shipped apples, pecans, and peaches all over Kansas and Missouri, Mr. Tollison made most of his money from the grapes he pressed and used to make wine. The winery operated during the winter months, when fruit didn't grow on the trees. If Mr. Tollison couldn't make wine anymore, he'd lose a goodly portion of income. "Lawsy, that sho' would mean a heap o' trouble fo' you now, wouldn't it?"

"It would mean 'a heap o' trouble' for a lot of people, Simon." Mr. Tollison's voice took on an edge. "If I'm not making wine, I won't need nearly as many workers. Do you understand what I'm saying?"

Simon nodded hard, the worry he'd pushed aside earlier returning to turn his belly into a quavering puddle. "I sho' do, suh. Yessuh, I do."

A slight frown creased Mr. Tollison's face. "Seeing as how we all stand to suffer if that vote passes, I'm asking you to talk to your people."

Simon knew Mr. Tollison meant the black workers.

"Encourage them to go to the poll and cast their vote against prohibition. It's a fine privilege you people have, to be able to cast your vote. The last thing I want to do is shut the winery down, put good men like you out of a job, but I won't have much choice if Governor St. John has his way in outlawing the making and distributing of alcoholic beverages."

Simon nodded slowly. "I'll be talkin' to the men 'bout castin' their votes. But, suh . . ." He pinched his lips into a grimace, hoping Tollison wouldn't take offense by what he planned to say next. "I gotta be right honest with you 'bout somethin'. Our preacher, the Reverend Wolfley, he talks pretty plain from the pulpit 'bout the evils o' strong drink, an' there be some men who are dead set against any kind o' liquor."

Mr. Tollison's brows lowered. "Is that so?"

Simon waved his hand as if shooing flies. "Oh, now, don't be worryin'. They works hard for you here. 'Preciate the job an' all. But inside, they got convictions 'bout drinkin'. Now me, I got no thirst for somethin' that'll gimme a fuzzy head, but I don't reckon I should be tellin' somebody else not to be indulgin' if they's a mind to. All that's to say, suh . . ." He pulled in a big breath, gathering courage to complete his thoughts. "I can sure tell the men to go vote, an' I can even tell 'em things could change a heap around here if you cain't make wine no mo', but I cain't make no promises all them men'll vote to keep sellin' liquor. Like I say, some gots strong convictions."

"Strong convictions won't provide food and shelter for their families. You can tell the men so." The boss clapped Simon's shoulder. "Your family and mine go way back. It would be a shame if some law made by a hoity-toity teetotaler forced me to close the vineyard and send you away. I'm counting on you, Simon." He turned and strode to the big house.

Misery gnawed at Simon's insides. His boss had surely put

him in a hard spot. What would Pappy do, if he were here? His appetite gone, Simon hitched his way to the grove of trees on the far corner of the property where half a dozen crosses marked the final resting spots of former workers.

With effort, Simon lowered himself to one knee and put his hand on the cross etched with the name Ezekiel Foster. "Pappy, you taught me to honor Mistuh Tollison, sayin' the Lawd done expects a man to do his work just like he was doin' for the Lawd Hisself. But Mistuh Tollison, he be askin' me to do somethin' that goes against my spirit. If I refuse, an' if that law the boss tells me about gets passed, I'll be out o' a job faster'n butter melts on Ruth's hot molasses cake. Who else'd hire me with this shriveled foot?" Simon dropped his head low. "Sho' wish you was here right now, Pappy, to give me some words o' wisdom."

Simon listened, but Pappy didn't call advice from the clouds. Simon listened harder, hoping, but all he heard was the voices of the men carrying from the dinner barn and wind whispering in the trees. He sighed. "Reckon I gotta figger this one out on my own. But I'll be prayin' on it, Pappy, just like you taught me."

When Simon returned home that evening, he left Ransom drowsing behind the little house, still in his traces. Might be he'd need to ride on back to the big house and talk to his boss before bedtime. Before he made it halfway across the yard, the children raced out to meet him, all clamoring for hugs and to be the first to share the details of their day.

Despite the concerns that tied his stomach in knots, a grin teased its way to Simon's lips. How could anybody stay sad when surrounded by his children's happy faces and cheerful voices? He walked in the midst of them, little Naomi swinging his hand and the boys walking backward, jabbering away like a pair of magpies. Simon caught only bits and pieces of what they said, what with their words tripping all over each other, but he understood they'd gone into town and visited with Joss Brubacher's wife. Simon did his best not to frown, but Ruth's intention to learn reading from the white woman was another concern.

"You all go take Ransom a bucket o' water an' some fresh-picked dandelions. I gotta talk to your mama."

Giggles ringing, the three scampered off.

Ruth stepped into the yard and greeted him with a hug and moist kiss. She took the dinner pail from his hand. Scowling, she tugged the cloth aside and peeked into the pail. "Simon Foster, you di'n't eat your lunch." Irritation faded to worry. "You ailin'?"

"I ain't sick, but we gots trouble, Ruth." He shared everything Mr. Tollison had told him, including the possibility of losing his job if the prohibition bill passed. "Need to do some hard prayin' over the next coupla days so's I know for sure what to do. Don't wanna let down Mistuh Tollison aftuh he done been so good to my family an' all, but don't wanna be doin' somethin' that'd be dishonorin' God, neither."

Ruth planted another kiss on his cheek, then wove her arm through his. They moseyed toward the house, their strides matching up perfectly. "Prayin' is 'xactly what we need to be doin'. An' I'll set Tarsie to prayin' on it, too. Seein' as how her man works at the vineyard, whatever happens out there'll be affectin' her, too. An' she gots a real strong faith, Simon."

"You done went to see her again this mornin'?" Simon tried not to show his disapproval, but Ruth shot him a look that said she saw right through him.

"I sho' did. An' she sent me on home aftuh we have a little talk."

Simon sat on the edge of the bed and kicked off his shoes. As much as he wanted his children to learn reading and writing, he still couldn't decide if Tarsie's offer was a blessing or a curse. Either way, to think she might have gone back on her word rankled. "Why she send you home? She decide she don't wanna teach you aftuh all?"

"No such thing!" Ruth clanked pots around on the stove. "She gon' teach me, just like she say. But she wants to do it in the evenin' 'stead o' durin' the day."

"How's come?"

"'Cause we got chores keepin' us busy durin' the day." Ruth aimed a mock scowl at him while dishing up steaming greens with fatback. "You think we womenfolk just set aroun' all day, puttin' our feet up an' bein' lazy?"

Simon chuckled. "No, ma'am. Wouldn't nevuh think that o' you."

She rewarded him with a twinkling smile. "Evenin's bettuh. 'Specially with these long summer days stretchin' out. Our chillun can all run in the yard togethuh, wearin' themselves out for sleep, an' you an' Joss, if'n your work is done fo' the day, can be buildin' a wall, an'—"

Simon held up his hand. "Wait, woman. Wha' did you say 'bout me an' Joss?"

"I said you'uns can be buildin' a wall." Ruth blinked, her face all innocent. "Joss, he needs some extra hands to be puttin' up walls for a sleepin' room. I figure, me an' the chillun gotta go, you might as well come, too. While Tarsie's givin' me my lessons, you menfolk can be workin'. An' while you's workin', you can be turnin' an ear to the teachin' an' mebbe pickin' up a thing or two, too." She rushed at him and plopped onto his lap, pinching his earlobes gently between her fingers. "Wouldn't you like to learn to read, too, Simon? Just think how proud E.Z., Malachi, an' Naomi'd be, to have a pappy who can read to 'em from storybooks an' newspapers an' the like."

Simon gently disengaged her hands. He wasn't going to be wheedled into agreeing to her scheme. No, sir. But being able to read—the Bible, newspapers, voting ballots—all the things a man needed to understand to make good decisions. That would be fine. Mighty fine.

He growled. "Woman, you's a sure enough troublemaker. What makes you think Joss Brubacher's gon' take my help buildin' a wall?"

Those dark lashes of hers swept up and down, her wide eyes turning all liquid and soft. "Why, 'cause Tarsie an' me done prayed togethuh about it an' we both felt the Lawd givin' His 'uh-huh' on the idea." With a chortle, she pranced to the table and plopped the plates in a circle. "Go call the chillun in to eat."

Stifling a groan, Simon shuffled to the door, but before he could step into the yard, Ruth called his name. He turned back. All the teasing was gone. A solemn yet confident expression gave evidence of her deep faith.

"It's gon' be fine, Simon. You just wait an' see. Ain't nothin' gon' go wrong."

❋ 23 ❋

"J ust hold it steady." Joss talked around two nails caught in the corner of his mouth. He pinched a third nail between his thumb and forefinger and took aim with the hammer. After a dozen sharp whacks, the nail sunk to its square top in the old wood. He gave a brusque nod. "I can do the rest now. Step back."

Simon shuffled backward two steps, cooperative and uncomplaining, then watched Joss pound nails in the middle and far end of the board to hold it in place. The man's unwavering gaze—the same intent look that observed Joss's movements at the vineyard—set Joss's nerves on edge, but he had to admit that having an extra pair of hands had proven helpful. Though he'd balked when Tarsie'd said Simon would be coming over to help portion off half of the little house for sleeping areas, he wouldn't have made nearly as much progress the past four evenings without Simon's assistance.

Of course, he hadn't missed the disapproving stares of his neighbors when Simon's family came trooping into the yard. And Emmy'd mentioned the neighbor kids had stopped coming by during the day to see if she and Nathaniel wanted to play. Irked him, the neighbors' attitudes. Spending time with a colored man didn't change who he was, deep down.

In the midst of the blunt thuds of boards clunking together and the sharp ring of the hammer on nails, Tarsie's and Ruth's voices reached Joss's ears. Bits and snatches of the reading lessons. Envy burned through his gut as Ruth dutifully named the letters, tracing their shapes on his tabletop with her finger and repeating the sounds they made.

"Y says *yuh, yuh, yuh.* Z says *zuh, zuh, zuh.*"

Joss chanted the sounds in his head but then chased away the chants by whacking another nail into place. He glanced in Simon's direction. "Need another board." Simon limped out of the house, and Joss stepped back to examine the shoulder-high wall constructed of wagon boards set horizontally. Behind him, Tarsie's lesson took a turn.

"All right, Ruth, you've done well learning all the sounds. Now it's time to put sounds together. That's how words are formed. You ready?"

"Oh, I's ready, Tarsie. Uh-huh, I be ready!"

Tarsie's laugh—a light, joyful, eager trickle of sound—sent pleasure tiptoeing up Joss's spine. He kept his face aimed at the wall but listened intently to a soft *whish-whish* that indicated the pages of a book were being turned. Then Tarsie's voice again. "Look here at this word. Only three letters. Sound it out."

"Lemme see. There's G. An' O. An' D." Concentration deepened Ruth's husky tone. "An' them letters, they say . . . *Guh. Awww. Duh. Guh-aww-duh. Guh-aww* . . ."

Joss held his breath, awareness dawning just before Ruth proclaimed, "God! That say *God!*" Clapping erupted while laughter rang.

Simon dragged a board into the house and handed it to Joss. "What's all the hoorawin' for?"

Joss hefted the board into place. "Ask your wife." He placed a nail and began banging, but Ruth's ecstatic voice carried over his ruckus.

"Simon, lookit this! See this word? It say *God*! Simon, I can read my Maker's name!"

Something pulled at Joss. Not a physical hand—not anything he could define—but an invisible cord wrapped itself around him and pulled him in the direction of the table. His muscles tensed, fighting the urge, but it won. His gaze found the open Bible, and he followed the line of Ruth's finger pointing to a single word: God. A tingle crept across Joss's scalp. G-O-D . . . God. He could *see* it.

"Get the chillun in here," Ruth commanded, flapping at Simon's chest with both palms. Her smile beamed bright, tears rolling down her face. "I want E.Z., Malachi, an' Naomi to read it, too."

With an indulgent chuckle, Simon hop-skipped to the door and hollered for the youngsters to come see what their mama'd learned. All of the children came running—the Foster young'uns and Emmy and Nathaniel, too—and the little room got so crowded Joss didn't have space to swing the hammer. But it didn't matter. He wouldn't have been able to lift it anyway. He felt as though every bit of strength had drained from his body. Yet something new and powerful pulsed through his middle.

God. He could read it! *God.*

❈

Tarsie tucked the light quilt beneath Emmy's chin and whisked a kiss onto the little girl's forehead. On the other side of the sleeping mat, Nathaniel already slept, his lips slightly puckered. The little boy'd tuckered himself out chasing with E.Z. and Malachi.

"G'night now. Pleasant dreams," Tarsie whispered.

"G'night." Emmy's thick lashes swept up and down in slow motion as she battled tiredness. "You comin' to bed soon?" Over the past few days, the children had grown accustomed to Tarsie sharing their mat.

Tarsie smoothed her hand over the child's hair. "Soon."
She pushed to her feet and crept through the gap in the newly
constructed wall. Although it was simply built—a few beams
upright from the floor to the ceiling and then some side-
to-side boards marching from the floor to just higher than
Tarsie's head—the wall created a fine privacy barrier between
the sleeping room and the main part of the house.

Joss had used up all of the lumber from the wagon, so
he intended to hang a blanket to separate the sleeping area
into two spaces until he could afford to buy enough wood
to build another wall. Considering the coarse materials he'd
been forced to use, he'd done a fine job. When she reentered
the main room of the house, where he sat at the table with a
cup of coffee between his palms, she told him so.

He jolted. Coffee sloshed over the rim of the cup and
dribbled onto the tabletop. Two dark splotches landed very
near Tarsie's Bible, which still lay on the table. He swept the
droplets away with his hand, then wiped his hand on his
pants. His eyes on the black leather-bound book, he mumbled,
"Reckon it'll do." With jerky motions, he raised the cup and
took a noisy slurp.

Tarsie poured her own cup and seated herself across the
table. In less than a week, they'd each adopted a spot. Tarsie and Emmy shared one bench, Joss and Nathaniel the
other, with the children and adults sitting diagonally from
one another. It worked well to keep their feet from tromping
on each other's, but it put distance between Tarsie and Joss.
Sometimes Tarsie appreciated the space.

Tonight, however, she wished she had the courage to slip
over next to him. Put her hand over his and tell him she'd seen
his expression when Ruth cried out in exulted understanding. Longing had filled his eyes. Not even his stiff stance as
he stood with his back pressed to the wall could hide it. But
pride would keep him from admitting it.

She took a sip of her coffee, then set the cup down and pretended interest in prying loose a sliver on the table's edge. "When I walked Ruth and Simon to their cart, Simon told me there's some saplings growing along the creek behind his pappy's place."

Joss peered at her over the rim of his cup, his brows low. "What do I need with saplings?"

"You could cut them down and use 'em to be buildin' bed frames." She flicked a glance in his direction. "If you've a mind to be buildin' bed frames."

Joss took another swig, then plunked the cup onto the table. "And why would I want to build bed frames?"

Tarsie offered a slow shrug. "It seems as though building things pleasures you. You built this fine table an' benches, and now a wall. I thought, since you'd gotten a taste of . . . buildin' things, it might've made you hungry for . . . more." She held her breath, her thoughts shifting to the taste he'd been given of reading.

He nodded. "I've seen rope beds. I could put one together. But I've got no axe to chop down saplings."

Tarsie beamed at him. "Why, that's no problem at all. Simon has an axe an' a sharpenin' stone. He told me so."

"'Course he did."

She pretended not to hear his sarcastic remark and reached for his empty cup. "Tomorrow after supper, we'll walk to Simon and Ruth's place. It's a goodly walk, but a summer evening—especially now that the rains have stopped—is a fine time to be going for a long stroll. You an' Simon can be cuttin' down saplings and stripping 'em while I'm giving Ruth another lesson."

She carried both of their cups to the washstand and placed them gently into the tin basin. With a sigh, she turned to face Joss. "Now that Ruth knows all the letters an' their sounds an' how to string them together into words, there'll be no stopping her. She can be reading anything. Learning anything." She paused, hoping he might forget his pride and express a desire to read, too. No man, no matter how stubborn, could have witnessed Ruth's elation and not want it for himself.

Joss sat staring straight ahead, his jaw at a stern angle.

"Joss?"

"Reckon it'd be good to get the young'uns off the floor." He still didn't look at her. "But Foster's place is too far for 'em to walk."

Tarsie tensed, expecting him to tell her he'd go by himself.

"After work, when I take the horse to the livery, I'll see about borrowing a buckboard from Keller so we can ride over. We'll need some way of totin' the cut saplings back here anyway."

Clasping her hands beneath her chin, Tarsie tried to rein in her delight. "So . . . we'll all be goin' to Ruth and Simon's place tomorrow?"

"Reckon so." He rose and headed for the door, arms swinging. "I'll go outside so you can get changed for bed. Blow out the lantern when you're done so I know I can come back in."

He stepped out and clicked the door shut behind him without so much as a glance in her direction. But Tarsie skipped to the partitioned-off sleeping area, her happiness spilling all the way to her toes. He was softening! Oh, he didn't show it in his tone or in the way he stomped around as if ants were under his feet, but he cared about his children or he wouldn't be fetching a wagon to save them from having to walk so far. He cared about her desire to teach Ruth or he wouldn't take her along. He cared—he truly did.

Tarsie quickly donned her nightgown, then slipped to her knees. Folding her hands, she squeezed her eyes shut and poured out her gratitude to God for the changes she'd witnessed in Joss. She finished, "Keep moldin' him, Lord, just as You've been doing. Keep drawing him closer and closer to You, just the way Mary wanted him to be. And help me honor my promise to Mary, Lord—be giving me the strength to be loving. Even when he's irksome. Amen."

She hurried back to the main room and blew out the lantern. On tiptoe, she skittered to the sleeping area and slipped in next to Emmy before Joss entered the house and caught her sneaking around in her nightgown. As she laid her head on the pillow, a worrisome thought captured her. When Joss made the children a rope bed, it likely would be large enough for both of the children . . . but not for her, too. Her mouth went dry. Maybe building beds wasn't a good idea, after all.

※

Tarsie worried about the youngsters bouncing off the back of the wagon, since no high sides offered protection, but they arrived at Simon and Ruth's little house safely. The Foster children were waiting in the yard and ran to the wagon, their faces alight. E.Z. cupped his hands beside his mouth and bellowed, "Ma! Comp'ny's here!"

At once, several faces poked from neighboring doorways. Tarsie noted narrowed eyes and firmly set lips. A chill crept across her scalp. Joss had warned her the white neighbors might think less of her for spending time with a black woman. For the first time, she wondered if Ruth might pay a price for befriending Tarsie. Her stomach churned.

Ruth charged across the yard, hands outstretched. "Climb on down, girl! Didja bring your Bible?"

Tarsie groaned. "I forgot. Joss was in such a hurry . . ." Hearing the complaint in her voice, she clapped her hand over her mouth.

Ruth chuckled. "Oh, lawsy, it's no trouble. I gots that one belonged to Simon's pappy. We can use it instead."

Tarsie climbed down while the children dashed around the corner in a happy cluster and Simon loaded an axe and an odd-looking two-handled saw in the back of the wagon.

"Be back afore sundown," Simon said, leaning in to deliver a kiss on Ruth's cheek.

Tarsie averted her gaze, embarrassed by their affection. No matter how much Joss changed, she couldn't imagine him ever kissing her cheek right out in broad daylight.

Ruth waved to the men. "Be careful, now!" The moment the wagon rolled off, she looped her hand through Tarsie's elbow and aimed her for the house. "I baked some molasses cookies, an' I got a pot of tea brewin' so's we can have a li'l treat while we study."

Tarsie glanced quickly at the nearby houses. People remained in doorways, staring at her. She lowered her voice to a whisper. "Are you sure it's all right for me to be here, Ruth? I don't want to be causin' trouble for you."

Ruth drew back, her brows crunching together. "Trouble?" Then she looked, too. She let out a little snort. Stepping away from Tarsie, she waved at the nearest neighbor. "Howdy there, Myrtle Mae. You gon' come ovuh an' meet my friend? Gettin' a look-see in the sunlight'll give you a better idea on how pearly white her skin be."

Tarsie gasped. The woman Ruth addressed as Myrtle Mae backed quickly into her house and slammed the door. The others followed suit, sending off a series of bangs that reminded Tarsie of Fourth of July firecrackers. Chortling, Ruth sashayed to Tarsie and took her arm again. She ushered Tarsie into the little house and pulled out a chair.

"Set yo'self down."

Tarsie did so.

Ruth headed to a roughhewn stand in the corner and lifted a plate of brown, crumbly-looking cookies. "An' take that worrisome look right off yo' face. You don't need to be frettin' one bit ovuh those nosy folks." She slapped the plate on the table, then stood with her hands on her hips. "They's just jealous is all. Word's got aroun' that you's teachin' me.

Whole lotta people'd like to be takin' the lessons, too, but I tell 'em they gotta wait. Soon as I got it all down real good, I'll be openin' up a school an' share what I learnt."

She tossed her head, making her wiry hair bounce on her broad forehead. "They's a few callin' me uppity, but we's used to that. They already fling that word at my Simon, an' at his pappy befo' him, 'cause Mistuh Tollison make them bosses at his vineyard." She yanked out a chair and plopped down. "But I nevuh pay no mind to foolish talk, an' you shouldn't neithuh. The good Lawd, He say, 'Tarsie, you teach Ruth to read,' an' you say, 'Lawd, Yo' child hears an' obeys.' He's gon' bless us for obeyin', an' that's that. Now let's you an' me have some o' them cookies, 'cause once the chillun give up their game an' come scroungin' for food, there won't be nothin' left but crumbs."

Tarsie laughed, charmed by Ruth's no-nonsense approach to life. She reached for a cookie, and she and Ruth munched, jabbering about the kinds of things women discussed—the funny comments their children made, recipes, and the new fabric on display in the window at the mercantile. Then Ruth's face turned serious. "Tarsie, what's Joss gon' do if that vote on pro'bition shuts down the vineyard?"

Tarsie scowled. "What vote?"

Ruth scowled, too, her lower lip poking out. "You mean to say Joss ain't said nothin' to you? It's got to be weighin' heavy on him, same as it is on Simon."

"He hasn't said a word." Tarsie knew what prohibition meant—alcohol would be illegal. The thought delighted her, given Joss's past penchant for indulging. Mary'd convinced Joss to come to Kansas to take him away from the saloons, and now it seemed as though he'd be permanently removed from the opportunity to drink. A shiver of delight quivered through her belly. She hugged herself. "Oh, I wish I could vote! I'd vote for prohibition."

Ruth swept cookie crumbs onto the dirt floor, releasing a disgruntled huff. "Women ain't nevuh gon' have votin' rights. Men, they don't think women's got enough sense for politics. But what they haven't figgered is women is the ones tellin' the men how things oughta be done." She tipped her head, her brow furrowing. "You'd vote fo' pro'bition? 'Cause shuttin' down that vineyard, it'd put a whole lotta people outta jobs. Includin' Joss." A sigh heaved from Ruth's lips. "Me an' Simon, we been prayin' on it, seekin' the Lawd's leadin' 'cause we sho' want to do what's honorin' to Him, but to Simon it's a fearful thing to mebbe lose the job an' home you've had for your whole life. He thinks nobody else'll want him, him havin' that bum foot an' all."

Tarsie nibbled her lip as she considered Ruth's concerns. "Maybe it's being selfish for me to want no more alcohol. I didn't stop to think about how it would affect other people. I was just thinking of myself and my family." She aimed her gaze at her lap, uncertain of Ruth's reaction when she shared a secret. "Joss, in times past, has had too much of a taste for liquor. It was hurtful for his wife."

Ruth grabbed Tarsie's hand. "Joss hurt you?" Her tone held both fury and disbelief.

Tarsie shook her head. "No, not me. His wife—Mary." She told Ruth how they'd all left New York together at Mary's request, about Mary's death, and about her and Joss's agreement to wed to honor Mary's last wish. "Mary'd dance a jig in heaven knowing Joss would never have another drink. It's what she wanted for him."

"My, my, my . . ." Ruth shook her head slowly, her dark eyes wide. "Well, 'course that 'splains why them chillun calls you Tarsie 'stead o' Mama. I just figger, hmm, well, they's white folks an' white folks sometimes be diff'rent." She chuckled softly to herself before scowling once more. "But that about Joss . . . That sho' opens up my eyes. Simon say Joss, he a' good workuh but crusty—short o' temper. A man who's filled hisself with liquor an' then don't have it no mo' is bound to be a little wrought up." Hunching her shoulders, she angled her face closer to Tarsie's. "Can I be tellin' this to Simon? Might be knowin' that about Joss'd help him decide what he's meant to do 'bout this vote comin' up."

Tarsie hesitated. Joss'd been softening, but he might turn hard as steel if he knew she'd shared something so intimate with Ruth. She opened her mouth to ask her friend to keep Joss's past between the two of them, but other words popped out. "Tell Simon." A wave of peace followed her simple proclamation, and then a voice whispered through her heart: *Prepare for change.*

Tarsie looked around the room, startled. Had someone crept in, unnoticed, and spoken those words to her? No one lurked in the room. She pressed her palms to her chest where her heart thudded a wild double-beat. *Prepare for change.* What did it mean?

❋ 24 ❋

Joss tossed the last ten-foot-long sapling, which he'd stripped of its branches and roots with Simon's axe, into the buckboard. It clattered on top of the others, rolled, and settled. Brushing his hands together, he examined the pile. Ought to be enough there to make the frames for three beds plus a couple of chair frames. Furnishing the house—even if they were only handmade, simple furnishings—made sense. The more he did to make the place comfortable for Tarsie and the youngsters, the less likely she'd be to pull up stakes and chase after him when he left. An odd weight settled in his belly at the thought.

Simon limped up beside Joss, the two-man crosscut saw bouncing on his shoulder. "That gon' be enough, you think?"

"Yep." Joss added gruffly, "'Preciate the use of your tools. Don't have any of my own."

Simon's lips twitched into a sad grin. "I wouldn't neither 'cept my pappy had 'em, an' I got his things when he passed on to glory a month back." He laid the saw in the buckboard's bed, then traced his fingers along the tarnished blade. "Him an' me, we sho' sliced up lots o' trees fo' firewood in our time. Now I reckon I'll be teachin' my E.Z. to man the other end o' that saw. He be named for his grandpappy, so it's only fittin' he be the one to use the ol' saw."

Joss frowned. "Your pa's name was Ezekiel? Did the workers at Tollison's call him Ol' Zeke?"

Simon nodded. "Yup. Ever'body at Tollison's knew Pappy. Liked him, too." His eyes turned liquidy, and he sniffed. "I sho' do miss 'im."

Joss crunched his brow so tight his forehead hurt. Not once in the month he'd worked with Simon had the man said a single word about mourning his father. Of course, Joss hadn't mentioned mourning Mary, either, but he hadn't smiled and laughed and gone on like he didn't have a care in the world the way Simon had. Joss blurted, "You don't act like it."

Simon blinked at Joss, his dark face reflecting surprise. "What you mean?"

Joss snorted, irritated with himself for spilling his thought. "We pass Ol' Zeke's grave every day, walking from the vines to the dinner barn. Never've seen you stop there, or even look over at it." If he were in White Cloud, he'd be at Mary's grave. A lot. He wouldn't be able to stop himself. "So if you miss him so much, who don't you . . . visit him?"

Simon stared into Joss's face. His dark eyes, all moist with unshed tears, seemed to glow with a compassion Joss didn't understand. "I don't visit 'cause he ain't there."

"Ain't there?" Joss barked out a harsh laugh. "Why'd you put that cross up if he's not there?"

Slowly, Simon shook his head, meeting Joss's gaze the whole time. Simon had a way of looking at a man that made it seem like he could see under the skin. "His body's there, fo' sure. We done buried his shell. But his soul, it be in heaven with his Lawd an' Savior, Jesus Christ." His eyes glimmered. Partly from moisture, but partly from something else. Something within. Something Joss interpreted as joy.

Envy twined through Joss's middle, erupting in an angry outburst. "And it's fine with you that he's dead and gone? That you'll never see him again?"

"Oh, I'll be seein' him again." Simon placed his hand on Joss's shoulder, his grip warm and firm. "On the day I leaves my shell behind, I'll be goin' on up to heaven, too. I'll have eternity with Pappy. An' with my ma an' all the saints who've gone before me. When I get to missin' Pappy too much, I think on that, an' it perks me right up. You see"—he squeezed Joss's shoulder, then let his hand drop away—"what time we got down here? It's just a tiny little drop in the mighty ocean compared to eternity. In no time at all, I'll be seein' Pappy again. Until then, well, I just carries him right here." He placed his palm on the center of his chest.

Joss wanted to hold his own chest. It ached like a bad tooth. Instead, he stomped toward the wagon. "We're done here. Let's get back."

He didn't utter a single word on the drive to Simon's house. When they pulled into the yard, Simon's two boys and Emmy came running.

"Papa," Emmy called, a bright smile lighting her face, "Miss Ruth made 'lasses cookies, an' I saved you one. Come eat it."

He held tight to the reins. "Get Nathaniel an' Tarsie an' let's get."

Emmy's face fell. "You don't want your cookie?"

"Just come on!"

Tears welled, and Emmy hung her head.

Joss turned away from her dejected pose, images from his own childhood rising up to strangle him. Why'd he speak so rough? He hated hearing his pa's voice come out of his own mouth. Hated himself for using it. But he still did it over and over.

Simon climbed down from the seat and hitched the few feet needed to reach Emmy. Joss watched out of the corner of his eye as the black man rested his hand on Emmy's tangled hair. "Come inside with me, little'un. We'll fetch yo' brother an' Miz Tarsie like yo' papa wants, an' we'll ask Miz Ruth to wrap up that cookie in some paper so's you can take it with you." Simon's voice, so gentle, stung Joss.

"Papa don't want it."

"Aw, now, honey, yo' papa's just too tired from hard workin' to chew right now."

Emmy flicked a resentful look in Joss's direction. "He's not tired. He's just mean." She turned and raced into the house. E.Z. and Malachi followed her, their apprehensive gazes pinned on Joss.

Simon stared after the children for a moment, rubbing his hand up and down on his pant leg as if trying to convince his legs to work. Then he crossed to stand by the wagon and curled his leathery fingers over the edge of the seat. "Joss, I ain't yo' pa, or even yo' preachuh. Right now we's just two men, all sweaty from labor, 'stead of a foreman an' one o' his workers. . . ."

Joss bristled, narrowing his gaze.

Simon didn't flinch. He didn't even blink. "But I gots to tell you, you's gon' do a heap o' damage if you keep barkin' at your chillun 'stead o' lovin' 'em. The Good Book tells fathers not to provoke their chillun to wrath but to bring 'em up in the love an' admonition o' the Lawd Hisself." He leaned in, his eyes blazing with conviction. "If chillun don't feel love from their pappies, they go lookin' for love in places that ain't so healthy for 'em. I don't reckon you wanna send yo' sweet little Emmy into the arms o' some man who ain't worthy of her, now, would you?"

Joss set his jaw to hold back words of indignant fury. That Simon—so sure of himself. So righteous. So *right*. But how could Simon know how Mary's pa had beat her nearly every day in drunken rages, then pushed her out the door to fend for herself? She'd married Joss out of desperation. Oh, she'd come to love him. He never doubted that. Why else would she have stayed with him after that street preacher convinced her to give her heart to Jesus and all those feelings of unworthiness and shame from her upbringing melted away? Mary had been too good for Joss, and Joss knew it.

Simon leaned in, his eyes nearly sparking. "Would you?"

At the insistent question, Joss whirled on the man. "'Course I want more for Emmy. But if you're so all-fired smart, how come you haven't figured out I don't know *how* to give her more? Not like fellas go to school to learn daddyin', now, do they? A man does what he knows, an' that's all he can do." He straightened in his seat and faced forward. "Go get my woman an' young'uns. It's time we got outta here."

✳

Simon lay wide awake, staring at the shadowy ceiling beams overhead. Ruth, nestled close with her head on his shoulder, breathed slow and steady. Sleeping soundly. Her hair tickled his cheek, but he made no effort to pull away. He needed her closeness tonight. It comforted him after his argument with Joss.

Maybe he shouldn't call it an argument. Mostly he'd talked and Joss hadn't listened. But at least he thought he now understood why Joss had such closed ears, such a sour face, and so much anger burning in him. *"A man does what he knows, an' that's all he can do."* Being raised with anger, of course Joss would be full of it himself. Only made sense.

Ruth shifted slightly, burrowing, and Simon moved his arm to pull her closer. As his fingers closed on her rib cage, her eyes popped open, settling on his. "Why ain't you sleepin'?" She smacked her lips, the scent of spices from the rich molasses cookies wafting on her breath. "Been a long day between workin' at Tollison's an' then cuttin' them saplings with Joss. You gotta be plumb wore out."

"I am. But I cain't shut down my thinkin'."

Ruth pushed herself up on one elbow and used her other hand to rub circles on Simon's chest. "Thinkin' 'bout what?"

"What you tol' me 'bout Joss bein' a drinkin' man. An' what Joss tol' me 'bout just doin' what he knows when it comes to bein' a papa to his chillun. It's all tied together somehow, an' he's a man in need o' fixin', but I cain't wrap my mind around how to fix 'im."

Ruth's low chuckle rumbled. She gave him a little pinch, then went back to making lazy circles with her palm. The touch felt good. Comforting. "Simon Foster, if there's one thing you learned from yo' pappy more'n anything else, it's that God's the only fixer. We's just helpless people. We got no power to change nobody. Leastways, not on our own."

"But Joss, he ain't gon' look to God for fixin'. You oughta see him get all prickled up when we talk o' God or Jesus. Ooo-wee, his hair just almost stand out like the tail on an angry cat. Nope, he ain't gon' look where he needs to, an' those chillun o' his, they's gon' be the ones to carry all that anger onward 'cause they ain't gon' know no bettuh."

Ruth settled back into the curve of his neck, draping her arm across his torso. "They's learnin' bettuh from Tarsie. She's lovin' to 'em, an' she knows the Lawd."

"Gon' take more'n Tarsie. They needs a man to lead 'em." Simon toyed with a loose thread on Ruth's nightgown, his thoughts tumbling onward. "An' Joss needs a man to lead him . . ."

A soft snore told him Ruth had drifted off again. He kissed her forehead, then rested his cheek against her hair, falling silent. On the other side of the house, his children slept, peaceful and content. Beneath his arm, Ruth slumbered. Outside, wind teased a lullaby from the trees, and a lonely coyote sang a mournful song. And still Simon couldn't sleep.

He sighed, aiming his gaze at the square windowpane that offered a view of the dark night sky sprinkled with stars.

Behind those stars was the One who never slept, whose ears were always open to His children, and who held the answer to any question Simon might ask.

"Lawd," he whispered, "don't make no sense for me to stew ovuh a man like Joss Brubacher who don't care nothin' 'bout me. An' 'cause it don't make no sense, onliest thing I can figger is You planted that carin' in me. Ruth's right—I cain't be fixin' that man. But I learned good from my pappy how to be patient an' lovin' with my chillun. I learned good to teach 'em to love an' serve You. An' it just seems to me, since Joss didn't nevuh learn it when he was a young'un from his own pa, he needs to learn it now, from somebody else. Somebody who knows."

Simon jolted, and Ruth released a little moan of complaint. She rolled over, pushing her backside against his hip. He gave it a few pats, hardly aware of the action, his focus inward. He licked his lips, swallowed, then braved a query. "Lawd, do You be layin' on me the task o' showin' Joss how to be a lovin' daddy to his chillun? An' if You is givin' me that task, how'm I gon' do it if Mistuh Tollison's vineyard gets shut down an' we all lose our jobs?" He lay, tense and waiting, for some response. But nothing came.

Simon sighed, shifting to curl his body around the form of his slumbering wife. "Awright, Lawd, 'nough pesterin' for one night. You can be tellin' me in the mornin'."

❋ 25 ❋

Tarsie set a plate of fried eggs, fried mush dripping with butter, and toasted bread in front of Joss for breakfast Saturday morning. She smiled when his eyes widened in surprise. "Sneaked them past you, didn't I?" She patted her apron's flat pocket. "Carried eggs home from Ruth and Simon's last night. So we have a treat for breakfast today."

Joss didn't reply, but he picked up his fork and dug in, licking his lips. The gesture of eager anticipation stirred a flutter of pleasure in Tarsie's middle. She poured coffee for him and then puttered around the small space while he ate, waiting for him to finish so she could ask the question that had kept her restless much of the night. Why hadn't Joss mentioned the upcoming vote concerning prohibition in Kansas? She didn't know a great deal about marriage, but it seemed as though a man should share his worries with his wife.

A man and wife should share lots of things—none of which had entered her relationship with Joss. Would they forever be man and wife in name only? Would she never know the true meaning of being joined with a man? Heat rushed into her face. Such a brazen thought . . . But after witnessing Ruth and Simon's ease with each other—gentle teasing, simple touches, tender glances—she realized anew how much she wanted, maybe even needed, such a relationship with the man to whom she'd pledged herself.

She couldn't honestly say she loved Joss. Not yet. But all of her prayers asking God to help her honor her promise to Mary had resulted in a softening toward him. An acceptance. Maybe even an affection. And that was a start.

"Got any more eggs? Those were real good." Joss's hopeful query startled Tarsie from her reverie. She turned toward the table. He must've used his bread to mop the plate clean. It didn't even look used.

She lifted the remaining eggs from a little bowl on the back of the stove. "I've got these. Did you want me to fry them for you?"

He gazed at the pair of creamy eggs cradled in Tarsie's palm. "That's it? Just two more?"

Tarsie nodded.

Joss sighed. "Then . . . nah. Feed 'em to the young'uns."

Tarsie's heart gave a little flip at his unselfishness. "I've got plenty more mush. I can fry up some more slices for you, if you'd like."

"That'll do."

Tarsie reached for his plate, and he handed it over. Her fingertips brushed his, and fire ignited in her face. She whirled away from him before he could witness roses bloom in her cheeks, thankful the stove sat in the corner so she could keep her back to him while she browned the slices of cold mush in lard. By the time the slices were crisp, brown, and hot, she felt as though she'd gathered her senses about her, so she slid onto the bench opposite him while he ate. "Ruth told me there's a vote coming up soon. If it passes, Kansas won't allow liquor to be made or sold in the state."

"I heard about it." Joss chopped free a hearty bite with his fork and carried it to his mouth, his head low.

"I'm surprised you haven't said anything. It's got to be

worrying you, knowing you could be losing your job if the vote passes."

"Fellas at work say if it passes, change won't come 'til January of next year. So . . ." He shoved the final bite into his mouth, then pushed the plate toward her.

Tarsie fiddled with the edge of the plate, watching him up-end his coffee cup and drain it dry. "But this is August already. Won't be long to January of 1881. Knowin' it's comin' so quick, that doesn't . . . bother you?"

He lowered the cup, sending her a puzzled frown. "Why should it?"

They'd enjoyed a pleasant morning. She didn't want to spoil it, but she had to know. "Only a few more months and maybe no more job. And for sure, no more liquor. *Never* a chance to . . . drink." She almost whispered the final word, so much meaning being placed within the confines of five letters.

For long seconds Joss gazed at her, his unsmiling expression giving away nothing of his thoughts. Then he shrugged. "Don't matter."

Joy exploded through Tarsie's middle. Had Drayton Valley worked its magic? Had his thirst for alcohol been washed away beneath the wide open skies? "It . . . it doesn't?"

"Nope." He pushed away from the table. "Gotta get to work." He grabbed his hat from its nail, plopped it over his thick, unruly waves, then reached for the door. Before stepping through, he glanced back. "I get paid today. I'll see about buyin' some chicks. Put up a little pen out back. Be good to have eggs every day."

Tarsie darted to the door, linking her fingers together to keep from adjusting his hat at a rakish angle over those thick, dark waves. "That'd be fine."

"All right, then. Bye."

"Let me get your lunch!"

He hovered in the doorway while she dashed to the stove

and snatched up the little pail that held his sandwi
the molasses cookie Emmy had brought back from
She pressed the handle into his waiting hand, experiencing
an urge to rise up on tiptoe and deliver a kiss on his cheek the
way the neighbors' wives did when sending their husbands
out for the day. But of course, she didn't do it.

"Have a good day, Joss."

He bobbed his head in a quick farewell, then headed down
the hill toward town. Tarsie stood in the doorway and watched
him stride away, his shoulders square and arms swinging, as
if ready to take on the world. Words of thankfulness winged
their way from her heart to the heavens. "He's changin', Mary.
Your prayers an' mine, they're bein' answered."

Joss swung onto the horse's back, acknowledging the animal's snort of protest with a pat on its neck. "I know you're
tired of totin' me back and forth every day, but don't worry.
Won't be long and I'll be hightailin' it outta here. You won't
have to tote me again." The statement, once intended to offer
encouragement, weighed heavy on Joss's mind as he aimed
the horse for the road leading to the Tollison Vineyard.

The elation he'd seen on Tarsie's face that morning haunted
him. He knew what she'd been thinking—she couldn't hide
anything with those big green eyes of hers. She thought it
didn't bother him that he'd have no access to liquor if prohibition came to Kansas. She couldn't know it didn't matter
because he wouldn't be here.

He sucked in a big breath of humid morning air. Early yet,
but already hot with mosquitoes buzzing thick in the brush
that lined the roadway. The pests dove at his head and whirred
in his ears, as annoying as the guilt that plagued him. Tarsie
turned more wifely every day, fixing up that little house, caring for his youngsters, preparing his meals and keeping his

clothes clean and mended. And he'd come to like having her see to his needs. Liked knowing she'd be there at the end of a day, a smile ready no matter his mood. He even liked when she got saucy with him. He would never have thought it possible to find her penchant for standing up to him amusing, but it added a little spice to his life.

He slapped at a mosquito that had the audacity to bite him on the back of the hand. The sharp sting served as a reminder that Tarsie wasn't "his" woman. "I oughta tell her," he muttered. But he knew he wouldn't. Not yet. Not until he had all the furniture finished, a few chickens pecking in a pen, the summer's garden harvested, and enough money set aside to cover her rent for at least three months. He wouldn't tell her until he could assure her that she and the youngsters'd be fine without him.

A question—one so unexpected his body jerked as if he'd been struck with a tree limb—roared through his mind: Would *he* be fine without *them*? An aching emptiness followed the thought. The question pestered Joss all day while he worked.

Over the past weeks, the vines had grown into a sea of green, bearing leaves almost as big as a man's hand, leaves that shaded clusters of tiny deep-purple and pale-green grapes. He'd learned the purple grapes were turned into red wine, the green ones into a pale Chardonnay that they seasoned in oak barrels to give the wine a rich flavor. Simon said it'd be another month at least before they harvested, giving the grapes time to fully plump and sweeten, but already the scent when the sun beamed down was heady. Almost intoxicating. But oddly, up until now, it hadn't stimulated any desire for drink. For the first time in years, Joss had a clear head, and a part of him gloried in it. Today, though, with the uncomfortable question niggling in the back of his mind, he discovered a strong desire to lose himself in a bottle. To forget, just for a while.

Although he hadn't swallowed one drop of liquor since leaving New York, he knew where he could indulge. On the outskirts of town, near the river where the loading dock had once stood, fellows had pointed out a little shack where they gathered from time to time to shoot craps and tip a glass. He'd avoided the place—desire to honor Mary had kept him from venturing there—but all day he battled a fierce temptation to break the alcohol fast. Just once. Get rip-roarin' drunk. Numbing drunk. Didn't he deserve it after working so hard? Sure he did.

At the close of the day, he fell in with the others to collect his wages. He'd taken his time ambling out of the fields, putting him last in line to receive his pay. By the time Simon slipped the brown envelope into his hands, he was twitchy with eagerness to ride into town and spend a bit of his hard-earned money on something that would fill the emptiness he carried inside.

Simon closed a little tin box with a snap and shot him a smile. "An' you be the last'un. Glad you came up last—gives me a chance to talk to you without holdin' up the line."

Joss slipped the envelope into his shirt pocket without checking inside, the way most men did. He had no reason to suspect Simon of shorting him. He inched backward, his bootheels stirring dust. "Whatcha need with me?"

"You started buildin' them beds an' such yet?"

Foolish question. He'd just carted the saplings to the house last night and he'd been at work all day. When would he have had time to work? "'Course not."

Simon's smile broadened, apparently unaware of the sarcasm Joss inserted in his tone. "I can come in with Ruth an' the chillun this evenin'—Tarsie's givin' Ruth another lesson. I'll lend you a hand if you's wanting to get started on those beds. Got some sturdy rope good for stringin', an' when I tol' Ruth you's thinkin' on buildin' some chairs, she said she'd be glad to weave some seats outta reeds. She's right clever when it comes to weavin'. Those chairs'd stand up real fine for you'uns."

Joss fidgeted in place, two desires warring inside of him. Oh, how he wanted a drink. But he also wanted to get everything finished for the house so he'd be free to leave. Once he was in Chicago, he could drink as much and as often as he took a mind to without it affecting anybody.

"C'mon in with Ruth, then."

Simon tucked the tin box under his arm and limped around the little table he used for distributing pay envelopes. "We'll head out aftuh we eat. Less'n you'd like us to bring some food ovuh an' all eats togethuh. Prob'ly give us a little more workin' time, were we to share a meal."

Joss could accept Simon's help in building, but sitting down to eat with him indicated friendship. He wasn't ready to stoop to that level. Another pang of guilt struck. Joss took a giant backward step. "After you finish eatin' is fine. There'll be plenty daylight hours yet. I can stay up late if I want to, since no work tomorrow."

"But there's service." Simon scuttled after Joss, his dark face serious. "Ain't you started takin' yo' family to service on Sunday mornin', Joss?"

The same longing that gripped Joss when he'd glimpsed the word *God* claimed him again, increasing the empty ache in his middle. He folded his arms over his chest. "Don't got time. When else am I gonna get things finished at that house except Sunday? I work every other day."

Simon's smile returned. "But Sunday, it be the Lawd's day. A day o' rest an' refreshment. If we honor the Lawd by keepin' His day holy, like He tells us to in His book, then He gives us the time an' strength we need to get ever'thing else done that needs doin'. Mebbe that's why He's been promptin' me to lend you a hand. So's you can feel freed up to go to Sunday service with yo' wife an' chillun. I know they's wantin' you to go."

Joss knew they wanted him to go, too. Although Emmy and Nathaniel had stopped asking out loud, he saw their begging faces as Tarsie led them down the hill to the chapel. Tarsie'd never stopped asking, though. She asked and asked. Almost harped. A grin tugged at his lips. She sure was a stubborn one.

Simon broke into his thoughts. "'Sides that, I been thinkin' on what you tol' me 'bout you not knowin' how to daddy yo' chillun."

The word *daddy* shot like an arrow through Joss's gut. "What about it?"

His shoulders raising in a slow shrug, Simon took another shuffling step toward Joss. His words were low, quiet, and fervent. "You say there's no school for learnin' daddyin', but you's wrong, Joss. There be a school—best place evuh to learn what'n all a man needs to be a good husband, a good daddy, a good *man*. That place, Joss? It be called church."

❋ 26 ❋

Tarsie walked between Nathaniel and Emmy, holding each one by the hand. Her leather satchel, once used to carry herbs, hung over her shoulder, weighted by her Bible. The little packets of herbs sat in the bottom of a trunk, nearly forgotten. After witnessing the deaths of the mother and baby on the journey and then losing Mary, Tarsie had no desire to use the herbs. Although she didn't use them, she hadn't been able to discard them. Carefully gathered in Aunt Vangie's memory, she couldn't toss them out. But neither would she offer them as a solution to anyone's sickness. She couldn't risk another failure.

Instead, she poured herself into these children. She glanced down at the pair of blond heads, their hair shimmering gold in the sunlight. A lump filled her throat. How she loved them. As much as if she'd given birth to them herself, she was sure. Mothering them was better than nursing strangers to health. She welcomed her new calling.

She sampled the word "calling," playing over the minister's message to the congregation that morning. He'd indicated that when people didn't follow what the Lord had called them to do, they never found joy or fulfillment. Instead, they spent their lives always seeking happiness in things that could never satisfy and eventually died sad and discouraged. He'd claimed every man's first calling was to accept the love of God into his life by acknowledging Jesus as Savior—then God could open his heart to his purpose in this world.

During prayer time, she'd asked God to reveal His calling for her life to her, and behind her closed eyelids, an image of Emmy and Nathaniel had appeared. The realization lifted her heart. Yes, caring for these children—raising them to love and serve the Lord as Mary would have done—was now Tarsie's purpose.

But where did Joss fit in her calling? She'd sought the Lord's wisdom concerning Joss. She'd committed to showing Him God's love, as Mary had asked her to do, but might God intend more? "Oh, heavenly Father, be leadin' me because I'm just a bundle of confusion. . . ."

"Huh?"

Not until Emmy turned her face upward and gave the puzzled query did Tarsie realize she'd spoken aloud. She released a light laugh, swinging Emmy's hand. "Oh, never mind me, wee one. Just talking to myself, is all."

Emmy crinkled her nose. "That's silly, talking to yourself. Then do you answer, too?" The little girl launched into a make-believe discussion, tipping her head this way and that and using her free hand to stir the air. "Why, hello, Emmy Grace, how are you today? I'm just fine, Emmy Grace, thank you for askin'. What're you doin' today, Emmy Grace? I'm just walkin' home from church with Tarsie an' Nattie. What're *you* doin' today? I'm doin' the same thing, Emmy Grace! Fancy that!" She laughed, her eyes twinkling with mischief.

Tarsie pretended to scowl, *tsk*ing at Nathaniel's grin. "Listen to your sister's blather now, Nathaniel. Is she a silly one or what?"

Nathaniel grinned, hunching his shoulders.

They continued onward, the sun warm on their heads and a breeze tousling the children's hair. Sweat beaded on their noses, and Tarsie hurried them a bit as they neared the yard, ready for the shaded interior of their cozy home. "Change into your playclothes," Tarsie directed as she sent the pair over the threshold. "I'll be puttin' some lunch on for us quick as a wink, an' then we can take a rest."

Emmy chased Nathaniel to the other side of the dividing wall, then she reappeared in the gap, hands on hips. "Hey! Where's Papa?"

Tarsie paused in retrieving a pot from the shelf. "Isn't he on the pallet?" He'd stumbled behind the wall as they'd left for church, claiming a monstrous headache. Tarsie hadn't believed him until he flopped onto her sleeping pallet, rolled onto his side, and promptly fell asleep.

Emmy shook her head hard, her curls bouncing. "He ain't there." She dashed to the window. "Oh, there he is—sittin' under the tree."

Tarsie crossed behind Emmy and peered out. Sure enough, there he sat, knees bent and widespread, his head drooping low.

"I'll go get 'im." The little girl turned as if heading for the door.

Tarsie caught her shoulders. "Go get changed, like I told you." She aimed Emmy for the sleeping area with a little nudge. "You an' Nattie set the table once you've changed your clothes. Then stay inside. I'll be seein' to your papa."

Emmy let out a huff of complaint, but at Tarsie's frown she scurried to obey. Tarsie headed outside. She clipped around the house at a quick pace, but when she reached the corner she paused. For reasons she couldn't understand, sweat broke out across her body. There was something about his pose—droopy, defeated—that gave her pause. A bitter taste filled Tarsie's mouth. A wife would certainly know how to approach her husband regardless of the state in which she found him, but Tarsie was only floundering and uncertain.

Tangling her hands in her skirt, she licked her lips and then braved a single-word query. "Joss?"

His head bounced up as though yanked by a string, then bobbled slightly. His mouth hung slack, and his red-rimmed eyes squinted as if he found it difficult to focus. "Huh?"

A sick feeling filled her stomach. She moved toward him, her narrowed gaze searching his face. The lack of muscular control, the red eyes, and the smell emanating from him told her everything she needed to know. Drunk. The man was drunk! She dropped to her knees before him. "Oh, Joss . . ."

"What?"

The word slurred out on a belligerent note that stirred Tarsie's anger. How dare he sit there disheveled and disgraced on the Lord's day and use that tone with her! She clenched her fists and pressed them to her thighs lest one of her hands chose to clop him upside the head. "Where'd you get a bottle?"

He slumped low and plucked at blades of grass growing between his unlaced boots, his motions clumsy. "Place by the river. Bunch o' fellas there last night."

Tarsie sucked in a sharp breath. Last night? He'd crept out while she and the children lay sleeping? It would be an easy thing to do, what with her and the youngsters on one side of the dividing wall and him sleeping on the other. It rankled that he'd taken advantage of her trust. "So you sneaked down there in the cover of dark like a fox raiding a henhouse an' got yourself pickled, did you?"

"No!" He jerked his head upright and glared at her. "Only had a couple o' shots." He held up three fingers. "That's all."

"That's all." She raised her face to the gently-waving tree branches overhead and released a snort of derision. Looking at him again, she said, "Don't be fibbing. You couldn't still be this drunk after only a couple of shots. You must've had an entire bottle."

Joss squinted at her, one eye completely shut. His lips

quivered into a lopsided grin. "Did have a whole bottle. Finished it this mornin'. Such a headache." He grasped his head with both hands as if holding it on his shoulders. "Best cure is the hair o' the dog that bit ya. That's what my pa allus said." He dropped his hands away from his head and let them flop on the grass.

One of his hands lay palm up very near Tarsie's knee. She stared at it, battling tears. Thick fingers, leathery palm dotted with calluses. The hand of a strong man who worked hard. A hand capable of building tables and walls, of swinging a child through the air into the back of a wagon, of cupping a woman's cheek in tenderness. So much potential for good in that hand. But he'd used it to lift a bottle to his lips while she and his children attended Sunday services.

Fury and disappointment rolled through Tarsie's chest. All these weeks of trying so hard to be a godly example to him—all the moments of hope—seemed pointless now. Because he chose to use his hands for ill instead of good. She blew out an aggravated breath. "You oughta be ashamed of yourself, Joss Brubacher. I know I'm ashamed of you. And Mary—she'd be the most ashamed of all."

His face crumpled. "I know. I know."

"If you know, then why'd you do it, Joss? Why'd you give in?"

He shook his head. His bleary gaze pinned itself to hers. "I was missin' Mary so"—he gulped—"bad. Didn't know what to do. Don't know what to do without her." He slumped forward and rested his head on Tarsie's shoulder. "Only good in my life, an' she up an' died. What'm I s'posed to do now?"

Tarsie wanted to feel compassion for him. So lost, so lonely. But revulsion coiled through her instead. Revulsion and a deep sorrow. She planted her hands on his chest and pushed him away, then bolted to her feet and glared down at him. "What you're supposed to do, Joss Brubacher, is take care of your children. Give up the foul drinking that broke Mary's dear heart. Live in a way that'd make Mary proud instead of wallowing in self-pity and excuses. For two cents I'd dump you headfirst into a vat an' let you drown, but I made a promise to Mary an' I intend to honor it. But right now . . . right now . . ." She growled and spun away from his detestable beaten puppy expression. "Right now I must get away from you before I dishonor both Mary an' the good Lord above by sayin' something I'll regret."

She charged to the house where Emmy and Nathaniel sat at the table, swinging their feet. They'd laid out the plates, just as she'd asked, and they beamed up at her, expecting praise. Tarsie snapped her fingers at them. "Get up from there an' come with me."

They scrambled from the benches, their eyes wide. "What about dinner?" Emmy asked.

"We'll eat later." Tarsie grabbed them each by the hand and stormed outside, dragging them with her.

"Ain'tcha gonna feed Papa?"

"Feed Papa?" Nathaniel echoed his sister's question, then started to cry.

Tarsie didn't break stride. Eyes aimed ahead, she barked out, "Your papa's belly is already filled up. Nothin' more I can give him." And then she came to a halt, realization slamming down on her as effectively as a wall of bricks.

Filled up . . . The minister's message about man's attempts to fill himself in ways that could never bring satisfaction returned. Joss's bleary, empty expression flashed in Tarsie's memory. He was trying so hard to fill his empty places with work, with building things, and with liquor. But until he answered the Lord's call on his soul, he'd always be empty. Always be seeking. Always be less than what he had the ability to be.

Nathaniel's confused sobs finally penetrated Tarsie's anger.

Dropping to her knees in the roadway, she gathered both children close. "Shh, shh, wee ones, don't cry." She swallowed her own tears. She'd failed again, letting her temper take control. She was no better than Joss, who gave in to temptation to drink. *Forgive me, Father.*

"But you ain't gonna feed us, an' we're hungry." Emmy pushed away from Tarsie's grasp, her lower lip quivering.

"I am going to feed you." But Tarsie couldn't go to the house. Not now, with Joss all liquored up and blubbering. The children shouldn't witness their father's weakness. Mary had always protected them. Tarsie must, too. "But instead of eating at home, we're gonna have dinner with Mrs. Ruth and Mr. Simon. All right?"

Nathaniel rubbed his fist under his nose and nodded. Emmy tipped her head. "They know we're comin' to eat with 'em?"

They didn't know, but they'd welcome her. Ruth and Simon wouldn't turn them away. The thought brought a measure of comfort. Instead of answering Emmy's question, Tarsie said, "It's a far walk. Do you think you can make it?"

"I can!" Emmy proclaimed. "I'm big enough."

Nathaniel squared his skinny shoulders. "I'm big."

Tarsie gave them each another quick hug. "All right, then. Let's go."

✳ 27 ✳

"He was drunk, you say?"

The dismay in Ruth's voice matched the heaviness in Tarsie's heart. Tarsie gazed out the open door to the grassless yard where the children used sticks to stir up mud pies in a battered tin bowl. Looking at little Nathaniel, hair standing on end and a beaming smile on his face, a mighty lump filled her throat. So innocent and carefree, but over time, would he become like his pa? Bitter and dependent on alcohol to meet his needs?

Turning back to Simon and Ruth, who sat on the opposite side of the cleared table, she sighed in frustration. "I thought he'd been doing better. Was changing. But seeing him liquored up that way . . ." She hung her head. "He hasn't changed. Not really." Disappointment had chased away her fury. Disappointment was harder to bear.

Simon shook his head. "He's doin' what he knows, Miz Tarsie. He be a grown man now, so I ain't makin' excuses for him. He oughta be able to see that his pa's way didn't do nobody no good an' choose a better way. But to choose a better way, he's gotta have one laid out in front o' him."

Tarsie shot Simon a defensive look. "But that's what Mary spent her life doing—being a living, breathing example of godly actions an' attitudes for her husband. An' she gave

223

me the responsibility right before she died. I . . . I know I fail sometimes." Remorse smote her as she recalled the number of times she'd allowed anger to get the best of her. "But I try."

"Oh, we knows you do, honey." Ruth patted Tarsie's shoulder. "Me an' Simon, we done seen how you give an' give without 'spectin' nothin' in return. Nobody's faultin' you."

Tarsie's defensiveness fizzled. She heaved a heavy sigh. "I'm not enough. If he can be sneaking out at night while his children lie asleep, he hasn't changed at all from the man he was in New York."

From the yard, childish voices exploded in an argument, and a wail followed. Ruth jumped up. "That's Naomi's 'I-be-upset' cry. I'll go settle the chilluns." She bustled out.

Simon clicked his tongue on his teeth, his sorrowful eyes pinned on Tarsie's face. "I's sho' sorry, Miz Tarsie, for your heart-achin', but I gotta confess . . . you comin' here today an' tellin' 'bout Joss an' his downfall done give me the answer I been seekin'."

"About what?"

"Pro'bition. An' how I's s'posed to vote." He paused, his brow furrowing. "You see, I was feelin' plenty torn. On the one hand, I got a boss who's been real good to me an' my family. Mistuh Tollison's daddy, he buy my pappy's freedom an' brings him here to Kansas, where there ain't no slaves. I's born a free man thanks to ol' Mistuh Tollison's kindness, an' my pappy always tol' me we owe the Tollisons a mighty big debt."

Tarsie listened intently, marveling at some men's inhumanity—enslaving others—and other men's kindness—setting slaves free. The Tollison family had her respect, though she'd never met a single one of them.

"I lived my whole life right here, an' Mistuh Tollison, he

give me a job managin' the vineyards. Managin' white men."
Simon's eyes widened in wonder. "You know any other white
man who'd give a colored man such a job?" He shook his
head, whistling through his teeth. "No, ma'am, it don't happen. Not even in free states befo' the war what ended slavery.
But it happened here"—he jabbed his finger at the table—
"thanks to Mistuh Tollison. But now . . ."

Tears flooded Simon's dark eyes. Tarsie's heart pinched
in response to his obvious distress. Without thinking, she
placed her hand over his. The difference in their skin color
seemed more pronounced, so close. She knew many people
would condemn her for daring to touch a black man. But she
left her hand there as a symbol of their friendship. Of their
kinship as children of the same mighty God.

Simon cleared his throat. "I been prayin' an' prayin' on
what God would have me do—vote against pro'bition an'
honor Mistuh Tollison, or vote fo' pro'bition. An' now I
knows. Even to please the man who done give me a 'portant
job, I gotta vote to get rid o' alcohol in our state. Long as
men can buy it, they'll be seekin' answers in a bottle 'stead o'
where they oughta." He chuckled. "Oh, I's not fool enough
to believe some men won't still find a way to drink. Men'll
always find a way to indulge the flesh. But if it ain't legal, it'll
be a heap harder to wallow in evil. So . . ." He sat up straight,
slipping his hand from beneath Tarsie's. "I'll be castin' my
vote in favor o' pro'bition."

Tarsie nibbled her lower lip. As much as she gloried in
Simon's convictions, worry still plagued her. "But what of
your job, Simon? If the vineyard closes, what will you do?"

Simon drew in a deep breath that raised his shoulders a
notch. "I'll trust. That's what—I'll trust. Took me a while
to wrap my mind around it—I ain't educated like some
men, so I be a mite slow in thinkin'—but while you was
talkin', just seemed like God was sayin', 'Simon Foster, I

allus met your needs in the past. Why you wastin' time wor-ryin' about the future? Do right an' I'll see to the rest.'" He smiled, flashing white teeth. "God'll provide, Miz Tarsie. Same way He'll provide for you an' Joss an' your chillun. Wait an' see."

Ruth stomped into the room and stopped in front of Si-mon's chair, hands on hips. "Them boys o' yours . . ."

Simon chuckled, rising to his feet. "If they's mine, they's been into mischief."

Ruth snorted. "Mischief an' then some. They got to flingin' mud patties at one another an' caught their li'l sister in the middle of it. She'll be needin' a dip in the creek fo' sho' to get all the mud outta her hair."

Simon ambled toward the door. "How's 'bout I take all the chillun to the creek. Let 'em do some wadin'. Hot day like this, that watuh's bound to feel mighty good."

"Take 'em." Ruth flapped her hands at Simon, then sank down at the table. "Splash the ornery out of 'em while you's there."

Simon laughed and headed out. As soon as he'd departed, Ruth folded her hands on the edge of the table, her smile bright. "Now that it's quiet 'round here, you reckon the Lawd'd mind if we done work on His day? Sho' would plea-sure me to study on a few mo' words. I already knows how to spell the name o' my Maker. Now I wanna learn my Savior's name. Can you teach me how to spell Jesus?"

Tarsie grinned, eager to move on to happier topics. "Fetch your Bible."

The women bent over the book and, for the next half hour, studied the first chapter in the book of Luke.

Slowly, painstakingly, Ruth read aloud the glorious words of the angel who visited Mary. "'. . . behold, thou shalt con-ceive in thy womb, and bring forth a son, and shalt call his name Jesus.'" Eyes closed and nostrils flaring, she drew in a breath as if savoring the name. She turned to face Tarsie. Tears glistened in her eyes. "Ah, I nevuh knowed such pleasure as this, bein' able to read fo' myself the very Word o' God. Thank you, Tarsie. Thank you fo' teachin' me."

Tarsie started to tell Ruth the pleasure was all hers, being allowed to share reading with her friend, but before she could speak, the patter of footsteps intruded.

E.Z. bounded into the house, his brown eyes wide and fear-filled. "Mama! Miss Tarsie! Pappy says come quick! Nathaniel—he done hurt hisself real bad!"

※

Joss awakened with a start. He blinked into bright sunlight, confused. Why was he under the tree? The sun hurt his eyes, and he cupped his hand to shield himself from the rays, trying to make sense of his whereabouts. Slowly, realization crept over him. Buying that bottle Saturday night, creeping into the yard after Tarsie and the youngsters left for church, drinking the entire thing. A sour taste filled his mouth, and he smacked his lips, trying to rid himself of the foul flavor. How could something that tasted so good going down leave such an unpleasant aftertaste?

He squinted skyward, noting the position of the sun. Late afternoon already. He'd near slept the day away. He'd meant to string ropes on the frames he and Simon had built the evening before so Emmy, Nathaniel, and Tarsie wouldn't have to sleep on the floor anymore. But he wouldn't get them done now. Tarsie'd surely be putting supper on the table soon.

His stomach spun. He hadn't eaten a thing, avoiding breakfast because of his headache and then sleeping right through lunch. Clutching his belly with one hand, he pushed to his feet and staggered into the house. He stood for a moment, studying the table with its plates set out in a circle. The plates meant a meal was coming. But no food simmered on the stove.

Where was Tarsie? She usually rested on Sunday afternoons, just like the young'uns, but she ought to be up already, getting their supper cooked.

Dragging his heels, he crossed to the dividing wall and paused. "Uh . . . Tarsie?" No answer. He spoke again, a little louder. "Tarsie?" Only silence greeted him. She must be sick, to sleep so sound. He peeked behind the dividing wall, then drew back, startled. Her pallet was empty, as were the children's. Where could they be?

He snorted. Of course. Where else would they be except out at the Foster place? He couldn't recall her words—the whiskey still muddled his mind—but he remembered Tarsie kneeling in front of him, harping at him, looking angry. And sad. His stomach twisted again, but this time for reasons other than hunger.

He dropped onto the bench, lowering his head to his hands. Pain throbbed in his temples, and his tongue felt dry and swollen. Why did he do this to himself? The brief escape he received from numbing his brain—was it worth all this? No. But he never could seem to remember the ill affects when he was craving a bottle. He'd be forever trapped in his desire to drink. Just like Pa had been.

With a snarl, he pushed the table aside and bolted to his feet. He'd go fetch Tarsie and the young'uns. He could wait for them to walk back, but that'd take too long. He wanted supper now. To rid himself of the flavor of his morning's binge now. Cringing at the fierce pounding in his head, he stumbled out the door and down the hill toward the livery.

※

Nathaniel screamed like a banshee, his face so red and veins so purple Tarsie feared he might burst something. For a small child, he proved amazingly strong, flailing his arms and legs with such force it took both Ruth and Simon to hold

228

him still long enough for Tarsie to examine the cut on the sole of his foot. Bile filled the back of her throat. Although a clean slice, it was deep. She glimpsed bone.

"He'll need stitches for sure." She cringed, thinking about poking a needle through the little boy's flesh.

Nathaniel's screams turned to harsh sobs. Emmy's wails carried from the yard, where Simon had instructed the other children to remain when he'd carried Nathaniel back from the creek. Tarsie should go comfort Emmy, but she needed to tend to Nathaniel first. A woman needed at least six arms at a time like this. Thankfully, Simon and Ruth could help.

Simon shook his head sorrowfully. He smoothed Nathaniel's sweaty hair from his forehead while the child continued to buck weakly in Ruth's restraining arms. "Sure am sorry you got hurt, boy." He lifted his gaze to Tarsie. "Wish I'd've seen that busted glass in the watuh. All the rain we had last month done muddied things up—watuh ain't clear like it used to be. I sho' di'n't see it. Not 'til Nathaniel starts howlin'."

"Ain't yo' fault." Ruth pressed Nathaniel tight to her bosom and rocked. "I sent y'all down to that creek. Shoulda known, what with all the ruckus we heard from there a few nights back, there might be busted bottles."

She pursed her lips, her big hand patting Nathaniel's bottom as she rocked forward and back, forward and back in rhythmic movements. "Fool men anyways. Oughta know chilluns use that pond for wadin'. Oughta not be breakin' their bottles on the rocks. But what do they care? Just little colored chillun, they think. Who cares if one of 'em gets hurt? When them men's all liquored up, they care even less'n usual 'bout anybody 'sides themselves, an' that's the truth."

A shadow fell across the floor, and Tarsie shifted her gaze from Ruth to the doorway. She gasped. Joss stood in the opening, Emmy clinging to his leg. Had he heard what Ruth said?

His eyes bounced past Tarsie to his son cradled in Ruth's arms. A fierce scowl marred his face. "Emmy said Nathaniel got cut." His flat, emotionless tone revealed nothing of his thoughts, but he cupped Emmy's head with his hand, his fingers gently stroking.

Tarsie swallowed tears. "It needs stitching." She gazed into Nathaniel's sweet little-boy face, still red from his wild crying. He was quiet now, but he wouldn't be once she put a needle and thread to work. She looked at Joss again. "I'll need help."

Joss set his mouth in a grim line as he stared at Nathaniel. Her husband held his body so taut and still Tarsie wondered if he even drew breath. Then he gave a brusque nod. "Let's get him home. I got the horse out here so I can carry him back."

Ruth glanced in Joss's direction, and her arms curved protectively around Nathaniel's little form. "You sho'? Here, Tarsie's got me to help her with this'un. At home she's only got . . ." She didn't need to complete the sentence. They all knew what Ruth was asking.

The muscles in Joss's jaw clenched, and his eyes squinted for a moment. But then he said, "I'm sure." He turned to Tarsie. "Better to fix him up at home. Then you can tuck him into bed . . . afterward."

Simon limped toward Joss. "I'll hitch Ransom to my cart an' tote Tarsie an' Emmy. Only take a minute." He shuffled out.

Joss set Emmy aside and strode forward. He stopped in front of Ruth, his hands balling into fists and then opening, as if testing their ability to function. Tarsie, watching him, marveled anew at his size. Such a big, powerful man—and handsome, too. He reminded her of the biblical man named

Samson who possessed great strength. What might God accomplish through Joss if he used his strength and ability to bring God honor?

Joss's arms stretched out. His hands slipped beneath Nathaniel's armpits. He lifted, and the boy tumbled, unresisting, into his father's embrace. Without looking at Tarsie, Joss turned toward the door. "Let's go."

❋ 28 ❋

C an't you hurry?" Sweat dripped from Joss's forehead, stinging his eyes. But the sting in his heart was worse, hearing his son's pained cries while Tarsie stitched the gash closed. How could someone so small fight so hard? Although Nathaniel couldn't move his arms or legs, trapped in his father's embrace with Joss's leg thrown across Nathaniel's much smaller ones, he continued to screech and buck his body, determined to free himself.

"I'm doing the best I can considering his squirmin'. Glad we battled his britches off of him. At least I'm not having to push his muddy pant legs out of the way anymore. . . ." Tarsie's face looked white in the harsh light of the lantern. Joss hoped she didn't pass out before she finished. He wouldn't be able to poke that needle through his son's tender skin. He also hoped Nathaniel didn't damage his lungs with all the screaming. He was getting hoarse.

Tarsie tied off the black thread, then sat back on her heels, a sigh slumping her shoulders. "There. All done." She held out her arms. "Let me have him."

Instead, Joss stood and swung Nathaniel around. The boy's arms flew outward, wrapping around Joss's neck. Joss held him close and paced back and forth across the floor while Nathaniel continued to cry—wracking sobs of hurt and frustration.

Emmy scuttled out of the corner where she'd hunkered, crying softly, during her brother's ordeal. She threw herself on Tarsie, and Tarsie soothed the little girl the same way Joss tried to soothe Nathaniel. Emmy quieted a lot quicker, though. For a moment, Joss considered handing Nathaniel over to Tarsie. Maybe he'd settle down faster if she took him. But he wanted to be the one to calm Nathaniel. He *needed* to calm him—needed to know if he could.

So he walked and patted and murmured nonsense while Tarsie moved to the stove, Emmy holding on to her apron, and started chopping potatoes into a pot of water. By the time steam rose from the pot, Nathaniel's harsh sobs had faded to jerky hiccups. Relieved, Joss leaned over to set the boy on the bench at the table, but Nathaniel wailed, "Nooo!" He gripped Joss's shirt in his fists.

Joss started to jerk Nathaniel loose—to tell him he'd done enough crying. But just as his fingers tightened on Nathaniel's arms, a memory surfaced—his father's hand, flying out to smack Joss hard on the cheek. His mind echoed with Pa's snarl: *"Didn't I tell you to stop that snivelin'? No more, or I'll give you somethin' to snivel about!"* The remembered pain and humiliation of that moment roared over Joss as harsh and strong as if it were happening now.

He caught Nathaniel's hands and gently disentangled them from his shirt. "I'm not goin' nowhere. Gonna sit here beside you." He heard his growly tone and cleared his throat. "You'll be all right." Joss sank onto the bench next to his son, and the little boy curled against him.

"Foot. Owie. Hurts."

"I know." Joss slipped his arm behind Nathaniel, holding him close. Had he ever held the boy this way before? He couldn't remember. Amazing how Nathaniel allowed it. Amazing how good it felt.

Joss glanced at Emmy, who watched from a safe distance,

her eyes—blue, with thick lashes just like Mary's—fixed on him. He offered his daughter a hesitant smile. "Come sit, too, Emmy."

She shook her head.

Resentment pricked. He opened his mouth to insist she get herself over there now, but once again he caught himself. After drawing a few breaths, he said, "Nathaniel'd probably like it if you would."

For a few moments Emmy stood, hand curled around Tarsie's apron strings, her face puckered with indecision. Then she released the apron and scampered to the bench, wriggling in next to Nathaniel. She held her brother's hand. The three of them sat, Joss giving Nathaniel little pats now and then and Emmy flicking puzzled glances at her papa. Joss understood her confusion. He didn't quite understand himself, either.

Tarsie ladled bowls of potato-and-green-bean soup with a few chunks of ham floating in the thin broth. Joss did his best to encourage Nathaniel to eat, but, fussy, the boy barely finished three bites. Tarsie ate in silence, her pensive gaze shifting from Joss to the children and back again. When they'd finished, she cleaned up the dishes without a word, leaving Joss to carry Nathaniel to his pallet and help him into his sleep shirt. Emmy dressed herself and then climbed in with Nathaniel.

He should've gotten those beds done so the children could sleep separately. Tangled up so close together on that pallet, Emmy'd probably be kicking Nathaniel all night long. "Don't bump your brother's foot tonight," Joss said.

"I won't."

Emmy's indignant tone reminded Joss of his own, and he grimaced. Simon was right. Children did what they learned. He sure hadn't taught them much good. He pushed up from his knees and stood for a moment, gazing down at the blond-haired pair. Who was he fooling, playing papa? He'd never be more than his own pa had been. These kids'd be better off without him. Sooner he left, the better for everybody.

"Sleep good," he ordered in his familiar gruff tone, then returned to the main room of the house. Tarsie washed dishes in the dented basin set on top of the dry sink. He crossed to her and leaned against the wall, arms folded. "You didn't put any herbs or wrapping on Nathaniel's foot. Don't you think you ought to?"

Color splashed her cheeks. She slapped a clean bowl onto a towel she'd laid across the corner of the stove. "I'll be watchin' his foot for signs of infection. If I see reason for concern, I'll take him straight to Drayton Valley's doctor." She gave him a sour look. "Probably should've had a doctor stitch him up, too, but I boiled that thread an' needle beforehand, just like a doctor would've done, so I'm trustin' all will be well."

"Why didn't you tell me you'd rather have a doctor stitch him up?"

Eyes on the sudsy water, she spoke through clenched teeth. "And when have I ever known you to be willin' to fetch a doctor for something like this?"

Joss's body jerked reflexively. Guilt rose, followed by a wave of anger. "I can't change none of that now, Tarsie."

"No, you surely can't." She yanked her hands from the dishwater and dried them on her apron. Then she faced him, her eyes sparking. "Just what do you think you're doin', Joss Brubacher?" Her words came out in a low-toned hiss.

"What're you talkin' about?"

"Bein' all kindly an' attentive toward those two wee ones after years of ignoring them. Are you tryin' to break their little hearts?"

He stared at her, openmouthed. "Of course not!"

"Well, it just seems odd to me, how you sneaked out last night an' got yourself pickled the way you used to do in New

York, an' now you're bein' all nicey-nice. . . . Those poor wee ones won't know what to expect from you tomorrow." She balled her fists on her hips. "Just what can we be expectin' tomorrow, Joss? A drunkard or a sober man? A man who holds himself aloof an' barks orders or one who tugs his child close an' soothes his hurt? 'Cause truth be known, I'm befuddled myself, an' I'm a grown woman. I can't imagine what those children'll go through if you bounce back the other way after an evenin' of kindness."

Had he really thought he appreciated her sauciness? He snorted and lifted his foot to stomp away.

She caught his sleeve. "Don't be misunderstandin' me, Joss. The way you were tonight with the children, that's what I've prayed for—what Mary hoped for all along. A part of me thrills to see you reachin' out to them. But it also scares me. 'Cause it needs to be more than a one-time action that stems from you feelin' guilty about what you did earlier in the day."

Joss wanted to pull loose, but he felt as though someone had driven stakes through the toes of his boots. He remained still as a statue as she continued.

"Those children need you to be a lovin' father to them every hour of every day. They need to be able to trust you. To depend on you. Do you understand what I'm sayin'?"

Even though Joss had decided on his own he didn't have what it took to be a good papa to his youngsters, it riled him more than he wanted to admit to have someone else say it. He shoved her hand loose, then took a step away. "I understand what you're saying. And I already know you're right. Those kids—they need more'n what I can give 'em. I tried to tell you that when Mary died. Didn't I try? I wanted to send 'em to an orphans' home where they'd have a chance of a different life. But you concocted this crazy idea of me marryin' up with you. Well, now look what we've got. Two miserable kids and two miserable adults. It didn't fix nothin', did it, Tarsie?"

His head began to ache again. Clutching his temples, he moaned. "What'm I doin' here? Should never've come."

He needed a drink. With a snarl, he whirled toward the door. But just as he grabbed the crossbar and raised it, a little voice trembled behind him.

"Papa?"

He glanced over his shoulder.

Emmy stood in the gap of the dividing wall. Tears swam in her eyes. "I accidentally bumped Nattie's foot. It's bleedin'." She held out her hand. "Will you come?"

Joss turned his gaze forward, away from his daughter's pleading face. "Tarsie'll see to him." And he strode out into the night.

※

Although Tarsie lay awake well past midnight, Joss didn't return that night. Or the next morning. On Monday evening, Simon, Ruth, and their children came for Ruth's lesson—this time on numbers—and Simon strung ropes on the bed frames he and Joss had constructed. When Tarsie asked, he said Joss'd been to work that day and showed no signs of having been drinking, but he didn't know where he'd gone afterward.

Tarsie spent most of Monday night praying he'd come back so she could apologize for her outburst. Her anger over his choice to drink had made her harsher than she'd intended. She didn't feel badly for asking the questions—he needed to understand how his behavior affected his children—but she wished she hadn't turned the questions into an attack. She'd driven him away, and guilt wore on her as heavily as a necklace of boulders.

Tuesday morning, she opened the front door to allow in a breeze and found a little drawstring pouch on the stoop. It contained four silver dollars. Her heart leapt as she held it, and she searched the neighborhood, seeking signs of the man who'd left it. But Joss was long gone. Heartsore, she fixed breakfast and avoided the children's questions about their papa.

By Wednesday, worry had created a constant ache in the center of her stomach. How long did Joss plan to stay away? His parting words—claiming he should never have come to Kansas—tormented her. How she wanted to set things right with him, but how could she if he didn't return?

Thursday afternoon, she and the children went to the mercantile to purchase a few staples. Tarsie carried Nathaniel. Although his foot was healing nicely and he'd learned to tiptoe around the house to avoid stepping on his heel, he couldn't wear a shoe. She couldn't expect him to tiptoe barefooted all the way to town and back, so she carried him. With his weight in her arms, she couldn't hold anything else, which forced her to limit her purchasing, since Emmy had to be the one to tote the items home. But she did buy a half pound of the pungent white cheese Joss preferred. Just in case he came home. Oh, how she prayed he'd come home!

Friday evening, Ruth arrived for another lesson alone in Simon's little cart—no husband or children in tow, much to Emmy's and Nathaniel's disappointment. She stayed late, waiting until Tarsie tucked Emmy and Nathaniel into their new beds. After the children fell asleep, Ruth said, "Pour me another cup o' your good coffee, girl. Then let's you an' me have us a talk."

Tarsie's heart skittered into nervous double-beats. "Is it . . . is it about Joss?"

"Yes'm, it is. But coffee first."

❄ 29 ❄

Tarsie's hands trembled as she poured the last of the coffee into two tin cups. She settled across from Ruth, both eager and apprehensive about what her friend might say. Drawing in a deep breath, she squared her shoulders. "I'm ready."

Ruth laughed softly, her low chuckle a comforting sound. "Now, it ain't all bad. Just di'n't want the chillun listenin' in. Some things is best left to the grown-ups." She angled her head, her brows dipping low. "Emmy an' Nathaniel, they been askin' for their papa?"

Tarsie took a sip of her coffee, her head low as sadness struck. "Not since Monday. It's as if they don't expect him to be here for them. Breaks my heart, Ruth. It truly does." She jolted as pain stabbed through her chest. But not for the children's loss. For her own. Not until that moment did she realize how much she missed Joss. The awareness both frightened and elated her.

Ruth's gaze turned knowing. "Mm-hmm." She cleared her throat. "Well, Simon, he ask me to tell you where Joss is stayin' so you won't be worryin' over him. He's just fine. Seems he's been sleepin' in Mistuh Tollison's summer kitchen—set hisself up a little pallet in there." Her forehead crinkled into a series of furrows. "But he tol' Simon somethin' that don't make much sense to us. Maybe it'll mean somethin' to you. . . .

He say he shouldn't be sleepin' over here 'cause you an' him, you ain't hitched."

Tarsie reared back. "Not . . . not hitched? Of course we are." Memories of that day at the riverbank and the simply dressed preacher leading them to state their vows washed over her. Her throat had caught as she'd pledged herself to Joss, but she'd done it for Mary, even while she longed to feel *something* for the man she would call her husband. She swallowed, her pulse pattering erratically. When had those feelings she'd wanted on that day crept into her heart?

She bounced up and retrieved her Bible, opening it to the page containing the marriage record as she returned to the table. She held out the Bible. "See?" She read while Ruth frowned at the page. "'This certifies that Treasa Raines and Joss Brubacher were united in holy matrimony on the 21st day of April in the year of our Lord 1880 in White Cloud, Kansas.' We've been husband and wife for three months now." Three months laden with living, growing, changing . . . even loving.

Slapping the Bible closed, Tarsie glared at Ruth. "How can he be saying we aren't wed?"

Ruth shrugged. "I dunno. Just know what he tol' Simon, that's all. Guess you gon' have to ask him yo'self."

Tarsie hugged the Bible to her breast, her mouth dry. "I need to talk to him."

"You sho' do." Ruth released a little snort. "But you's prob'ly gon' hafta go to him." She quirked her lips into a disapproving grimace. "Simon, he says Joss has settled hisself in good there at Mistuh Tollison's, an' he figgers Joss'll just . . . stay there. Leastways, until we know how that vote's gon' go. If pro'bition comes an' the vineyard closes, most all the men'll be findin' someplace else to be. Simon, he figgers Joss'll just scoot on outta Drayton Valley if pro'bition comes."

Tarsie pushed aside the last part of Ruth's statement, her focus on now rather than what could happen later. "I can go to him if someone watches the children for me. Could you come in again tomorrow evening so I can go see Joss?"

"Tomorrow's Saturday. I was plannin' on spendin' all day cannin' my beans an' tomaters." She puckered her lips. "You reckon you could come out to my place instead? Chilluns can entertain themselves while I's workin'."

Tarsie sank onto the bench, her spirits plummeting. "Not with Nathaniel's foot still so sore. It nearly wore me out carrying him to the mercantile an' back. I'd never make it all the way to your place an' then home again."

"Well, now . . ." Ruth rubbed her chin with her fingers. "How about this? I can ask if Simon would come in here after he finishes tomorruh an' tote you all to our place. He might even take you on out to Tollison's in his cart, if'n you like."

The thought of riding rather than walking appealed. "Yes, please."

"All right, then." Ruth slurped the final drops of coffee, then rose. "I best be skedaddlin' home now. Simon knew I'd be stayin' late, but that Naomi, she won't lay down no more 'less I read a li'l out o' that storybook you done give us. Simon'll have his hands full, keepin' her quiet 'til I gets there. She's got flat-out spoiled by my readin' to her, that one has." Pride burst across her face.

Tarsie walked Ruth to the cart and rubbed the mule's nose while Ruth climbed aboard. "Thank you for telling me about Joss. I've been so worried, wondering where he was. And thank you for watching the young'uns tomorrow evening so I can go talk to him."

"You's welcome, Tarsie. I hopes you can get it all figgered out. Sho' 'nough seems like a jumbled-up mess." She flicked the reins, and the cart creaked away, moonlight shimmering on the mule's swayed back.

Tarsie sat on the stoop and stared into the gray night. She never tired of looking at the stars in the endless Kansas sky.

Such a different view than the tiny slice of smoke-smudged black visible between buildings in New York. She loved it here. Loved the wind, the rolling hills, the towering trees, and the openness that made her want to raise her hands in the air and sing praises for God's glorious creation.

Ruth had said Simon indicated Joss wanted to leave Kansas. Her chest constricted at the thought of leaving. Would he go back to New York? What else did he know? She had no desire to return to that dirty, crowded, crime-infested city. But as his wife—if she really were his wife—she'd go, too. It would be her duty to follow him wherever he went.

The ache in her chest increased as she admitted to herself she'd follow him for more reasons than duty. She'd follow him because she loved his children. She'd follow him because, despite what he'd done and despite his faults, he'd become woven into her life's fabric. She'd unravel without him.

"Oh, Lord . . ." She buried her face in her hands. "Ruth was right. We've got ourselves a jumbled-up mess. How can we make it all right?"

※

Joss received his pay envelope at the end of the week from Simon, made his scribbled mark that served as a signature on the paper, then moved aside while the remaining workers stepped up for their wages. He opened the envelope and spilled the money into his hand—two paper five-dollar bills and two silver dollars. He mentally added what this week's pay needed to cover for both him and Tarsie. Eight dollars for August's rent at the house in town, fifty cents for the horses' care at the livery, and maybe two dollars for groceries. That left—he wrinkled his forehead—a dollar and four bits.

If he ate carefully, as he'd done this week, living on canned beans and leftovers handed over by Tollison's cook, he could add another dollar to the old sock holding his savings. The sock already held almost ten dollars. He wanted to leave thirty for Tarsie, and he'd need some for traveling. He'd need to save a little more each week to have enough by the end of the year to get out of Drayton Valley for good.

The last man ambled away from the table, and Simon plopped the ledger and money box inside a little wooden crate. Joss hurried over, the bills from his envelope wadded in his hand.

"Is Ruth still taking those reading lessons with Tarsie?" He wished he'd picked up a little more of those lessons, listening in. Mary'd always done any reading for him, and then Tarsie, but now that he was on his own, being able to read would sure be helpful.

Simon balanced the crate against his stomach. "She sho' is. Figgers on openin' her school come Septembuh." Simon fixed Joss with a steady look. "That Tarsie, she be a fine teachuh. She be a fine *woman*." His gaze narrowed, and Joss squirmed, imagining what words Simon was holding behind his closed lips.

He jammed his hand, bills clenched in his fingers, toward Simon. "Wouldja give this to Ruth to give to Tarsie? She's gotta pay rent next week. There'll be enough there to cover it."

Simon stared at Joss's hand but made no effort to take the money. "You givin' all that to Tarsie? To some woman who ain't even yo' wife?"

Joss gritted his teeth. Why'd he admitted such a thing to Simon? He'd gotten far too relaxed around this colored man who spoke softly, walked on a gimpy leg, and still seemed stronger than nearly any other person Joss had ever met. He bounced the money. "Why shouldn't I give it to her? She's carin' for my young'uns, an' her bartering with the neighbors won't pay the rent. So will you give it to her or not?"

Simon chewed his lower lip, his brows crunched as if deep

in thought. Finally he huffed out a funny little sound—half sigh, half laugh. "Drop it in my box here. I'll see she gets it."

"Thanks." Joss tossed the bills into the crate, watching them flutter to the bottom and settle. Assured Simon would be true to his word, Joss started to head to the summer kitchen. But the thought of sitting all by himself in that stuffy room that smelled of onions and sour milk didn't appeal. So he stood in the patch of shade from the towering maple, watching as Simon shifted the crate to one hip and used his free hand to grasp the lip of the little table.

He darted forward. "Lemme help."

Simon shot him a funny look, but he offered a shrug rather than an argument. Turning toward the house, Simon set off in his foot-dragging way of walking. Joss trailed behind, the table gripped so hard his fingers ached. Watching Simon's body jerk with every step made him feel guilty for having two good legs. He'd spent a lot of his lifetime complaining. About the weather, about the price of suspenders, about some men not carrying their fair share of the workload . . . All of it seemed petty in light of the crippled man's troubles.

They reached the back door of the house, and Simon opened it without knocking. Joss followed Simon into a small, square room with floor-to-ceiling bead-board paneling painted white. A gaslight with three globes burned overhead, shining on the white paint as bright as sunlight at midday. Two walls bore closed doors, one with a glass pane on its upper half giving Joss a view of a kitchen, and one solid wood with a highly polished brass knob and locking mechanism.

Simon, humming, crossed to the solid door and shifted the crate to one hip. He removed a key from his pocket, unlocked the door, and then glanced at Joss. "You can set that table ovuh there in the cornuh." He opened the door. The hinges creaked loudly, as if bemoaning carrying the door's weight.

Joss shoved the table into the corner, as Simon had asked,

but he angled his body to peek at what was kept behind that heavy, locked door. It seemed to be a closet with shelves—what folks called a pantry. Brown pay envelopes were scattered across the upper shelf, and the bottom one was empty. The contents of the middle shelf captured Joss's attention—a black iron box, the kind of box bankers used, only smaller.

Joss held his breath while Simon spun a little dial and then pushed down on a silver handle. The door on the front of the box opened. Simon slid the little cash box he used to divvy out wages into the open space beside several stacks of bundled bills and a lumpy cloth bag. Joss's pulse doubled. He'd never seen so much money in one place.

Simon gave the door a push, and it slammed closed. Joss jumped at the resounding clang. He backed toward the door leading outside as Simon slid the crate onto the bottom shelf. "Guess I'll be goin' now."

Simon spun around. "Where you goin'?" Then he laughed—an odd kind of laugh. Forced-sounding. "What I mean is, you got plans to head into town or somethin'?"

As much as he'd like to visit that little shack by the river, he wouldn't. He couldn't waste his money that way. Not again. For a moment, he halfway hoped Simon might invite him over for the evening just so he wouldn't be all by himself. Crazy idea. "Nah. Turnin' in early. Been a long week." A long, lonely week.

"So you's headin' to the summer kitchen, then?"

Something in Simon's tone and the innocent way he held his eyes wide open, as if he'd forgotten how to blink, raised a prickle of awareness across Joss's scalp. He answered slowly. "That's where I'm stayin' now, so . . . yup."

Simon gave a quick nod, then flashed a smile. "Sounds fine, Joss. Mighty fine. You have a good evenin' now." He turned to the door and inserted the key in the lock, once again humming.

Joss left the house and strode across the quiet grounds toward the summer kitchen. He let his arms swing, trying to give the appearance of having not a care in the world. But underneath, his stomach churned. That Simon was up to something. He just knew it.

❋ 30 ❋

Tarsie held to the edge of Simon's cart as it bounced across the ground between buildings at the Tollison vineyards. She'd been amazed at the size of the Tollison house—she'd never imagined someone in a riverside town like Drayton Valley owning such a fine home. For a moment, she felt sorry for Mr. Tollison. Prohibition would certainly rob him of this mansion. Would a wealthy man like him be satisfied with less?

Simon drew the cart to a stop behind the big house, then pointed ahead to a square, wood-sided building with two stove pipes poking skyward from its red slate roof. Simon pointed. "That there's the summuh kitchen, Miz Tarsie. Joss, he'll be inside."

The summer kitchen's door, centered on the wall facing the house, yawned wide open. The aromas of onions, roasted meat, bread, and something sweet drifted on the breeze. Apparently the cook had prepared quite a feast for Mr. Tollison's supper. Had the cook fed Joss, too?

Tarsie's stomach fluttered. As much as she'd wished for an opportunity to see Joss, to apologize and set things right, now that the moment was upon her, she hesitated. How would he react when she stepped through the doorway? Oh, how she longed to see his usually stern face light with joy that she'd come.

247

Simon cleared his throat. "You want me to stick aroun'?"

Tarsie considered asking Simon to come in with her. The thought of facing Joss alone suddenly seemed overwhelming. But a wife—and she *was* his wife!—should have no fear in confronting her husband. "I'll walk to your place when we've finished talking. But I'd appreciate it if you'd be praying I can convince that stubborn man to go home with me."

Simon grinned. "Sho' thing, Miz Tarsie."

Tarsie clambered off the cart, holding her skirts to keep from catching the fabric on the wheel. She waited until Simon rolled past, then shook the dust from her dress, smoothed stray wisps of hair into place with her fingers, and sent up a quick prayer for strength. She marched forward, her chin high even though a million butterflies flitted wildly in her tummy.

She paused on the little concrete slab that served as a porch, uncertain if she should knock or simply call out, since the door stood open. Peering inside, she searched for Joss. Sunlight slanted through the windows, creating shafts of yellow that broke through the gloom of the small space. She finally spotted him in the corner between a shiny black stove with six cook lids and a tall pie safe. He lay on his side on a pile of folded blankets with one elbow propping him up. An open booklet of some kind lay in front of him, and he appeared to be studying the pages.

She watched him, hoping he might sense her presence and look up. Head low, sleeves rolled to his elbows, sunlight dancing on his tousled dark hair, he seemed much younger. He flicked a page, and his finger traced a line. His lips moved, but no sound came out.

Tarsie linked her hands and drew a fortifying breath. "Joss?"

His head jerked up, his eyes wide. In an instant, he'd shoved the booklet aside and leaped to his feet. He ran his fingers through his hair, sweeping it back from his forehead, then stood glowering at her. "What're you doing here?"

That was not the welcome she'd hoped for. She swallowed a lump of disappointment. "May I be comin' in?"

He didn't move. Not even a muscle. He simply stood there, feet set wide, hands balled at his sides, unsmiling face aimed in her direction. Then, as if stretching awake after a long hibernation, he poked out his foot and kicked the booklet into the shadowy place beneath the stove. "Ain't my house. I'm just staying here. You can do what you want, I reckon."

What she wanted was to run into his embrace. To feel him hold her close the way he'd held Nathaniel. And Mary. The desire took her by surprise. Her breath releasing in nervous little puffs, she stepped into the kitchen. The strong odor of onions assaulted her, making her eyes burn. How did Joss sleep in here? She blinked rapidly against the moisture distorting her vision.

He took one step forward, his shoulders stiff and his lips set in a firm line. "Why're you here?"

Tarsie licked her lips. Maybe she should have asked Simon to stay. Here, alone with an angry Joss in this half-dark room with the awful odor clinging to every surface, unease gripped her. "The young'uns . . . and me . . . we were worried." The moisture in her eyes increased, but these were tears of remorse. "I didn't mean to send you away, Joss. I only wanted you to . . . to not change back to the way you were before. I wanted you to keep being kind, because that's what the wee ones are needin' from you, but I said it all the wrong way. I'm sorry."

He looked past her, his jaw muscles twitching.

A long, scarred trestle table stood between them. She inched around it, her gaze fixed on his stoic face. "I know you're upset with me. But don't be punishing Emmy and Nathaniel for my errant tongue."

"That's what you think? I'm punishing them?" He blasted a laugh—the most cynical laugh she'd ever heard. Shaking his head, he stared at the floor. "Try to do right for the first time ever, an' this is how it's seen. As punishment . . ." The ugly laugh barked out again.

Tarsie darted forward and caught the front of his shirt. She gave the plaid fabric a good shake, wishing she had the strength and courage to shake him instead. "What else would it be but a punishment?"

"I'd call it a . . . gift."

Tarsie's ire raised. "It's a *gift*? The best you can offer . . . to abandon your wife and children?" She shook his shirt again. One button popped loose and flew across the room. "What kind of a man are you, Joss Brubacher?"

He grabbed her wrist and pushed her hand aside. Storming to the other side of the table, he spun and faced her. "You know what kind of man I am. I'm a man who drinks. A man who gambles. A man who lacks patience." He pressed his palms to the sturdy wood surface, assuming a menacing pose. "Selfish. Spiteful. Prone to fits of rage." He spat the words, fire sparking in his eyes. Suddenly the bluster went out of him. His shoulders collapsed, and his chin dropped low. "I'm exactly like my pa and his pa before him. That's the kind of man I am."

Understanding bloomed through Tarsie's heart. She held one hand toward him. "Joss—"

"And I'm a liar, too. But it's time to set that straight."

Tarsie's hand froze in midair. "W-what do you mean?"

"We ain't married." He lifted his face just enough to peer at her through the heavy hank of hair falling across his forehead. "That man who led us in sayin' 'I do' . . . he wasn't no preacher. Just a bartender."

A bartender? Dizziness assailed her. Gooseflesh broke out across her arms and back. Her knees felt weak. She stumbled forward, gripping the table for support. "You mean . . . all this time . . . ?"

He gave a grim nod. "Only did it 'cause Mary's kids—"

She bolted upright. "*Your* children!"

"—needed somebody to raise 'em right. Mary said you were honorable. A good friend. The best kind of friend." He grimaced as if something pained him. "So I did what I had to do to make sure those kids had somebody lookin' after 'em." He snorted. "I sure can't do it. Never could. Never will." The last words rasped out on a note of regret.

"You're wrong, Joss." Tarsie inched around the table, fearful of approaching him yet unable to remain distant. "You can be carin' toward them. I've seen it. The way you were the other night with Nathaniel, holding him close and givin' him comfort—"

"One time." He jammed a finger upward, fury and something else—something Tarsie recognized as despair—glimmering in his eyes. "That don't mean it's gonna be a habit. My habits are set. Don't you understand that? Even Simon knows—he told me my young'uns are gonna grow up to be angry, Emmy searching for a man to love her and probably finding the wrong kind, because I'm such a lousy papa."

Tarsie couldn't believe kind, gentle Simon would say such a hurtful thing. Joss must have misunderstood. But before she could offer her thoughts, he rushed on.

"If I stay in their lives, they'll learn nothin' but wrong. It's better for me to leave 'em. You keep 'em, Tarsie. Raise 'em. Teach 'em to be decent people. Mary said I could trust you, so I trust you with Emmy and Nathaniel. You takin' 'em? That'll be giftin' Mary."

Tarsie knew what Mary wanted. And she'd promised. Her heart ached, knowing how she'd been fooled. For weeks she'd seen to Joss's needs, envisioning them as a family, opening her heart to him . . . falling in love. But he'd never felt a thing for her. Her pride urged her to walk out the door and pretend Joss Brubacher didn't exist—that her time with him was all a bad dream. But her love for Mary nailed her feet to the floor.

Forcing her mind back to the day of Mary's death—a painful place—Tarsie offered a silent prayer for God to guide her words and to open Joss's stubborn heart to understanding. "Joss, I told you Mary's final wish was for me to care for your children. But . . . but I lied, too."

His eyebrows crunched downward.

"I was too embarrassed to tell you her real last words. Maybe I was afraid, too. Afraid they'd anger you or . . . hurt your pride. I know you're a proud man, Joss."

In response, his chin rose a notch.

"But I need you to be knowin' what your Mary was thinkin' as she lay in that wagon with life slipping away from her. She was thinkin' of you."

Joss's chin trembled. He set his jaw, stilling the movement.

"She knew how poorly you thought of yourself . . . and why. And she knew what needed to be done to change it." Tarsie spoke softly, soothingly, the way one might comfort a colicky babe or a frightened horse. "So she asked me to love you . . . the way she'd tried to love you." She gulped, her pulse leaping into a gallop. "She'd tried to love you the way God loves you. Because she wanted you to be seein' yourself as someone worthy of receiving love."

Joss spun around, showing Tarsie his back. The muscles of his shoulders bunched and released under his shirt. When he spoke, his voice came out harsh and strangled, as if a fist squeezed his vocal cords. "Ain't no way God could love me. Not the way I am."

Tarsie darted to Joss's side. She reached to touch him, but then she clutched her hands together and pressed them to her rib cage instead, unwilling to have him push her aside again. "He can, Joss! And He does! But . . ." She gathered her courage and placed her fingertips gently on his taut arm. "He loves you too much to leave you as you are, because He knows you can't be happy wallowin' in sinful behavior."

He stepped away from her touch. "And just how does He change a man, Tarsie?"

An image flooded Tarsie's memory. She scuttled after him. "Joss, do you remember the morning on the trail when Mary's moans woke us?"

He cringed. He remembered.

"Remember what you did? You picked her up. You picked her up in your arms and you carried her all around the camp." She tipped her head, looking into his stormy eyes. "Why'd you do that, Joss?"

Joss clamped his jaw so tight the muscles bulged. For a moment, Tarsie thought he'd refuse to answer, but then he stuffed his hands into the pockets of his pants and said, "I wanted to take her pain away."

Tarsie nodded, a smile lifting her lips as tears filled her eyes. "And don'tcha see, Joss, that's exactly what God wants to do for you. He wants to pick you up, hold you so close you can be hearin' His heartbeat in your ear, easin' away the pain you've carried from being mistreated by your pa. When you let Him pluck out all that pain, Joss—the pain you've tried to numb by pouring whiskey down your throat, it'll leave an opening for Him to slip in an' change you from the inside out."

Joss's stern expression didn't change.

Tarsie dared to move in again, lifting her hand to place it softly, tenderly, deliberately over his heart. The force of his pounding pulse beat against her palm. "Let Him in, Joss. Let Him change you into the kind of papa"—she withheld the words *and husband*—"He'd have you be. He'll help you, Joss, if you'll just lean into His arms."

They stood in silence, her hand pressed to his chest, his

hands deep in his pockets. She gazed into his sternly set face, praying for him to soften, while he stared past her head to some unknown point behind her. His lips parted and she held her breath, anticipating the sweet moment when he'd finally acknowledge his need for God in his life and pledge to change.

"Get on out o' here now."

Tarsie stumbled backward, tears spurting into her eyes. Although his words were soft—gentle even—he couldn't have hurt her more if he'd slapped her.

"Go see to Mary's children. Don't be stewin' over me." He pressed his lips together as if a deep pain stabbed him. "No matter what you say, I ain't worth stewin' over." He stomped to the corner and flung himself down on the blankets with his face to the wall.

Tarsie stared at him for a moment, hardly able to breathe her chest ached so badly. *Strength, Father* . . . Gathering the tattered edges of her dignity about her, she did as he'd commanded.

❋ 31 ❋

J oss was awakened Sunday morning by someone kicking the soles of his feet. Even without looking, he knew who'd done it. He grunted in response, then sat up, groggy and grumpy. "I know, I know. I'm leavin'."

Tollison's cook, a rotund woman with a bulbous nose and three chins, waved a rolling pin. "And be quick about it. I need wood chopped—enough to last through tomorrow's baking."

Joss tugged on his boots, then squinted upward. "Got coffee goin' yet?"

"You'll get your coffee with your breakfast. Now scat— don't want you underfoot while I'm cooking."

Muttering under his breath, Joss scuffed into the soft glow of predawn. One lone bird chirped from a treetop. A sharp, scolding chirp that reminded Joss of the cook's harpy voice. He'd wondered a time or two over the past week whether three meals and a place to sleep was worth putting up with her crotchety attitude. She acted too much like—

He stopped in his tracks. She acted like Pa. And like him.

Tarsie's words—the same words that had haunted him far into the night—returned. *"When you let Him pluck out all that pain, Joss—the pain you've tried to numb by pouring whiskey down your throat, it'll leave an opening for Him to slip in an' change you from the inside out."*

Joss had grown up hating his father, yet he'd become his father. Deep down, he wanted to change. For Mary. For Emmy and Nathaniel. Even for Tarsie, who'd had every right to rant and rave and throw pots at his head for his trickery. He'd come so close to asking her how to let God fill that place inside of him that always felt empty, but pride—and guilt over fooling her into thinking they were married—rose up and stopped him. He'd sent her away instead. And she'd stay away. Not even a promise to Mary would let her come back after all he'd said and done.

"You!"

A familiar voice blasted from behind him, scaring him half out of his wits. The bird shot off with a raucous chirping as Joss turned around. The cook stood outside the summer kitchen, red-faced and glowering. "Why aren't you chopping wood? You want any breakfast today, you better get busy!"

Joss swallowed a sharp retort and took off at a trot toward the woodshed, where a chopping block, axe, and pile of tree trunk sections waited his attention. He worked up a sweat turning round chunks into splintery wedges that would fit the cookstove's belly. The cook rewarded him with coffee, three fried eggs, a big scoop of grits with gravy, and two biscuits. He might complain about her prickliness, but he couldn't fault her cooking.

He ate outside, seated on the stoop with the plate balanced on his knees, as the sun crept from its sleeping place behind the horizon and crawled skyward to peek at him from behind tree branches. When he'd finished, he returned the plate and fork to the kitchen but held on to his cup.

"Can I have more coffee?"

The cook scowled, but she sloshed the strong brew into his cup. As Joss raised the cup to his lips, she said, "You ought to mosey to the creek this morning and give yourself a dunking." She yanked up the bar of soap that sat next to the washbasin and dropped it into Joss's shirt pocket. "You're starting to stink up this place with your sweat odor."

Joss raised one brow, resisting a snide comment. His sweat couldn't smell worse than the onions she fried for every meal and even in between. Who ate onions six times a day? But as much as her statement irritated him, he couldn't deny a dip in the creek—and a good all-over wash—would feel mighty good. He drained his cup, dropped it in the basin without a word, and aimed himself outside.

Little Beaver Creek, which fed into the Missouri River, wove its way all along the northwest edge of the Tollison land. The colored workers lived along Little Beaver Creek between Tollison's place and town, but the creek ran enough distance that Joss could avoid the cluster of houses. He intended to give his clothes a good scrubbing when he went in for his bath, which might take a while, and he had no desire for someone to come along and spot him, stark naked, rubbing his britches on a rock. It being Sunday, the colored folks would be gathering for a service. He'd just make sure to be done before they let out and maybe decided to cool their toes in the creek.

He worked his way along a deer-carved pathway through a stand of trees and brush so thick only slivers of sunlight penetrated. The sunbeams formed slanted pillars of shimmery dust. It was quiet there away from everything and everyone, cooler with the heavy cover of shade. Peaceful. Or it should've been peaceful. But the aching emptiness in his gut—the emptiness that had increased with Tarsie's visit—traveled with him. Maybe the cool, sparkling, clear water would wash the uncomfortable feeling away.

But even after washing himself from the top of his head to the soles of his feet, using the soap to scrub the majority of grime from his long johns, britches, shirt, and socks, and taking a leisurely swim to give his clothes a chance to dry out before he dressed again, he still hadn't managed to rid himself of the dirtiness inside. He splashed his way to the bank and sat on a large rock, staring across the water with his chin propped up by one fist. All the scrubbing with the strongest soap couldn't penetrate below his skin. The realization left him out of sorts. And more sad than he wanted to admit.

The sun shone directly overhead when he wriggled into his damp clothes. Cook would have dinner going—probably something extra special, it being Sunday. After he ate, he'd take a nap. Maybe make up for some of the sleep he'd missed last night, lying awake fretting over his conversation with Tarsie. As he ambled along the narrow path, he heard voices—childish ones laughing and then a woman gently chiding followed by a man's throaty chuckle.

He tried to duck back out of sight, but he hesitated a moment too long. Simon Foster, his wife, and their children came up the path right toward him. The children skipped in the lead, with Simon and Ruth close behind. A large basket hung from Ruth's arm and Simon carried a ratty-looking quilt. Heading for a picnic, no doubt. A coil of longing twined through Joss's middle. How many meals had he eaten with Mary, Tarsie, and the young'uns on the trail? It'd been nice, all clustered together on a quilt on the ground.

The two little boys, who led the pack, stopped and gaped at Joss. The biggest one pointed. "Ain't that Emmy an' Nattie's pappy?"

Ruth reached out and pushed the boy's hand down. "Ezekiel Foster, you gots better manners than to be pointin' at folks."

The boy poked his bare toe against the ground, shamefaced.

Simon limped past his family, his smile wide. "We's gon' have ourselves a picnic down by the crick."

Joss squirmed in place, wishing he'd managed to escape

before they spotted him. "I figured as much." The scent of fried chicken reached his nose. Unconsciously, he turned his gaze on the basket. "I'll get out o' the way so you all can head down."

"Why don'tcha come with us?" Simon's face glistened with a fine sheen of perspiration. It was shady here in the trees, but the long walk on his bad foot must tax him. "Ruth, she wrung the necks o' two birds yestuhday. Got plenty."

Ruth's face briefly reflected disapproval, but the expression disappeared so quickly Joss thought he might have imagined it. "Why, sho'," she said. "We'd be right pleased to share."

Joss stood, uncertain. Chicken sounded good. The idea of not spending the afternoon all alone with his thoughts sounded better. And Simon knew God—how many times had Joss inwardly accused the man of sounding like a preacher? Maybe Simon could answer a few questions . . . if they had a chance to sneak off and talk. He wouldn't say much in front of Ruth. She'd repeat it all to Tarsie.

Tarsie . . . Joss swallowed hard. He sure wished things could be different for him and Tarsie. But if he'd messed things up with God, he'd messed things up even worse with Tarsie.

Simon's boy—the one they called E.Z.—sidled up beside his daddy. Simon's hand rose and descended on the boy's wiry hair. Gave it a pat. A loving pat. A lump filled Joss's throat. Much as it pained him to admit it, he could learn an awful lot from Simon.

"Thanks for the invitation," Joss finally said. "I . . . I think I would like to have a piece of that chicken."

※

Joss's response couldn't have surprised Simon more if the man had picked up a rock and chucked it at E.Z.'s head. The way he stared at the boy, with his forehead all creased and angry-looking, Simon half worried Joss wanted to take after little E.Z. But then he agreed to eat with them. Would wonders never cease?

"Well, c'mon then." Ruth gave him a little nudge from behind. "This basket o' food's pullin' on my arm. I'm ready to toss out that blanket an' have us a set-down."

The children giggled, then dashed up the path, nearly trampling Joss's feet as they passed. Ruth came alongside him, and Joss held out his hand.

"Lemme carry that for you."

Ruth seemed to freeze for a moment, her lips flapping a bit as if fighting for words. But then, with a self-conscious chortle, she handed it over. "Thank you. It ain't the chicken so much as the jars o' pickles an' such I put in there that's weighin' it down."

"It all sounds real good," Joss said, his voice quiet and serious.

Ruth scuttled on up the path, holding her skirts up above her bare ankles, and Joss followed. Simon trailed behind, shaking his head in puzzlement. A week away from Tarsie had surely broken something inside that man. Talking soft and gentle instead of loud and angry. And being willing to eat with a black family? Simon would never have imagined it.

They reached the creek, and the children darted straight for the water. Simon called out, "You be careful, now—watch where you step. 'Member that busted glass little Nathaniel got hisself cut on."

"We'll be watchful, Pappy," Malachi responded. He took Naomi's hand and the pair waded in together with E.Z. splashing more exuberantly a few feet away.

"They'll be fine." Ruth took the quilt and spread it on the mossy ground. "Bunch o' men came down an' cleaned up all that glass. Must o' been four, five bottles worth in all! I ain't heard no hoorawin' down here since, so I reckon we's safe."

She snorted under her breath, taking the basket from Joss's hand. "Fo' now, anyways."

Simon sent a sidelong glance toward Joss. The man stood to the side, his solemn gaze on the children. What was he thinking, listening to Ruth disparage men who'd come down to the creek, drank themselves silly, then tossed their bottles aside without a care for who might come along later? He'd probably never know. Joss was one closemouthed man.

Ruth filled the center of their quilt with the contents of the basket. Crisp fried chicken, biscuits, hard-boiled eggs, and jars of pickles, spiced peaches, and okra. Simon's mouth watered in eagerness. He struggled down on one knee to lay out the plates. He placed them just so, then frowned.

"Whoops. Only got five plates."

Joss cleared his throat and took one step toward the path. "That's all right. I don't gotta eat with y'all. I'll just—"

Ruth bounced up and caught his arm, drawing him to the quilt. "Me an' Naomi'll share a plate. Men." She shot Simon a mock glare. "Allus seein' problems where none exist. Sit down, Joss." She turned to the creek and hollered, "You chillun get on up here now. We's gon' eat!"

They came and flopped down at the edge of the quilt—Naomi in Ruth's lap, Malachi between his folks, and E.Z. next to Joss. He beamed up at the big man, poking his tongue through the gap where a tooth had fallen out last week. To Simon's surprise, Joss didn't rear back. He didn't smile, either, but he lifted his hand and gave E.Z. a little pat on the back. Hesitant. Like he wasn't quite sure how to go about touching a child. The gesture made something burn in the back of Simon's nose. How he wished the good Lord had given him the ability to read minds. He'd love to know what Joss was thinking right then.

Ruth bumped Simon's elbow. "Say the blessin', Simon, so's we can eat. These young'uns . . . an' Joss . . . 're hungry."

Simon started to bow his head, but Joss spoke, startling his head upward again.

"An' when we've finished eatin', maybe you an' me . . ." Joss swallowed. "I mean, Simon an' me, could have us a little talk."

Simon gave a quick nod, then closed his eyes to offer thanks for the meal. While he prayed, though, his thoughts tripped ahead. He'd wondered what was going through Joss's head, and now it seemed he'd get to find out. He added a silent postscript to his prayer: *Lawd, whatevuh it is he's wantin'— an' I'm afeared he might try to get me tangled all up in his an' Tarsie's troubles—give me wisdom in answerin' him. Whatevuh's gon' be, let it be pleasin' to You, Lawd.*

✳ 32 ✳

"Hitch up Ransom, Simon. I's gotta get straight to town an' tell Tarsie."

Simon couldn't stop grinning. Ruth nearly twitched right out of her skin. She looked like a young girl again, eyes all twinkling and cheeks rounded up with her smile. But he caught her hand and drew her back down on the little bench tucked beneath the kitchen window of their house.

"Now, Ruth, you know what I shared with you 'bout my talk with Joss is private. He'll nevuh trust me again, you run in an' spout it all to Tarsie."

Ruth's bright smile turned into a pout. "But it's only fittin' she knows, her bein' Joss's wife an' all. 'Specially since she's prayed so hard he'd go seekin' the Lawd."

"Oh, she's prayed—I'm for certain sho' o' that. But they ain't married up." He explained the trick Joss had played, watching disbelief bloom across Ruth's face. Then he added, "An' 'sides that, Joss di'n't make no decisions. Oh, he asked lots o' questions. I answered 'em best I could. Gave 'im plenty to think on, I reckon." Simon sighed, recalling the way Joss's eyes had lit, then dimmed as he wrestled with accepting the truth that God loved him. Really, really loved him.

Simon took Ruth's hand. "You knows that story in the

Bible—'bout seeds gettin' dropped an' some sprouted but some di'n't?"

"Sho' do. I can even read most o' it on my own now, thanks to Tarsie."

Simon gave his wife's hand a squeeze, proud of her accomplishment. Maybe someday she'd teach him. He sure would like to read the stories out of God's book all by himself. "Well, today I tossed a handful o' seeds on Joss's road. Others've tossed 'em befo'. He tol' me his wife, Mary, she was a believuh. An' o' course we know Tarsie's a believuh. So there's been lots o' seeds tossed. Now we's just gotta pray Joss'll let them seeds sprout.

"But you cain't say nothin' to Tarsie." Simon turned firm—something he rarely did with Ruth. "Joss, he don't know what he's gon' do. Pro'bition comes an' the vineyard closes, he says he cain't stay 'round here. An' Tarsie, she don't wanna leave Kansas. So they might be partin' ways. You go runnin' tellin' her Joss done talked to me 'bout the Lawd, it might give her false hope. No sense in that."

Ruth released a deep sigh. "I s'pose you's right. But it sho' would give her a lift to know he's at least askin'."

"Ruth . . ."

Ruth waved both hands in the air. "I hears you! I hears you! I ain't gon' say nothin'." She grinned, her eyes sparkling with mischief. "But I sho' is gon' pray, long an' hard, that them seeds get to bloomin' in Joss's heart. For the Lawd, but also for Tarsie. 'Cause, Simon, sho' as the sun sets in the west, the girl be in love with that man."

Oh, Lord, why'd You let this love blossom in my heart for Joss when You knew he'd misled me?

Tarsie used a sharp knife and turned the cheese she'd purchased for Joss into thin slivers that she layered on buttered bread. Two whole weeks, and he still hadn't come home. She'd wanted to have the cheese ready and waiting for him, knowing it was his favorite, but if she didn't use it soon, it would spoil. She'd already had to carve away fuzzy mold from the outer edges. It made no sense to throw out the entire block just because Joss was being stubborn. Tears stung her eyes as she created the sandwiches. Two of them—enough for the children. She wouldn't be able to eat a bite of Joss's favorite cheese without breaking down.

She poured milk—canned milk, since the neighbor had decided not to trade with her anymore—into tin cups. Then she called the children in from the backyard, where they had spent the late part of the morning playing with the chickens in the newly built wire coop. Emmy had named them all, although Tarsie couldn't determine how the little girl could tell Rosie from Posey. The chicks, with their oversized feet and prickly white feathers growing in over their yellow down, all looked alike to her.

"Come here, now. Wash your hands and then climb up to the table." She gave the directions kindly, but she heard the tiredness in her voice. The children had stopped asking her to play games or dance jigs with them. Somehow, she'd lost an element of joy for living. Even Ruth had expressed concern when she came in, alone, for her evening lessons, telling Tarsie, "You gots to buck up, girl—ain't doin' you or them chillun no good to have you mopin' aroun' all the time." Tarsie knew her friend was right, but losing Joss had stolen something from her, and she didn't know how to retrieve it.

Emmy and Nathaniel dried their hands on a towel and dashed to the table, eager to eat. Nathaniel continued to use his toes to support his injured foot, even though the wound had healed nicely. She supposed she should insist he stop babying the foot, but she was too weary for a battle. So she helped him onto the bench and then prayed with them. At their chorused "Amen," she moved back to the stove, pretending busyness so she wouldn't have to sit down and think about the meals when Joss had sat catty-corner across from her and helped Nathaniel cut his meat or carry his cup of milk to his mouth.

She stared out the window, lost in thought, dimly aware of the children's chatter behind her. Despite the fact that he'd sent her away when she went to see him, she knew he cared about her and the children. A man who didn't care wouldn't arrange to have a dozen chicks and a bundle of chicken wire delivered, or hire someone to build a pen for the little cluck-clucks, as Nathaniel called them. A man who didn't care wouldn't leave the bulk of his pay on the stoop where she'd find it so she and the children could live in a little house while he slept on a pallet in the corner of a summer kitchen. A man who didn't care wouldn't stay in a town in which he hadn't wanted to live just so he'd be close enough that he could make sure her needs were met.

He cared. And she cared about him. But he'd still sent her away.

"Why?" she whispered for the hundredth time in the two weeks since he'd stormed out the door. But she didn't receive an answer.

"Tarsie?" Emmy's voice cut into Tarsie's musings.

"What?" she responded without turning around.

"Can we go to the mercantile today? Remember you need buttons to finish my new dress. I wanna pick some out."

Had Joss been able to replace the button she'd torn from his shirt?

"Can we go, Tarsie? Huh?"

Tarsie sighed and offered Emmy a weary smile. "If Nathaniel will be wearing his shoes and walk all the way there and back again, then we can go. I can't be carrying him." She barely had the strength to carry herself these days.

"He'll walk, won'tcha, Nattie?" Emmy grinned and shoved the last bite of her sandwich into her mouth. "I want pink pearl buttons for my dress."

"As long as they don't cost more than plain."

Tarsie tied Nathaniel's shoes, loosening the bows when he complained. Emmy fetched the big shopping basket Ruth had made, and they set out. When they reached the edge of the business district, Emmy pointed.

"What's that?"

Tarsie squinted against the sun and peered ahead. Some sort of red-and-white-striped tent had been erected in the middle of Main Street. An American flag hung from one side of it, flapping in the breeze. Men stood in a line under the sun, talking softly with one another and scuffing their boots on the ground. Although no sign indicated the tent's purpose, Tarsie knew.

"It's a voting tent." She searched the line for Joss, her heart leaping with hope. She wouldn't be able to miss him, taller than most and with that thick thatch of dark, wavy hair. He would always stand out in a crowd. But no tall man with broad shoulders and a rakish mustache held a place in the line.

"Can we go in it?"

"Go in it?"

Both children pulled at Tarsie's skirt, begging. Tarsie pushed their hands away. "No. It's for grown-ups."

Which way were the men casting their votes—to outlaw liquor or to keep it? She wished she could go in and peek at the ballots. But of course she couldn't, so she cupped the backs of the children's heads and gave a little push. "Come along, now."

With chins low and lower lips poked out, they complied. Emmy cheered up, however, when Tarsie allowed her to select a card with six pink pearl buttons from the little drawer in the dry goods area. They cost one cent more than plain buttons, but Tarsie decided it was a small price to pay to see such a beaming smile on Emmy's face. However, when the children clamored for gumdrops, Tarsie remained firm in her refusal. Buttons were necessary to fasten Emmy's dress. Candy they could do without.

She stepped up to the counter and waited for the mercantile owner to finish whatever he was doing in the back room so she could pay for the purchase. The children leaned against her legs, pouting, but she ignored them. As she dug through her little coin purse, Emmy began yanking on her skirt again. Tarsie sent a stern look at the little girl. "Emmy, I said you cannot be having candy. Stop your pestering now."

But Emmy wasn't looking at the candy jars. Instead, she peered toward the mercantile's screen door, her eyes wide and an uncertain expression on her face. Bringing up one hand to shield her mouth, as if telling a secret, she whispered, "Tarsie? Papa's here."

※

Joss froze in the doorway of the store when he spotted Tarsie and the youngsters at the counter. The other vineyard workers who'd already gone through the voting tent waited near the wagon that would carry them all back to work—Mr. Tollison had arranged their transportation, thereby ascertaining they'd all have the chance to vote. But Joss had wanted to get out of the sun, so he'd ducked into the mercantile. He sure hadn't reckoned on encountering Tarsie.

Part of him wanted to back out—pretend like he hadn't seen her. But Emmy stared right at him, her blue eyes round and full of questions. Nathaniel leaned on Tarsie's skirts, halfway hiding, with one finger in his mouth. Sadness gripped Joss's heart. Simon's youngsters ran to their papa but his youngsters hung back.

He shifted his focus from the children to Tarsie and discovered the same apprehension pinching the children's faces shimmering in her green eyes, as well. The sight pierced him—pierced him deep—and he searched for some way to erase the sad unease from her countenance. He never would have imagined caring about how she felt. She was, after all, Mary's friend. Someone to look after his children. But she'd become more. Much more. And he didn't know what to do with the feelings boiling inside of him.

He lifted his foot to turn around and escape, but then Emmy spoke.

"Guess what, Papa? There's a mouse in our house."

Nathaniel popped his finger free of his mouth and nodded, his round eyes serious. "Mou-ouse." The word carried great meaning.

A burble of laughter formed in Joss's throat. "Th-that so?" He dared a glance at Tarsie. She stood, silent and somber-faced. He gulped. "Didja buy a trap?"

"We bought buttons," Emmy answered.

Joss looked at his daughter. "Buttons?"

"Tarsie made me a new dress. But I needed buttons." She twisted back and forth, making the skirt of her little yellow-flowered dress sway. "She lemme get pink pearl ones."

"Th-that's right nice of her." Joss wished he could quit stuttering. But he felt stupefied, standing with a good ten feet of planked boards between them and a thousand unsaid words floating in the air.

"Uh-huh. The neighbor traded Tarsie yard goods for doin' wash, an' Tarsie sewed me a dress an' some aprons 'stead of sewin' herself a dress." Emmy jabbered on, talkative as Joss had ever seen her. "She's gonna use my old dress to make Nathaniel a shirt. She said boys can wear blue gingham."

Joss swallowed a chortle. He'd've been mortified to wear a blue gingham shirt made over from somebody's dress when he was a boy, but he wouldn't say so. He was enjoying listening to his daughter. Why hadn't he ever realized how adorable she was? How could he have just handed something so precious to someone else? And how could he reverse it now?

Emmy pointed at Joss's chest, her little brow puckering up in concern. "You gots a button missing." Then she brightened. "But Tarsie can fix it for you." She swung her grin in Tarsie's direction. "Can'tcha, Tarsie?"

❁ 33 ❁

Tarsie drew upon every bit of self-control she possessed to remain at the counter rather than running across the floor to Joss. She didn't know what she'd do when she got to him. Pound her fists on his chest and wail? Fling her arms around him and cover his face with kisses? Neither would be acceptable. So she stood as still as a scarecrow on a windless day, heart thudding erratically in her chest and stomach whirling, while she listened to Emmy prattle on about everything and nothing.

Until the little girl turned the question on her.

Joss remained just inside the door, his handsome face aimed in her direction, his expression both sheepish and hopeful. He appeared to hold his breath, waiting for her reply to Emmy's innocent query.

Her tongue felt stuck to the roof of her mouth. She needed to answer. But what should she say? Pulling in a quick breath, she found her courage, unstuck her tongue, and blurted, "Sure I can fix it. There's buttons"—she flopped her hand in the direction of the dry goods corner, her gaze never wavering from Joss's—"over there. Find one that matches and then . . . then be bringin' me the shirt. Won't take but a minute or two to . . . to . . ."

Won't take but a minute or two . . . Her words echoed in

her head. How she wished his shirt bore a jagged tear or his pants had a hole in the knee. Something that took *time* to fix. Maybe if they had time together, they could repair the damage their budding relationship had suffered.

Joss shuffled in place, his eyes darting from Tarsie to the children and back again. "That'd be fine. I . . . I'd appreciate it." He pushed his hands inside his pockets but then pulled them out again to finger the place where a button should be. "Can I maybe come by this evening?"

Eagerness exploded through Tarsie's chest. "Sure. You can be . . ." The dryness plaguing her mouth made it difficult to form words. ". . . coming early in the evening. Eat with us."

He ducked his head, seeming to examine the scuffed toes of his boots. "Nah. I'll eat at Tollison's." He flicked a glance at her. "Seven? Seven-thirty? That be all right? Then I can be outta there before you tuck the young'uns into bed."

Disappointment sagged her shoulders. He didn't want more than a minute or two with her. She nodded silently, afraid of what might come out if she opened her mouth.

Joss looked over his shoulder, and he jolted. He edged backward, bumping the screen door open with his back pockets. "I gotta go. Wagon's leavin'. I'll—" His gaze fell on the children, and a tenderness crept across his hard features—"I'll see you tonight."

"Bye, Papa," Emmy and Nathaniel chorused, their voices matching their somber faces.

"Bye." Joss scurried out the door as if a grizzly bear were after him.

The mercantile owner bustled from the back room, swishing his hands together. "Thorry for makin' y'all wait. Dumped a bag o' beanth on the floor an' hadda thcoop 'em up."

Tarsie gave herself a mental reminder to wash well any beans she purchased in the future, then assured the man the wait was no trouble at all. But she told a fib. Seeing Joss had certainly been trouble. And tonight she'd see him again. To fix his shirt. Something a wife would do.

While she and the children walked home, she plotted what she would say to Joss. If she had only a few minutes with him, she needed to make every word count. She didn't want to rail at him in fury, but she needed answers. She needed to understand why he held his distance but saw to their needs. Did he care, or did he only feel guilty?

God, give me words, an' give me the courage to speak them plain.

Tarsie finished Emmy's dress that afternoon. The little girl insisted on wearing it right away, and although Tarsie preferred her to save the dress for Sunday, she couldn't refuse the child's sweet begging. But she insisted the children not play outdoors lest the dress be soiled. So Emmy sat at the table, humming happily in her new pink calico frock with its row of pink pearl buttons, and drew pictures on the edges of a catalog page with the stub of a pencil. Nathaniel, also content, played with blocks on the floor.

Tarsie went about her duties, the hours to evening stretching endlessly before her. Needing something to occupy herself, she decided to bake. She checked her supply shelf, and thanks to Joss's generosity in leaving money on the porch each Saturday, she discovered she had plenty of flour, sugar, and baking soda left in their bags. A swap earlier in the week with Ruth for butter and eggs gave her everything she needed to bake a cake.

She tapped her chin with one finger, thinking. Why not make it an extra-special cake? She could add walnuts harvested from a tree growing near the river, cinnamon and cloves, and maybe even some chopped dried apples. How wonderful a cake laden with spices and apples would smell. Wouldn't the aroma be welcoming for Joss when he came?

Suddenly, she dropped the little tin of cinnamon onto the

shelf and buried her face in her hands. A groan found its way from her throat, creating an ache as it escaped. She must stop thinking of ways to please Joss. He'd made his choice clear. He didn't want her. Didn't want his children. Somehow she had to forget a man named Joss Brubacher existed and find happiness without him.

Letting her hands slip away from her face, she straightened her shoulders and drew in a deep breath. *Mary, I'm so sorry, but I'm afraid I failed you. I can't love Joss for you. Not anymore. It's just too hard.*

❄

The cake was cooling on the windowsill, flavoring the air, by the time Mary's beautifully carved clock showed the hour as seven. Tarsie had hurried the children through supper, determined to have dishes washed and put away and the house in perfect order before Joss arrived. Emmy's mention of the mouse that had found its way in through a tiny hole in the north wall niggled in the back of her mind—she hoped Joss knew she checked their food supplies and beds for anything a mouse might leave behind before making use of any of it. A clean, tidy house would reassure him. She wouldn't have him thinking his wee ones weren't properly cared for.

Nathaniel, dressed in his nightshirt, came around the corner from the sleeping area. He crossed directly to the open window where the cake perched. He licked his lips and pointed, beseeching Tarsie with his eyes.

"What is it you're wantin', Nathaniel?" Tarsie prompted, even though she already knew.

Emmy bounced from the sleeping area, her hair free of the little braids Tarsie had fashioned earlier in the day. "He's wantin' cake. I want some, too."

Tarsie clicked her tongue on her teeth. "Emmy, darlin',

you've got to let Nathaniel use words himself instead of talking for him or he'll never learn to speak."

Emmy wrinkled her nose. "Can we have cake now?"

"When your father gets here," Tarsie said, her throat closing at the mention of Joss. She glanced at the clock. Five minutes past seven. Her heart hiccupped. This waiting was torturous!

At twenty after, she relented and sliced into the cake. The children climbed into their familiar spots on the benches and forked up moist bites, following each mouthful with a sip of milk from their cups. They each were digging in to a second—albeit smaller—piece when a tap at the door signaled Joss's arrival.

Tarsie felt strangely uncomfortable opening the door to him. He paid the rent for this house. His children resided under the roof. Yet he was a visitor. Everything felt backward. Especially the way her stomach turned a somersault at the sight of his tall form, standing just outside the door, the familiar wool cap in place over his hair. He had one hand behind his back, his feet widespread, giving him a very formal bearing.

"Good evening, Joss." Tarsie creaked the door a little wider. "W-won't you come in?"

He tipped sideways slightly and peeked past her to the table, where Emmy and Nathaniel paused in their eating to look back at him. Milk mustaches, spotted with crumbs, decorated their faces. Tarsie nearly moaned. She should have cleaned their faces before opening the door!

A grin twitched Joss's lips. "Got any more milk?"

Tarsie blinked twice. What kind of greeting was that? "Do you want a cup?"

His grin grew, and he pulled his lips back down with one finger, the other hand still hidden behind him. "I don't . . . but he might." And he brought his hand around. A small bundle of orange fur with pointy ears and white whiskers splaying out like dandelion tufts nestled in his large palm.

Emmy squealed, leaping from the bench. "A kitty!"

Tarsie stepped back as Joss went down on one knee and presented the kitten to Emmy. Emmy cradled it beneath her chin, laughing in delight, while Joss grinned at her.

"He's just a baby, but he'll grow fast," Joss said, his voice gruff, the way Tarsie remembered it, but gentleness showed in the fine lines around his eyes. "In no time at all he'll be able to take care of any mice that sneak into the house." He sent a quick look at Tarsie. And he winked. "Lots cuter than a trap, huh?"

Tarsie's face became a roaring inferno.

"Where'd ya get him, Papa?" Emmy nuzzled the kitten.

"Oh, there's lots of cats out at Tollison's. Pret' near fill the barn, so the boss said I could pick one out for you." Joss lifted his attention from the kitten to Tarsie, his expression sheepish. "That's why I'm late. Wanted to pick just the right one."

His eyes seemed to linger on a strand of hair falling alongside Tarsie's cheek. Embarrassed but unsure why, Tarsie anchored the strand behind her ear. His gaze followed her fingers, increasing her feeling of discomfiture.

"What's his name?" Emmy plunked the kitten on Joss's knee, where it hunkered, looking around the room with round green eyes.

Blessedly, Joss shifted his attention to his daughter and the cat. He rubbed the kitten's chin with his knuckle, and the little thing started up a loud purr. "He don't have one yet. I thought you'd wanna name him."

Emmy lifted the kitten again, holding it at arm's length and giving it a good look-over. "He's orangey-colored, so I think I'll call him . . . Marmalade." She gave a satisfied nod, tucking the kitten beneath her chin again. She beamed at Tarsie. "This is Marmalade, Tarsie. Papa brung him to us."

Then she turned slowly, sending an uncertain look at Joss. "Is he gonna stay here forever?"

Tarsie thought her heart might break in that moment. Mary's death and Joss's departure had shaken the little girl's base of security. As much as Tarsie had longed for this evening with Joss, she now wondered if she'd made a mistake, allowing him to come. Would his leaving again inflict an even deeper scar on Emmy's heart?

Joss ran his big hand over Emmy's hair. "You take good care of him, an' he won't want to go anyplace else."

I took good care of you, Joss Brubacher, and you still left. Tarsie held back the protest. She couldn't say such a thing in front of the children. Curling her hands over Emmy's small shoulders, she turned the child toward the center of the room. "Pour the rest of your milk into a bowl for Marmalade. I'll be fixin' him up a little pallet between your beds in a bit. But first I need to"— she swallowed—"take care of your papa's button."

Emmy skittered off to obey.

Joss finally stepped all the way in, pushing the door closed behind him. He swept his hat from his head and pressed it to his chest, sniffing the air. "You been baking?"

Tarsie nodded. "Spice cake. With walnuts and apples."

"Sounds good."

She dared examine his face. Not smiling exactly, but neither did he frown. He maintained a pleasant expression. A little apprehensive, yet open. He puzzled her. "Would you like a piece?"

A small smile tipped up the corners of his mouth, lifting the edges of his mustache. "I've never been one to turn down a sweet."

Flustered by his strange behavior, Tarsie waved both hands at the table. "Well then, sit." She dashed to the stove, where she'd left the cake on the smooth top, and carved out a good-sized square for him. When she carried it to the table, she discovered he'd taken his old spot next to Nathaniel. He sat with his arm around the boy's narrow shoulders, alternately smiling at his son, who busily tamped up crumbs with one finger, and at Emmy, who crouched on the floor next to Joss's booted foot and watched the kitten slurp its milk.

They looked so sweet—so *right*—there together that tears spurted into her eyes. She slid the plate and fork on the table, then backed away, unwilling to intrude upon the pleasant family scene.

Joss lifted his head and sent her a startled look. "Aren't you gonna sit, too?"

She wound her hands together. "I . . . I need to be fixin' that button for you." He still wore the shirt. More heat flooded her face. "Can you . . . give me your shirt?"

He grimaced. "I didn't get a button at the mercantile. I . . . I had to leave."

Yes, she remembered his abrupt departure. "I have buttons in my sewing box. I'll be finding something."

After a moment's pause, he shrugged out of the shirt. He wore a long-sleeved undershirt beneath, the ribbed sleeves pushed above his elbows in a bulky wad. Tarsie couldn't help noticing the bulge of his biceps as he handed the shirt to her. She clutched it and scurried to the trunk in the corner where she kept her sewing items. Her stomach fluttered worse than tree leaves in a stout breeze. Why'd the man have to be so attractive? It'd be easier to keep her distance if he were a homely man.

To her great surprise, she realized, on this evening at least, Joss's attractiveness went beneath his pleasing exterior. His kindness to the children, the way he smiled at them when they weren't even looking at him, the way he'd set his gaze on her with admiration and . . . something more . . . ignited a fire within Tarsie. This . . . *this* was the Joss she'd longed to see. Attentive. Tender. Giving.

But how long would it last?

That was a question she dared not explore for fear of being disappointed once again. She selected a spool of white thread and a needle, then dug through her little button box for one identical to those on the shirt. Although she couldn't locate an exact match, she found one similar in color and identical in size. It would do. But instead of sewing it in the second spot, where everyone would notice its difference, she snipped the button from near the tail, where it would be tucked into the waistband of Joss's trousers, and used it to replace the missing one. Then she sewed the mismatched button at the tail.

While she stitched, Joss ate his cake and the children played with the kitten. A delightful feeling of peacefulness coiled through Tarsie's middle. Joss had claimed he didn't know how to be a father, but right now, before her eyes, she watched him step into the role with ease. She heard his low voice instruct Nathaniel not to pull the kitten's tail—firm yet kind. She watched him stroke Emmy's tangled hair from her face. When Nathaniel bounced up and leaned his elbows on his father's knee, Joss leaned forward a bit—stiffly, but purposefully—and placed a kiss on the top of Nathaniel's blond curls.

Somehow in the past weeks, Joss had uncovered a hidden part of himself. And Tarsie witnessed the loving side of him unwrap right before her eyes. A lump filled her throat, a prayer of gratitude building in her heart. Joss *could* care for his children—he possessed the ability.

But he wouldn't as long as there was someone to do it for him.

By the time Tarsie nipped the thread from the second button, she knew what she must do. It wouldn't be easy. Her chest ached just thinking about it. But it would be best. For Emmy, for Nathaniel, and for Joss. And Mary would be so pleased.

Forcing her lips into what she hoped was a bright smile, she crossed the floor and offered the shirt to Joss. "There you are. Good as new. Well . . ." She giggled, the sound shrill. "Almost new."

Joss pushed up from the bench and shrugged into the shirt. Deftly, he fastened the buttons, leaving the tail out. He smoothed his hand down the placket, then sent Tarsie a lopsided grin that nearly melted her insides. "Thanks. It looks real fine." He drew in a big breath, his gaze wandering to the door. "Well, I guess I should—"

"Could you be staying a few more minutes?" Tarsie pressed her palms to her jumping stomach, certain her face must be blazing red. "I . . . I need to use the outhouse, and . . ." She gestured to the children.

Joss's eyebrows flew upward. "Oh! Yes. Sure." He sank back onto the bench, pink stealing across his whiskered cheeks. "Go ahead. I'll stay with 'em."

"Thank you, Joss." Her voice quavered, but he didn't seem to notice. He'd leaned forward with his elbow on his knee, tickling the kitten with his fingertip. The children giggled.

At the doorway, Tarsie peered back for one long moment, memorizing the sight of them. The dark-haired man and the blond-haired children, all playing together with a marmalade-colored cat. She smiled. *It's perfect, Lord—exactly what Mary always wanted.* And then she slipped out into the evening gloaming, knowing she'd never see them again.

❋ 34 ❋

Nathaniel yawned, his face stretching comically. Then he rubbed his eyes. "Tired . . ."

Joss glanced at the clock. Forty after eight? He'd lost track of time, playing with the kitten and listening to his children's chatter and laughter. "Let's put you down for some sleep." He scooped Nathaniel off the floor, giving him a little swoop that made him shriek.

Emmy bounced up, her hands reaching. "Me too! Swing me, Papa!"

Happiness danced in his chest, hearing the eagerness in her voice. He hitched Nathaniel onto one hip and ruffled Emmy's already bedraggled curls. "Lemme tuck this one in, then I'll getcha."

He stepped behind the dividing wall and blinked through the shadows. Three beds stood in a row, two smaller ones close together on the left, and a bigger one tucked against the wall on the right. Apparently Tarsie'd found someone— mostly likely Simon—to finish the beds. He felt torn between gratitude and guilt. He should've been the one to do it.

"Which one o' these is yours?" he asked Nathaniel. The little boy pointed, and Joss plopped him onto it, deliberately releasing him a few inches above the folded blankets that served as a mattress. He grinned at Nathaniel's giggles.

Then he spun and grabbed Emmy, who'd trailed behind him in impatience. She squealed in delight, nearly piercing his eardrums, but he laughed. A loud laugh. A real laugh. It felt good to let it come out.

He laid Emmy more gently onto her bed, figuring Emmy wouldn't want too much roughhousing. Simon didn't roughhouse with his little girl the way he did with the boys. Joss'd spent every evening since last Sunday with Simon's family, and he'd learned a lot about daddying just by watching. Simon was a good teacher.

Emmy wriggled into her bed. "I want Tarsie to come tell me good night."

"Tarsie," Nathaniel echoed.

"I'll send her in." Joss drew up their light covers, then brushed a kiss on each sweaty forehead, breathing in their scent. His children . . . his and Mary's. Tears stung behind his eyes as love for the towheaded pair swelled in his chest. He'd wasted an awful lot of time. And he had a lot to make up for. If only Tarsie would let him.

His pulse sped as he thought about everything he wanted to tell her. Starting with how he'd voted. Wouldn't she be happy to know he'd made his X in the box for prohibition? He'd seen the damage drinking could do. He'd seen it in himself, and he'd seen it in the people he loved. Nathaniel's bleeding foot and Tarsie's disappointment on top of Mary's sorrow had pretty much destroyed any desire he had to up-end a bottle. Oh, his flesh still wanted it—as Simon said: "The spirit, it's willin', but the flesh sho' be weak." He'd battle the urge in his flesh probably for the rest of his life. But if liquor wasn't easily available, it'd be a lot easier to let his spirit win out.

He whispered good night to Emmy and Nathaniel, then moved through the main room to the front door. Marmalade pranced at Joss's heels, batting at a loose thread dangling from the hem of his britches. He picked up the cat and tucked it in the crook of his arm as he went in search of Tarsie. A contented sigh heaved out. He appreciated how she'd left him alone with the youngsters so he'd have a little time with them. He'd sensed her eyes on him, watching as he played. But instead of watching with apprehension, like she was afraid he'd do something hurtful, she'd watched with approval. He'd *felt* it. And he wanted to thank her.

On the stoop, with Marmalade's whiskers tickling his hand, he called, "Tarsie?" Dusk had fallen, the blue sky fading to a washed-out grayish-purple, and long shadows covered the ground. He looked in every direction. Tarsie was nowhere to be seen. He raised his voice a bit and called again. "Tarsie?" He tipped his head, listening. A cricket chirped, and voices drifted from open windows of neighboring houses. But Tarsie didn't answer.

He stepped off the stoop and walked around the house, searching. He remembered how she'd looked inside in the lamplight. Shining hair—its reddish color a shade darker than the orangey-yellow of the cat—pulled up in a loose bun, a few spirals falling along her neck. She'd worn a familiar dress. Cream-colored with sprigs of green. The green matched her eyes. He'd always liked that dress. And the light color should be easy to spot even in the muted light.

He moved past the garden plot, where dark splotches marked the locations of plants in the earth. The outhouse stood well behind the garden, its door with the half-moon cutout pushed inward a good six inches. He stopped, frowning. She wouldn't be in there with the door unlatched. Where was she? Marmalade squirmed in his arm, but he held tight to the little animal and bellowed, "Tarsie?"

The kitten mewled and climbed his arm to his shoulder, where its claws dug into his neck. He waited for a few seconds, holding his breath, but when no answering call came he plucked the cat loose and headed for the house at a trot.

Worry created an unpleasant taste on the back of his tongue. Had something happened to her? He'd put Marmalade inside, grab a lantern, and start searching. But once he stepped inside again, he realized he couldn't traipse off looking for Tarsie. He couldn't leave Emmy and Nathaniel untended. And he didn't want to drag them all over the place in the dark.

Joss sank onto the closest bench. Marmalade wriggled loose of his grasp and dashed under the stove, where he peered out at Joss with round eyes. Joss rubbed his jaw, forcing himself to calm. Silly to worry. Tarsie was a grown woman, not a child. She was familiar with Drayton Valley. She'd probably gone for a walk or to visit a neighbor. How often did she get the chance for a few minutes to herself? He recalled Mary sometimes needing a little time alone.

Yes, surely she'd just taken a walk. Probably wandered farther than she'd intended with no children tagging along. And now, with it being dark, it was taking her a little longer to get back. But she'd be back.

Crossing to the stove, he checked the coffeepot. It was cold, but it contained a good two cups of liquid. He poured some into a cup from the shelf, plucked out a chunk of the cake with his fingers, then sat back at the table to wait. He took a nibble of the cake, watching crumbs bounce down his front. Cinnamon chased the unpleasant tang of worry from his tongue.

She'd be back soon. Sure she would.

※※

Tarsie moved along the uneven ground toward the little cluster of houses where Ruth and Simon lived. Away from town, the total darkness of the landscape with leafy tree branches creating a canopy overhead and the moon hiding behind a milky smudge of clouds made her shiver, even though the night was pleasant.

Twice she'd been startled by rustling in the brush, but both times it had proven to be small animals foraging. Even so, she worried she might encounter something larger than a raccoon, so she picked up her pace, determined to reach Ruth's place and safety.

Perhaps it had been foolhardy to simply walk away. It was certainly irresponsible, but underneath, she believed she'd done the right thing. Emmy and Nathaniel had already lost their mother. They needed their father. And, based on what she'd seen this evening, he needed them. She was just an outsider—Mary's friend, brought along to provide care as it was needed. Well, her services weren't needed any longer. So she would move on. And they'd be fine.

An owl hooted, and then a coyote howled. Tarsie hugged herself and continued walking. The little community of colored folks should be close. She'd left town behind nearly an hour ago. Although she'd never made this journey in the dark, she knew she had the correct roadway. The sweet song of Little Beaver Creek, which ran on the other side of the thick brush, accompanied her. It would guide her to Ruth.

The wide dirt pathway led uphill, and when she topped the rise she spotted the dark shapes of houses below. But no lights burned in any of the windows. Not even at Ruth and Simon's place. She moved slowly along the narrow, uneven pathway that wove between the houses. Should she tap on their door and awaken them? They wouldn't be angry. But they'd certainly have questions, and their talking might awaken others.

Then she remembered Ruth saying Simon's father had lived in the little house beside theirs. Ruth intended to turn it into a school when September rolled around. Tarsie stifled a giggle, recalling how Ruth had fussed, *"But befo' I can make it ready for teachin', Simon's gon' hafta move ever'thing out o' there. Ol' Zeke, he gots that place so cluttered up with stuff there ain't hardly room to turn aroun'!"*

As far as she knew, Simon still hadn't gotten around to clearing out the little house. So there'd be a bed available. She doubted Simon kept the house locked. She would spend the night in Ezekiel's house and talk to Ruth in the morning.

The decision made, she moved directly to the door. Dangling from a little hole was the string that would lift the crossbar on the other side. She gave the string a pull. Wood squeaked on the other side as the bar slid upward. But just as she cracked open the door, she heard the *click* of a shotgun hammer being cocked right behind her. Then a voice growled, "Who are you, an' what'choo think you's doin' sneakin' 'round here?"

※

Simon's knees wobbled as he pointed the barrel of Pappy's shotgun at the stranger. When Ruth had poked him and said she heard somebody wandering around outside, he'd thought she was dreaming. But a peek out the window revealed a ghostlike figure moving toward Pappy's house. So he fetched the gun and made it outside in time to see the person—a female, judging by the clothes—open Pappy's door. He didn't like the idea of pointing a gun at a woman, but nobody had any business in that house.

Bobbing the gun, he made his voice as snarly as he could and repeated his question. "I says, what'choo want 'round here?"

The woman turned very slowly, her hands held away from her body. "Please . . . don't shoot."

The slanted roof covering the warped porch on Pappy's house put her fully in shadow, but he knew that voice. He squinted through the inky night. "Miz Tarsie, that you?"

"Simon?"

He heard the relief in her tone. Letting the barrel of the gun drop so it pointed at the ground, he limped forward till his toes bumped the edge of Pappy's porch. "Girl, what'n tarnation're you doin' out here at this hour? I come pret' near to blastin' a hole through your middle!"

She moved to the very edge of the porch, letting a little moonlight touch her. She wrung her hands together. Her eyes looked bright—probably from unshed tears. He hated to have scared her so much, but she'd scared him, too. A black man never knew who might bring mischief to his doorstep.

"I need a place to be spending the night. I didn't want to disturb you and Ruth, so I just thought I'd sleep in your father's old house."

Simon scowled, befuddled. "But you got a nice place in town to stay." He looked around, his confusion mounting. "Where're the chillun? You di'n't leave Emmy an' Nathaniel all alone, did you?"

"Joss is with them."

Simon's jaw dropped. During their evening talks, Joss had 'fessed up about wishing he hadn't given his youngsters to Tarsie. Not that he thought she didn't take good care of them, but he missed them. It had heartened Simon to see Joss changing, bit by bit, as they talked about how God could help him become a pa who set a good example.

He whistled through his teeth. "My, my, my . . . I knew he was thinkin' on it, but I sho' di'n't figger he was ready to take 'em on already." Simon propped his hand on the weathered porch post. "But it don' seem right for Joss to send you out in the middle o' the night. Ain't safe, Miz Tarsie, for you to be out here. Tell you what, I'll hitch Ransom an' tote you back—"

"No!"

Simon jolted. This girl was plain wrought up. "Why not?"

"I can't be going back." She folded her arms across her stomach. "Please, can't I stay here tonight? I won't bother your pa's things. I promise."

Simon stared hard at her, trying to decide the best thing to do. If word got out he'd been talking to a white woman in the middle of the night and had put her up, it could cause a heap of trouble for him. But he couldn't very well refuse her. She couldn't spend the night wandering around the countryside.

He blew out a breath. "All right, all right. You head on in there. You, me, an' Ruth—we'll have us a talk in the mornin'. Early." Before any of his neighbors woke. "An' I'll be expectin' you to make more sense than you's makin' right now."

"Thank you, Simon." Her voice trembled.

Shaking his head, Simon turned and scuffed back to his house. He put the gun on its hooks, tiptoeing as best he could to avoid waking his slumbering family. The moment he crawled into bed, Ruth grabbed his nightshirt and gave it a pull.

"You was gone a long time, an' I heard voices. Ever'thing all right?"

Simon patted her hand. "Ever'thing's fine." Leastways, he hoped it would be. "Sleep now. I'll tell you all about it in the mornin'."

Ruth's grip loosened, and she snuggled into the pillow. Soon her steady breathing let him know she'd drifted back to sleep. But Simon laid wide awake, fear holding his eyelids open. He'd just offered shelter to a white woman.

Lawd, I'm countin' on You to protect me ovuh this.

❄ 35 ❄

Joss plopped lumps of cornmeal mush into three bowls. Even after sprinkling on a good pinch of brown sugar and splashing in the last little bit from the can of milk Tarsie'd left sitting on the windowsill, the food still looked unappetizing. But they'd have to eat it. He didn't have time to make anything else. Actually, he didn't know what else to make. Tarsie always did the cooking.

Another stab of worry pained his gut. Where was she?

He set the bowls on the table and slid in next to Nathaniel. The children sent sour looks at the bowls' contents. Before they could fuss, Joss said, "Hurry and eat now. I gotta get to work. No time to dawdle."

Emmy blinked at him. "But we gotta pray first."

Of course they'd want to pray. Mary'd always prayed, and Tarsie had, too. As many times as he'd listened, Joss ought to be able to speak the words, but it didn't seem right. He wasn't in good standing with God. The realization stung. "Well then, go ahead."

Without pause, Emmy bowed her head and folded her hands. "Thank You, God, for this food." She sneaked a peek in her bowl with one squinted eye. "An' please make it taste good. Amen."

"'Men," Nathaniel echoed.

The pair took up their spoons and dutifully dug into the lumpy mess. They made faces, but they ate without complaint, sending surreptitious glances at Joss between bites. Joss knew what they were wondering: *Why is Papa here and not Tarsie?*

He'd been shocked to find himself slumped over the table when fingers of dawn sneaked through the window and poked him awake. But the mighty crick in his neck confirmed he'd spent the entire night sitting on that hard bench with his head on his arms. A peek behind the dividing wall confirmed Tarsie hadn't come back at all. As soon as he'd tended to the children, he planned to send out a search party.

"Hurry now," he prompted again. After they'd finished eating, he'd get them dressed, hustle them to the sheriff's office, and report Tarsie as missing. Then he'd . . . what? He had to go to work. And he couldn't leave the youngsters alone. He nibbled his lower lip, wishing someone could give him some answers.

Then Joss remembered something Simon had told him. *"No matter what we's needin', God can provide. Thing is, Joss, we's sometimes just too all-fired stubborn to ask Him."* Joss paused with his spoon dipped in his bowl. *All-fired stubborn*—that description sure fit him. He carried his stubborn pride like a shield. And even though it was a heavy burden at times, he didn't know how to lay it down. Could God show him how to do even that? Holding his breath, Joss dared to let the question drift from his heart to the One Simon claimed always listened: *What'm I supposed to do with these young'uns today?*

Emmy pushed her bowl aside. A little dribble of milk formed a winding creek in the bottom. "Papa, can I give the rest to Marmalade?" The kitten still slept in the rumpled covers on Emmy's bed.

"Just set it on the floor there. He'll come get it when he's hungry."

Emmy climbed off the bench and crouched to place the bowl on the floor under the table. Then she tipped her face to Joss. "Papa? Where's Tarsie?"

Joss shook his head. "Not sure."

"She comin' back?" Emmy's voice quavered.

Joss forced a grin and tousled his daughter's hair. He needed to find a hairbrush and get rid of those tangles. "Sure she will." His confident tone belied his inner concern. "But I'm not sure when, so we gotta figure out where you an' Nathaniel are gonna go while I'm at work. Maybe Mrs. Bliss next door—"

Emmy made a face. "She don't like us. She shouts at us when we play in the yard."

Joss chewed the inside of his cheek. He wouldn't leave the youngsters with someone who wouldn't be kind to them. Maybe one of the other neighbors—would they be any more willing? Most of them had started turning up their noses when Tarsie began to teach Ruth.

Stretching to her feet, Emmy placed her hand on Joss's knee. "Can we go to Mrs. Ruth's?"

Why hadn't Joss thought of Simon's wife? The children knew her, and he trusted her. And while he was there, he could ask Simon and Ruth if Tarsie had contacted them. Was Emmy's suggestion of going to the Fosters God's way of answering Joss's question? His heart bumpity-bumped against his ribs. "Sure, honey. But you gotta get dressed. Help Nathaniel, too. Then I'll take you to Mrs. Ruth."

While the children dressed, Joss stacked the dirty bowls with the pan in the washbasin. He didn't have time to wash them if he was going to visit the sheriff before toting the children to the Foster place. His hands froze mid-task, awareness dawning. He planned to leave his children in the care of a colored woman. And the idea didn't sour his stomach.

When had he stopped looking at Simon and Ruth with

derision and started counting them as friends? A smile tugged at his lips as he considered how pleased Tarsie would be at the change that had taken place inside of him. Then the smile faded, gooseflesh erupting over his entire body. Why didn't he think how pleased Mary would be? When had Tarsie stepped into such an important spot in his life?

He had to find her.

Turning from the basin, he called, "Emmy, Nathaniel, hurry now—we gotta git!"

❀

"So you see, I had to leave." Tarsie kept her voice low to avoid disturbing the Foster children, who still slept in the corner. She gave Ruth and Simon her most emphatic look. "If I stayed, Joss'd never step into fully caring for his children. And those wee ones need him." A lump filled her throat. "They need him more than they need me. I'm just a . . . a person who cooks and cleans. He's their papa."

Ruth squeezed her hand. "You's a heap more'n a cook an' housekeeper, Tarsie, an' you knows it." She sighed, turning her dark-eyed gaze on Simon, who'd sat stern and silent all through Tarsie's explanation. "But she's right 'bout Joss. 'Less he has to, he won't start bein' a papa to those chillun. Gots so much fear built up inside o' him, 'cause o' the way his own daddy treated him. But with Tarsie away, he'll hafta do his duty."

Tarsie leaned in, hesitant hope rasping her voice. "So you'll help me? You won't tell Joss where I am?" If Joss found her and asked her to return, she'd go. Even as much as she believed she shouldn't, she'd do it for love of Mary and for love of the children. And—she forced herself to accept the truth—for love of Joss. But she'd be miserable. She could no longer live a farce. To protect herself, she had to stay away. Loving him and not being loved in return would eventually kill her spirit.

"I won't tell," Ruth vowed. She continued to look at Simon.

Simon drew in a slow breath. Deep lines formed furrows across his forehead. He spoke to Ruth as if Tarsie weren't sitting across the table. "You know how much trouble this's gon' bring down on us? You forget we's colored an' she's white? So far folks've only frowned at us fo' takin' up with Miz Tarsie. Knowin' she's teachin' you to read an' write, an' knowin' you'll be teachin' others, they's pret' much held their tongues. But this's goin' beyond learnin' from her. This is housin' her. Hidin' her. You think folks 'round here gon' keep silent on that? Nuh-uh, they's gon' speak right up. An' when they do, others'll get wind of it. An' trouble—*big* trouble, more'n we've ever known befo'—is gon' come marchin' right up to our door."

While he spoke, his low tone increased in intensity until the fine hairs on Tarsie's neck stood up. Although he didn't define the kind of trouble he expected, Tarsie could surmise. There were always those who viewed any person of color as inferior. Joss's attitude on the trail had rankled her, and his reaction—holding his distance, speaking with superiority when addressing their black co-travelers—was mild compared to stories she'd heard of white men's cruelty to colored men.

She pushed up from the table. "I can't be bringing trouble on you. I'll—"

"You's gon' stay put." Ruth's firm voice held Tarsie in place. She whirled on Simon, grabbing his hand and giving it a good tug. "All this time you been preachin' at Joss 'bout trustin' God. 'Bout lettin' God meet his needs. 'Bout believin' God can make changes in a man's natural inclinations. An' now you're sayin' God cain't change folks' inclination 'round here if'n they start to get riled?" She snorted, pushing his hand aside. "Shame on you, Simon Foster."

For a long moment, she sat glowering at her husband's low-slung head. Then she sighed and curled her hand around the back of his neck, her thumb gently caressing the spot below his ear. "I's sorry, Simon. You be a good man. I know you's only thinkin' o' yo' family right now—wantin' to protect us, an' I loves you for it. But this here's a chance to show yo' chillun what it means to stand firm an' do what's right, even when it might cost you somethin'. We cain't turn Tarsie away. It'd be the coward's way, an' no place in God's Book does it call us to be cowards."

Simon looked deep into his wife's face. Uncertainty showed in the set of his lips and his puckered brow. But slowly his expression softened. He plucked Ruth's hand from his neck and gave it a long squeeze. "Aw right then, woman . . ." A steely determination crept across his features. "Tarsie can stay in Pappy's house long as she needs to so's Joss'll go back to his place, where he belongs. An' we'll be prayin' God'll work ever'thing out to our good."

"An' His glory," Ruth added.

Simon gave a solemn nod.

Tarsie eased back into the chair. "I only intend to stay long enough to collect my few things. Then I'll be makin' my way elsewhere."

Ruth gawked at her. "Not all the way back to New York!"

A shudder rattled Tarsie's frame. "Never there." She forced a carefree shrug. "But there're many cities in Kansas where a woman can settle an' be makin' her own way. I'm handy with a needle an' thread. I won't go hungry." Her bravado faded a bit, thinking of being alone again. How she'd come to depend on Mary's family to provide companionship for her. Then she set her chin at a determined angle. "Just as Simon's been teachin' Joss, God will be meetin' my needs." For food, shelter . . . and companionship. She tossed her head. "I'll be fine. Just fine."

Joss kept one hand wrapped around Nathaniel's middle and the other on the reins. Emmy's small hands clutched his waist, her little knees snug against his hips. He'd nearly held his breath the entire distance from town to the little community of colored folks' shacks, afraid one of the youngsters would bounce off the horse's back before they reached their destination. Or that Marmalade would wiggle loose of Nathaniel's arms and disappear in the brush. But there was the group of houses ahead, and no mishaps involving children or kitties thus far. A thank-you hovered on his heart, and he came close to saying it out loud, surprising himself. Because he knew Who he wanted to thank.

As soon as he dropped off the youngsters with Ruth, he'd gallop on to Tollison's and tell the boss he wouldn't be able to work today. He'd best steer clear of the summer kitchen. The cook had gotten used to him seeing to morning chores—she'd be put out with him for spending the night away, but it couldn't be helped. He wouldn't have left his children untended.

A wave of protectiveness swept over him, his hand automatically tightening on Nathaniel's round belly while his elbow pressed down on Emmy's little hand. These kids came first. Then Tarsie. Then Tollison. He just hoped his boss would understand.

Black faces watched him warily, whispered voices reaching his ears, as he rode through the center of their little community. He bobbed his head in a silent hello to anyone who met his gaze, hoping his casual behavior would give them no cause for apprehension. He didn't want them taking out their fear on Emmy and Nathaniel when he wasn't looking.

The door to Ruth and Simon's place stood wide open, and Joss glimpsed the three Foster youngsters seated around the table. He drew the horse to a stop, then caught Emmy's arm and swung her to the ground. "Go fetch Miz Ruth," he said.

Nathaniel leaned to hop down when Emmy scampered into the house, but Joss held on to him. "Just wait a minute, son." Nathaniel leaned into Joss's arms and poked a finger in his mouth.

Moments later, Ruth followed Emmy into the morning sunlight. She peered up at Joss, her mouth set in an uneasy smile. "G'mornin'. Emmy here ask if she'n Nattie can spend the day."

"That's what I was hoping. Tarsie's . . ." He whisked a glance at Emmy's innocent face. He didn't want to worry her. "Not around today. An' I gotta . . ." He shook his head. He couldn't go into details with the youngsters listening in. "Can they stay with you? I . . . I don't know anybody else."

Ruth's gaze landed on the cat. "That thing stayin' too?"

Emmy gasped. "That's Marmalade! He's ours!"

Ruth *tsk-tsk*ed, but she reached for Nathaniel. The boy, cradling the kitten, slid into her arms. She set them both on the ground. Emmy immediately took Marmalade from Nathaniel, who set up a howl. "Here now, 'nough o' that," Ruth said. The boy quieted, and Ruth cast a smile across both children. "You'uns go on in. We's eatin' flapjacks. I'll fry you up some in a minute."

Emmy, with Marmalade dangling under one arm, caught Nathaniel's hand and the pair darted into Ruth's house without a backward glance at their papa.

The horse pranced in place, and Joss pulled back on the reins to settle the animal. "Thanks. Can't say for sure when I'll be back. Tarsie took off last night. I've told the sheriff and he said he'd look around town." Sheriff Bradley's lack of concern still irritated Joss. The man didn't care about Tarsie's well-being. Not the way Joss did. Somebody needed to hunt *hard*. Like it mattered. Hunt until they found her. And that's exactly what he intended to do. "I'll come fetch the young'uns quick as I can, but it might be after dark."

He waited for Ruth to ask why he thought Tarsie might've run off, but she didn't. Instead, an odd expression bloomed across her face. Joss couldn't be sure, but he thought she looked guilty. Apprehension gripped him. "Ruth?"

"Well, now, don't you worry none 'bout Emmy an' Nattie. I'll take right good care of 'em." Her promise chased away the niggling disquiet. She flapped her pink palms at him, backing up. "Go on about yo' business an' don't give us'ns a thought."

Joss decided that asking questions would only delay his leave-taking. He nodded, then dug in his heels, urging the horse into a trot. The sooner he reached Tollison's place, the sooner he could ask permission to take the day off so he could search for Tarsie.

What if he couldn't find her? Releasing a huff of aggravation, he pushed the errant thought aside. He *would* find her. He had to.

36

Tarsie watched out Old Zeke's dusty window until Joss rode away. By pressing her ear to a crack in the window frame, she'd managed to hear most of what'd been said. Ruth hadn't given away her hiding place, but Joss hadn't asked about her, either. Disappointment weighed heavily in her heart. Why hadn't he asked?

She gave herself a little shake. Isn't this what she'd wanted? For Joss to take responsibility for his children and not rely on her? So why did it hurt so much that he hadn't seemed interested in her whereabouts?

Before she left for good, she'd pen a letter to the children—something they could keep that would let them know how much she loved them. Her heart ached, thinking about leaving them forever, but she knew she was doing the right thing.

She waited until she was certain Joss was far enough away he wouldn't look back and catch a glimpse of her. Then she sneaked out the front door, inching her way around the far side of the house in case Emmy or Nathaniel looked out a window and spotted her. She needed her things from the house in town—her clothes, her sewing items, and her Bible. She had few belongings. Ruth's basket should hold them all. Once she'd collected her things, she'd head down the river toward White Cloud. The ferry could take her across to the

Missouri side. She'd surely find work in the big cities over there. And she'd still be close to Kansas and the people she loved.

Behind Old Zeke's house, she made a quick dash for the brush at the far edge of the property. And then, with a silent prayer for God to let her move swiftly, she took off at a brisk pace for town.

※※

Simon nodded as Mr. Tollison explained that Joss would be gone for the day. He'd suspected as much when he'd seen Joss come barreling in on that horse and jump up on the porch to pound on the door. His stomach whirled, wondering if Joss would seek him out and ask him about Tarsie, but after talking to their boss, he'd just swung himself up on the horse's back and taken off again.

"Get Stillman to take Joss's place in the vineyard today," Mr. Tollison finished. He pressed his hand to his chest and coughed. Long and hard.

Simon gazed at his boss in concern. The man's face turned bright red with all the coughing. "You all right, suh?"

Without answering, Mr. Tollison turned and made his way back to the house, bent forward as if drawing a breath pained him. Simon waited until his boss was safely inside, then went in search of Stillman. He whistled under his breath. Stillman wouldn't be happy to be pulled from his usual duties in the packing house to standing out in the sun, flicking bugs from leaves and checking for rotting fruit. But what Mr. Tollison said, Simon would do, for as long as he had this job.

As he'd suspected, Stillman crunched his face into a fierce scowl. "Why me? Why not Rouse or Maher or Russell? They ain't been here any longer'n I have."

Simon held out his hands, hoping to appease the aggravated worker. "I's just tellin' you what Mistuh Tollison tol' me. You gots trouble with it, you can go up to the house an' talk to him yo'self."

The man released a disgruntled snarl, but he yanked his straw hat low on his forehead and strode out of the packing house. Other workers watched him go, a murmur rolling through the wood building. Simon sealed his ears against the mutters—wasn't like he hadn't heard them before—and hitched his way back into the sunshine.

Simon went about his duties, the job so familiar he could perform the tasks in his sleep. He checked on the men in the vineyard, instructed Todd to watch the burn pile closely—things had dried out in the harsh heat of August and he didn't want any sparks igniting more than the snipped vines—and carted a few bushels of harvested grapes to the winery for pressing. The morning passed quickly, and he was startled when Cook clanged the noon bell, calling men in for dinner.

He drove his cart, careful to stay behind the workers who walked in from the field. Watching the men clomp along on two sturdy legs always raised a longing in his chest, but he'd learned long ago to be thankful for two good hands, a cart to tote him wherever he needed to go, and a boss who didn't hold his crippled leg against him. He might not have legs and feet that matched, but he had a lot for which to be thankful. He sent up a quick prayer of gratitude as he pulled his cart in next to the dinner barn and reached for his lunch bucket.

Just as his hand curled around the handle, someone behind him barked out one word: "Simon!"

Simon spun around, tipping his bucket and nearly losing his balance. Mr. Tollison strode toward him, fury contorting his face into a scowl. Simon scuttled to meet him, aware of the workers' eyes following him. Tollison grabbed Simon's arm. His boss had never been forceful with him before. Fear rose in Simon's belly, creating a bitter taste in his mouth.

"Yessuh? What is it?" Simon maintained a respectful tone

he hoped would calm the angry man, who held tight to his arm.

"Have you been in the back room today?"

He never entered the back room except on payday, to put away the cash box. "No, suh, I ain't."

Tollison's eyes narrowed. "Are you sure?"

Drawing a steadying breath, Simon posed his own question. "Have I evuh been known to lie to you, suh?"

At once, Tollison's fingers fell away from Simon's arm. He heaved a sigh. "Of course you haven't, Simon. I . . . I apologize for my behavior. But . . ." He peered toward the dinner barn's opening. Simon followed his gaze. A dozen men peered out, curiosity on their faces.

Catching Simon's sleeve again, he drew Simon to the porch of the big house, out of sight and hearing of the men. "Simon, I went to the back room to retrieve some larger bills to take to the bank and exchange to fill tomorrow's pay envelopes. I discovered someone had tampered with the lock on the door. When I opened the closet, I saw that the safe was gone."

Simon's legs went weak. He staggered to the side, catching the edge of the house with his hand to steady himself. "The whole safe? But that thing's gotta weigh . . . what? Two hunnerd pounds?"

"One fifty empty," Tollison confirmed. "I chose a lightweight Whitfield's safe to make it easier for me to transport."

Simon shook his head, reeling. "So somebody done stole away with yo' money?"

Tollison nodded, his expression hard. "Cook said Brubacher wasn't in the summer kitchen when she went in this morning. She said he left for town after supper last night, saying he had personal business to attend to. Do you know anything about it?"

Simon squinted at his boss. "You ain't thinkin' Joss Brubacher stole that safe."

"Did he know it was there?"

Simon chewed over his boss's inquiry. Joss had helped him put away the table that one time, watched him open the closet and the safe. Uncertainty wiggled through Simon's chest. Would Joss do such a thing? When he'd first come, he was all-fired eager to stash away cash money and skedaddle on out of Kansas. But over the past weeks, Simon had seen a change in the man. He couldn't believe Joss would steal from Mr. Tollison.

Still, he had to answer honestly. "He seen me open that closet an' put things away once. But—"

"So him needing today off after being gone all night seems very suspect. I'm riding into town and alerting the sheriff." Tollison held his chest, his breathing coming in short puffs. "Go tell Todd and Fenn to ready my buggy. I want the top up, and I'll want Fenn to drive me."

Simon hesitated. He wanted to tell his boss about Joss's queries about God. Surely it would alter Mr. Tollison's suspicions. But who else knew that safe was there? And Joss, he was a big man. A strong man. He could pick up that safe and carry it a good distance just in his arms. Simon hated himself for keeping silent, but he didn't know what to say.

"Go!" Tollison swung his hand toward the dinner barn, then broke into a fit of coughing.

Simon trotted off as quickly as his bum foot would allow, with his boss's wheezing breaths echoing in his ears.

✳

Late in the afternoon, hunger drove Joss to Drayton Valley and the little house he rented for Tarsie and the children. Sweaty, tired, and discouraged from his fruitless search, he needed to eat something. As soon as he'd filled his belly, he intended to set out again. He reined in the horse next to the house where it could munch grass, and he aimed his feet for the front door. But frantic cheeping captured his attention—the chickens. They needed to be fed and watered.

Groaning, he trotted around to the backyard. The bag of feed, now half empty, sat in the outhouse where he'd directed the man who delivered the chicks and the wire for their pen to leave it. He scooped out a tin cupful of feed and scattered it on the ground inside the pen. The half-grown chicks began pecking wildly. While they were occupied, he snagged their watering dish and filled it. With the chicks' needs met, he headed for the house.

He stepped inside and moved directly toward the shelf where the food stores were kept. But he came to a stop in the middle of the floor as an uneasy feeling gripped him. He turned a slow circle, examining the room by increments, and when his gaze fell on the washstand, a tingle attacked his scalp. The pan, bowls, and spoons he'd left stacked and dirty in the basin weren't there. He zinged his attention to the shelf. There they were, washed and put away. Tarsie had been here!

His heart thudding, he stumbled around the room, seeking other evidence. The trunk of clothing had been riffled through, and her dresses and other items of clothing were missing. Her sewing box and the pouch of medicinal cures she'd carried from New York were also gone. He spun toward the door and his gaze fell on a folded piece of paper, tacked to the doorjamb. He stumbled across the floor and yanked it loose. Hands trembling, he unfolded the paper and stared at the neat lines of flowing script. He scowled at the message. A full page of words, but his limited reading ability stymied him. However, he understood one of the words in the last line: *Good-bye.*

Holding the paper tight in his fingers, he crossed back to the trunk and sank down, defeated. Tarsie hadn't met with an accident or gotten lost. She'd chosen to go. He slapped the note onto the trunk beside him and placed his head in his hands. Regret and sadness claimed him. How would he tell Emmy and Nathaniel they'd lost yet another mother?

"She's gone and it's my fault. Again, it's my fault." He'd kept Mary from seeing a doctor who might have been able to cure her cancer. He'd held himself aloof from Tarsie. Lied to her. Taken advantage of her. She was as gone to him as Mary was. And he had no one to blame but himself.

Emptiness, all encompassing and dark, drove him from the trunk to his knees. He raised his face to the ceiling and groaned out in anguish, "My selfishness has cost so much. How do I change it, God? What do I do?"

In the far fringes of his mind, he recalled Tarsie's advice. *"When you let Him pluck out all that pain, Joss . . . it'll leave an opening for Him to slip in an' change you from the inside out."*

"God . . . God . . ." The name croaked out from a throat so tight it ached. "I'm broken. I'm nothing. But, please, help me . . ."

Simon's voice now eased through his memory, replacing Tarsie's gentle instruction. *"The good Lawd done come to this earth fo' one thing, Joss—to save us from ourselves. All we gots to do is tell Him we wants Him, an' Jesus, He washes all the ugliness away an' makes us clean as fresh-fallen snow in His eyes. Then ever'thing's new."*

Clasped hands held up like an offering, Joss begged, "I want You, Jesus. Fill me. Change me. Make me new."

Slowly, like a flower unfurling beneath the warmth of the morning sun, something within Joss opened and allowed the touch of God to whisper through his being. A tenderness moved from the top of his head and inched its way to the soles of his feet. His body trembled with its gentle force. Tears flooded his eyes and rolled down his cheeks in warm rivulets.

Eyes wide open and fixed on the beamed ceiling, he shook

his head in wonder as the long-held emptiness in his soul became a basin overflowing with a love so intense he could hardly bear it. He began to sob in joy, knowing no other way to respond to a fullness of rapture beyond understanding.

Still on his knees, he threw his hands wide. "Thank You, Lord! Thank You!" For long minutes, he continued to praise the God Mary, Tarsie, and Simon called Father. The same God he could now call Father. Then his prayer changed. "Dear God, I've made so many mistakes with Tarsie. I need to ask her forgiveness. But first, I have to find her. Will You please guide me to her? Give me a chance to fix things." Uncertain what else to say, he finished simply, "Amen."

He pulled himself onto the trunk, completely spent yet utterly filled. No longer hungry, he rose, prepared to go once more in search of Tarsie. Grabbing up her note, he folded it and jammed it into his pocket. As he turned toward the door, a fierce pounding came from the other side. His heart leaped in hope. Had she returned? He bounded to the door in two big strides and flung it wide. But instead of Tarsie, he found the scowling sheriff on the stoop.

The man grabbed Joss by the arm. "Brubacher, you need to come with me."

❋ 37 ❋

An unpleasant sight greeted Simon as he pulled his cart into the yard. Myrtle Mae Ulsh faced off with Ruth. Emmy and Nathaniel clung to Ruth's skirts, hiding their faces. He nearly groaned aloud. He'd feared something like this would happen if they kept those youngsters.

Simon limped up behind Ruth as she spouted, "Myrtle Mae, if I wasn't a good Christian, I'd poke you right in the nose for bein' so hateful. These two chillun ain't hurtin' a thing by bein' here. They's just young'uns. Cain't you have a li'l compassion?"

Naomi's wail carried from inside the house. The child was probably part scared, part jealous. She'd been fussy ever since Emmy and Nathaniel had come to stay, wanting her mama's attention to her own self. Truth be known, Simon was feeling the walls close in on him, too, having two extra ones underfoot at night, but what else could they do? With Tarsie heaven only knew where and Joss sitting in a jail cell, somebody had to keep track of those two little ones.

But those little white faces sure stuck out in the community. After seeing his neighbors' scowls at the pair of yellow-haired children sitting between him and Ruth on their bench at Sunday services yesterday, he'd suspected they'd get a visit soon.

Simon gave Ruth a little nudge. "Take 'em inside. I'll deal with Myrtle Mae."

With a *hmmph*, Ruth bustled the children into the house. That little orange cat they'd brought with them scampered along behind. Simon turned to Myrtle Mae, who'd been joined by a handful of neighbors. All of them glared in Simon's direction. *Lawd, I could sho' use Your help right about now.*

Myrtle Mae balled her fists on her beefy hips. "Simon Fostuh, you's gon' bring ruination down on all o' us if you don't get them chillun out o' yo' house."

Len Troxell moved in behind Myrtle Mae. "We's all worryin', Simon. It ain't that we's hardhearted—Lawd knows them young'uns cain't take care o' theirselves—but ain't there a white family in town who can take 'em in?"

The soft-spoken man with snow-white hair rarely complained about anything. To have him voice concern let Simon know how much the children's presence affected his neighbors. "Won't be long an' their pappy'll be back to get 'em." Simon spoke with confidence, but inside he wondered if he was telling a lie. Sheriff Bradley seemed convinced if he let Joss sit and stew long enough he'd finally confess where he'd hidden Mr. Tollison's safe. Joss kept claiming he didn't take it, but so far nobody'd been inclined to look in any other direction.

"Gon' be *too* long if folks in Drayton Valley get wind we's got white chillun out here." Myrtle Mae's comment rose an answering murmur of agreement. Fueled by their support, she leaned in like a rooster ready for battle. "We all kep' quiet when yo' wife took up with that white woman. 'I just learnin' to read,' she says. 'I gon' teach all o' yo' chillun to read, too,' she says. An' we all close our lips, thinkin' good's comin'. But now that white woman takes off an' leaves these

307

yellow-haired chillun on your doorstep. No amount o' readin' is worth the trouble it could bring."

The murmurs increased, more neighbors inching up to voice their thoughts on the situation. From the back of the crowd, Preacher Wolfley called out, "Lemme through here. Lemme through."

The people parted, allowing the man to work his way to the front.

Myrtle Mae whirled on the reverend. "You tell him to get those chillun out o' here, Preachuh. He won't listen to nobody else."

Preacher Wolfley put his arm around Myrtle Mae's shoulders and gave a pat. "Settle yourself down here, Myrtle Mae. Between your temper an' the blazin' hot temp'atures, you're gon' give yourself apoplexy."

A ripple of laughter rolled through the small crowd. The reverend faced Simon, and his expression turned serious. "Simon, I'm right proud of you for wantin' to take care of those little ones. Jesus Himself said whatsoever ye do to the least of these, you also do fo' Me."

The people crowded near began to hang their heads, some of them toeing the ground in embarrassment. All but Myrtle Mae, who stood beneath the reverend's arm as stiff and unsmiling as ever.

Preacher Wolfley went on. "But I do wonder at the wisdom of keepin' 'em." Myrtle Mae opened her mouth to speak, but the reverend gave her shoulder a pat, and she snapped her mouth closed. "They're white chillun. I know in God's eyes, chillun is chillun, but most folk don't bother to look through God's eyes. Times bein' what they are, it might be bettuh fo' those two young'uns—as well as fo' you an' yo' family—to give 'em over to a white family."

Myrtle Mae beamed in triumph. Some others nodded in agreement or said, "Uh-huh. Tha's right."

The reverend went on. "How 'bout this, Simon? I can go into town an' talk with one of the ministers there. Ask him to help us find a family willin' to provide for them two chillun. Then you'll know they's cared fo' by a good family. What you say?"

The crowd leaned in, all eyes pinned on Simon. It got so quiet he could hear a bee buzzing in the bushes nearby. Simon searched his heart for an appropriate response. It'd be mighty easy to pass off those children on someone else. They weren't his responsibility, and he had plenty of his own children already.

Lawd, what would You have me be doin'? He tipped his head, listening for a response. And he felt a smile building. He aimed it at the reverend.

"As ya'll know, my Ruth's been learnin' to read. Ever' night she practices her readin' by openin' up my pappy's Bible an' sharin' somethin' with us. Last night she read from the Book o' Mark. 'Member the story? Jesus' disciples, they was fussin' at folks fo' bringin' their chillun to Jesus an' askin' Him to bless 'em. But Jesus, He tells His disciples to let them chillun come. He said"—Simon lifted his head and spoke Jesus's words boldly—"'fo'bid them not.' So I says to you now, fo'bid them not. God done brung them chillun to my doorstep, an' I cain't tell the Lawd no."

The crowd mumbled, but nobody hurled angry words at Simon. Not even Myrtle Mae. One by one, they turned and ambled back to their own houses until only Simon and Preacher Wolfley remained.

The reverend put his bony hand on Simon's shoulder. "Simon, I ain't gonna fight you on this. You got to follow what God lays on you to be doin'." His fingers tightened. "But I'll be in prayer fo' you. Fo' all of us. Fo' protection. 'Cause I've sho' 'nough seen plenty of ugliness in my life. An' I don't want to see more of it brought right here."

Simon gritted his teeth as he bobbed his head in reply. He'd be praying, too.

※

Sunlight slanted through the small window above Joss's head, painting a gold square high on the opposite wall. He leaned against the rough rock wall, his heels caught on the edge of the lumpy cot that served as the only piece of furniture in the small cell tucked at the back of the sheriff's office. Elbows draped over his raised knees, he sighed. This town was so small it only had one cell . . . and he was moving into his fourth day of calling it home.

When would they finally believe he had nothing to do with the theft at Tollison's and let him go? He'd heard Simon out in the office twice, arguing on his behalf, but nobody wanted to listen to him. In years past, Joss would've discounted anything a black man said, too. The realization shamed him. What a fool he'd been to let himself make judgments based on the color of a man's skin. He'd never had a better friend than Simon Foster.

Despite Simon's fervent pleas, the sheriff had refused to let Simon see Joss. Then he'd chased Simon out of the office, claiming they had enough circumstantial evidence to hold Joss over for trial. Joss understood enough about prejudice to see why the sheriff wouldn't listen to Simon, but he didn't understand how they could call his spending the day away from work evidence that he'd stolen. He also didn't understand how Mr. Tollison could accuse him when Joss'd worked faithfully. Mostly, he didn't understand why God let this happen. He'd no more than handed God his life, and trouble descended. Was this how God showed love to His children?

He let his feet slide off the mattress, the thump of his bootheels on the rock floor sending a shock up his calves.

But the sting in his legs was mild compared to the ache in his heart. Flinging an accusing gaze upward, he said, "I asked You to let me find Tarsie. How'm I supposed to do that from in here?"

The iron door clanked and then swung open. The deputy stepped through, holding a tray with a tin cup of coffee and a plate with a red-checked napkin draped over it. "Breakfast." He flicked the napkin aside, revealing a mound of corned beef hash and two dry biscuits. The same thing he'd brought for every meal so far, morning, noon, and evening. Whoever cooked for the prisoners could learn a thing or two from the cook out at Tollison's. Or from Tarsie.

Joss's stomach clenched. "When'm I gonna get out of here?"

The deputy placed the tray on the edge of Joss's cot, then backed up. "Sheriff already told you. Not 'til the district judge makes his rounds out here and we can hold trial."

Joss lifted a rock-hard biscuit and tapped the edge of the plate with it. Crumbs broke off and danced across the tray. "When'll that be?"

"'Nother week. Maybe two."

Joss flung the biscuit onto the hash and leaped up. "I can't wait that long!"

The deputy darted out the door and gave it a slam. Holding to the bars with both fists, he peered in at Joss. "You got no choice."

Joss paced the length of the small space twice, growling under his breath. His prayers to God were going unheeded. He couldn't get out and find Tarsie himself . . . What else could he do? He whirled on the deputy, who remained holding tight to the bars as if prepared to use them as a weapon if need be. "Can I have visitors?"

The man shrugged. "Depends."

Sinking back onto the cot, Joss said, "Fetch a minister. An' make it quick."

❈

The rumble of wagon wheels captured Tarsie's attention and her heart gave a leap of hope. Her journey had taken longer than she'd expected after twisting her ankle on the first day. A good soaking in the river brought down the swelling, and wrapping it with the skirt from her apron allowed her to walk. Even so, an unceasing ache forced her to stop frequently and let the ankle rest. A ride would be a blessing.

She brushed at her skirt with her hands, scowling at the rumpled fabric and clinging bits of leaves. Without any kind of shelter, she'd slept beneath the trees, staving off her hunger with berries and watercress she found along the way. She must certainly appear bedraggled after her days of walking, but maybe the people in the wagon would take pity on her and let her ride the remaining distance. Poised at the side of the road, she watched as a pair of horses emerged from around the bend and clopped toward her. She raised one hand, waving as the wagon approached.

A rough-looking man with scraggly whiskers and a low-tugged, misshapen hat held the reins. Tarsie quickly lowered her hand, scuttling backward. Even so, the man drew the team to a stop and scowled down at her. Tarsie licked her lips, apprehension weaseling its way through her middle. She'd hoped for a farm family or perhaps a delivery wagon. She should have hidden in the bushes until she knew for sure who drove the wagon.

The man bounced a nervous glance up and down the road. "Hey there, girlie. What you doin' out here all alone?"

As she sought a suitable answer, a second man suddenly sat up in the wagon bed. Just as unkempt in appearance as the first one, his narrowed gaze swept over her and made her feel as though bugs crawled under her skin. She needed to escape quickly.

Swallowing the taste of fear that lingered in the back of her throat, she angled her chin high and assumed a bravado she didn't feel. "I was down by the river—gathering berries. My . . . my husband was to meet me. I thought you might be him." The lie didn't roll easily from her tongue. She hoped the Lord would forgive her. She also hoped the men believed her. "But I see you aren't. So I'll just—"

The man in the bed leaped out and darted at her. She released a cry of alarm as he snatched her basket of belongings from her arm. He held it aloft to the man on the wagon seat.

"She's lyin'. There ain't no berries in here, Lloyd."

Tarsie reached for the basket, which possessed all of her worldly goods. She couldn't allow this grubby man to take it from her. "Here, now! You'll be returnin' that to me right now!"

The man laughed, holding the basket well out of her reach. "Well, now, ain't you the feisty little thing!" Quick as a striking snake, he grabbed her arm. She fought against him, but he twisted her arm behind her. Tarsie bit down on her lip to keep from crying out in pain. He had her trapped. Swinging her basket with his other hand, he said, "What you want me to do with her, Lloyd?"

Lloyd tapped a dirty finger against his lips, frowning. "Now that she's seen us, we can't just leave her here."

Tarsie's mouth went dry. Who were these men? What would they do to her? *Oh, Lord, please help me!*

Lloyd patted the seat beside him. "Put her up here."

With a gleeful chortle, the man propelled her across the ground. Fear and her injured ankle made her clumsy, and she couldn't manage to climb aboard. The man behind her snorted. "C'mon, girlie. Get on up there." He planted his hand against her backside and gave a heave. Tarsie fell face-first into Lloyd, who caught her arm and helped her sit up. He kept his fingers wrapped around her upper arm, preventing her from jumping down again.

The other man plunked her basket into the back next to a mound of hay, then clambered in. He hung over the seat's back, grinning. "What we gonna do with her?" His gaze raked across Tarsie, raising memories of the hungry looks men on the streets of New York often cast at her. She knew what he wanted. She shivered.

Lloyd scowled at his buddy. "Sit yourself down, Coot, an' wipe that eager grin off your face. Folks in town see you pantin' like that, they'll wonder what's got you so all-fired het up."

The man named Coot set his lips in a deep frown. "Aw, c'mon, Lloyd, why can't we have a little fun with her? She sure is a purty thing. . . ." He toyed with a loose strand of tangled hair hanging alongside Tarsie's cheek. She gasped.

Lloyd released Tarsie's arm and clopped Coot on the side of his head. Coot's hat flew off, and he yelped in surprise. Lloyd pointed at him. "You know what happens to men who molest women. 'Member ol' Luther?"

Coot's eyes flew wide in horror.

Lloyd nodded, his expression grim. "You don't wanna end up like him. So get your mind offa stealin' pleasure from this girl an' remember what we got in that box. You'll be able to buy all the pleasurin' you want from women who don't mind sharin' soon enough."

With a maniacal chortle, Coot plunked down on his bottom, facing the back of the wagon.

Lloyd turned to Tarsie. "Now, don't you be worryin', girlie. Coot an' me, we're . . . on the run, but we ain't gonna hurt you—not so long as you do what I say."

"W-what are you wantin' me to do?"

"Just sit up here an' make like we're a man an' wife comin' to town for shoppin'."

Another cackle came from Coot.

Lloyd snapped down the reins, making the wagon jolt forward. Coot's feet flew in the air and he rolled onto his back, still laughing. Shaking his head, Lloyd apologized to Tarsie. "We gotta get through White Cloud to the Missouri side o' the river without nobody checkin' to see what we're carryin'. Lawmen'll be less likely to suspect a man an' wife. So you're gonna be our decoy."

"'Course, if'n you knew what we had, you might just wanna stick with us. Then you'd be rich, too!"

"Coot, you talk too much." Lloyd shot a glare into the back of the wagon, then looked at Tarsie again. "Chances are the law's already moved on. We been layin' low, bidin' our time to cross over to Missouri. But just in case, you're gonna be a good girl an' playact like we're just any other man an' wife goin' about our business. Understand?"

Tarsie glanced at Coot as he sat up, whirling around to pat the pile of hay. Some of the hay slipped, revealing a glimpse of something made of black iron. Tarsie squinted at the patch of black. "What is that?"

Lloyd barked, "Cover that thing, Coot!"

Coot snatched up a wadded quilt from near his feet and tossed it over the pile of hay. Using the mound as a pillow, he linked his hands on his chest and closed his eyes.

Tarsie turned forward, examining the stern set of Lloyd's whiskery jaw. Men on the run, hiding something from view. She'd fallen in with thieves! And they intended to use her to outsmart the law. She couldn't be a party to something illegal. Clutching her hands together in her lap, she searched her mind for a means of alerting the authorities to these men's unlawful activities.

Lloyd shifted on the seat. His unbuttoned jacket swung back, and she spotted the butt of a gun sticking out of his waistband.

Tarsie swallowed, her throat so dry it ached. Lloyd had protected her from Coot, making her believe he didn't want to harm her. But if she double-crossed him, would he seek revenge with that pistol?

❋ 38 ❋

"A ll right, girlie. Now just act natural," Lloyd hissed
through gritted teeth as he guided the team down the
middle of White Cloud's busy main street.

Tarsie searched the faces of people bustling here and there
on the boardwalk, praying someone—anyone!—might meet
her gaze so she could signal for help. But, caught up in their
own needs, no one so much as glanced at the wagon rolling
by. She held to the seat, her breath emerging in tiny puffs of
panic. What should she do? If she boarded that ferry and
accompanied these two ruffians to the Missouri side, they'd
have no further need of her. No matter what Lloyd had said,
what would keep him from doing away with her?

The wagon creaked along, passing places of business, and
a swinging sign caught Tarsie's attention: SHERIFF OFFICE.
Lloyd must have seen it, too, because he flicked the reins to
hurry the team. She only had one chance.

Gathering all her courage, she grasped the brake handle
and jammed it forward. The wheels groaned, the wagon
jolted, the horses reared up while nickering in protest, and
Lloyd grabbed at her hands. She held tight whimpering in
fright. He raised his fist, his snarling face only inches from
hers. "Girlie, whatcha think you're doin'?"

Ducking from his swinging hand, Tarsie let out a shriek

317

that brought half a dozen men running. Lloyd yanked out his gun. Coot bolted from the back and took off. Tarsie scrambled over the edge of the seat, crying out, "Help me! Help me!" A shot rang, shouts erupted, and fear claimed Tarsie. With one more whimpered plea for help, she fainted in the street.

✻

The minister—he'd introduced himself as Reverend Mann—sat on a straight-backed chair outside of Joss's cell with a Bible draped open over his knee. For nearly an hour, he and Joss had talked, and the man's patient response to each of Joss's questions calmed the frayed edges of Joss's heart. But Joss had one question left unanswered.

Cross-legged on the cold floor inside the cell, Joss curved his hands over his knees and met the minister's steady gaze. "Why am I in here? I didn't steal that safe. It's not fair to be locked up. If God can do anything, He could've kept me from being arrested. Why didn't He?"

Reverend Mann licked his finger and flicked a few pages in his Bible, then gave a nod in Joss's direction. "Listen to this. From the eighth chapter of Romans—'For we are saved by hope: but hope that is seen is not hope: for what a man seeth, why doth he yet hope for? But if we hope for that we see not, then do we with patience wait for it.'"

Joss scratched his head and released a rueful chuckle. "Those're real pretty words, Reverend, but I'm not sure what they're saying."

The man leaned forward, bringing his face very near the bars that separated them. "What I believe, Joss, is often God allows things to happen that are confusing to us to give us a chance to discover if we really trust Him or not. If we could understand everything, why would we need faith?"

Joss stared hard into the minister's face, letting his words soak in. "So you're saying my sitting in here is kind of a . . . a test? A way for God to find out if I trust Him or not?"

"Perhaps." Reverend Mann sat up, closing the Bible. "Or maybe He needs you here for some reason we don't yet understand." He smiled gently. "God's ways aren't our ways, Joss. Sometimes He uses unexpected means to bring about His will. But I do know this." He stretched his hand between the bars and placed it over Joss's shoulder. "Everything He does is out of love for us. It's to make us stronger or draw us closer to Him. Don't question His love, Joss. Trust Him. Will you do that?"

Joss let his head sag. "I'll try. But I gotta tell you, I'm going a little crazy in here, worrying about things. If they send me to prison, what'll happen to my young'uns?" He'd once wanted to send them to an orphanage. Now he feared that fate awaited them. His chest ached. God had to let him out so he could be a real father to Emmy and Nathaniel.

He bounced his face upward to look at the minister. "Would you ride out to the black settlement and check on my children? They're staying with Simon and Ruth Foster. Tell 'em . . ." He gulped, a fierce sting attacking the back of his nose. "Tell 'em I miss 'em and I'll be with 'em again as soon as I can."

Reverend Mann squeezed Joss's shoulder and pulled back. "Sure I will. Anything else you need?"

I need someone to read Tarsie's note for me. He pushed to his feet and reached for his pocket. But when he spoke, other words spilled out. "I need a good lawyer, I think."

The reverend rose, tucking his Bible into the crook of his arm. "I'll look into that for you." He stuck out his hand, and Joss shook it. "I'll be praying for you, Joss. You hold on to your faith now, you hear? God has a plan for you, and one day you'll look back at this time and understand why you had to sit here. I'll come see you again tomorrow, all right?"

Joss hoped he wouldn't be there tomorrow, but he said, "Sounds good." His fingers grasping the cool iron bars of the cell, he watched the minister leave.

❋

Tarsie sat next to Deputy Pierce on the seat of the wagon, her basket in her lap and the Whitfield's safe pressing against her leg. Behind her, in the wagon's bed, which resembled a large birdcage with its metal bars stretching up the sides and across the top, the two men who'd hauled her into their wagon as a decoy now slumped against the wall of the cage. She sensed their murderous glares on her back, but she refused to turn around and look at them. Such a sorry sight they were in their filthy clothes and darkly whiskered faces, their ankles circled by iron bands bearing thick chains that rattled with every bump in the road. The clanks, such eerie sounds, made Tarsie shiver, even though the midafternoon sun beamed down brightly.

She hadn't wanted to return to Drayton Valley, but the White Cloud sheriff insisted she'd be called upon to testify when the men went to trial. Since the theft took place in Drayton Valley, the trial would also take place there. So here she sat—after finding the courage to leave, she was being carted back.

Lloyd's and Coot's capture would set free the man they'd previously arrested for the theft of the safe. The sheriff in White Cloud indicated a worker from Tollison Vineyard had spent several days in jail already, apparently falsely accused. Tarsie imagined how eager the innocent man would be to escape a dreary cell. As much as it would pain her to see Joss, the children, and Ruth and Simon again—and then leave them again—at least she'd have the chance to do something good. She consoled herself with the knowledge as the wagon rolled steadily toward Drayton Valley.

When Deputy Pierce drew the wagon to a halt in front of the sheriff's office, a man with a silver badge on his chest approached from the Drayton Valley café, carrying a tray. He glanced into the back of the cage and grimaced. "Here already? Just got the wire a couple of hours ago about these fellas being apprehended. Didn't figure they'd arrive until tomorrow."

The driver wrapped the reins around the brake handle and hopped down. The keys on his belt rattled. "Sheriff Travers was eager to be shed of these two. Figured Mr. Tollison was eager to get his safe back, too."

"Reckon you're right about that," the man on the boardwalk said. He bobbed the tray. "Only thing is, I didn't get food for three prisoners." Then he grinned, shrugging. "'Course, if we're lettin' loose the one we already got, we won't have to feed him, so these two can share his meal. C'mon in."

Deputy Pierce assisted Tarsie to the ground. The arrival of the caged wagon attracted attention, and a small crowd began to gather in the street. The deputy ignored the onlookers and escorted Tarsie into the office, leaving the two men to be gawked at like a pair of circus animals. Despite the scare they'd given her—as well as their illicit activity—Tarsie experienced a pang of sympathy for them.

"Sheriff Bradley?" Deputy Pierce stuck out his hand to the man who rose from behind a large wood desk in the corner of the office.

"That's right." The two shook hands, their faces solemn. Then Sheriff Bradley's gaze flicked to Tarsie. "Is this the young woman who notified the sheriff?"

Deputy Pierce nodded, urging Tarsie forward. "Yes, sir. Sheriff Travers took down her statement in White Cloud." He withdrew several crumpled papers from his shirt pocket and placed them on the desk, then gave Tarsie an approving look. "Wish I had a medal to give her. Took a lot of courage, hollering like a banshee. One of the fellas started shooting—injured one of our deputies." He blew out a breath, shaking his head. "But if those men had made it to Missouri, we might've never found Tollison's safe. We owe this little lady a mighty debt of gratitude."

Sheriff Bradley raised one brow and looked Tarsie up and down. She wanted to hide, knowing how unkempt she appeared—no better than the two thieves in the wagon outside. But she forced herself to stand square-shouldered and unashamed as he reached for the papers and unfolded them. Scowling, he perused the written account she'd given the sheriff in White Cloud, his lips moving silently as he read. Suddenly his startled gaze bounced to meet hers. "You're Tarsie Raines?"

Surprised by the vehemence in his voice, she offered a weak nod.

"Tarsie Raines was reported missing five days ago."

Tarsie drew back, an odd feeling creeping through her middle. "B-by whom?"

The sheriff rustled through a disorganized stack of pages on his desk. "Joss Brubacher."

Hope rose in Tarsie's chest. Joss had reported her missing? Then he'd at least been concerned about her. Could it possibly mean . . . ? As quickly as it had risen, the elation crumbled. No doubt he only wanted her to care for the children so he wouldn't have to. She hung her head, battling tears.

Sheriff Bradley read the paper, underlining words with his finger. "Said you went out the night before and didn't return. He came in here demanding we start a search."

Tarsie swallowed. "I'm sorry to have caused trouble. I . . . I just intended to . . . move on."

Slapping the pages onto the desk, the lawman grunted. "We thought he made it all up to get us all scouting for you so he could make his escape while everyone was focused elsewhere."

Tarsie lifted her head, confused. "His escape?"

The sheriff snagged a silver loop holding a brass key from a peg on the wall and marched toward a door on the back wall of the office. "Guess he was telling us the truth all along. And it's time we let him out."

Realization exploded through her mind. She rocked in place, desire to see Joss battling with the despair of another parting. Desire won. She darted after the sheriff, wincing at the ache in her foot, her heart pattering three beats for every step she took.

Behind a wall of bars, Joss sat on a little cot with his elbows on his knees. He rose when the sheriff charged through the doorway, resignation sagging his features. Then his gaze shifted to her, and his jaw dropped. He dashed forward, grabbing the bars. "Tarsie?"

The sheriff jammed his thumb in Tarsie's direction. "Guess it's a good thing she took off. She stumbled upon two men with Tollison's safe in tow. That means you're free to leave . . . with our apologies, of course." He unlocked the door and stepped back.

But Joss didn't move. He stood inside the cell, wide eyes pinned to Tarsie's face. He seemed to have aged in the past few days, thick whiskers dotting his cheeks and chin, new lines of worry etched across his brow. But the scowl she'd come to expect didn't appear. Instead, a sheen of tears brightened his eyes. He swallowed, his Adam's apple bobbing in his throat.

Sheriff Bradley balled one fist on his hip. "You comin' out of there, or you want to stay with the two hooligans we've got waiting in the wagon?"

Finally Joss moved. Not toward the door—not toward freedom—but toward Tarsie. Slowly. Deliberately. Each footfall echoing in the rock room. Tarsie sucked in her breath and held it, watching Joss's slow approach. His eyes roved her face, and heat rose in her cheeks as she remembered her tousled hair littered with bits of dry leaves. She lifted one hand to smooth the stray wisps, but he took one giant step forward and captured her wrist. He held it, his fingers smooth and warm, while she wondered if he counted her pulse beats.

He gave a gentle pull, and her stiff body stumbled forward in response, her chin colliding with his firm chest. His arm snaked around her middle, sealing her in place, and the hand holding her wrist rose, propping it on his shoulder. Then he buried his face in the curve of her neck and clung, his hands curving her spine to fit her frame snugly against his arched body.

Tarsie's breath whooshed out. Her hands coiled around his neck, clinging, and she turned her face to his cheek. His sharp whiskers pricked her skin, but what did she care? Could a few pricks distract from the wonder of being held in Joss's arms? She was disheveled, sweaty, with days of grime caking her skin . . . and still he held her. Held her the way a dying man held to life. The way a lover held his beloved. Her fingers tightened on his taut neck, glory filling her so completely tears spurted.

A clearing throat intruded. "You two'll have to scat." The sheriff's droll command broke through the sweet moment of reckoning. "I need to bring the prisoners in."

Joss released her by increments, his fingers sliding from her spine to her waist and then away. A shiver shook her frame as he took a backward step, putting a good two feet of distance between them. He ran a hand through his hair, his gaze darting around the room as if uncertain where to land.

Tarsie clutched her fingers together, watching him. Would he touch her again? Place his hand upon her back and escort her from the jail? She waited, yearning and hopeful, and his hand lifted. Her heart skipped a beat.

The old Joss—the distant Joss—returned in the blink of an eye. He gestured to the open doorway. "Let's go, then."

Fresh tears gathered in Tarsie's eyes. Tears of disappointment. Whatever had compelled him to draw her close had slipped away. Defeated, she hugged herself and scuffed out the door, her shattered heart aching within her chest.

❄ 39 ❄

Joss followed Tarsie through the sheriff's office, careful to
keep several inches of distance between them. What had
he been thinking to grab hold of her that way? Varying emotions—relief that she was safe, gratitude to God for answering
his prayer, appreciation at being released—had propelled him
forward. But he shouldn't have embraced her. It was selfish
of him to seek comfort in her arms, and he'd determined to
give up selfish actions. From now on, he'd keep his hands to
himself.

They stepped onto the boardwalk, and Joss drew in several
lungfuls of air. After breathing the stale air of the jail cell, the
hot Kansas wind tasted wonderful. He might sleep outside
tonight, just to enjoy the openness afforded by that vast sky.
But first, he needed to go see his children. They'd be thrilled
to have him and Tarsie back again.

Tarsie moved stiffly to the wagon and reached for the woven
basket Ruth had crafted for her. Joss darted forward and
snatched it off the seat. His gaze connected with the two men
in the wagon who waited under the evening sun for someone
to release them. To his surprise, a tiny coil of compassion
wiggled through him at the sight of their grim faces framed
by iron bars. They'd done him a mighty disservice, stealing
that safe, but he knew how it felt to be locked up. He wouldn't

wish it on anybody. Did that mean God was already softening him, the way the preacher'd said would happen? Oddly, he didn't mind the idea of being a little tender. The compassion sat comfortably within his chest.

Tarsie reached for the basket. "I'll be takin' that now."

Her sweet Irish lilt carried a hint of sadness. Joss wanted to cup her cheek with his palm and ask why she looked so bereft. Common sense claimed his fingers, and he slipped his hands into his trouser pockets. "Now that I'm free"—what a wonderful word!—"I need to ride out to Simon's and fetch the young'uns. Will you meet me at the house?"

She stared at him, alarm widening her eyes. "W-why?"

For a moment, aggravation captured him. Didn't she realize she owed the children a proper good-bye? He started to tell her so, but something held his tongue. Reverend Mann had told him to ask God to give him words when his own failed, so he sent up a silent plea for help.

"Because Emmy an' Nathaniel'll want to see you." He sounded gruff. He swallowed and tried again, more kindly. "Don't you want to see them?"

Longing broke across her face. She ducked her head. "For sure I'm wantin' to see them. They're . . . they're so very dear to me."

"Then go to the house. I'll bring 'em to you."

Sheriff Bradley and Deputy Pierce charged out of the office, forcing Joss and Tarsie to step aside. Joss had no desire to see the men with their chained ankles paraded past. He took several shuffling steps toward the livery. "Meet us there, Tarsie." Then he paused, his heart pattering. "Please?"

※

The gently worded entreaty—*"Please?"*—proved to be Tarsie's undoing. She could resist a harsh, demanding Joss. But this tender, pleading one? She surrendered.

"I'll be there when you bring the wee ones."

A smile burst across his face, and he turned and trotted off.

A crowd had gathered to stare at the prisoners, so Tarsie crossed to the opposite side of the street before aiming herself toward the little house that had been her home for the past months. The closer she got, the more anticipation built within. How could she have left this place? The dirt street beneath her feet, the flower-dotted yards, the towering trees, the gently rolling hills leading to the river—she loved every inch of this town.

She waved at neighbors as she passed, noting their bobbing heads or waves in reply. Although she hadn't formed close friendship with any of them yet, she still discovered a sense of belonging as she passed their yards, recalling moments of fellowship that now held a sweet essence in her memories. Coming back to the familiar house, with its Joss-made table and benches and simple self-sewn curtains in the window, elated her. She didn't want to leave again.

But she would. To preserve what was left of her tattered heart, she would go.

When she reached the house, she headed for the well and drew a bucket of water for a much-needed wash. But once inside, she stood unmoving in the middle of the room, simply absorbing. Remembering. Reliving. She allowed herself several minutes of reflection before she carried the bucket behind the dividing wall—letting her palm drift down the length of rough wood as she passed—and discarded her filthy dress. The cold water refreshed her, and she even dipped her hair, relishing the feel of droplets trailing down her back from her soaked tresses.

Her wet hair hanging loose and a clean dress in place, she returned to the main room and started a fire in the stove. Neither she nor Joss had eaten supper. She could prepare something. And after they'd eaten, she'd say her good-byes and take her things to the hotel on Main Street to await the trial. A knot of sorrow filled her throat. *Strength, Lord.*

Joss arrived with the children just as she removed a pan of corn bread from the oven. The aroma filled the room, increasing the feeling of *home.* Tears stung when the children charged across the floor to her, their voices chorusing her name. She dropped to her knees and held them tight to her breast, kissing first one tousled head and then the other again and again until they finally pulled loose.

Emmy wadded her fists on her hips. "You left us. You went away." Hurt mingled with accusation in her tone.

Nathaniel cupped Tarsie's face between his little hands and gave her a stern look. "Tarsie no go 'way. Yes?"

Tarsie looked over Nathaniel's head to Joss, who stood with Marmalade lying upside down on his arm as Joss stroked his stomach. If the children's father voiced the same request, she'd agree. She waited, hoping.

He cleared his throat, setting the cat on the floor. "You can't go."

She listened, ready to leap into his arms.

"Not 'til after the trial."

She struggled to her feet and turned her back on him. Once again he needed her. He'd needed her to care for his children. He'd needed her to keep his house. Now he needed her to clear his name. But he didn't need *her.* He only needed what she could do for him. It would never be enough.

Moving to the stove, she lifted a knife to cut the corn bread into wedges. "Yes, I have to testify. And when the trial is over . . ." A sob found its way from her throat. She pressed her fist to her lips, holding back any others that might try to escape.

Hands descended on her shoulders. Strong hands that turned her around. Fingers gripped her trembling chin, lifting her face. Joss gazed down at her. He spoke, his deep voice growly yet somehow tender. "When the trial is over . . . what then?"

She stared into the face of the man she'd grown to love. There was something different about him. The same dark hair fell across his forehead in unruly waves. The same mustache slashed across his upper lip. The same dark eyes peered at her from beneath heavy brows. But a flicker of something new—something wholly appealing—also existed. She wished she could recognize it.

"And then I must go."

"But why?"

Once again, his tenderness took her by surprise. If only the demanding Joss would return, she could remain firm. But the kindness she'd seen bestowed on the children was now aimed at her, and she was defenseless against it. Tears stung her eyes. She pulled away from his gentle grip.

"The corn bread's getting cold." She scooped a wedge onto a tin plate and handed it to him.

He took the plate but didn't step away. Rooted in place, he gazed at her, his expression unreadable. She busied herself carving out a wedge of the mealy yellow bread for herself, pretending not to notice his scrutiny but nearly dying beneath it.

Finally he sighed. "All right, Tarsie. We'll eat." He started to step away, but then he leaned in, his breath caressing her ear. "By the way, you're beautiful with your hair down."

Tarsie sat at the table with a plate in front of her, but she couldn't eat a bite. Joss's sweet words filled her so completely, she didn't have room for anything else. What had come over him? Part of her wanted to ask, and part of her was afraid of the answer. So she picked at her food, chopping the wedge into pieces without carrying a bite to her mouth.

Joss ate three pieces, however, and when he finished he washed the dishes and put them away, encouraging Tarsie to spend time with the children instead. She read them their favorite storybooks and then tucked them into their beds. When she returned to the main room, she carried her basket with her.

Joss rose from the table and glanced at the basket, a frown creasing his brow. "Where are you going?"

"I can't stay here." Tarsie injected defensiveness in her tone. She had to protect herself somehow. "We aren't married. It isn't appropriate."

He bowed his head. "I know. I'm sorry I lied to you. It was wrong of me."

She nodded. "Yes, it was. It was hurtful, Joss."

He met her gaze. "God's forgiven me for lying to you."

She gasped, the importance of his statement smacking with such force her knees buckled.

His gaze never wavered, his eyes smoldering. "Will you forgive me?"

Stunned by his proclamation of finding forgiveness from God, she couldn't answer. Joss remained on the other side of the table, but he might have been inches in front of her. Her skin tingled with awareness.

"When I realized you'd left—that I'd run you off—I did some deep thinking. I knew I had to change before I lost everyone I cared about. So I asked God to help me, and . . . He answered, Tarsie. He met me, right here."

He pointed to a spot on the floor near the trunk, and tears shimmered in his eyes. He stared at the spot for long moments, as if reliving something precious, and then he looked at her again. "I wanted to go find you and bring you back, but I got arrested. They stuck me in that cell and I couldn't go after you." A grin tugged his lips. "But guess what? God didn't want me to find you. He knew where you'd be, and what you'd hear, and that your testimony would set me free. So He let me wait and see how He had things worked out. It was a good lesson."

Tarsie wished she could speak, but she'd gone mute. This was Joss speaking of God? Joss proclaiming he wanted to change? And what might he say next?

"When I picked up the young'uns from Simon's, he told me Tollison said the vote had come in. Prohibition passed. So the vineyard'll be closing—or at least they'll be getting rid of most of the workers." Joss heaved a sigh. "It worries me, but I'm gonna try trusting instead of worrying. God fixed things for me to get out of that jail cell. I reckon that means He can fix things for us men who've been earning our keep at Tollison's to find another way to make a living." He paused, tipping his head boyishly. "Right?"

Tarsie found her voice. "R-right." Then she fell silent again, her mind moving backward through everything he'd said. He'd indicated he cared for her. He'd bemoaned losing her. He questioned where she would go next. But the thing she most needed to hear remained unspoken. He hadn't asked her to stay.

She turned toward the door, her heart heavy. "I better go now."

He dashed around the table, his hand extended but not touching her. "No. You stay here tonight. I'll walk to the livery, bed down there." A teasing smile curved his lips and brightened his eyes. "You've done enough wandering the hillsides for a while."

"But—"

"Tarsie, please. Stay with the young'uns. You have to stay somewhere until the trial's over. Why not here? I'll stay out of the way so there's no question about propriety. Stay . . . please?"

He'd finally asked, but not for himself. For the children. Even so, when he asked so sweetly, she had no ability to refuse. She gave a weak nod.

"Thank you." He moved to the door and grabbed the

crosshatch. Then he looked back at her, his expression con-
trite. "And, Tarsie? About me grabbing on to you like I did
in the jail . . ."

Heat rushed to her face. She gulped.

"I shouldn't have done that. I was just . . . so relieved." He
drew a deep breath, his chest expanding with the indrawn
air. "You don't need to worry. It won't happen again." He
slipped out the door.

Tarsie held to the door's edge, staring after his tall form
moving down the hill. What would he do if she told him her
greatest fear was that he'd never hold her again?

❋ 40 ❋

The circuit judge wired that he'd be in Drayton Valley the second Friday in September to preside over the trial of the two accused thieves. With no courthouse, court would be held in the community church. Simon drove his boss to town for the trial. Mr. Tollison usually had Thurman Fenn drive him, but he'd said he needed to talk to Simon and the drive would give them privacy. Simon, never one to disregard an instruction, readied the buggy and pulled up in front of the big house to retrieve his boss.

Instead of climbing into the back of the four-seat buggy, the way he usually did, Mr. Tollison sat next to Simon on the driver's seat. Dust from the horses' hooves flew in their faces as Simon headed down the lane, and Mr. Tollison held a white handkerchief over his nose.

Simon cast a worried glance at his boss. "You sho' you don't wanna get in the back? Less dusty back there."

Mr. Tollison shook his head, coughing a bit behind the hankie. "If I sit back there, I'll need to raise my voice to be heard, and yelling is harder on my lungs than breathing a little dust."

Simon pulled the reins, slowing the big pair of roans. Maybe a slower pace would mean less dust. "You do lots o' coughin'." He hoped he hadn't insulted the man, but he cared. "You seen a doctor 'bout that?"

Mr. Tollison chuckled, bringing on another bout of coughing. "I've seen several doctors, Simon, and they all tell me the same thing: I need to live in a dry, warm climate. So far I've managed to survive Kansas by using more onion poultices than I can count, but with that vote . . ."

Sorrow weighted Simon's shoulders. He'd known Mr. Tollison his whole life. He'd never heard the man sound defeated. But he did now. "Gon' hafta shut things down, ain'tcha?"

"I am."

They rolled on in silence for several minutes. Simon wiggled his nose against droplets of sweat that rolled from his forehead while the horses *clip-clopped* a steady beat.

Finally Mr. Tollison shifted in the seat to half face Simon. "I don't want to leave you and your people without a means of providing for yourselves. My father brought you here. I won't sell the land out from under you. I've already drawn up papers to make sure the property where your houses are built transfers to your names."

Simon heaved a sigh of relief. He admitted to some worry about what might happen. "That's right good o' you, suh."

"And I intend to sign over the orchards to you, Simon."

Simon jerked, yanking the reins. The horses neighed in protest. He chirped to them, giving them an apology, then gawked at his boss. "Sign ovuh? You mean so's I be ownin' all them trees an' such?"

"That's right."

"But . . . but . . ." Simon shook his head, unable to conceive what he was hearing.

"I know it's a huge responsibility," Mr. Tollison went on, his voice muffled by the protective square of white. "But you know how to operate the orchard. The grapes will be plowed under—the governor's edict stipulated that had to happen before the year's end—but there's no reason to destroy the apple, peach, or pecan trees. More than half of my income has come from the wine. A fine income, allowing me to live well and set a goodly portion of money aside. I have enough that I don't need to sell the orchards, and the trees will continue to provide an income for you, your family, and your friends."

Simon marveled at the man's generosity. He bit down on his lip for a moment, but he had to ask a question. "What about the white men workin' fo' you? You gon' provide for them, too?"

Mr. Tollison chuckled. "Well, Simon, that's up to you. The orchard will be yours. I imagine a few of them won't be interested—"

Simon could surmise which ones.

"—but you can hire whomever you'd like to work with you."

Simon knew who he'd ask first. "I don't rightly know what to say, Mistuh Tollison."

"Say you'll take care of the trees. My grandfather planted them, and my father tended them. He meant them to be my inheritance. But this foul consumption . . ." He coughed again, long and hard. When he finished, his face was white and his breath wheezed. "Prohibition is a blessing in disguise, Simon. I would never have left the place if I wasn't forced to. Maybe my health will improve once I've left Kansas."

"Me an' Ruth'll sho' be prayin' fo' that, suh. An' me an' mine, we'll take special good care o' them trees fo' you an' yo' pappy."

Mr. Tollison laid his hand on Simon's shoulder. "I know you will, Simon. I know you will." He shifted in the seat, facing ahead. "Now let's hurry this team. I want to see those two men who wreaked such havoc brought to justice."

When Tarsie finished testifying about what she'd experienced, she left the church. Joss, Emmy, and Nathaniel sat out on the steps, waiting for her. Joss rose when she emerged.

"It's over already?"

"Just my part."

"You don't want to stay . . . hear the verdict?"

Tarsie shook her head. She'd stayed long enough. Too long. The past weeks had been sweet agony, caring for the children's needs, fixing meals for Joss, teaching him the alphabet and celebrating words coming to life for him, feeling her love grow deeper day by day, minute by minute. Then watching him stride away every evening. Now that she'd fulfilled her obligation to the sheriff, it was time to pack her bag and go. It would break her heart to leave Mary's family, but she knew the children would be well cared for.

Joss's ability to read had blossomed daily, as had his relationship with God. Many times tears filled her eyes as she received glimpses of God's amazing transformation in his actions and speech. Between Simon's example and Joss's desire to change, he was becoming the kind of father Mary had always wanted him to be. Tarsie had been a witness to a miracle, and her heart rejoiced. But at the same time, she mourned. Because loving him and the children wasn't enough. Being loved by the children wasn't enough. She wanted Joss—this new, changed Joss—to love her, too.

They walked to the house, the children scampering ahead, their giggles ringing. Tarsie memorized the sound, her heart aching. If she never had the joy of motherhood, at least she would have these memories to recall and treasure. She sighed, and Joss looked at her.

"Glad it's over?"

She knew he meant the trial, but his words carried a deeper meaning for her. "Yes . . . and no." How could one small heart hold so many mixed emotions? She sped her steps, eager to retrieve her belongings and leave so she needn't prolong this torment.

He caught her arm, drawing her to a halt. "Tarsie . . ."

She didn't want to look at him, but she couldn't stop herself. Just as she'd tried to memorize the sound of the children's laughter, she now memorized Joss in that moment. Always handsome with his thick hair, square jaw, and broad shoulders, the softening of his features only increased his attractiveness. He gazed down at her, his expression serious, a shadow of whiskers darkening his tanned skin. His fingers still held her arm, the touch as gentle as a summer breeze. Tarsie swallowed.

"What is it you're wantin', Joss?" *Please, say it and then let me go. Let me go. . . .*

He toed the ground, letting his hand slip away from her arm. "I know you said as soon as the trial was over you intended to move on. Start over someplace else. But . . ." He whisked a glance ahead to the children, who crouched in the dirt by the side of the road, examining something. "I wondered if I could talk you into . . . not going."

Tarsie took a deep breath, ready to argue.

He hurried on. "Those two love you. Love you as much as they loved their ma. And they need you. I couldn't find someone better to raise 'em right if I searched a hundred years. I know you love 'em. You said so in your letter."

Her eyes flew wide, and he nodded, his face serious. "Uh-huh, I read it. Every word of it." Pride squared his shoulders. "But even if you hadn't written it down on paper, I'd already know. I see it on your face every time you look at them." His brow pinched. "Can you really leave 'em, Tarsie?"

Tarsie gazed at the pair of blond heads close together, little shoulders hunched, whispers carrying on the breeze. Her heart constricted. "I have to."

"But what about that promise you told me you made to Mary?"

Her head zipped around to look up at him. "Don't be throwin' my promise at me, Joss Brubacher. You know I've done my very best to honor it! But Mary, she asked too much of me, I can't do it anymore!"

"Can't . . . or won't?"

She folded her arms over her chest. A bird chirped from a tree nearby, and two gold leaves let loose and spiraled downward. Tarsie stared at them, their hue the exact color of Emmy's and Nathaniel's soft curls. And Mary's hair. Tears burned behind her nose.

"Why'd you stay as long as you have?"

"You know why."

"Tell me." Joss brushed his fingers from her shoulder to her elbow.

Tremors shuddered through her entire frame. She hugged herself harder and whispered, "For love of Mary." She swallowed. "And Emmy. And Nathaniel. And . . ." She couldn't finish. *Wouldn't* finish. Wouldn't humiliate herself here in the sunshine on a glorious fall day.

He leaned close, his voice dropping low. So low she almost thought she imagined its tenderness. So sweet it washed over her like a dew-kissed morning. "But you didn't only vow to love Emmy and Nathaniel. You vowed to love me, too. The way God would love me—unconditionally. Isn't that what you told me?"

Mesmerized, she could only nod—one slow bob of her head.

"Then are you leaving because of me? Because you can't do as Mary asked and love me unconditionally?" Pain formed a sharp V in his brow. "I know I've wronged you. Lied to you. You have reason not to forgive me."

"But I have forgiven you!" The words burst out, shrill and louder than she'd intended. The bird shot from the tree, its wings beating the air. She ducked her head. "I'm not going because I'm angry with you, Joss. I'm going because . . ." *Oh, Father, strength!* Unless she told him the truth, he'd never let her go. Meeting his gaze, she drew back her shoulders and stated boldly, "Because I can't be stayin' here while I'm lovin' you and not havin' you love me in return. There! Now will you please let me go?"

She marched forward, arms swinging, determined to reach the house and escape before she could suffer any further mortification. A laugh exploded from behind her. She whirled around to see Joss holding his stomach, his face crinkled in mirth. She jammed her hands on her hips. "Don't you be makin' fun o' my feelings, Joss Brubacher! You an' your stubborn ways. You just had to push an' push until—"

Three long strides brought him to her. That grin still stretching across his cheeks, he caught her by the upper arms, drew her up, and captured her lips in a kiss so strong and sure her head spun. He stood upright, his hands still holding tight, which was a good thing or she might have collapsed out of shock.

Staring into his grinning face, she spluttered, "W-why'd you go and do *that?*" She wriggled her shoulders, a feeble attempt to free herself.

His hands slipped to her shoulder blades, drawing her close. With her snug against his frame, he smiled down at her. A warm, tender, filled-with-promise smile that had an even greater effect on her senses than the kiss had. Which she hadn't thought possible.

"I'm not much of a man for words. It's hard for me to say what I feel." His breath brushed her cheek, his palms roved her spine, and his eyes glowed with emotion. "But I don't want you to go. That kiss was meant to say . . . stay." His voice dropped to a throaty whisper. "Please, Tarsie. Stay."

She gathered the remains of her courage and placed her palms flat against his chest. Depending on what he said next, she would either draw him near or push him away. "To be your children's caretaker?"

"To be my wife." He brushed a kiss on the tip of her nose. "Because I love you, Tarsie Raines."

Gliding her hands upward, she wove her fingers through the thick hair at his temples and pressed her cheek to his chest. His heart beat in her ear, the steady thrum as comforting as a lullaby. "Yes, Joss. I'll stay."

✻

Tarsie married Joss a week later, with Ruth and Simon as their witnesses, in the yard at Tollison's place. Reverend Mann presided, and when he asked Joss if he would take Tarsie to be his wife, Joss's lips twitched teasingly as he proclaimed, "For sure I do." Then he winked at Tarsie, filling her cheeks with enough heat to inspire a rosy glow that would last a year at least.

Tarsie scratched out the old date in her Bible's marriage record and penned the correct date above. Joss signed his name with a flourish, planting a kiss on Tarsie's lips immediately afterward with a whispered thank-you for teaching him to write it correctly. Mr. Tollison's cook, who'd cried copiously throughout the entire ceremony, set out a buffet that ensured no one would want food again until the next evening, and a lean, white-haired black man played the fiddle so they could all dance. The merrymaking went on until dark, and then they returned to the little house where, together, they tucked the children into bed and Joss prayed with them.

Listening to her husband pray with the children was the

most joyous moment of her life. Until they crept beneath the covers together and she discovered in a completely new way how much Joss loved her.

Sunday morning, Joss awakened her early with a gentle nuzzle behind her ear. "I'd like pancakes for breakfast before we leave for service."

Tarsie giggled. "Then you'd best be fetchin' the eggs instead of tickling your wife."

"Yes, ma'am," he drawled.

Their morning passed quickly, with much laughter, and when the little hand on Mary's clock pointed to nine, they headed out their door in their nicest clothes. The early fall breeze was crisp but not cold, the air scented with smoke from cookstoves and nature. Tarsie breathed deeply, savoring the delicious scent of this Kansas September. She stopped to pluck up a particularly beautiful leaf that lay in her pathway, and Joss and the children kept going.

She straightened, poised to catch up, but then she paused, watching, as Emmy and Nathaniel each caught one of Joss's hands and the three fell into step together. They walked, hands swinging, Kansas sunlight glistening on one dark head and two blond ones, little feet skipping and Joss's larger boots moving purposefully. Guiding the children in a direct path to the church steps.

Tears flooded Tarsie's eyes, turning the sweet scene into a dreamlike vision made all the sweeter because it was real. "Oh, Mary," she whispered, joy and grief exploding in one rush of emotion through her heart, "how I wish you were here to be witnessin' this miraculous sight." Then peace eased its way through her frame. She aimed her gaze to the endless blue sky above. "You know, don't you? Somehow, you know . . ." She turned her attention back to Joss and the children in time to see them stop at the bottom of the steps.

Joss looked over his shoulder. An endearing smile curved

his lips. "Are you comin'?" He and Emmy dropped hands, each extending their palms toward her in invitation.

A bubble of joy rose from Tarsie's chest and erupted as a giggle. She nodded. Then, with a prayer of thankfulness filling her heart, she joined her family.

Acknowledgments

To *Mom, Daddy, Don, my girls, and my precious grandchildren*—Thank you for your support and encouragement. I could not meet the demands of this ministry without your assistance.

To my mom-in-love, *Shirley Sawyer*—This was the first manuscript completed without a phone call from you asking "How's the writing going?" I missed that, but I suspect you're marching around heaven telling everybody about my books, just like you did down here. Thanks for always being one of my best encouragers.

To my wonderful critique partners, *Eileen, Connie, Margie, Darlene, and Donna*—Thank you for your suggestions, your prayers, your cheers, and especially your friendship. What would I do without you?

To my choir and church family—There are too many of you to list, but you know who you are. Your prayers and encouragement are so precious to me. When I am weak, you hold up my arms. I appreciate you more than you know.

To my traveling buddy, *Beverly*—Thanks for making that trip to the far corner of Kansas. The day was hot, windy, and *long*, but I had such fun and it helped so much. I appreciate your willingness to accompany me.

To my editor, *Charlene,* and all the wonderful folks at Bethany—What a delightful journey we've had together. I am so grateful to be a member of this publishing house and to partner with you in the ministry of my heart.

Finally, and most importantly, to *God*—You fill me in every way, meet my every need, and hold me in Your capable arms. Thank You for working in and through me. May any praise or glory be reflected directly back to You.

Kim Vogel Sawyer is the bestselling author of more than twenty novels, which have sold more than one million copies. She has won the Carol Award, the Gayle Wilson Award of Excellence, and the Inspirational Readers Choice Award. Kim is active in her church, where she leads women's fellowship and participates in both voice and bell choirs. In her spare time, she enjoys drama, quilting, and calligraphy. Kim and her husband, Don, reside in central Kansas and have three daughters and nine grandchildren. Learn more at

www.kimvogelsawyer.com
writespassage.blogspot.com

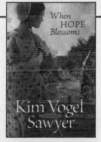

If you enjoyed *A Home in Drayton Valley,* you may also like…

Driven to fulfill an unbreakable promise, Alyce finds help in an unlikely ally. But can she trust this man with her secret—and her heart?

At Every Turn by Anne Mateer
annemateer.com

In the picturesque Amana Colonies, two very different young women are looking for answers. But secrets run deep there, and the truth could alter everything.

A Hidden Truth by Judith Miller
HOME TO AMANA
judithmccoymiller.com

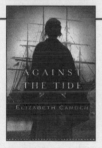

When Lydia's translation skills land her in the middle of a secret campaign against dangerous criminals, who can she trust when her life—and heart—are in jeopardy?

Against the Tide by Elizabeth Camden
elizabethcamden.com